PRAISE FOR *THE VANISHING MAN*

"Fiction readers who crush on blue-blooded British detectives will fall hard for Victorian-era sleuth Charles Lenox. . . . Jump into the carriage with Lenox and hold on tight."   —*The Washington Post*

"Finch's nimble prose, edged with humor, makes this twelfth in the Charles Lenox series a pure delight."   —*Booklist* **(starred review)**

"Rich in period minutiae, [*The Vanishing Man*] unveils the frightening power of the uppermost classes."   —*Kirkus Reviews*

PRAISE FOR *THE WOMAN IN THE WATER*

"A cunning mystery."   —*New York Times Book Review*

"Finch is an elegant stylist. . . . A persuasive portrait of Victorian England."   —*The Washington Post*

"An excellent addition to an already terrific series."

—*Library Journal* **(starred review)**

THE VANISHING MAN

THE VANISHING MAN

Charles Finch

MINOTAUR
BOOKS
NEW YORK

Published in the United States by Minotaur Books, an imprint of St. Martin's Publishing Group

www.minotaurbooks.com

The Library of Congress Cataloging-in-Publication Data is available upon request.

ISBN 978-1-250-31137-5 (trade paperback)
ISBN 978-1-250-31138-2 (ebook)

First Minotaur Books Paperback Edition: January 2020

10 9 8 7 6 5 4 3 2 1

For Emily, with greatest love

ACKNOWLEDGMENTS

With every book I write, I seem to wind up thanking the same people, and yet my debt to them continues to grow. Should I give up and just start selling these spots? Watch this space. In the meanwhile, I am, as ever, grateful foremost to my inimitably generous and wonderful editor, Charles Spicer, and to my agent, Elisabeth Weed, whose calm, intelligent, and affectionate guidance is what every writer deserves but too few have. I know how fortunate I am.

Neither works alone: at Minotaur, Andy Martin leads a spectacular team, including Sarah Melnyk, Hector DeJean, Sarah Grill, Paul Hochman, and David Rotstein, while Elisabeth has in her corner at The Book Group the kind and capable Hallie Schaeffer.

I want to give special thanks to Martin Quinn, whose ingenuity and enthusiasm and great cheer have turned him from an acquaintance into a valued friend and an invaluable colleague as we've worked more closely together.

In my personal life, I'm again overrun with people I should name. But let me just use this occasion to point out some of the amazing people I've met during my time in Chicago's literary community: Rebecca Makkai, Kim Brooks, Sasha Hemon and Teri Boyd, Rebecca George, Elizabeth Taylor, Jennifer Day, and of course everyone who was at Ragdale, along with the people who run it. Each of you is extremely dear to me.

Readers, you've given me a career. I don't think I deserve it, and I don't know how I ended up here. But you are in my heart as I write these books, truly. Plus, without talking to you on Facebook I might go crazy.

Finally, to my family, near and far: I love you so much.

THE VANISHING MAN

CHAPTER ONE

Once a month or so, just to keep his hand in the game, Charles Lenox liked to go shopping with his friend Lady Jane Grey.

On this occasion it was a warm, windy day in early June of 1853, quiet, the gently sunny hour of late morning before the clerks would fill the streets on their way to take lunch. The two friends were next-door neighbors on tiny Hampden Lane, in the heart of London, and he was waiting on her steps at ten o'clock precisely. At five past, she came out, smiling and apologizing.

They left, eventually turning up Brook Street and walking past the little string of streets that ran parallel to their own, talking.

"Why are you checking your watch every ten seconds?" she asked after they had gone about halfway.

"Oh! I'm sorry," said Lenox. "I've an appointment at noon."

"I hope it's with someone you've hired to teach you better manners."

"The joke's on you, because it's with a duke."

"The worst-mannered wretch I ever met was a duke," Lady Jane said. As they crossed Binney Street, Lenox's eyes stayed for an extra moment on a man painting an iron fence with a fresh coat of black paint, whistling happily to himself. "Which one is it?" she asked.

"Out of discretion I cannot say."

"I call that disagreeable."

Lenox smiled. "It's a case."

She turned her gaze on him. It had been a long drought since his last case—more than a month. "Is it? I see."

Though both considered themselves tenured veterans of London now, anyone observing them would have seen two very young people, as young and resilient as the summer day. Lenox was a tall, slender, straight-backed young bachelor of twenty-six, bearing a gentlemanly appearance, and with, whatever Lady Jane said, a courteous manner. He was dressed in a dark suit, hands often behind his back, with hazel eyes and a short hazel beard. There was something measuring and curious in his face. As for Lady Jane, she was five years his junior, a plain, pretty woman of twenty-one, though she had been married for fully a tenth of those living days, which gave her some obscure right to self-regard for her own maturity. This told in her posture, perhaps. She had soft, dark curling hair; today she wore a light blue dress, with boots of a tan color just visible beneath its hem.

They had grown up in the same part of the countryside, though until he had moved to London, Lenox had never considered her part of his generation. By the time he'd noticed she was, Lady Jane had been engaged.

They neared New Bond Street, where the shops began, as the church clocks chimed the quarter hour.

In truth it was not altogether customary that *she* went shopping quite so often as she did—in most households like Lady Jane's, the task would have fallen to a maid—but it was one of the things that she liked, and Lenox liked it for that reason.

The meeting at noon was continually on his mind, even as they walked and spoke. Lenox was a private . . . well, what word had he settled on! Investigator? Detective? It was a new endeavor yet. Three years could count as new, when the field was one of your own rough-and-ready invention, and when success had been tantalizingly close at moments but remained mostly elusive.

A duke might well bring it close enough to hold with two hands.

This intersection was vastly busier than their peaceful street. She stopped at the corner and looked at a list. After she had been studying for a moment, he said, "What do you need today?"

"Are you going to bother me with questions the whole time?" she said, trying to decipher, he could tell from many years of knowing her, her own handwriting.

"Yes."

She looked up and smiled. She pointed to the window next to which they were standing. It was a barber's. "Shall we buy you some mustache grease?"

"Oh, no," he said, looking at the sign that had inspired the question. "I make my own."

"How economical."

"Yes. Though it puts you in the way of quite a lot of bear hunting."

"You are in a very amusing mood, I suppose, Charles. There—I've made it out. Let's go to the greengrocer's first."

He bowed. "Just as you please, my lady."

They made their way carefully down New Bond Street, stopping in at every third or fourth shop. Jane was very canny, while Lenox shopped almost at random; at the confectioner, as she was remonstrating with Mr. Pearson over the price of an order of six dozen marzipan cakes she wanted for a garden party she was having, Lenox decided with little prompting to order a cake to be sent to Lady Berryman, who had invited him to the country for August.

"That reminds me," Jane said to the baker. "I have an odd request. Could I order an eggless cake from you? Vanilla. It's for my husband's aunt. I wrote down the recipe she gave me. She's lord-terrified of eggs, I'm afraid."

"Why on earth?" said the baker, so moved by this horrible information that he forgot himself.

"Can you think I have asked her, Mr. Pearson?"

"Blimey," he said. Then amended himself. "Blimey, my lady."

She raised her eyebrows. "I know. Imagine being married to her."

"I couldn't," said Pearson fervently, which was true for several different reasons.

Lenox was just about to interject that he knew the lady in question, a larger person, and that he would stand on his head if she had ever refused a dessert in her life. But as he was about to speak, Jane threw him a look, and he knew to keep mum.

In the street again, after they'd gone, she explained that she had read a recipe for an eggless cake from Germany and wanted to try it, but didn't dare insult the baker.

"You could have made it at home."

"No—no. He has the lightest hand in London, Mr. Pearson," she said. "Speaking of which, how is Lancelot?"

He made an irritated face at her, and she laughed. Lancelot was a young cousin of Lenox's on half-term from Eton and therefore in the city for two weeks of what his family had optimistically called *seasoning*. "I would prefer not to discuss it."

"Does he still want to come with you on a case?"

"Ha! Desperately."

"Has he gotten you with the peashooter again?"

"Please leave me in peace."

They proceeded past the cobblers, then the book stall—BACK IN STOCK, EXCLUSIVELY IN ALL OF LONDON, *Uncle Tom's Cabin*! a sign declared excitedly—before arriving at the dressmaker. Here Lady Jane went inside alone to have a word, as Lenox skulked outside, feeling like a schoolboy. Soon, though, he was meditating on the upcoming meeting.

The Duke of Dorset!

He thought of the title with a tightening in his stomach, and then of the letter that contained the entirety of his knowledge of the case thus far: *His Grace has discovered that a possession upon which he places high value is missing. He would appreciate your advice regarding its potential recovery.*

He checked his watch and saw that it was ten past eleven. They were near the end of their ramble, and he felt a quick flicker of melancholy. When he was with Lady Jane, he generally forgot himself; just at the moment, a welcome oblivion.

If Lenox's first year in London after moving down from Oxford had been characterized by his tenacious, mostly fruitless search for work as a detective, the subsequent eighteen months had been more complex and difficult. In part it was still to do with the scorn his profession drew from his peers, as they advanced steadily onward in their fields—and in part it was to do with the lonely feeling that all around him his friends were marrying, having children even, while he was still by himself.

But most of all, of course, it had to do with the death of his father. At first he had borne up under this misfortune well, he thought. Fathers were supposed to die before their children, he supposed, and he knew any number of friends who had been orphaned long ago. But recently, especially in the last six months, his grief had shown itself in odd, unexpected ways. He found himself losing minutes at a time on train platforms and in gardens, thinking; he found himself dreaming of his childhood.

Perhaps it had to do with the fact that they had never been especially close. He had loved and revered his father, but the easier friendship had been with his mother. Had he assumed there would be time, later on in life, for their relationship to grow? His father had been only sixty-one when he died; for his second son, it had been, surprisingly, not as if some venerable building in London disappeared, which was what he had always imagined—Parliament, for instance—but as if London itself had.

This past year he felt the loss more keenly with each month, n less, and he was sure that was unnatural. For the first time in his life, he woke each morning with a sense of dejection—a sense that, well, here was another day to be gotten through—rather than happiness.

CHAPTER TWO

Of all people, Lady Jane perhaps sensed her friend's state of mind most delicately. When she came out of the dressmaker's, a look that was difficult to read passed across her face, as if she knew where his thoughts had turned.

"Everything acceptable?" he asked cheerfully.

"Yes, they're still making dresses."

They resumed their stroll. A few shops down the long boulevard, they passed the optician. "I really would like a barometer above anything," Lenox said longingly, pausing before a beautiful brass one in the optician's window. "Ah, well."

"What a waste of money it would be," she said.

"They say it is good to have friends who support one's interests," Lenox replied, studying the barometer.

"You are dead in the center of the largest city on earth. When was the last time you even saw a ship?"

"Ha! There you're going to feel foolish, because I see them nearly every day on the Thames."

"From a cab." She pulled his arm. "Let's go, you can't be late to your duke."

They proceeded down New Bond, talking of this and that. It

seemed Lady Jane had a kind word for every person they passed, and it occurred to Lenox that just as he had been struggling to find his feet in his profession, she had perhaps felt something like an impostor in her first years in London—in the very earliest days of her grand marriage, to an earl's first son. Perhaps this was why she shopped for herself; perhaps it gave her a sense of intimacy with their leafy, occasionally intimidating London neighborhood, making a community of it. Like him, she belonged, from the first, to a small place, a village. Now she had made a small place here, in the biggest place. A village of its own.

They spent some time discussing the duke. A duke, after all! The whole of the United Kingdom, in its population of thirty million, possessed just twenty-eight such creatures. The least of them was a figure of overpowering consequence. Yet even among their rank were finer gradients, and the man Lenox was shortly to see held one of the three or four greatest dukedoms.

Theirs was the highest tier of the nobility, the dukes, first in the land beneath the royal family. Not only that, but in their innermost souls not a few dukes and duchesses would have pointed to their lineage (the title of "duke" had come into existence in 1337) and claimed a greater stake in the leadership of Britain than the comelately family currently chattering around the throne in German accents.

After them, it went so: first the marquesses, thirty-five of these, and their wives, the marchionesses. Then earls—and there it became complicated, because the title of "earl" was nearly oldest of all, originating as long ago as the year 600, historians said, when each shire of England had a *jarl* (Norse for "noble warrior"), which was the reason that in England each earl was still entitled to a small crown: a coronet.

Many earls in England (including Lady Jane's father, Lord Houghton) would not have admitted for a second to being beneath a duke. Their wives were called countesses, because nobody had ever thought to name them earlesses—which had struck many schoolboys memorizing these facts as extremely stupid indeed.

Thereafter it got greatly simpler. Viscounts were next, nearly a hundred of these, common as church mice, the poor devils. Finally came barons, last rank in the peerage.

"And there you'll be, at the very top of the heap," said Jane.

"I doubt he'll make me a duke there on the spot," Lenox said.

"Probably just a baron or something."

"I do wonder what he wants. *A possession upon which he places high value.* I only hope it's not his lucky kilt, or something like that."

Lady Jane laughed. "And the laundress has lost it, yes. I could see that being the calamity, I fear."

Lenox himself held none of these titles. Just to confuse things, there was still one title left over, and it was here that he entered the picture: Baronets were called "sir," as Lenox's older brother, Sir Edmund, had now been in the eighteen months since their father's death.

A knight was also called "sir," but his children couldn't inherit the title. It belonged to a sole person and died with him, a great writer, say, or artist, or dear intimate of the Queen's ninth-favorite cousin.

All of these gentry taken together with their families numbered not more than ten thousand, but Lenox, as the second son even of a very old, landed, and honored baronetcy, was as far down the slopes of the mountain of aristocracy from the Duke of Dorset as the thirty-millionth Briton, drunk in a ditch, was from Lenox himself.

It was an absurd system. Almost nobody believed in it as more than a matter of chance, except for the very old aunts and uncles who kept the genealogies. Yet all of them also, somehow, believed in it implicitly.

Strange to be an Englishman, an Englishwoman.

At last they reached the turn of New Bond Street, where they saw the most dignified shop in the whole row, housed inside a handsome stone building with purple wisteria climbing its white face. This was the leecher's—the best leecher in town, people generally agreed, where they boxed the living leeches in boxes bound with blue ribbon, as if they were marzipan cakes themselves.

Despite this enticement, Lenox and Lady passed by the leecher's in favor of their own favorite shop, which stood just around the corner, behind a short porch made of plain, unsanded boards. Over the door it said nothing but BERGSON in plain white stenciled lettering.

They pushed the door open and saw Bergson himself in a chair behind a broad counter, looking infernally grumpy and making absolutely no movement to rise and greet them. A duke or an earl or a murderer or anyone on God's green earth could have walked in and his reaction would have been the same.

He was a silent old Swede, Bergson, who had spent most of his life in America and then, for reasons known only to himself, come to London and set up an exact replica of the shop he had once owned in the Wisconsin territory.

An exact replica, truly exact, which meant that there were items of no conceivable use to a Londoner, like two-hundred-pound bags of cornmeal (enough to last a long cabin winter, in lesser demand here), mixed with those of delightful novelty and tireless fascination.

"Look!" said Jane, handling a necklace with a large polished turquoise at the end of two rubbed-leather ropes. "These are the fashion right now, Duch says."

Lenox looked at it doubtfully, then at the stone-faced Bergson, who, in bib overalls of a denim that was either very dark or had never been washed, did not look even adjacent to the world of fashion. Some people said he had lost his whole family to a fever, others that that he had left America when Wisconsin had become a state five years before, because he had murdered another man over a plot of property once and could not survive a land with laws.

Lenox suspected him simply of being shrewd; this was one of the most popular shops in London, its stock replenished just often enough to be endlessly fascinating.

Bergson was not telling—he barely deigned to speak to his customers—but he did sell Charles and Jane a variety of items: bars of pine soap, bags of sifted brown sugar, rough lumps of silver, a woven fishing creel that Lenox thought he might give his brother, Edmund. Lady Jane bought a handsome leather cap for her husband, who was due back from India with his troops in August. Lenox considered a tinderbox before buying Lancelot an arrowhead, silvered with mica.

"See, you do like having Lancelot," said Lady Jane as they left.

"In fact I do not, but I love Eustacia very dearly." This was Lancelot's mother, Lenox's first cousin. "As for Lancelot, he'll slit my neck with this arrowhead tonight."

She mulled this over. "Better than the tinderbox, then, all things considered, since our houses are side by side. Look, it's eleven forty, Charles. You had better go and see about your duke."

CHAPTER THREE

He arrived at Dorset House twenty minutes later, taking off his hat in the doorway and listening very attentively to Theodore Ward, the duke's private secretary, who was leading him inside.

"Just to clarify once more, our expectation, His Grace's expectation, is that we may trust in your absolute discretion, Lenox. Really, your absolute—well, you understand. You do, don't you?"

"I'm scarcely liable to change my answer the ninth time you ask, Theo."

Ward's brow darkened, and for just an instant they were two boys on the cricket pitch at school again, arguing over whose turn it was to bowl. "I say, Charlie, it really is the most highly—"

Lenox held up a hand. "I'm sorry. You have my word. My absolute word. My rock-solid bottom-of-the-ocean heaven-swear-it word. Honestly."

Ward was mollified. "Good. It's only—I don't think I have ever even seen the duke perturbed."

"I understand."

He did. In his work, Lenox had seen people of all stations experiencing the most frantic moments of their lives. Having encountered wrongdoing or violence, none of them, from scullery maid to stiff-chinned major, could stay unchanged.

"Just wait here a moment, then, if you wouldn't mind."

Lenox smiled. "I could live here comfortably enough for a while if you like."

The secretary followed Lenox's gaze across the enormous entry-way. They had just come in from the noisy streets of London, but the cavernous silence made it like stepping into a house recessed deep in the pine-tree countryside: the vast checkerboard marble floor, the curling staircase, the high arched ceiling, a mahogany settle with the proportions of a dinghy.

"It's something rather else, isn't it?" said Ward.

"They would have slept thirty of us on that stairwell at Harrow."

Ward laughed. "They did cram us. At any rate, stay here. Find a chair if you like." He gestured toward a row of twelve of them. "Have a gander at the paintings. I'll be back when I've made sure His Grace is prepared to see you now."

Ward left, and Lenox looked around the hall.

He had seen paintings before—most of them, in his limited experience, seemed to be of streams, cows, or fine personages, and these were no exception—so instead he turned back to the entrance through which they had just come.

On either side of the heavy front door was a large vertical window. He stood close to one and looked out at the Thames, which glimmered gold under the summer sun.

He was in what some people reckoned London's most beautiful house. It was a white marble citadel built four hundred years before, sitting not all that much more than a thousand yards or so west of the Houses of Parliament and Westminster Abbey, the only private residence on this stretch of the city. The Thames faced its front door; Buckingham Palace was a five-minute walk from its back one.

Standing there, Lenox was perhaps just conscious of a slight feeling of fraudulence. He had dressed in too warm a gray wool suit and a somber maroon tie—serious clothes, to indicate his seriousness, though in his sober face was a betraying trace of self-doubt. He was only twenty-six, and while he was passionately interested in this work, the number of serious crimes he had investigated could still be counted on one hand.

After perhaps five minutes, Ward returned, and Lenox strode back to the center of the entrance hall. He was shorter and sturdier than Lenox, Ward—a boxer in the deepest places of his heart—and there was no levity left in his manner.

"Just this way," he said. "His Grace will see you at the place of the—in his private study. His real private study."

"Is there a made-up one?" Lenox asked in a quiet voice, because now they were proceeding up the stairwell.

"There is a *public* private study, where he takes large meetings," Ward replied, equally quietly.

"I see."

And he was a duke, after all. Even Jane, whom very little impressed, the daughter of an earl, some distant day destined to be the wife of one when her husband's father died, had given Lenox a second look when he said the name Dorset. Aside from a handful of people—the Queen, Prince Albert, the old heroic red-faced Duke of Wellington, still just alive—there weren't many more powerful inhabitants of England. The Archbishop of Canterbury? Probably not. If you took the whole power of Oxford University it might compete with the duke's.

But not with his wealth.

Theodore Ward (a well-born commoner, son of a squire, which is to say a sort of untitled baronet, and grandnephew of a marquess, bound someday for Parliament in all likelihood—hence this prestigious post) was conscious of this, it was clear. He led Lenox down a red-carpeted hallway of Dorset House as carefully as if they were bound for St. Peter's gates.

When they reached the duke's study, he tapped gently upon the door. "Your Grace?"

"Come in," a voice called after a moment.

Lenox wondered again, briefly, whether there had really been any crime at all. A duke seemed a prime candidate for a cry-wolf. In they went, however.

"Charles Lenox, Your Grace," said Theo, bowing slightly.

His Grace looked up from behind his desk. His face was impassive. "Good afternoon, Your Grace," said Lenox.

"Come in," Dorset said. "You may sit."

It was a spectacular little room. One wall was entirely covered in windows, which overlooked the river and the bankside. Two others were taken up with bookshelves, which held innumerable small treasures; Lenox saw a scored and battered Anglo-Saxon broadsword laid along a velvet runner.

The final of the room's four walls, directly behind Dorset's immaculate French desk, was the scene of the crime.

Lenox and Ward sat in two ebony chairs, upholstered in pale green, facing the duke.

"Ward tells me you have set up as a private sort of police officer."

"Well—after a fashion, Your Grace, yes, I suppose that's correct."

The duke studied him. "He also tells me you are trustworthy."

There was no point in modesty here. "Yes, Your Grace."

The duke paused once again. He was thin, aged about fifty-five, Lenox would have said, and wore a navy suit with a gray waistcoat, like a schoolboy. He had trim gray hair, firmly set blue-gray eyes, and a mustache. He held a gold pen in one hand.

There was something ethereal in his lined face, as if a lifetime of holding his position had somehow insubstantiated him individually, his personality absorbed partially into his station. And his expression was the expression of a man who has heard the word "yes" many, many times in his life, and expects to hear it many more still, yet who is also trained to the strictest self-discipline. It was the expression of a man with dozens and dozens of servants whose existence was dedicated to him and of whose individual existences he was only loosely aware.

"I knew your father in Parliament before his death."

Lenox was a stoic, like all of his class, and only said, "Did you, Your Grace," without a question mark in the reply.

"He was a man of principle."

"He certainly was, Your Grace."

"Yes, I liked him very much. I dislike it when the ministries are out of the House of Lords, but I would have been happy to see him in a cabinet."

"He declined several posts, I know, Your Grace."

The duke barked a laugh, as if Lenox would have to dig much deeper to surprise him. "Yes, I know."

"My apologies, Your Grace. Of course you do."

Dorset gave him one final, appraising look, as if he were a horse up for a prize at a county fair, then nodded. "You had better leave us, then, Theo," he said.

CHAPTER FOUR

When the private secretary had left, the Duke rose and walked to a discreet stand of variously shaped crystal decanters. "Whisky?" he said.

Lenox's father's guideline flashed through his mind: Upon a first meeting, always accept the offer of a drink from a man lower in rank than yourself, never from a man higher in rank than yourself.

"Thank you, no, Your Grace," Lenox said, still sitting.

"As you like it." The duke stoppered the bottle he had opened. He turned back to Lenox. "How do you generally proceed in this kind of matter?"

"Ward told me very little."

The duke strode back to the desk. "Good. He knows very little."

"Given that, Your Grace, perhaps it would be best if you began at the start and told me as much as you could."

Lenox expected some further cavil or hesitation, but instead, after resuming his seat, the Duke launched directly into his story. Once he had taken a decision, he moved forward without reservations, apparently. Lenox stowed that away as a potentially valuable piece of knowledge.

"It's about a painting," Dorset said.

"So I had guessed, Your Grace."

The duke looked at him sharply. "Mr. Lenox?"

"The one piece of information I had from Ward was that you were missing a possession you valued." Lenox nodded to the wall behind the duke. "There are normally eight paintings on your wall, four on each side of you. At the moment there are seven. The empty space is conspicuous."

"I see. But for all you know it's been taken away for cleaning, and what's missing is a string of diamonds."

Lenox shook his head. "No, Your Grace. One of the two nails upon which the painting was hanging is ripped halfway out, the other is gone, and there is a fresh wound in the wood where it was. You can see raw wood under the varnish."

The duke turned back to look once again. "So you can."

"Not even your most careless footman would handle a painting from your study that way. Or the wall's paneling."

The duke looked at him, neither impressed (as perhaps Lenox had hoped he would be) nor displeased.

"This is your trade, then," he said curiously. "Observation."

"It is, Your Grace." Lenox hated that word, "trade," but of course it *was* his trade. Still, he couldn't help but add, "I believe that one must take money in exchange for services or goods for work to be properly considered a trade, if one wished to be technical, however."

Dorset looked surprised. He pulled a gold case, engraved with his coat of arms and clasped with a ruby, from his waistcoat pocket. He drew a small cigar from it and closed the case again. "You don't take money?"

"No, Your Grace."

"I see. You are a hobbyist."

"No, Your Grace. My practices are professional. But I am—"

He hesitated. How to explain it, quite?

But the duke understood. "No, I see." He lit the cigar from a safety match struck against his lampstand. "Be that all as it may—you are correct that it is a painting that has been stolen. You may also wish to know that I want to know who took it very badly."

"Naturally, Your Grace."

"No, not naturally."

"Excuse me?"

"*Who*, I said. I only care about the *who* of the thing. The painting itself is of little consequence to me."

Lenox nodded. That was unusual. "May I assume that the painting is"—he gestured at the seven pictures still on the wall—"also a portrait?"

"It is. A portrait of my great-grandfather, the fourteenth duke."

"I would imagine that you might value the object itself in that case."

Dorset shook his head. "There you would be wrong. He had his portrait painted oftener than most. We have a dozen more scattered here and there. One is hanging in my club, where I see it every day, and another in the Lords."

Lenox squinted at the paintings. There was something wrong about them, though he couldn't yet put his finger on what.

He returned his attention to the duke. "Perhaps you are worried about your safety, then?"

"I am not," said Dorset. "New locks have been installed on the windows and door of the study, and the staff is on alert. Listen here, however. What were you looking at? Just now, behind me?"

What had he been looking at? He stared at the paintings again. Then he realized: One of them was wrong.

From left to right the pictures might have been numbered one through eight. With, as Lenox had said, four on either side of the duke's desk. The missing one would have been numbered six in the sequence.

The first, all the way to the left, hung closest to the large windows overlooking the Thames. Lenox's inexpert eye dated it roughly to Elizabethan times. Going left to right, the paintings grew one by one slightly more modern, concluding with what he felt sure was the current duke's own father.

But one of the paintings was wrong.

"I take it that these are other of your predecessors, Your Grace," he said, pointing to the four paintings on the left.

"They are, yes. Dukes of Dorset."

Then Lenox's eyes looked past the duke and to the right side of the room, where the missing painting had hung. "And the last two are, as well—like the missing one."

"Yes."

"The farthest to the right, next to the whisky you very kindly offered me from the bookcase"—the one that Lenox had numbered eighth in his own mind—"being, I would hazard, of your own father."

"Yes," said the duke again.

"But that one." Lenox pointed to the painting just over the duke's left shoulder. Number five. Just next to the missing painting, number six. "That one is very different, Your Grace."

"Different."

"The other six, I can see, are all almost exactly the same in size. This one is half as large. It is also darker, and it is less—I suppose the sitter looks less distinguished than your other ancestors. Forgive me for saying so, Your Grace."

The duke looked a shade amused for a moment, and then more serious. He gazed at Lenox for a long time.

At last he spoke. "But that painting is not the one that's missing."

"No," said Lenox. Then he added, "My instinct with crime is always to look for anything that seems off. The painting merely seems off. We needn't discuss it if you prefer."

"No. It is quite bound up in why you are here. But it is—well, I was unwilling to call in Scotland Yard for a reason. The matter is too serious. And it has to do with exactly this painting, the fifth."

So he thought of it as the fifth, too, and the stolen one as the sixth, perhaps. "I am very curious, Your Grace."

The duke leaned back in his chair, crossing his legs with the shush of very expensive cloth. "Very well. Today is Wednesday."

"Yes."

"On Monday, that is June first, the Duchess and I had planned to depart for Ireland. I have a house on Lough Leane. My son, however, who was to travel with us, fell ill that day with a fever. Out of an excess of caution—he is my only son and my heir—we delayed the date of our proposed departure to yesterday, Tuesday. He refuses to see a doctor, the stubborn fool."

Lenox took a notebook from his pocket. "The second. Might I take notes?"

"If you wish." The duke went on, his straight, slender body standing over the chair, as if he himself were posing for a portrait. "It was then, the second, yesterday morning, that I came into my study. It was just before seven o'clock. The painting was gone."

"Did you come in for any specific reason? A noise?" asked the young detective.

"No. I generally breakfast alone here, answering letters."

"What did you do when you saw the sixth painting was missing?"

The duke smiled enigmatically. "Looked at the fifth and heaved a sigh of relief."

"And then, Your Grace?"

"Rang the bell, and quickly questioned every servant I could find. None of them had seen or heard anything. My manservant, Craig, has questioned them all at greater length, and confirmed the same."

Lenox nodded, pondering this. "When was the last time you had been in the room?"

"Late the previous evening. Everything was in order then."

"Was anyone from the household in the room after you, Your Grace?"

"Only Craig. He is a Scotsman who has been with me thirty years. Before that he was in the army. He tells me that the room was in perfect order when he left, after tidying it."

"Was there any sign of how the thief might have gained access to the room?"

"Nothing could have been clearer. The door was locked when I came in yesterday morning, but the thief left a window open. They had very definitely been shut."

Lenox looked over at the windows, which were locked now, with thin curtains tied away from them to either side. He nodded. "I see. Did the missing painting have any value?"

"I think it probably the least valuable painting on the wall," said the duke, with an odd satisfaction. "Even if it were not stolen but freely sold by its owner, myself, its worth would not exceed fifteen or twenty pounds at auction."

"Is that all?"

"If more, only because its sitter is a Duke of Dorset, perhaps. Its painter has been forgotten. Next to it, you see, is a Joshua Reynolds of my grandfather, which would obviously be a different matter." Even Lenox knew Reynolds. "Nor was my great-grandfather—who was in the sixth portrait, the missing one—a great political leader, like his own father. Or mine. He was a quiet man."

Both of those men had served in the cabinet of Parliament with relatively little distinction, Lenox knew, though that was not an opinion he would share in this proud household, where they were evidently remembered as Ciceros of the Embankment.

His eyes returned to the much smaller, smokier painting. Number five.

It was in a wood frame, not gilt like the others, and its sitter wore a plain dark shirt, open at the neck. He had a small gold earring, in the fashion of the 1810s. But the painting looked a bit older than that to Lenox's (untrained) eye. The sitter held a delicate flower carelessly by its stem, and his gaze was directed at the viewer.

There was an intelligent watchfulness to him. In the empty space by him on the canvas were a few lines of cursive writing, as you sometimes saw in old French pictures of Christ.

"Who is this, then?" Lenox asked, nodding toward the painting.

Dorset smiled, at last. "There you ask to know something that Ward does not know—that, if I am not mistaken, three people on earth know. I suppose you think I may rely upon you to be the fourth."

"I will keep it a secret, Your Grace."

It was a half-truth. He would tell Graham—of course. But the duke needn't know that.

"Very well," Dorset said. "That is the only existing oil painting from life of the writer William Shakespeare."

CHAPTER FIVE

S ome hours later, at twilight, Lenox stood in the doorway of a very different sort of room than the beautiful little study by the Thames. He paused, surveying the grizzled inhabitants along their low-slung deal benches, their pint pots of ale in hand, their amiable conversations gathering into a low indistinct rumble, until a pair of heavy sailors pushed through the door and past him, carrying him partway inside.

This was a pub in Cannon Street called the Dovecote, and he was in search of a fellow named Bonden.

The sinewy, angular old landlord walked out from behind the bar to one of the pub's tables, holding four pewter jugs in each hand, foam rocking tautly atop each of them, then placed them on the table with a thud, spilling nary a drop. He returned with the table's empty tankards and laid them in a pan of sudsy water. When he was done, he looked at Lenox, who asked whether Thaddeus Bonden was there.

"Tad Bonden? I can check."

Lenox nodded. "Thank you."

The Dovecote sat squatly near London Bridge, where, being

close to two dockyards, it served primarily a naval clientele. A naval clientele, at that, drawn from before the mast, the hammock rather than the officer class, rough, rough-tongued, easy with their money, generous to those they liked, violent to those they didn't.

Presumably those characteristics were also possessed by Bonden, and Lenox was on his guard.

"How'd you hear of him?" the proprietor asked eventually.

A stool at the bar had been vacated. "Could I have a pint of bitter, please," said Lenox, taking it.

The old server briefly smiled. "Lock-jawed, then," he said. "Fair enough."

As he spoke he was already turning toward the tap with a jug in hand, as automatically as if he were only a large piece in some large mechanical contraption designed to serve beer and gin to men.

"Your bitter." The old man looked at him levelly for a moment. "Well, Bonden, he's here, or he ain't, if you catch my meaning. You'll know which in five minutes. Find a table if you like."

Lenox followed these instructions and watched the barman disappear from sight, then return without looking at him. He waited nine minutes, and when that much time had elapsed, he stood, lifted his hat to the proprietor, who nodded back without a change in countenance, and left.

He was a bit disappointed, a bit relieved. Bonden would have been a risk.

It was a long westward trek back across town to Mayfair, but Lenox walked it, the six-odd miles. He had a good deal to consider.

London was a very different place at this hour. The business of the day was done, and everyone but the few lone souls upon the streets had returned home from the diligent, hectic, forgetful city. Yet the late pale violet light made the houses—whose quality improved just perceptibly from street to street over the course of his walk to his own neighborhood—look so sad, cold and alone, the world an arcing, skybound, unknowable place. Those who remained outside were thrown back, with every shop shuttered, every street hawker headed to their hearths, upon little but their own thoughts.

Lenox didn't quite mind that melancholy feeling; and he needed the thoughts. The Romans, in their phrasemaking way, had hit upon it: *Solvitur ambulando*, all problems are solved by walking. In the times when Lenox had been most puzzled during his short career, it was often a long walk that had suddenly galvanized his mind.

And the duke's problem was a significant puzzle, both in itself and because it belonged to the Duke of Dorset.

The walk took him a little more than ninety minutes. His own tall, handsome home came into view when he turned off Grosvenor Square and onto Hampden Lane.

"Graham?" he called when he had reached it and unlocked the front door. "Graham, are you there?"

Nobody answered, but he heard a footstep on the stair. Then he felt a sharp crack on his face, as sudden as a bee sting. He lurched backward.

"Ha!" cried a triumphant young voice.

"You fiend!" Lenox shouted. He had been the victim of this same peashooter four times thus far. "Lancelot! Come here! I'm going to thrash you, I swear on your life!"

But this was apparently insufficient enticement; Lenox's young cousin was already thumping up to his lair on the third floor.

It was hard to conceive of a person belonging less to his name, this Lancelot being, down to his deepest essence, an instrument of mischief. Lenox loved—truly loved—his cousin Eustacia, Lancelot's mother, who had married a fine country-souled man named Stovall and led a loving, charitable, and blameless life in the far west reaches of Cornwall, near the sea.

But Lancelot made it difficult to remember that. He was a child of twelve, with continually dirty knees, brown-blond hair that spiked in every direction regardless of the ministrations it received, and a face that looked mostly innocent, but from time to time flashed a deep cunning. It was just the week before that they had celebrated his twelfth birthday, Lancelot gorging himself that day on chocolate torte in a way that would have made a French courtesan blush.

"Lancelot!" Lenox shouted up the stairs.

But the only response was silence. After these attacks the boy liked to hole up in his room, which was tactically intelligent, given that, alas, it locked from the inside. According to Graham, he had turned it—the best guest room!—into a midden of discarded clothes and lurid illustrated magazines about the bloodiest subjects imaginable, werewolves, vampires, unrepentant murderers. (Lenox had swiped a few of the last. He had research to conduct.)

Lenox shook his head and hung up his hat, rubbing the welt on his cheek and scanning the floor for the projectile.

He found it. A pebble! That was hardly sporting. Really, now. As he examined it there was a far quieter footstep on the stair, and Lenox looked up to see the house's butler, Graham, a compact, sandy-haired man of roughly his own age.

"Good evening, sir. I heard a noise."

"Did you! What hearing you must have!" said Lenox bitterly. He shook his head, removing his jacket. "What does the law say about killing your cousin?"

"It's illegal, sir."

"Still!"

"I believe so, sir."

"And they call this a civilization."

Graham held forth a patched, smoky tweed housecoat, into which Lenox deposited himself, arm by arm. "Your supper is in your study, sir," Graham said.

"Oh. Thank you. Would you care to sit with me while I dine?"

Graham tilted his head. "With pleasure, sir. The Dorset case?"

"Yes. It's a good one."

Graham would not smile, indeed would not inquire further than he already had, but Lenox had known him for eight years, and from a very minor compression of the valet's lips could tell that he was extremely glad to hear it—that they had a case—for from the starting gun they had been strange, friendly partners in this business.

Passing, in the long hallways from which his study branched to the right, the table that bore his silver card-stand, Lenox saw that several people had left their calling cards while he was away that afternoon.

One of them was Sir Richard Mayne, the head of Scotland Yard.

"Mayne didn't come here himself?" he said to Graham.

"No, sir. The card was left on his behalf by a constable."

"Did he have a message?"

"He said that Sir Richard would appreciate a call when you have spare time. There is no rush."

This was mere politeness. Lenox needed the goodwill of Scotland Yard, and he would go to Mayne in the morning. He was in a position that required him to treat his few allies respectfully.

Lenox's career as a detective had been, thus far, a mixed success. The first obstacle to overcome had been the lack of work, but he had chipped steadily away at that. There were long stretches when he had nothing to do, not a case in sight, sometimes until he was very near indeed to the brink of despair. He satisfied himself during such periods with carefully designed courses of study—on poison, firearms, fraud, every criminal subject—but they never felt a substitute for a real case.

Still, something always arrived at last, as it had now. Harder to manage, and harder to bear, was the ridicule visited upon him by members of his own class.

In truth he understood their attitude. Had he been to Harrow and Oxford for this absurd shamming police work? Had he been raised to the manners of the aristocracy, ridden horses with royalty, been invited to the balls of the great metropolis and England's immortal country houses, been flattered by the mothers of young women who knew he had money and position, had he been *Charles Lenox*, only to throw it away?

No, it was agreed, by all but his close friends. Perhaps even some of them secretly agreed.

And on his other flank there was the ridicule of the police. They considered him a mere enthusiast, an amateur; a nuisance.

This was despite the two notable successes of his three-year tenure in London. The first was the case of the Thames Ophelia; the second, the bizarre matter of the businessman in Maida Vale who had gone into a top-drawer butcher's shop, come out with a pound of mutton wrapped in wax paper for his family, and upon reaching the outdoors again immediately taken a pistol from his pocket and shot himself.

Lenox alone could claim credit for solving that one.

He wondered why Mayne wanted to see him. It might well be about the duke.

There was a knock on the front door. Lenox turned, curious, having come about twenty feet into the house. He felt a sharp hunger— he could smell the cook's fragrant leek-and-potato soup, and it had been a long six miles—and hoped the caller would make no very determined demand upon his time.

Graham answered the door, spoke a few words, then closed it gently. "It is a gentleman named Mr. Bonden, sir. He asks if you'll meet him in the street."

Lenox felt a prickle across the back of his hairline. He had been followed home.

CHAPTER SIX

Tell him I'll be with him in a moment."

"Yes, sir."

In the instant this exchange took, Lenox and Graham came to a quick, silent understanding: Graham should follow them if he could.

Lenox looked into the ancient brass stand by the door, scrolled with lions, where a walking stick and two black umbrellas stood in loose order. He took up the scarred calabash walking stick, which had been his grandfather's. Then he looked outside.

On his steps, with one foot higher than another and his hands in his pockets, was a man of an age very near the duke's, but in all other respects completely different.

He had a weathered face and wizened, piercing eyes. Despite the warmth he wore a long sealskin jacket. He held a pipe.

"How d'you do," he inquired in a low, powerful voice.

"Mr. Bonden?" Lenox said.

"I understand that you wanted a word with me."

Lenox noticed that Bonden had not used his name. Likely he didn't know it, then. But it would not be hard for him to learn it now that he had Lenox's address.

"I did," he said, putting out his hand. "I'm Charles Lenox."

Bonden returned his handshake, then stood back and considered this information unemotionally. The embers in his pipe glimmered faintly orange, as if they, like he, were cool on the outside but very much alive inside.

"It's not a name I know."

Lenox closed the door behind him, Graham on the other side of it.

"There's no reason it should be."

"Yet you know mine," Bonden said. "That is an uncomfortable situation in some lines of work."

"Listen—shall we take a walk?" Lenox asked, gesturing up the street toward the square.

He was thinking of Lady Jane next door, the odds of running into her and her giving away their closeness, something that would put him and, worse, her in Bonden's power. Not that he had cause to think Bonden a bad man. But he was an unknown one and, perhaps given the way he had followed Lenox here, had something menacing to him.

They started west down Hampden Lane. Lenox's walking stick was clamped tightly under his right arm. He had no idea what to do with it if the cause arose, except swing as hard as he could. That would have to do.

He wondered if it had been unwise to seek help. In the Maida Vale suicide attempt, one of the two cases he could claim to have solved for Scotland Yard, he had worked alone. He'd only been invited in because the police had decided he was merely mad, the gentleman, Quentin Wilkie, who had stepped outside of the butcher's and shot himself. (He had *lived* somehow, Wilkie, but was still comatose.) But Wilkie's wife had insisted that he was quite sane. It was she who had sought out Lenox's help.

Lenox, believing her, had painstakingly reconstructed the scene in the street from eyewitness accounts. One figure had slowly emerged out of those murky overlapping memories: a fellow with a diamond ring on each thumb and a bone-deep tan. Not a typical pedestrian.

Lenox had tracked him down based on the description; he was one Everett Botham, diamond miner from Cape Town.

Thereafter the story came together quickly. During a cave-in, Quentin Wilkie had chosen to haul a fortune in diamonds out of the mines with him rather than Botham, his partner, whom he left for dead. Wilkie returned to London, a rich man. But Botham had reappeared five years later, a still-richer man, and bent on either justice or revenge.

Wilkie must have known instantly when he stepped outside of the butcher's that his life would end either at Botham's hand or on the gallows.

Something like that, at least—police were still untangling the details. Among the men on the case was Mayne, who had been openly grateful to Lenox in a way none of the Yard's inspectors had.

Bonden and Lenox walked in silence for perhaps two hundred steps or so before Lenox said, "I have been wondering about the Dovecote. Why would a naval pub call itself that?"

"Before we venture onto the terrain of etymology," Bonden replied, "perhaps you could tell me why you were looking for me there."

There was a muted authority in his voice.

Lenox stopped and looked at Bonden in the shifting gaslight. They had reached the corner of Hampden Lane and Brook Street, a busy thoroughfare.

"I have been told that you are an expert at finding things, and I need something found."

"Could you please be more clear, on both counts?"

"I have heard your name twice, once from a friend inside Scotland Yard, once from a shipping officer on a case in which I was involved."

"A case?" Bonden looked up at the alabaster houses surrounding them, a smile on his face for the first time. He had taken his pipe in his hand. "You are the highest-living police constable I have met."

"I am in private business."

"Private business," Bonden repeated. He studied Lenox. "You do not have a criminal face."

"Ha! That is convenient to me, since I am not a criminal."

"Are you not? A valuable thing to know."

Lenox laughed shortly. "Listen, Mr. Bonden, we have gotten off to a poor start. I am a practicing detective, with a client who is willing to pay you for your time. My own circumstances have been mine since birth—you may ask after my identity if you wish to verify that—and I am not living on Hampden Lane as the result of any lucrative criminal enterprise. I am interested in police work, yet I am not suited for Scotland Yard. It's as simple as that."

"I see."

"What's more, I'm not after any trouble. I am looking for a specific object and hoped to enlist your aid. That is the whole of it."

Bonden again set his unnerving gaze upon Lenox.

Charles was himself headstrong at times—he was young and bright, after all, and he could have been in Baroness Lieb's parlor at that moment, with amiable company around him, or at the theater with his friend Hugo, or dining quietly with Lady Jane. He only tolerated this inspection now because of what he had heard of Bonden.

Both men—Sir Richard Mayne at the Yard, Willoughby Clark in the navy—had described him as a fellow with a nearly magical ability to locate the mislaid, the stolen, the long forgotten. Neither could account for his abilities; only swear to them. Bonden had once been a seafarer, Clark had told Lenox, but was now settled in London and possessed a reputation, at least in the strange overlapping criminal and official spheres that were conscious of his existence at all, for achieving the impossible. At last Bonden seemed to come to a decision. "Not this time, Mr. Lenox," he said. "But thank you for your interest." He glanced back down Hampden Lane. "You needn't have had your valet follow us. I intend you no harm."

Very abruptly he turned and walked away.

Lenox watched him go, then peered back down Hampden Lane himself. For his part, he couldn't see Graham anywhere.

He sighed. "Damn," he said to himself.

He walked back down the street in the direction of his house, and called out to Graham to show himself.

The valet emerged from a shadowed doorway. "Sir," he said.

"He spotted you."

"Did he?" Graham frowned. "My apologies."

"Oh, don't apologize. I don't know how he managed it. Uncommonly good hearing, perhaps? I should have talked more."

They returned to the house. "That was the Mr. Bonden you have had occasion to mention, sir?"

There was little Graham didn't know of Lenox's professional life. "Yes. I hoped he might assist us on the duke's case. He declined."

"Then the duke is missing something, sir?"

"He is. No matter, though. We'll find it on our own."

And indeed Lenox believed they would. The two of them had been through a great deal in the years since Lenox came to London from university, collaborating every day, out in cold and hot together upon false trails and real ones. Aside from his brother there was nobody in the city that Lenox trusted more.

"But not until I eat," Lenox said, opening the door to his house, peering in cautiously to be sure Lancelot wasn't waiting to spring. He slotted the walking stick back into its brass stand. "I'm starved. In fact I'm happy that Bonden has turned us down, blast him."

"What was the crime to do with, then, sir?" asked Graham, as they proceeded down the long central hall.

It was kept lit to a perfect lulling low candlelight by Lenox's redoubtable housekeeper, Mrs. Huggins, who with any luck had locked cousin Lancelot into some dark, damp, and narrow closet.

"An assault upon a very august personage, in fact."

"Who, sir?" Graham.

"It will wait one moment longer—he's been dead two hundred and fifty years."

CHAPTER SEVEN

Lenox had recently taken to drinking strong tea with his supper. In the mornings he preferred to have Pekoe, the tea of his childhood, which, because it was made of the earliest spring buds, was light and fragrant; but for whatever reason, in the evenings he found that only the very black workingman's India tea, drunk by nine of ten households in England, would suffice. Taken with two spoonfuls of sugar, it gave him a few hours of vibrant energy to work before, for whatever mysterious reason, allowing him to drop into a sweet and effortless sleep.

That evening, as he ate first his leek-and-potato soup, then a very good chop with buttered potatoes and spring peas, he sipped his tea and felt himself slowly stirring into new life after his long day.

Graham sat opposite, hands closed together on the table, listening to Lenox as he described his meeting with the duke. He only interjected once, his eyes widening.

"Shakespeare!" he said.

This counted as a positive effusion from Graham, and Lenox smiled.

"Yes," replied the young detective. "I'm told he's quite famous."

Graham would not be drawn. "But that was *not* the painting stolen, sir?"

"No," said Lenox, eating his chop. "It's the poor old twelfth duke who's gone. The current one being the fifteenth."

"Perhaps the thieves took the wrong painting? A portrait of Shakespeare would be—well, priceless, of course, sir."

"The duke had the same initial thought, and so did I."

"But then, sir?"

Lenox stood up. There were madeleines on the sideboard, the specialty of his cook, Ellie. He took two, returning to the table and dunking one into his tea.

"The first thing I asked the duke was which three people's company I had joined in this knowledge, that there was a painting of Shakespeare from life sitting in the middle of London. I did not also say: if it was indeed a picture of Shakespeare, and this was not some dull, easily disproven family legend."

The duke had given Lenox his answer very simply.

"Myself, the Queen, and Sir Charles Locke Eastlake," he had said.

"Who is Sir Charles Eastlake, Your Grace?" Lenox had asked.

"The Surveyor of the Queen's Pictures."

Lenox had never heard of him before in his life. "May I ask you about your decision to confide in him, sir?"

"It was on the advice of Her Majesty. It is a national treasure, after all."

Almost involuntarily both had at that moment glanced at the painting.

And the truth was that Lenox had just then felt an odd sort of radiant power emanating from the shabby little portrait, though in itself it was nothing, the sort of three-quarters pose that you could find stacked by the dozen at any London marketplace on a Saturday morning. An art student might have bought it simply to paint over. It was surrounded by what even he could see was much finer art.

But Shakespeare!

There were few people in England to whom his works were not as intimately familiar as the stories of the Bible, and often, as with the Bible, through lovingly wrong retellings, plays put on at local fetes, bedside stories that missed and altered dozens of details— the sort of backhanded homages that make a piece of literature more than a piece of literature, stitching it instead into a nation's culture.

Beyond the work, there were the mysteries. Who was the dark woman of his sonnets? Had Shakespeare been a secret Catholic? Where had he been during his famous lost years? Why had he left his wife his "second best bed" in his will—as a snub or a compliment? Each was tantalizing, each impossible to answer conclusively. For Lenox—who had always preferred novels to the theater, and never quite understood the pure elation the playwright seemed to elicit in some people—they were more interesting than the work itself. Perhaps naturally, since he was a detective.

"And Sir Charles Locke Eastlake struck you as a trustworthy person, Your Grace?"

"He certainly seemed to be. Sober as a judge, very tedious. But when can one ever be sure?"

"Indeed, Your Grace."

Dorset looked at Lenox evenly. "You may have noticed several surprising people absent from that list of three. My wife, for instance."

"I had noticed that, yes, Your Grace."

"It is the great secret of the Dukes of Dorset, passed hand over hand from one to the next. It is a responsibility each duke has taken very seriously."

"And your son, Your Grace?"

"My solicitors hold a sealed letter to be given to my son in the event that anything happens to me. I shall tell him myself when he turns twenty-five. He is nineteen at the moment."

"What is his name, Your Grace?"

"Corfe."

Lenox nodded. There was a Corfe Castle in Dorset. "How did your family acquire the painting, Your Grace?"

"That is a long story, and not relevant." The duke stubbed out his small cigar and took another from the gold case. "But I hope you can now see why it matters more to me who took the painting than where the painting is?"

"I have a guess, Your Grace."

"Well?"

"Do you believe that the thief took the wrong painting?" Lenox gestured toward the wall. "The sixth, rather than the fifth, from the windows?"

Dorset looked satisfied. He checked his watch. "Yes."

Lenox, heart beating hard, said, "And yet I wonder, Your Grace."

"Eh?"

Lenox didn't speak for a moment, staring at the portraits. "Is the missing picture similar in size to the remaining ones, excluding the portrait of Shakespeare?"

"Identical. They are all modeled on the first."

They both looked toward the first and oldest portrait, next to the windows. "What gives me pause," Lenox said, "is that the Shakespeare is so very different in size, style, framing—in every detail—from the other paintings here. All of those are large, and very majestic, and very—well, ducal, Your Grace."

Dorset frowned. "But why would someone steal a painting from this room other than the Shakespeare? Or if they did, why on earth not the Reynolds?"

Lenox shrugged. "That I do not know, Your Grace. For that matter, why would they steal a painting rather than—just to take an example—your snuffbox there? Those are diamonds, if I am not mistaken?"

Dorset touched his fingertips to the box. "You are not, though I keep pen nibs in it, not taking snuff myself." He looked up at Lenox.

"If they were not after the portrait of Shakespeare, I have made an error telling you about it."

Lenox inclined his head noncommittally. "At least I can promise you that I will not compound the error by telling anyone else, Your Grace, if indeed it was an error."

"Thank you," said Dorset, though his mind was elsewhere.

"Had you contemplated Sir Charles Eastlake, Your Grace, as the possible thief?"

The duke glanced at him. "I had."

Lenox shook his head. "I believe we can safely rule him out, personally. If he were the thief, I imagine he would be absolutely and entirely sure to get the right painting. It would have been an insane risk, and he has a very great deal to lose. He would have made no mistake."

"Hm."

"Moreover, he would also know how immediately suspicion must fall upon him."

The duke wore the look of a man who had found himself in deeper waters than he thought and did not like it—though Lenox could tell there was also some relief in the possibility that the portrait of Shakespeare was not part of the robber's plan.

"Yes. True. He might have told someone still, however, though he very solemnly swore to me and to the Queen that he would not."

"He might have, Your Grace."

Dorset looked at Lenox. "The Queen, of course, was not scaling the water pipe of my house on a Monday evening."

"No, Your Grace. It would not have been very stately."

"Besides, it is hers for the asking," the duke murmured, in such a definite way that it surprised Lenox—this glimpse of the intense loyalty of the medieval nobleman, who considered his life worth staking on his sovereign's slightest wish.

Their conversation had not continued much longer, and now, many hours later, in Hampden Lane, slowly eating his madeleines,

Lenox sketched in its contours for Graham. He had asked for a detailed description of the painting, had inspected the windows (there was no evidence at all that they had been forced), then had inspected the room, without result.

After that, the 15th Duke of Dorset had rung for Ward and asked him to provide any general information that Lenox needed. As they left, Lenox thanked him, and the duke offered only a troubled nod.

It had occurred to Lenox how very alone he would be again in a moment.

Graham took all this in. "That is why you asked Bonden for his help, sir," he said at last.

Lenox nodded. "Yes. I wondered if there might be something about the missing painting itself, number six as I think of it, which is important after all. Perhaps nothing to do with William Shakespeare whatsoever."

"What will you do now, sir?"

"Go to sleep." Lenox smiled ruefully. "But in the morning, I intend to find this worthless painting, with or without Bonden's help."

Graham nodded but looked troubled. Both of them had it, Lenox could feel: the catch of irresolution, the absolute need to know what had happened, and why. The circumstances were too confused, too ambiguous.

"Very good, sir, though to remind you, you are engaged to have breakfast with Lady Jane Grey."

"Oh, I am, aren't I. Planning this garden party?"

"Yes, sir."

Lenox threw his napkin onto the table. "My life is a plague of obligations."

As if to confirm this bleak statement, upstairs there was a minor boom, which meant his cousin Lancelot was once again in motion— like a battalion marching under cover of darkness.

CHAPTER EIGHT

Lenox was up at the stroke of six o'clock the next morning. By quarter past, he was seated at the desk in his study, carefully reading through the papers, a pair of scissors at hand so that he could clip any article he thought relevant to his encompassing study of criminal activity in London.

It had taken him some time to be happy in this house; his rooms from the year he had first moved to London held a dear place in his heart, with their expansive view of Green Park. It was when he had made this large rectangular study comfortable that he had at last felt really at home. Now he couldn't imagine a better place to work. His books were arranged as he liked, history on one side of the room, fiction on the other. At the far end of the long chamber there was a fireplace surrounded by comfortable chairs; here, closer to the windows, was his desk, topped in red leather. From his chair he could turn and ponder the passersby a few feet below on Hampden Lane.

These morning hours were his most serious time of work. One of the reasons he had hoped to have Bonden's help was to add to his own education, to which he was ardently committed. He wouldn't have minded being a person who could find anything.

Mrs. Huggins came in. "Good morning, sir. Do you have enough tea?"

The housekeeper was a widow of approximately fifty-five, attractive and severe, with dark hair going gray in streaks—who kept house for him more exactingly than perhaps he would quite have preferred.

Lenox looked at the monumental teapot on the corner of his desk, which could have accommodated the needs of a party of eight, then at his own very small teacup.

"For now I think I'll be able to get on, Mrs. Huggins," he said, looking up at her earnestly. "Thank you."

"Mr. Graham is preparing your eggs, sir, and your toast is in the brazier."

"Thank you, Mrs. Huggins."

"If you had time to peruse a few matters of household—"

"Unfortunately it is a very busy morning, Mrs. Huggins. Could we put off the perusing until tomorrow?"

She knew very well what that meant—that he would try to put it off to the day of revelation, if he could. "Very well, sir."

He tried a slight smile. "Be sure to give me two or three reports before the food comes, though. I would like to be apprised of absolutely all this information as it becomes available."

Some days she was receptive to a joke; some days not. Today: not. "I thought you would like to know, sir," she said stiffly.

"I'm sorry," he said, "I would. I'm very hungry." Then, pressing his luck, he said, "I also much need to take something along with me to Jane's for breakfast—to Lady Jane's—but it slipped my mind to buy flowers, or what have you, yesterday. Do we have anything sitting around?"

"Sitting around, sir!" said Mrs. Huggins.

"Well, I mean, a savory cake, or something of that sort."

She looked at him almost sadly. He knew in these moments that he seemed to her an irredeemable specimen representing the lost ways of a whole generation. "A cake, sir."

"Or something. I did say, 'or something,' Mrs. Huggins."

"I could make a tulip cake in a pinch, sir."

"Might you? I would be extremely grateful."

"In that case Mr. Graham will have to be the one to bring you up your eggs and toast, though, sir! And see to it if you need any more tea!"

Graham could have done this blindfolded and backward. He had been Lenox's scout at Balliol for three years—even now was the person Lenox liked to make his soft-boiled eggs, a duty Mrs. Huggins had only conceded after the bitterest protest—but Lenox just said, "Thank you, Mrs. Huggins. You are a brick."

"I suppose such emergencies are part of being in service, Mr. Lenox," she said.

Before long Graham brought the eggs and toast, and Lenox tucked into them with a hearty appetite. The valet sat down in the chair opposite, with his own cup of tea and his own stack of newspapers, and was soon as absorbed as Lenox. This was their daily ritual—or their friendly competition, you might say. Each was put out if the other found a significant clipping that he had missed.

"These are cracking good eggs," said Lenox after a long period of silence, looking up.

"Thank you, sir."

Lenox laughed. "Eh? *Cracking?* Did you pick up on that?"

"Yes, sir."

"*Cracking.*"

"Almost painfully humorous, sir," said Graham, nodding.

Lenox frowned. "You need to get about more, Graham."

"It may well be so, sir."

Lenox glanced up at the clock on his mantel. It was close to eight o'clock. The rays of the sun were just beginning to fall more insistently across the room's dark carpet. "What time is the breakfast, remind me?" he said.

"Nine o'clock."

Lenox sat back. "I have just enough time to run out and call on Mayne. But I doubt he'll be in the office before eight thirty, and then I shall have to turn around. It's a nuisance."

"Indeed, sir," said Graham, though this time his sympathy was sincere.

Instead of leaving, Lenox took out his notepad. He flipped to the page where he had written the duke's description of the missing painting.

"The painting was thirty inches high by twenty-two inches across," Lenox said, reading. "Or at least the *frame* was, because he swore it was the same size as the other seven, and he had asked Theodore Ward, my old school friend, to measure one of those."

"Do you have any suspicions of Ward, sir?" asked Graham.

Lenox didn't look up from his notes. "No, none," he murmured. On the wall there was a portrait of Lenox's mother's uncle, an earl himself, sitting grumpily in a chair. Lenox had always liked it. He looked over at it. "Would you say roughly that size, Graham?"

"To a first approximation, sir, certainly."

"Not easy to conceal." He looked up at Graham from his notepad. "Whereas the Shakespeare couldn't have been more than fifteen inches high and twelve across. Scarcely much larger than a sheet of paper."

"Interesting, sir."

"The background was Dorset House, in the country—trees and that sort of thing, the duke said, a pillar. You know how those old portraits look."

Graham nodded. "Yes, sir."

Lenox frowned at his notes. "What is a jerkin?"

"A sort of sleeveless jacket, sir."

"Sounds asinine. Well, he's in a red jerkin and silver pants, this fellow, if you can credit that. Next to him is his favorite dog, a setter with long ears."

Graham nodded. "Anything else, sir?"

"It is signed by the artist very legibly, a person named Quincy Quinn. Oh, and the duke is smiling in it. That shall be a clue, if the jerkin doesn't give it away." Lenox flipped his notebook closed. "It sounds a picture of so little consequence. And yet someone went to the trouble of hiking up the side of that building, prying open a locked window, and stealing it. That is peculiar."

"You saw evidence the window was pried open, sir?"

Lenox shook his head. "No. But Dorset and his valet both swear that it was locked the night before. And it would have been far easier to break into the window than into the house, and then into the study, which itself has two locks."

"It only occurs to me, sir," said Graham, "that perhaps we are all overreaching. Perhaps it was merely one of the servants."

"I specifically asked about that possibility. Nearly the entire staff had gone to Dorset Castle ahead of the duke and duchess. Those that were left—the duchess's maid, the butler, the duke's valet, the cook—are employees of long standing."

"None with a grudge, sir?"

Lenox tilted his head philosophically. "It is always possible. But the duke told me specifically that he pays well over market rates. That includes Ward. Why steal a painting worth less than that difference and risk the sack?"

"True, sir."

"That is what I keep wondering—why that painting? It's too large, too personal, not valuable enough . . ." He glanced at his watch. "But we can resume this discussion in a bit."

He stood up and straightened out. He didn't really mind at all going to Jane's, though it did well to pretend; his heart, the stubborn old animal, beat a little faster at the thought of seeing her. The irony was that she planned breakfasts like this one partly to help him find a wife. It would be best to leave the city soon, he thought. Behind him on the wall was a map tacked to corkboard and covered with ink: the places he intended to travel.

"Graham," he called, when the tie was done. The valet appeared. "Is Lancelot awake?"

"Not yet, sir."

"You'll see him into Mr. Templeton's hands at nine?"

This was the pimple-covered young curate in charge of showing three young Etonians on their break the sights of London.

"Yes, sir," said Graham.

Before he left his study, Lenox went over to one of his bookshelves on the right side of the room and scanned it for about ninety seconds before finding the small, very soft brown leather book he was looking for. He opened it wholly at random and read a line:

> *I can easier teach twenty what were good to be done, than*
> *be one of the twenty to follow my own teaching.*
> —The Merchant of Venice

He frowned, considering this, then slipped the buttery-soft little book into his front pocket.

On the front hall table was the tulip spice cake, an object of perfect beauty, of course, still warm, wrapped in parchment paper, reposing regally upon a deep-blue plate.

"It's a capital cake, Mrs. Huggins!" he called out loudly. "Thank you! Good-bye!"

CHAPTER NINE

The garden behind Lady Jane's house was unusually wild compared to most of those on Hampden Lane, with vines that climbed the fences and a small sunlit knoll encircled by a few towering oak trees, shifting in the breeze.

There was a table on the flagstones outside with four places set, three occupied. Lady Jane waved to Lenox. "There you are! What a cake," she said, taking the plate from his hands. "How neatly it's iced."

"Well, of course," said Lenox with pride.

"Pass my compliments to Mrs. Huggins."

"I will not!" said Lenox indignantly.

She laughed. "You know the duchess, Charles." This was the Duchess of Marchmain, an older cousin of Jane's aged around forty-three or forty-four, very pretty, all that was amiable and kind. She gave Lenox her hand. "And this is my dear friend Miss Euphemia Somers, from Mrs. Clark's. She has just returned from a year in America with her parents."

"I'm charmed to meet you, Miss Somers," said Lenox, bowing.

She inclined her head. "And you, Mr. Lenox. My friends call me Effie."

If Effie Somers had been at Mrs. Clark's with Lady Jane—a girls' school where Lenox's friend had spent a year perfecting her French and painting sailboats—she was probably around twenty-two. She gave an impression of great ease and good nature. She was not unusually beautiful, but her smile was, and so was her hair, a dark chestnut blond that she wore in plaits, so notably beautiful, in fact, that one might have fallen in love with her for this single trait.

Lenox sat, and the duchess said, "I hear you have been calling upon Dorset."

Lenox peered curiously at her, smiling. "Where on earth did you hear that?"

"Not from me," Jane said.

"A little chickadee saw you going into the house, I suppose."

It would be easier to find privacy in a jammed lifeboat in the middle of the Pacific Ocean than in London. "He was an acquaintance of my father's," Lenox said.

Her husband was a very different kind of duke than Dorset, his title only two generations old and won on the battlefield. But there was a great deal of money in it. "I like him."

"He pinches cheeks," said Effie Somers.

"Does he!" said Lenox, surprised.

She smiled. "He did when I was eighteen, at any rate."

"Come clean, Charles," said Lady Jane, "why were you with him?"

"It really was a social call," he said, and took a covering bite of teacake.

"Just don't go hunting with him," said the duchess.

Jane laughed shortly.

"Why not?" he asked.

They glanced at each other. Miss Somers looked at them inquiringly, evidently in the dark, too. "I suppose he kept it quiet," said the duchess.

"Kept what quiet?" asked Lenox.

Lady Jane, who had before her a small, neatly drawn diagram of the seating arrangements for her garden party, nominally their reason for being there, looked down at it. "Shall we discuss seating?"

"Come now!" said Lenox.

"Even dukes deserve privacy."

Lenox might have let it rest there, except that Miss Somers, to whom he became instantly indebted, said, "But there are only two of us. I'll keep the secret."

"So shall I," Lenox put in right away.

Lady Jane sighed. "Fine. It was about five years ago. It was terribly sad, really. A group were hunting grouse in Dorset, the duke, General Pendleton, and their two sons, and the duke accidentally shot Pendleton's son. Pure bad chance."

"And he died?"

"He lived for a month," said the duchess, her cup of tea poised in her hand. "It was awful for Georgia Pendleton—awful. They have no other sons."

"Was there an inquest?" asked Effie Somers.

"Yes, with no fault found. Everyone present, including the groom, agreed that it was no more than an unfortunate accident."

Lenox reflected on this. "Pendleton commanded a brigade at Waterloo," he said. "He was made a knight for it."

"Your facts are out of date," the duchess said, "for the Queen made him a baron in the list last year. He doesn't come down from the country often, or you would have heard."

"He has no son to leave the title to," said Lady Jane.

"He has a nephew, at least," said the duchess, "with whom he has become closer. His younger brother's son."

Lenox took another bite of his teacake, which had a satisfying cracked-cinnamon sugar crust. He followed it with a sip of tea and looked up into the pure blue sky, thinking of his father and his brother for a passing moment.

"Was there bad blood between Pendleton and the duke?"

"They are not so close as they once were, of course," said the duchess. "But no, the general accepted the situation, ultimately. Of course the duke himself was heartbroken."

Lenox pictured the still, impassive face of the thin and finely dressed aristocrat.

"What a terribly sad story," said Jane's friend.

"Yes. I don't know why we brought up something so morbid!" replied Lady Jane, then with a businesslike tone went on, "Leave it aside—this seating plan. Here is where you are essential, Charles. I need to know everyone who has rejected everyone's proposals among your Oxford friends. It's vital. All the secrets, now, please."

"Why do you care?" he asked curiously.

Lady Jane looked at him for a moment with guilty happiness. "There is a chance the Queen may come. I'd like it to be perfect."

"You'd better cut those branches back, then," said Lenox, nodding upward. "It would be bad news if one fell on her."

"Leave the garden to me." Then, with sudden alarm, she said, "Lancelot will be gone in three weeks' time, won't he?"

"Yes, thank heavens."

"That's good news. It's one thing for him to target you with the peashooter, another Prince Albert."

"I'm offended at that," said Lenox.

"Who is Lancelot?" Effie Somers said.

"Don't ask," he and Jane replied simultaneously, and all three laughed, and the conversation turned decisively away from the Duke of Dorset.

Still, the story of the hunting accident stayed in his mind. And the name: Pendleton.

When they had finished eating breakfast, Lenox went inside to help Lady Jane fetch the cut flowers she was considering for the tables. He said to her, in the back conservatory, "You're about a quarter as clever as you think."

She stopped, surprised. "At least half, I would have said. But how so?"

"As if I knew more than you about who has proposed to whom! I can't even remember who's engaged."

"We have different friends," she said.

He shook his head and smiled. "I'm not going to marry Miss Somers."

Lady Jane paused, looking at him, then said, "But don't you like her? She was the dearest person I knew at Miss Clark's. Always the most popular—but never took sides, even against the worst of the girls. And her father, being a diplomat, has dragged her all over the world these last three years, meaning she's never been thrown in the way of a decent fellow."

"Well, she may be at your party. Say, look at this," he said, and pulled the small leather book from his study out of his breast pocket. "You'll like it."

She took it. "*Selected Quotations of William Shakespeare.* Why do you have it?"

"I just came across it. My father gave it to me when I went to Harrow. It was once his own."

She smiled, flipping through the pages. "There are stars by some of the lines."

"Those are his."

She read one and laughed, studying it. She was one of the people close to Charles who had known his father well.

Eventually she handed the little book back. "I'm very glad you have it."

"So am I."

Lady Jane looked him in the eye. "Don't you like her, Charles? Effie?"

He did, in fact; he liked her more with every passage of the conversation. She didn't have quite so sharp an edge as Lady Jane or the duchess, but there was something lovely about her—the effortlessness of her laugh, the ingenuousness of her wit, her clear intelligence.

He was about to say so, but there was a knock at the door. There were no servants immediately at hand, and he went to answer it himself. He saw, to his surprise, that outside was Theodore Ward.

"Hello, Theo," he said.

Lady Jane came up behind Lenox. "Hello, Mr. Ward."

The young secretary looked utterly changed. His hair was a dark upright shock, his collar loose and his face red. He only just managed to bow. "My Lady." Then he turned back to Lenox. "Charles. Thank goodness."

"What's the matter?" asked Lenox.

"The duke has been kidnapped."

CHAPTER TEN

L enox opened the door wide. "Kidnapped! What?"

Ward shook his head. "I don't know much. I have a cab waiting. Will you come?"

"Of course. Instantly."

Soon Lenox and Ward were down the stairs and into the waiting hansom. Ward gave the address of a busy corner near Pall Mall, the quarter of Mayfair that housed the private clubs and wine and gun and clothing shops that the city's bluest-blooded inhabitants frequented.

Theo had only heard the barest details of the incident. He knew the duke had been stepping from his carriage outside the august Carlton Club, which was the luxurious and exclusive game preserve of the conservative party. It was apparently where Dorset went nearly every morning, meaning the kidnappers might well have lain in wait for him there.

"Two large men in cloaks, collars turned up, shoved him into a different carriage that pulled right up alongside the duke's."

"Cloaks?" said Lenox, interrupting.

"Yes, why?"

He turned away and looked at the passing street. "Out of season," he murmured. "Go on."

"This second carriage had sped up the street before the doorman of the Carlton could even get down the steps," Ward said, though he had blown his police whistle instantly. There had been a large crowd upon the steps of the Carlton who watched the commotion.

"Where were you?" Lenox asked.

"Dorset House."

"Did any of them provide a good description of either the men or the carriage?" asked Lenox.

Theo shook his head unhappily. "You have heard all I know. I came to fetch you immediately. The duchess is at the scene of the crime, accompanied by her cousin Sir Japheth Miles. His Lordship, the duke's son, Corfe, would naturally have gone, but his health has worsened today. He has not left his room—delirious with fever from what I understand."

"Bad timing."

"It never rains but it pours," said Ward, resorting, in his plain unintellectual but not unintelligent way, to the closest cliché at hand.

"Chin up," Lenox said, resorting to his, for Ward looked bereft. "The duke is too important to stay kidnapped. Nothing could be more certain than that."

And indeed, when they pulled up to the Carlton there were no fewer than half a dozen police wagons present. The street was blocked off in both directions. They stepped down from the cab and walked the last hundred yards to reach the scene.

The first people Lenox saw there were Sir Richard Mayne, head of the Yard, and one of his chief inspectors, Warren Sinex. Sinex was a tall, hard, dangerous fellow, shrewd but given to flights of temper. Mayne, by contrast, was a gentleman to his fingernails, equable and hood-eyed, careful.

"Lenox," Mayne said, surprised. "What brings you here?"

"I have been consulting with the duke in the last few days. His personal secretary, Mr. Ward, fetched me."

Mayne's eyes went to Ward. "You are Theodore Ward? Very well, you two, come through the gauntlet if you wish."

Journalists were ringed around the carriage, which had the Dorset family's intricate arms in raised gold leaf on each of its four doors. Inside it, Mayne showed them, were two plush blue velvet benches facing each other.

One of them there bore a large dark stain.

"Blood?" Lenox said to Mayne.

"We think so," said Sir Richard. He turned to find the journalists pressing behind him and barked, "Clear out! Clear out! Constables, yes, you two, do a better job of keeping these men back or you'll be looking for another line of work. I mean that sincerely."

The constables didn't need a second telling, and with rough shoves pushed the protesting members of the press backward.

Lenox took the chance to lean in and feel the cushion. His fingers came away a rusty red. There was no doubt of it: blood.

He looked at Ward. "Not a great amount. That is some comfort at least," said Lenox.

Mayne and Sinex returned their attention to the carriage, Sinex hanging about half a foot behind his superior, glowering at Lenox, whom he strongly disliked.

"What happened?" Lenox asked Sir Richard.

Mayne offered an account similar to Ward's, filigreed with a few more details. The carriage into which the duke had been forced had four horses—in other words, was unusually fast, might easily be halfway to Scotland by now—and both men had looked "English," to the doorman.

"'No Indian or Negro buggers, begging your pardon, Sir Richard,' he told me," Mayne said. "I quote him directly, you understand."

"Did he notice anything about their clothes?"

"Not beyond the cloaks. But there's this," said Mayne. He took a notecard from his pocket and passed it over to Lenox and Ward.

Prepare ten thousand pounds in ready notes and ten thousand pounds in gold bullion. Await further instruction.

Lenox read it twice and turned to Ward. "I take it the duke can raise this kind of money?"

Ward, who had been pale throughout the encounter, at last had a use to which to put his nervous energy. He nodded. "Without even troubling his bankers, I should think," he said. "He owns—well, Dorset. You know that as well as I do."

It was scarcely an exaggeration. Hundreds of thousands of acres of that county were the duke's. Lenox had only asked to be sure there was no sudden, secret embarrassment in his finances.

What in all creation did this have to do with a stolen painting of a forgotten duke? What did it have to do with William Shakespeare?

"What are your men doing?" Lenox asked Mayne.

Mayne glanced up Pall Mall. "No tracks to follow, unfortunately. Cobblestones on this street; no recent rain regardless." He tapped the note against his knuckles distractedly. "I don't like the blood, obviously. Anyhow, why had you been consulting with the duke?"

Lenox, suddenly alert, said, "Do that again, would you?"

"What?"

"Hit your hand with the card, if you wouldn't mind."

The superintendent looked at him as if he belonged in an asylum, but bounced the thick notecard lightly against his knuckles. "Like this?"

"Yes." Lenox looked away, reaching for his tobacco in his waistcoat pocket. "Good. Thank you."

"Why?"

"Nothing. I was wrong," Lenox said. He had learned better than to tell the gentlemen of the Yard anything before he was obliged to do so. Motioning discreetly with his tobacco pouch, he said, "Is that the duchess?"

Ward followed his hand. "Yes," he said. "Her cousin is next to her."

This was a tall, older man who himself was very upright, with white hair and a clean-shaven face. "Perhaps I might have a word with her?"

"Better be a cautious word," Sinex put in, giving him a mirthless smile. "Don't want to be playing about in matters like this, Lenox. Liable to spill your own blood."

"Enough of that," said Mayne sharply. "Lenox, I'll walk you to Her Grace."

They left Ward and Sinex by the carriage doors. Their boots clicked on the cobblestones as they walked. "You received my card yesterday?" Mayne asked.

"I did. I had planned to call on you this morning, Sir Richard."

"Dorset wrote me to ask—well, commanded me, I suppose, to come to the Lords. He asked if you were reliable."

Ah, so that was why Mayne had sought him out.

"Did he?" said Lenox, who had lately learned, in conversations such as this one, too, the value of saying little.

"I asked him why he wanted to know. He would not tell. At last I gave him my reluctant recommendation."

"Reluctant on my behalf, or reluctant because you didn't know the reason it was requested?"

"The latter," said Mayne. "Mixed with some of the former, if I'm candid. You are, of course, not a police officer."

"No."

"I was also going to tell you this morning to be careful of him, Dorset. I have had cause to run across him in Parliament. He can ruin any man he pleases, and he has a streak of—" Mayne looked at the immaculate façade of the Carlton Club as they walked toward the duchess. "Not unkindness. But he believes that God made Victoria the Queen, then made him the Duke of Dorset."

"I see."

"If you feel you can tell me what he wanted I would be grateful."

"I need time to think, if you could permit it, Sir Richard. The duke entrusted me with a secret he held very close."

Mayne looked at him warily. "Very well. But if he winds up dead and you have held something back, it will go badly for you. I say that with sincere regard, Charles. I was fond of your father."

"Thank you, Sir Richard."

"Here is the duchess."

CHAPTER ELEVEN

The duchess was, to an almost unsettling degree of accuracy, a duchess.

Which was to say, first, that she had the cool self-possession of her position; second, had the odd ability to look downward at a person of any height whatsoever; and third, was very elegant and unruffled, even in these circumstances. Her dress was conservative and self-evidently expensive, dark blue with a very wide, graceful bell-shaped crinoline spreading out from her waist, just the fashion at the moment. It must have been the devil of a time to get through doorways.

As well as her cousin, two attendants stood at her side.

She greeted Lenox with little more than a nod when she heard that he had been working for her husband, until Ward mentioned his name.

"Oh," she said, rather surprised. "Charles Lenox. I know your mother, Lady Emma."

"Ah, yes," said Lenox, nodding.

His hands were clasped behind him, in deference both to her title and her situation. "I would go so far as to call her a friend," the duchess added.

"I will remember you to her, with your permission, Your Grace," he said.

She put out her hand, and Lenox took it. She applied a gentle pressure. "Please do."

Ward asked the duchess if Lenox might pose her one or two questions, and she nodded. "Has your husband mentioned Shakespeare to you recently?" he said.

She looked at him with a surprise that would have been difficult to feign. "Shakespeare. No. Why?"

"I ask for no important reason—a misplaced thought, Your Grace," said Lenox quickly and apologetically. "Had he done anything out of the ordinary recently, may I ask?"

This was what Lady Jane called his Victoria question. He fell back upon it whenever he needed to buy time to think. Every morning, in the course of her usual business, Queen Victoria gave the orders that her chefs make a serving of curry for forty-eight.

This was despite the fact that she herself despised curry. She did it because she wanted to be prepared in case a visiting dignitary of Asian descent called upon the Palace at random.

Or forty-eight of them, Lenox supposed. The forty-ninth would have to eat whatever the Queen herself ate. All he remembered from when he had dined at the Palace as a boy was that she had eaten with incredible speed and that everyone had to stop the moment she set down her fork, which meant that nobody would have gotten enough if there hadn't been, blessedly, twenty courses.

His question to the duchess was a catchall, but being both intelligent and exceedingly private, she swatted it away. "He has hired you, evidently. Otherwise, no."

He had been raised not to contradict any woman, much less one who outranked him, but he could not let this pass. "Not hired, Your Grace," Lenox said.

"Excuse me?"

"I am an amateur."

Her cousin Sir Japheth Miles, whom Ward had introduced secondarily, said dryly, "How comforting."

Lenox had already pegged Miles—a clubman. His acerbic tone in those two words confirmed him as such: worldly, neatly dressed, faultlessly connected, probably a bachelor with voluminous memories of the gay '20s. No doubt working on a memoir. Inwardly, Lenox sighed.

"Just one more question, Your Grace," he said. "Is the duke left-handed or right-handed?"

She looked at him oddly. "Right-handed. Why?"

"Another failed thought," he said, bowing his head deferentially. "Thank you for your time."

He left the duchess and spoke to the porter at the Carlton, celebrity of the moment, who confirmed that the carriage into which the duke had been forced had four horses and was colored black, with no markings. He added that the men were cloaked in black, too.

Their behavior toward him had been undeniably violent, the porter said—no chance he went willingly into their carriage.

The duke's own driver, who was in disgrace for his failure to intervene, confirmed that.

"Why didn't you follow them?" Lenox asked.

"They knocked me clear off the box when I was getting down for to assist 'is Grace, didn't they!"

The young detective saw a developing lump on the driver's forehead now. "I didn't know that."

"Oh, yes! And in the scrumble to get out from under the wheels—'orses may always bolt, and a man kilt like the snap of your fingers—I've seen it, Your Lordships—sirs—they was gone. My goodness," he added, shaking his head in wonder. "An innocent chap can't find an ounce of sympathy."

Lenox looked through the carriage itself. He asked the driver whether there was anything missing—all he had found was a top hat, in a box beneath one of the benches—and the driver said no, there was never anything kept in the carriage. He himself cleaned its bits and bobs out completely twice a day.

Lenox thanked him, then took a step away. He put one foot up on the steps of the Carlton Club and looked down St. James's Street in the direction of Piccadilly Circus, the busiest thoroughfare in London. A quick left or right turn there and the kidnappers could have melted into traffic without any trouble.

As he contemplated this, he vaguely listened to Ward engage in an increasingly fractious discussion with Sinex about their next steps (neither had any intelligent plan for what to do, and each was ferociously committed to it), and Mayne ordering the slow and probably hopeless but necessary process of having his constables spread about the neighborhood to question the populace.

Sir Japheth was just asking when they could expect some *action*, the kind of question only a man without specific experience of action could ask, when a thought came to Lenox.

He interrupted authoritatively. "We need to speak to that fellow Jacob who sells apples outside of Savile's. It will be fastest to reach him on foot."

Everyone looked at him. "What?" said Sir Richard after a moment.

"He is a simpleton—"

"Well, that's ideal, then," said Sinex. "You two should be able to converse on an equal plane."

Lenox gave him a dead-eyed stare. "But, as I was going to say, he has perfect recall. We are in possession of one piece of information of any value aside from the ransom card: that the carriage had four horses."

"And?"

"He is always on Jermyn Street. He will know whether a carriage with four horses has passed him today." Lenox pointed. "That is the only street between here and Piccadilly, the largest street in London, where if they went, of course, they are lost to us. If they took Jermyn, however, we have a chance of witnesses."

"How do you know this simpleton?" asked Sir Japheth.

"It is my job to know something of crime in London," said Lenox curtly.

"Fine," said Mayne, siding with Lenox. "Let us go."

It took only a minute or so to reach Jacob, a popular, hulking man who sold hot chestnuts and apple cider in the winter, quinces in the summer. He greeted Lenox with a grin and a touch of his hat.

He had seen twenty-three carriages that morning (he reported), and only *two* had no markings and only *one* had four horses, and all four were dark, though one had a white diamond on its nose and another white socks, and he was sure two were mares, and certainly the driver had been wearing a cloak. He had also seen—

He would have gone on endlessly, but Lenox stopped him to ask where that particular carriage had gone, the unmarked one with four horses.

"It took a right on Bury Street," said Jacob promptly.

A little breath went through their small group. This was the first right off of Jermyn Street, and Bury Street was the opposite of Piccadilly—tiny.

Lenox started to feel a tingle of excitement. "Well done, Jacob, thank you," he said.

The duchess, from her seat in the carriage, handed over a pound note. "Please give this to him."

Lenox did so. Jacob took the pound note happily, then tried to give a basket of quinces to Lenox, who plucked just one for himself from the top and said good-bye. He got back into the duchess's carriage (a light conveyance with two horses and two doors, prettily designed) and asked its driver to turn down Bury Street.

There were five people here, Mayne, Lenox, Ward, Japheth Miles, and the duchess. The first three men were all squeezed along the bench with their backs to the horses, since the standard etiquette was that no man who was not a relative ought ever to sit alongside a woman in a carriage.

"What now?" Miles said.

Lenox had a small map of London in his pocket, folded so many times that it was white and illegible at the creases.

He took it out and spread it over his knees. "If they took Bury Street, it can only mean one thing—they wanted to get into St. James's Park as soon as possible. And the only reason for that must be that they wanted to go down Birdcage Walk and cross Westminster Bridge."

"So they would have passed directly by Parliament," said the duchess grimly. "The Duke of Dorset trundled past the House of Lords itself like a sack of grain."

She seemed angrier at the impudence of this than worried.

"What is across Westminster Bridge?" asked Ward.

"A great deal. South London," said Mayne.

He and Lenox exchanged glances. The two of them knew very well what South London meant: crime.

"I would have a look in the opium dens," Lenox said.

"The opium dens!" said Sir Japheth.

"It is the easiest way of keeping a man sedated." This was something Lenox had learned in the course of his self-education. "It is not an uncommon method—stuff a wad of opium in a man's mouth, hold it shut until he blacks out, then leave him in a supervised daze."

"That really happens?" the duchess said.

"All the time," said Mayne, who was looking at Lenox, surprised perhaps to find him acquainted with this rough practice.

Lenox nodded. "If they have headed south, I believe it is our best chance."

And if the duke was still alive—he did not add.

CHAPTER TWELVE

They failed.

It was wretchedly hot in London by that night. Though it had been a warm, pleasant day, the evening papers reported that when the sun set the temperature was at a record high for London. This would have been bad enough, but the streets were also peculiarly breezeless, leaving the heat to radiate into the eerie air, unsoftened, from every city stone, every iron gate.

Lenox tossed and turned in his bed. He was uneasy. That afternoon at three, several dozen constables, assisted by thirty-five members of the Grenadiers sent by the Queen herself, had simultaneously raided the large and small opium houses of Battersea.

They had gone nine to each, cutting off front and back entrances, striking all at once so that nobody would be tipped off. But they hadn't found the Duke of Dorset.

Nor had any of the dozens of minor thieves or opium fanatics they'd turned out known anything—nothing at all, returned the reports to Mayne, at Scotland Yard, one after another after another, despite immense promises of reward and reprieve.

There was also a huge population of minor criminals in the clumped low-slung drinking holes that clung like gray old seashells around the south side of Westminster Bridge, respectable boatmen and bargemen, too, and not one of them had seen a carriage of the description they were seeking pass at any time around nine o'clock. Nor thereafter. Despite this being quite literally the only place besides Parliament or his own house to which Bury Street could have most quickly transported the kidnapped duke.

At eleven o'clock, Lenox gave in to his wakefulness and lit a candle. He felt as if he were baking—his windows open, but the air outside utterly dead, the leaves as still as statues.

Suddenly he realized somewhere within that it was going to rain before the night was out, one of those pieces of natural insight, left over from his childhood in the country, that he never quite knew where he stored. He wondered if a dozen streets away his brother Edmund felt it, too.

He paced the bedroom by candlelight, thinking. The block of ice in the basin on his bedside table was a pool of tepid water now. He dipped a small towel in it nevertheless and wiped his brow.

Finally, at midnight, he went downstairs. There he discovered that he was not alone in his sleeplessness.

"Hullo, Graham," he said.

"Good evening, sir," the butler said. He rose from the chair by the door, tucked into a miniature alcove, that he often used as a discreet way station. Despite the heat he was in a proper suit. He laid his book aside. "May I get you anything?"

"Oh, no, I'm just awake." Lenox's mind felt a little overheated by the weather, and by his doubts. "Awake, awake."

"Is it anything specific, sir?"

"Primarily the duke being kidnapped."

Graham, in the low light of the hallway, smiled. "Yes, sir," he said.

Lenox sat down opposite Graham, on one of the chairs that lined the hallway. "You know you can read in my study if you're up at night," Lenox said.

"Thank you very much, sir," Graham said, in a way that firmly rejected the notion.

Lenox sat for a moment, chin in his hand. "It's the matter of the carriage going down Bury Street that bothers me so much," he said. "Piccadilly was fifty yards ahead of them, and instead they *turned right*. Piccadilly would have meant certain safety. Whereas Jermyn Street, then Bury Street—either could have been blocked, and Bury Street brought them within sight, through the alley, of the Carlton Club, the very scene of the crime! Madness!"

"You believe the apple seller, sir?"

"Oh, without a doubt. I have tested his memory pretty thoroughly." He sighed. "It's such an odd decision. The only reason they would have made it is to get to the other side of the river, Battersea. And nobody there saw them. Someone should have."

"You feel sure of that?"

"Absolutely sure. Yet the constables were relentless, according to Mayne. *Nobody* south of Westminster Bridge saw a thing. They have turned over every rock."

"Perhaps the carriage didn't cross Westminster Bridge, then, sir," said Graham.

"Perhaps." Lenox sat there, contemplating this. "But nothing this side of the river is closer by Jermyn Street. It would have to have been someone who didn't know London in the slightest."

Saying this, he thought of Pendleton.

"Yes, sir."

They sat in silence for a little while, Lenox tracing triangles of geography in his mind, going over and over what Mayne had told him about the massive police effort to find the duke.

At times like this he felt a sort of nausea of confusion, the feeling a doctor must have when a diagnosis lies just beyond his grasp, a writer when the plot won't come together.

It inclined him to a broad and undignified kind of despair. He was twenty-six—how soon hath time, that subtle thief!—and he had

achieved nothing, he thought glumly. The police despised him, and any man or woman of his own class might dismiss him without a thought for this odd folly of his profession.

"Sir," said Graham, after a long silence.

"Yes?" Lenox replied, looking up after a beat out of the oceanic lethargy of his thoughts.

"I'm going to fetch a glass of water from the kitchen, if you'd like one."

"Oh. Why, all right. Thank you, Graham." He mustn't give in to melancholy. "I would eat some of that cold plum pudding if it happened to be in the larder, too."

Graham smiled. "Of course, sir."

Lenox pulled the little leather book of quotations from Shakespeare out of his pocket—he had found himself carrying it around all day—and, after stroking its soft cover with his thumb, opened it at random again.

> *Reputation is an idle and most false imposition; oft got*
> *without merit and lost without deserving.*
>
> —Othello

He read this carefully, but it did not strike him as particularly interesting. When he closed the book, rather, he thought of the duke's son, Corfe, whom he had visited earlier that afternoon.

He was a tall, fit lad, who was dressed but still very pale and keeping well back of the crowd, coughing, reclined on a sofa. Still, he had not seemed delirious, despite Ward's statement. He had been with the duchess and with his sister, Violet.

This daughter, who completed the quartet of the family, had returned from their house in the country by private train car when she heard the news of her father. Few women could have been more eligible socially, but at thirty it seemed exceedingly unlikely now that she would marry. Lenox had heard of her—of this misfortune-

before the duke had ever solicited his aid. Meeting her, Lenox observed that she was very sweet but painfully shy, with a large nose and small eyes: none of her mother's beauty and perhaps twice her kindness. Of the three it was she who had asked the most intelligent questions. It was also evident that her brother loved her dearly.

As Lenox went over the meeting in his mind, Graham returned with a tray bearing two glasses of water and two plates of cold plum pudding. "Would it be presumptuous of me to join you, sir?" he asked.

"No. Imagine asking that, Graham! How many times did we go divvy on a plate of chips from the caravan outside Balliol?" Lenox took a mouthful of the pudding, deliciously sweet and cool. "Ah, that's good."

They sat up for a while longer. At around one o'clock, Lenox at last went back upstairs and fell into an overheated rest, sheets kicked aside. At four he vaguely sensed, through sleep, that the heat had broken; it was raining.

The relief of the rain was enormous. Half still in sleep, skin cool, he knew that he could find the answer if he was just patient and didn't think too hard.

He lay there, listening to the hard rain, watching the branches lash around outside.

And then he had it.

He rang the bell for Graham's room—the hour be damned—and got dressed as quickly as he could. The valet appeared soon, dressed himself.

"Sir?" he said.

"Would you come with me somewhere?"

"Of course, sir," said Graham. "Shall I have the carriage taken out?"

Lenox looked into the rain. Rousing the groom and warming the horses at this hour would take twenty minutes. "We'll chance a cab if you have two umbrellas and a pair of decent boots."

If the duke hadn't been in South London, if nobody in the all-

seeing population of Battersea had spotted him in a single one of its nooks and hideaways, then—he wasn't in South London.

That was the crucial fact.

And where else could doubling back to Bury Street have led the kidnappers? Suddenly it all seemed as clear as the water of a stream, the clues snapping into place: 1) that improbable bloodstain, 2) the ransom note tapped against Mayne's knuckles, and 3) the driver's account.

The only thing he still didn't understand was how the stolen painting fit in.

A few moments later they were walking hunched under umbrellas down Hampden Lane, looking up and down the street for a taxicab. At last a slow old rambler passed by on Brook Street, its horse in very little hurry.

They got in. "Dorset House, please," Lenox said.

"V'good, sir," said the driver.

It was an open cab. "Not tired?"

He was an old man, who had an umbrella himself, hooked into his trap. "Sleep less, a' my age, sir. Specially on a night so infernal 'ot as this one used to be."

It was a wet but uneventful cab ride—until, just as they were turning through St. James's Park, Graham said, in a low voice, "I believe we are being followed by a hansom."

CHAPTER THIRTEEN

W e'll step out here," said Lenox to the driver of the hansom.
"Here?" said the man in a doubtful way. He turned back
to look at them from his seat on the box.

Lenox handed him a coin. "Thank you," he said, then added, "It's
not like that."

"Please yourselves," the old man muttered, tucking the coin into
his small waistcoat pocket.

St. James's was the trysting ground of the least savory characters
of the upper classes—Lenox's own. Any constable could levy an immediate fine of a pound—an immense sum, as much as a working-
class family's budget for the week—if he even suspected someone of
"loitering" there, such was its ill reputation. At White's, his club,
Lenox had often heard men say before supper that they were going
to draw a few pound notes from the bank before it closed.

They took off on a rapid clip down one of the stone pathways.
Under the moonlit rain, the park looked a bright beautiful startled
green, wild and innocent.

"Anyone following now?" muttered Lenox.

"No," Graham said.

"What did you see?"

"A young man, sir. Just a glimpse. He must have seen us hail the cab and pegged us for easy marks, followed us in his own."

Lenox stopped and looked around. There was only the rainy night behind him, but it was hard to see far. He held his cane firmly in his hand and surveyed the park.

They emerged from the garden and turned down Abingdon Street. Here there was no mistaking it, under the combination of moonlight and brilliant streetlamps: They were alone. Lenox breathed a little easier.

The enormous silhouette of Parliament stood behind them; soon they had arrived at the duke's house. Both young men moved as quiet as the grave. They approached the southwest corner of the great marble house and stood there for a moment. One story up its sheer white face, a window of the duke's study was ajar, despite the rain. There was no light on inside.

Lenox smiled to himself.

He turned to Graham. "Let's try the stables."

The door to the stables was unlocked. Stupid. The only person there was a small boy, sleeping among the horses, whose fault it was not.

"Where is Perkins?" Lenox said.

That was the driver's name—the one who'd been present at the duke's kidnapping. "At home," said the boy, rubbing his sleepy face. He peered at the heavy rain behind them, which Lenox and Graham were shaking off. "Blimey if it's not tipping down, isn't it?"

"At home?" Lenox said.

"He don't live in."

"We're going in to see Lord Vere," said Lenox. "The door is unlocked?"

The boy nodded obediently. He was too young, or it was too dark, for him to catch the subtle differences in attire that marked Graham as a valet. They must have all looked—men in suits—the same to him, like friends of the duke's son, Corfe, Lord Vere.

Lenox handed the boy five shillings, a princely sum. It was intended to mimic the aleatory tips of the drunken rich. He patted a flawless mare with a white diamond on her nose who was looking at them mildly. "Go back to sleep," he said to both horse and boy.

The detective and his valet slipped inside quietly.

Only when the door was closed behind them did Graham speak. "Is this wise?" he whispered.

"I'm wondering too," said Lenox.

There was nobody downstairs. They passed on the balls of their feet through the hard marble entranceway, leaving an unfortunate trail of moisture, before taking the carpeted steps upstairs.

Lenox led, turning left down the long hallway at the top.

They went into the duke's study. Empty. When his eyes had adjusted, Lenox could see, from the moonlight reflecting brilliantly off the Thames outside, old Shakespeare, undisturbed in his frame, fifth from the left, next to the empty spot where painting number six should be.

He struck a match against a brass candleholder and lit the new candle it held. That was life as a duke: new candles, continually replenished by an unseen hand, burning as cleanly as the conscience of the Christ child.

They stood there for a moment, and then Lenox said, in a voice low but distinct, "It's Charles Lenox, Your Grace."

There was a long, tense pause.

Then, from a closet at the far left end of the room, the duke emerged. He was in a tight-wrapped burgundy dressing gown, holding a pistol.

"What in seven hells are you doing here?" he asked, his face visibly furious even in the dim candlelight.

"I would be interested to know what you're doing here," Lenox responded.

"You're lucky you weren't shot. I have a pistol. My man Craig has a blunderbuss."

"Since we have survived, Your Grace, perhaps you could tell us why a man who was kidnapped earlier today is alone and quite at ease in his own private study."

What had come to Lenox in his half-sleep was something simple, prompted by Graham. If the carriage that had taken the duke had gone down Bury Street *without* crossing into South London, there was only one place other than Parliament on this side of the river that was closer by that route.

Here, Dorset's own home.

Now Lenox went to the duke's desk and pulled open the top drawer.

"What are you doing?" asked Dorset. "Who is this man?"

"This is my valet, Graham," said Lenox, looking with a frown of concentration through the drawer.

"What does he know about . . . about Shakespeare?"

Lenox paused and looked at Graham. "Graham?" he said.

Graham frowned. "Shakespeare, sir?"

"Shakespeare. What do you know about Shakespeare, His Grace would like to know."

"I recall that he wrote *Pericles, Prince of Tyre*, sir."

Lenox tilted his head. "It wouldn't be the first play I thought of."

"A company came to our town with it when I was a child, sir. A very engaging performance."

Lenox looked at the duke. He seemed mollified at least on this one subject; Graham was a persuasive actor. Lenox looked down into the second drawer he had opened.

He took out a notecard and inspected it—heavy, cream colored, unmarked.

He tapped it against his knuckles. "Very, very fine paper for a ransom note, isn't it?" he said. "Such as no thief or kidnapper could afford. A duke could, of course."

"Please leave," the duke said.

"That was the first thing that struck me as curious. The second was that there was so much blood *inside* your carriage, staining the cushion. If you were interrupted before getting in, as your driver and the porter testified, why would it have been there?"

"I asked you to leave," the duke said.

"You have cost the police force untold hours and your family untold worry with this absurd scheme," said Lenox. "You admit that you faked your own kidnapping?"

"Get out."

"What was it, pig's blood?"

The duke looked at him grimly. "I still believe that someone is after my family's most important secret—and very possibly after me," he said, glancing at Graham. "I thought my absence would embolden the thief to make a second attempt."

"So you arranged the kidnapping, and left your window open to entice him."

"Yes."

Paradoxically, this act of deceit proved one thing to Lenox, he thought: The duke himself was not guilty of the original crime, a possibility he had considered.

"Who were the two men in cloaks?"

"Loyal servants," said the duke brusquely.

"Did you not consider just going to the country? Wouldn't the thief be incredulous that a *second* criminal was after you?"

The duke, though briefly nonplussed, waved away this objection. "A man of my stature is under continual threat."

It was here that Lenox had a surprising revelation: The 15th Duke of Dorset was—though temperamentally suited to his rank—perhaps not especially intelligent.

"I see. Maybe. But who do you believe actually is after you, Your Grace?" asked Lenox. "It is not the Queen, nor Sir Charles Eastlake. Do you have enemies?"

"No."

"I would like very much to know how the Dorset family acquired this picture, Your Grace," he said.

Fury erupted in the duke's expression. Lenox had touched a nerve. "Please leave."

The duke knew no more than he did, but it must be possible that he entertained some suspicion, some inkling, based on the story of Shakespeare's portrait. Yet the question remained: Why the *wrong painting*?

Lenox looked at him for a long moment. He was still holding the notecard, and tapped it against his knuckles. He glanced outside. The rain had slackened, and the trees were swaying above the river.

He put the notecard in his pocket. "I am going to inform the Yard right now that you turned up at home safely overnight, without any idea of what happened. They will be able to stop expending their thinning resources on the search for you."

The duke smirked. "Do what you please."

"I consider it a courtesy to you, in fact, Duke. If you want any further assistance, you may let me know," said Lenox.

There was a subtle change there. "Duke" was how one addressed a social equal of that rank—and anyone might be a social equal to Dorset, by virtue of the subtle calibrations of money, fashion, and taste that dictated society's preferences. Lenox used the word with a feeling of recklessness. He was, in his young person's way, in a terrible haste to find the truth, and he hated the duke right now for slowing his way—for this sham of a path toward justice.

They left the study and then departed by the front door, the duke standing halfway down the steps, watching.

It would be up to him how to tell his family that he had arrived home safely.

Outside, the rain was reduced to a scattered drizzle, wonderfully cool. Across the way from Dorset's front door, leaning against the stone railing overlooking the Thames, was a man in a dark cloak. A little orange ember marked him out, not much more.

Lenox started across the empty street, under the gleam of the gas lamps. "You were right, Graham. We were being followed. Hello, Mr. Bonden."

"Good evening," said Bonden, the old seaman removing the pipe in his mouth. "I couldn't help my curiosity."

"I would be delighted to have your assistance," said Lenox. There were rays of dawn appearing between the buildings across the river. "We find ourselves in deep waters. It is a painting that we're searching for."

CHAPTER FOURTEEN

The next morning was a Saturday, which meant, per his custom, that Lenox was due, at eight o'clock exactly, in the most feared place in England.

At seven he sat in the little drawing room where he took his breakfast, a chamber directly opposite his study in which he occasionally entertained friends and family, if they numbered fewer than half a dozen. It had a fireplace and a cabinet piano, which, closed, showed a painting of Lenox House set in the countryside surrounding it.

Here he sat, a steady rain still whispering against the window-panes, eating eggs, toast, and porridge and having his tea. The morning's newspapers were in front of him.

PEER ALIVE AND WELL!
Duke of Dorset Recovered Safely; Police Mystified
No suspects taken into custody, questioned;
Duke recalls no details of captivity;
Ransom unpaid;
Reward of 500 pounds offered for capture of criminals

That was the loud, confused, and rather confusing set of head-lines stacked above a drawing of the 15th Duke of Dorset in the *Il-lustrated London Morning News*. This was a paper of greater vulgarity than the *Times*, and therefore often much more interesting. Not just to Lenox.

He looked away through the window and sat, eating his porridge and thinking. He and Bonden had spoken at length the night before and were going to meet again after the weekend. The young detective was determined to find the lost painting.

It was one of those mornings—the rain trickling down the win-dows, the gray skies—when for whatever queer reason he felt the loss of his father.

As he was meditating on this, Mrs. Huggins and Lancelot entered the room.

Lenox put down his fork. "What have I said about this room?" he said.

"That only Graham may enter it in the antemeridian, sir, but—" said Mrs. Huggins.

"And you told me that you'd use a shotgun on anyone who comes in but Graham, especially me," Lancelot added scrupulously.

"Sir!" Mrs. Huggins exclaimed. "Did you really? For shame, sir."

"I hate an informer," Lenox said darkly to Lancelot. "What is it, Mrs. Huggins?"

"Your brother is here, sir."

"Oh! Send him in."

"Yes, sir," said Mrs. Huggins.

Lancelot ran after her, no doubt to ask Edmund for money—which he would receive, since Edmund was, in the first place, a soft touch and, in the second, deeply grateful that he had not been imposed upon to house Lancelot for two weeks himself.

Sir Edmund Lenox had assumed his father's baronetcy eighteen months earlier, still a young man, birth-side of thirty. Nevertheless, he had subtly changed since inheriting Lenox House and the tangible and intangible legacies that came with it. He was still his cheerful, rather countryish self, stouter than his younger brother, and gentler, too, easier to smile, full of goodwill, never most at home in London.

But there was a new, decisive authority in him, and a note of service. He strove every day—silently, Charles knew—to be as good a squire to the land and its people as his father had been. It couldn't be easy.

"This is one of those nice surprises you hear about," said Lenox. "How are you?"

"Oh, very well," said Edmund, setting his cane and his hat on the windowsill. He poured himself a cup of tea. "This rain is a treat, isn't it? It was hot as Satan's hoof in Parliament yesterday."

"Lancelot is still here."

"Yes, he just asked me for a pound."

"Did you give it to him?"

"No. Four shillings. Had to draw a line."

"That's twice his weekly pocket money, you idiot," said Lenox. "I just wonder how they've kept him at Eton! Some of the stories he tells—they would have buried us alive when we were at school. Did you know he and his friend put a snake in the headmaster's study?"

"A snake!"

"Then gave each other alibis. He told me this with utter confidence that I wouldn't tell anyone. Which he's right about, blast him. Schoolboy code."

"Still, it's just another day or two," said Edmund sympathetically.

"You know very well it's six. I do wish he were staying with you. You're a father!"

Edmund took a piece of the stack of buttered toast between him and Charles. "I suspect that in fact Mother and Eustacia settled on you for exactly that reason."

"Please, help yourself to toast. But how's that?"

"Mother thinks you ought to be settling down."

Lenox laughed. "And that Lancelot will persuade me of it! What a scheme. If anything I'm going to spend the next several decades on a remote Greek hillside studying scripture in silence, like a monk."

"Not many murders there, unfortunately," said Edmund, who, perhaps exclusively among Charles's acquaintance, had never even once faltered in his support of his brother's idea of a career. "Coincidentally, on that subject . . ."

"Murder?"

"Well, no," said Edmund. "It's about Dorset."

Lenox frowned. "What about him?"

"He was at the Carlton this morning, apparently."

"Already! You weren't there?"

"Of course not." The Carlton was for conservatives; Edmund sat for the other side, in the family seat. "But the word reached me quickly enough that he was saying very foul things about you."

"Such as?"

"It was Capability Elliott who told me. I ran across him in Pall Mall and came straight here." Elliott was an ambitious young conservative, affable, full of the latest gossip. "Dorset didn't go quite so far as to blame the kidnapping on you, but he came close. Said he had asked you to consult upon a private matter, but that you were a pirate. That he had misplaced his trust, was thinking of firing his secretary. Is it really old Ward, from school?"

"A pirate!"

"Yes, Elliott emphasized that word."

This could only mean that the duke wanted his version of events spread early and quickly, to counter any tales he suspected Lenox might tell.

"Yes," said Edmund. "Of course, your friends will know that he's wrong."

"Not many people remain your friend if they have to pick between you and a duke," said Charles, smiling.

"Ah, but there is every kind of gossip abroad about him, you know," said Edmund. "His credibility is low. If I had to guess, I would say you stand a decent chance of coming out ahead."

"Hm." Lenox sat back, arms crossed. "Well, thank you for telling me. I'm grateful."

"In brighter news, I was hoping I might speak to you and Jane, actually—two birds and all that—about Molly's birthday. I thought it would be nice to have a party for her. A surprise. Jane is such a dab hand at that kind of thing."

Molly was Edmund's wife. "What a thoughtful soul you are, Edmund. Nobody would believe that you used to chase me with that cricket bat."

Edmund reddened. "You called me fat."

"You *were* fat that year."

"I was growing into my build, and it was rude of you to point out."

"I'll see if she can come."

Lenox got up and went across the hall into his study. He tapped on the wall in code: twice, once, twice. *Come if you can, but no rush.* Then he returned to the breakfast table.

Not two minutes later, Lady Jane arrived. Both brothers stood up, smiling happily at their friend.

"When it's raining, for shame," she said.

"Oh! I am sorry," said Lenox, and he was. "I hadn't even—"

"No, it's fine. But what is it? Hello, Edmund, dear fellow. How are you?"

"He wants help planning a birthday party for Molly."

Jane, in an overcoat, brightened. "A party! Oh, and for Molly. Nobody could deserve it more."

"I'll have to leave you two to the planning," Lenox said, taking a last sip of tea. "I'm due for an appointment."

"Where?" asked Edmund.

"It's Saturday morning. I'm—"

His brother made a horrified face. "Oh, don't say the name. Don't say it. I'd forgotten. Well, go if you must."

CHAPTER FIFTEEN

At five to eight, the broad iron gates of Bedlam opened to admit Lenox. He still hadn't grown quite inured to the sound they made when they closed behind him.

This hospital was only just twelve or twenty years younger than Oxford itself, and in an inverted way as august. In 1270 it had been founded as a house for the mad, the first in the world: Our Lady of Bethlehem. Within a century its name had been shortened to Beth-lem. By 1440 it was called, thanks to the local accents, Bedlam. In the centuries since then that word had lost its capitalization, and now people spoke of bedlam, of frenzied uproar, madness, mass confusion. But they also spoke of this dread place: Bedlam.

On a small plaque inside the hospital—and already he could hear the distant howls and cries of the inmates, guttural and horrifying—was a quote from the middle of the fifteenth century.

> **And in that place be found many men that be fallen
> out of their wit.
> And full honestly they be kept in the place; and some
> be restored onto their wit and health again.**

> **But some be abiding therein forever, for they be fallen
> so much out of themselves that it is incurable unto
> man.**

Fallen so much out of themselves—that was the phrase Lenox always paused upon in the hours after his weekly visits to the hospital. On one of his first visits he had asked the warden, Dr. Hansel, under whose protection he was here, why the hospital had chosen that plaque.

"Because we have hope, you know—all of us who work here—but our final faith must be placed in God. Else I think we all of us would go mad ourselves."

He was a humble, quiet man with graying hair, Hansel. He greeted Lenox this week just as he did each time, with a gentle reminder that he could leave whenever he liked. Lenox thanked him, but he would be in Bedlam for the next eight hours.

This was part of his commitment to his career. It had started with clipping newspapers, then with seeking out the dangerous low places where crimes happened. Finally his investigations into crime, into what made a crime, had fetched him here. He had tried to convince one or two of the more open-minded officers at Scotland Yard to come with him, but they had laughed directly in his face.

Yet what could be more constructive to understanding the criminal mind than to spend half an hour in casual conversation with a man like Henry Fairfax?

By half past eight they were sitting opposite each other. Each had a cup of tea. Fairfax was scrutinizing his closely, apparently without a worry on earth. He was a handsome man with jet-black hair, as tidily dressed as one could be in the flannel garments that Bedlam provided. He was relaxed and polite. He was also a murderer.

Hansel—not given to hyperbole—thought him the most dangerous man in the hospital.

Though Bedlam still housed men like Fairfax, it was nowhere near as terrible a place as it had been thirty years before, though, as Edmund's reaction showed, not many people knew that.

Back then, after centuries of neglect, it had been a true house of horrors. The final straw was a diabolical director earlier this century, a doctor; he had published extensively in the medical journals on the need to treat lunacy humanely, while in his private fiefdom of Bedlam he had been a figure of almost limitless cruelty.

That lasted until Wakefield's famous report of 1814, which roused public indignation and instant parliamentary action. The patients at Bedlam were treated as "vermin," Wakefield had reported. Wholly coherent men, who suffered from little more than nervous anxiety, were beaten and hosed every morning, then left naked to shiver in isolation, eating one meal a day. Women were locked up in their cells, also naked, sleeping on filthy beds of straw.

Being in a group was worse still: Wakefield described ten women, "each chained by one arm to the wall; the chain allowing them merely to stand up by the bench or form fixed to the wall, or sit down on it. The nakedness of each patient was covered by a blanket gown only, nothing to fasten it."

The worst of all was the fate of those who had fouled themselves, even once. They were kept together, regardless of their particular mental condition, murderers and mild depressives alike. He had seen dog kennels in better keep, he wrote.

Fortunately, now, the horrors of those days were in decline. Two men of science, Tuke and Pinel, had published theories of treatment around the time of the Wakefield report, and the world was bending toward their kinder methods. Tuke, a genius from York, had founded near his home a place that took the gentlest and most respectful care of lunatics. Dr. Hansel was attempting to catch up to his example, though the older guards were resistant.

Tea with Fairfax was an example of how Hansel had changed the culture here, however. There were no chains in sight.

"Thank you for meeting me again," Lenox said to Fairfax.

"Not at all, Dr. Carson."

That was Lenox's name within these walls. "Last week we spoke at some length about the methods of your crime."

Fairfax looked immediately wary. "I don't quite remember that."

"Perhaps I should have said . . . of the time in your life when you felt so troubled, unlike now."

Lenox had learned on his very first Saturday the violent reaction anything less than this kind of periphrasis could elicit.

"Ah, well," said Fairfax, calming. "Yes."

Four years before, Fairfax had been employed as a solicitor in Birmingham. One evening, after a normal day at the office, he had returned to the house where he boarded and spent twelve uninterrupted hours methodically murdering everyone there. In all, he took six victims. The details were so gruesome that even Lenox, who tried to be dispassionate, could not dwell on them. (Fairfax had grown up in Lincolnshire, and his face lit up when he described his memories of hunting, gutting, and skinning animals there.) He had ethered and then bound and gagged each victim, letting them wake up on their own, one by one, before proceeding.

"Perhaps this morning I could ask about the ether," Lenox said. "How long in advance did you buy it?"

"Two weeks," said Fairfax cautiously. But pride always got the best of him, and he added, "Two weeks to the day."

This conformed to a pattern that Lenox had slowly begun to discern. He thought it might prove important.

The men at the Yard defined all murders as being, because of their bloodiness, crimes of passion. Was it true? There could be no doubt that something hideous and visceral had driven Fairfax on the night of the attacks—but had that passion been in him two weeks earlier, too? Or could a murderer be methodical in a way that, for instance, a bank robber could? Sir Richard would have said it was impossible. But Lenox and Hansel, when they discussed it, agreed that the idea should be treated more scientifically.

Lenox had nine patients on his docket that day—among them a woman who'd slain her sisters, a wellborn and mannerly merchant named Jacobsen who had woken up one morning and killed every dog on his street, and a vagrant accused of no crime but who drew the most detailed, fond, and alarming pictures conceivable of humans butchering horses—and in all their cases he and Hansel agreed that fantasy preceded action.

If it was true, it was a compelling piece of knowledge. Could a murder be *prevented*? Just imagine.

"Two weeks," said Lenox. "Can you recall your thoughts on that day?"

"I just thought the ether might be useful," said Fairfax, mildly sipping his tea.

"Were you excited when you bought it?" Lenox asked in a quiet, distracted voice, eyes on his writing, as if he didn't especially care about the answer.

"Yes," said Fairfax.

"You were excited by the . . . sorry, just taking care of paperwork . . . the ether?"

Fairfax leaned forward. "I slept with the bottles every night. Once I used it to sleep. I bound my feet. I wanted to wake into the stupor that—"

"Yes?" said Lenox.

"That they would wake into," Fairfax said casually, looking away.

But that approached too closely to the crime itself, and Lenox steered the ship away, back to Fairfax's daily life in the solicitor's office, talk about his childhood (idyllic, in every respect, as he described it—but Lenox suspected the deepest of lies lay there), the weather on the day of the murders.

They spoke for perhaps forty-five minutes. After that, first nerves gone, Lenox went to work, a steady eight hours without more than a five-minute break to wolf down a sandwich.

By the end of these days, he was always shaken and exhausted—more than ready to leave. Today was no exception. He was due at a dinner party at nine, but thought he might send late regrets if he could not rally from this horrible sunken feeling.

Just before he departed, as he was packing away his notes, hoping they were worth what they cost him emotionally, a man approached the window. He had a tidy mustache and light, curious eyes.

"Dr. Carson?" he said.

"Yes."

"They never let me out on Saturdays." The man smiled grimly. "Because of you, I suspect."

"Me?" said Lenox.

"The name is Irvington. Captain Tankin Irvington. I am a post captain in Her Majesty's Navy. I am asylumed here under false pretenses."

They all were. "Oh?"

"If you could request to see me next week—I will tell you why it is wise never to let a member of the royal family fall in love with your wife."

Lenox looked at him curiously. "What?"

Just then a guard approached them and rapped Irvington sharply over the ear. The old methods lingered. "Back to your quarters, Belmont," the guard said, and very pointedly didn't look at Lenox as he chivvied the man away.

CHAPTER SIXTEEN

Lenox departed Bedlam's solemn gates at five minutes past five o'clock. He had politely declined his customary glass of whisky with Hansel, citing with half-accuracy his social commitment. It was at least an hour's carriage ride back to the center of London—that much was true.

He looked behind him, exhaling. Just inside the grounds of Bethlem was an unexpectedly beautiful expanse of green, washed gold now by the serene falling sun. Several inmates were playing a spirited game of bowls. One was Hellerby, among the most malicious men Lenox had ever met. His face was tight with happy concentration as he tossed his boule. He might have been on a quadrangle at Cambridge.

Lenox found his carriage a quarter mile down the road, greeted the driver, and after getting in flung himself back upon the seat, dog-tired. He spent the ride—south to north through Bromley, then on to Camberwell, before the Thames came into sight—recopying his notes from that day.

"Here will do, Robertson," he said, tapping the roof of his carriage when they were near Hungerford Bridge. He was a bit bilious from the heavy lunch Mrs. Huggins had packed. A walk would suit him.

"You can take the horses home. Please tell Mrs. Huggins I'll be along in about thirty minutes."

"Very good, sir."

"My satchel is in the back here, if you wouldn't mind having someone put it in my study."

"Of course not, sir."

"Thank you, Robertson."

Lenox got out, and soon he was walking, unencumbered and alone.

There was a feeling unique to Saturday evenings in London, when it seemed both emptier than usual yet also somehow fuller—full, at least, of *imminence*, as the restaurants set out their tables and the houses prepared themselves to entertain and people walked along, looking up at addresses, unused to whatever particular street they happened to be calling upon.

Lenox strolled, unnoticed, across the river. He stopped at a park along the northern embankment. There was a small bar here, where two men played Spanish guitars with rosewood fretboards whose inlays were of intricate and lovely ivory. The notes of each instrument stood out, yet they blended effortlessly. What did it remind him of? Perhaps of love, this beautiful sound, where you could at once pick out what you saw and heard, the tone of a voice, the fall of a lock of hair, but each individual beauty was nothing without the greater whole that contained it.

He was thinking of Lady Jane, he supposed.

"Drink, sir?"

Lenox turned, brought out of his reverie by a small Frenchman in a dark tie and waistcoat, sleeves rolled up, bearing a tray. "Oh, yes. What's coldest?"

"We have an excellent white wine from Vigny on ice, sir."

"Perfect."

On the wrought-iron fence where Lenox had been standing there was a wooden box bolted to the rails, which said in gold stencil TO

INSURE PROMPT SERVICE. The waiter pointedly did not look at it, and Lenox just as pointedly did not look at the waiter but found a half-shilling in his breast pocket and dropped it clattering into the box.

"Thank you, sir," the waiter said.

These boxes had shown up in all the tea gardens a few years before. The faddish thing to do was make an acronym of what the box said—*to insure prompt service*, "tips."

The wine was nicely sharp. The beautiful music continued. And the garden's flowers were in splendid form, huge purple irises bedded among the tiny speckled white flowers that they called London Pride, though Lenox's mother had always called them Whimsy, and the maids at Lenox House—Sussex girls—said everyone knew they were called Look Up and Kiss Me.

After fifteen minutes or so of quiet meditation, Lenox drained his glass, stood up, and started back through the waning daylight to Hampden Lane.

He arrived at his door and unlocked it, calling as he entered, "Lancelot, hold your blasted fire!"

His cousin—who had the unsettling gift of pretending that nothing had occurred prior to the very instant in which you happened to be conversing—said, "Fire?"

"You know quite well what I mean." Lenox paused, staring warily at the boy. "How is Mr. Templeton?"

"On Saturdays we have dancing lessons from Mr. and Mrs. Treway."

"Oh, right. Well, I jolly well hope you behaved yourself."

"We did, because Mrs. Treway had a cane."

Lenox frowned. That didn't sound quite right, even for Lancelot. "Did she cane you?"

"Oh, no. But you have to carry it if you misbehave. You look a fearful fool, and there are people everywhere, you know. Everyone being on hols. There must have been fifty people at the dance hall."

Lancelot was already turning away—his lair was the back

garden—but he stopped. "I'll bet you five pence you don't know the Queen's name," he said.

"Show me the five pence."

Lancelot pulled it out. "Now you show me."

"I don't need to. Alexandrina."

Lancelot's face fell. He handed over the coin. "That's ten pence I've lost today on that. I was sure it was Victoria, but a boy from Marlborough had a little card about her coronation."

"I know for a fact that Edmund gave you four shillings, so I don't feel badly for you in the slightest."

Lancelot grinned. "See you soon," he said.

"That always sounds like a threat when you say it, you know," Lenox shouted after him.

He checked his watch. It was just past seven. He decided that he would dine out as he had planned after all. Many of his friends would be at the party, including Lady Jane, their friend Hugh, perennially lovelorn, and possibly even Edmund.

He changed and left by cab, stopping in at his club beforehand for a drink and a game of billiards. In the bar he ran into an old acquaintance from Oxford, a happy fellow named Crisp, who would lift anyone's spirits, and they split a cheerfully banter-filled pair of games before Lenox had to beg off at about five till the hour.

On his way out, though, Lenox saw someone he hadn't expected at all: the Duke of Dorset, walking straight toward him at a rapid clip.

White's was the most exclusive club in London; in the front hall at the moment Lenox could see several people he knew, including the 2nd Earl of Munster, whose grandfather had been King William the Fourth; George Byng, one of the Prime Minister's closest advisors; and half a dozen other illustrious gentlemen who were preparing, themselves, to scatter into the fashionable dining rooms and salons of the West End that evening.

"Good evening, Your Grace," Lenox said, when there could no

longer be any question that the peer was approaching him specifically.

The rigid set of the duke's thin, aristocratic face now, his hands
holding his cane behind his back, all bespoke his distress.

"I was dining privately but heard you were here," the duke said
loudly. "I came to find you. I wanted to let you know that you are
released from your position."

There was a gasp and a murmur. No business was to be conducted
at White's. All eyes were fixed on the duke. "Excuse me, Your Grace?"
said Lenox.

"You are sacked. You have led me into disaster."

Lenox was trembling. He had to act forcefully, which was not his
strength.

But when he spoke it was in a loud, strong voice. "In the first place,
if you insist upon discussing such matters here, I never worked for
you. In the second, if you are in any way implying that I was at fault
for or complicit in your disappearance, I reject the claim outright,
and suggest we go jointly to Scotland Yard right now to take it up
with them." He gestured around the room. "All of these men are my
witnesses that that offer stands, and will not be withdrawn."

The duke's face did not change—he was too well conditioned for
that—but in his eyes was a flare of panic.

"I am implying none of that nonsense," he said stiffly. "I am merely
letting you know that you are superfluous to my needs. It was a
mistake to bring a commoner into a family matter anyhow."

Lenox stared him in the eye. "I was taught by my late father never
to let a man feel his inferiority of rank to my own," he said at last.

There were more murmurs around the front hall. Lenox's father
was remembered at White's. "I cannot pretend to care what you were
taught," Dorset replied.

"No, I suppose that good manners are not incumbent upon one
so exalted as a duke. Good evening, Your Grace."

CHAPTER SEVENTEEN

Lenox left, hot-cheeked, striding fast and unthinking across the genteel streets around White's in his top hat and Saturday tails, furious, sick with the feeling that he had just had an experience of great consequence but couldn't yet tell how it had gone.

His feet took him automatically to the house where he was to dine, a trek of thirty minutes or so—and indeed word of the encounter had beaten him there. By tremendous good fortune it was Lady Jane he happened to see first, standing in the hallway and handing her light shawl to a footman.

"Charles!" she said. "Have you been antagonizing dukes?"

Lenox could feel his own rapid pulse, but he answered as lightly as he was able. "Just the one. Why, did you hear something?"

"Indeed, I heard of what happened at White's word for word."

"That was quick."

Just then, their hostess, Lady Helton, sailed into the room. She was a much-courted widow who owned this small blue gem of a house on Berkeley Square. She was a year younger than Lenox, but she had two children, a husband in the ground, and a grouse farm in Scotland to manage, and thus felt herself to be, comparatively, as old as the Ganges.

"Mr. Lenox!" she said brightly. "I am so very glad you have come. I hope you can give us at least ten or fifteen minutes—at least—you young men being so much in demand on these nights, with the whole round to make. If only you could stay for dinner!"

Lenox bowed, knowing that he had been as good as slapped across the face. "You are exceedingly gracious, Lady Helton. In fact I only called to offer my apologies in person, for it emerges that I must dine elsewhere. My cousin Lancelot is in London and needs entertaining. I am most deeply sorry."

He had been explicitly invited to dine here—and while, social plans being very flexible, it was within his right to cancel his attendance even while in her house, it was a drastic demotion to be asked to stay for an aperitif when he had been invited to supper.

It could only mean that she, too, had heard of his words with Dorset.

"Oh! It is quite—quite all right," said Lady Helton, palpably relieved. "I am very, very sorry, of course, but I understand."

Lady Jane stepped forward. "And I'm afraid your footman has been too quick taking my things—I must go with him. I hope you won't be disappointed, Livia."

"Oh! What!" said Lady Helton, in a suddenly flustered voice. Lady Jane was a high prize of a guest. "Jane, no! Certainly, you—you mustn't go! Both of you must stay!"

"I have told you we will manage by ourselves," Lenox said to his friend.

But Lady Jane was already gesturing to the servant for her shawl. "Nonsense. I'm sorry, Livia," she said.

"Jane, you had—I had thought—both of you must stay," said Lady Helton desperately. "To dine."

The first thing Lenox said to Lady Jane, after the door had closed behind them, was that she of course ought to stay. She told him to shut up. They walked together through Berkeley Square, silent, contemplating, one sympathetically, the other miserably, Lenox's social disgrace.

"Where shall you go?" Lenox asked. There were a dozen parties that night. "I can take you in a hansom."

"Let's go to Chiltern's and call it a quit."

"Are you sure?"

"Of course," said Lady Jane.

This was a fallback for their crowd, a friend's open-ended Saturday salon. "I say, Jane, I am lucky to have you as a friend," he said humbly. "I know that very well."

"Tomorrow I am going to ask you for five pounds to go to the orphans of Surrey, so we shall see then if your tune has changed."

He smiled. "Put me down for ten."

"No, we don't want the orphans getting too comfortable," she said in a childing tone, then smiled back. "Anyway, I never once liked Lady Helton."

It was Jane's independent-mindedness exactly—her integrity—that had made her already an arbiter of London society, at this very precocious age. But Lenox could already tell that, whatever Edmund said about the duke's credibility, his own position was collapsed. A duke! There were not many of them, and their power was so encompassing, so unimpeachable, that even a few headlines had done nothing whatsoever to diminish Dorset's. Lenox thought of the famous Henry Moore, Earl of Drogheda, who had been so rich that he wrote his name through Dublin *in buildings*, each house forming part of a letter, so that a bird high above might have read it. And nothing, still, compared to a fellow like Dorset.

He stayed at Chiltern's long enough to be sure that Lady Jane was comfortably situated, then went home and to bed. He had confused nightmares about Bedlam and Shakespeare—and woke, fitfully, throughout the night, as the heat returned.

The next morning, there was a raft of correspondence on his desk. (The mail was delivered seven times daily in London, even on Sundays.) There were a few concerned letters from friends, many more "concerned" letters from assorted tattletales, and three very gracefully managed disinvitations. One of them stung. It was from an old friend of his father's, who had asked him to his box at Goodwood for the races in July.

There was a knock at the door. Mrs. Huggins answered it and returned with Jane, who often dropped round for breakfast. "I've had a letter from James," she said, referring to her husband. "The regiment is on half-rations at the moment for 'practice,' he says, in case they are ever under siege. Even he abides by it. Don't you find that appalling?"

"Toast?" Lenox said, gesturing toward the silver tray.

She laughed, took a piece, and bit it. "Yes. I might as well." She was holding a newspaper, too. "Then there's this. Someone sent it to me."

Lenox looked at the paper, which was one of the lowest rags, the *Challenger*. "Oh, botheration," he said.

She laughed. "Your oaths have stayed quite Sussex, Charles."

He didn't look up. "I am in the presence of a lady."

The article she had brought was a scurrilous and one-sided account—emphatically not Lenox's side—of the conversation he and the duke had had at White's. It called Lenox as good as a thief, connecting him, at the end, to the missing painting.

Lenox started reading it aloud in a very serious voice after he had finished, for comic effect. But when he was through he heard a kind of silence and looked at the doorway, where Lancelot was watching them, mouth agape.

"Is that true?" he said.

"Aren't you meant to be at church?" Lenox asked, frowning and not a little embarrassed.

Lady Jane shook her head. "Lancelot, come here."

He stepped forward. "Yes?" he said.

He was in short pants, a blue jacket, a gray tie, and black shoes, ready for church. For one of the few times since his arrival, he looked young to Lenox.

"Lancelot," she said, "you must know that the very *opposite* of this is true. The Duke of Dorset has behaved very badly, and your cousin Charles has behaved very *well*. Do you understand?"

He nodded. "But then why—"

"Because the duke is telling *lies* about Charles," she said. She nodded in response to his shocked expression. "Yes. Dukes can tell lies. I know there is probably a boy at your school whose father is a duke, and you all think it the grandest thing going, but dukes lie all the time."

"Cor," said Lancelot, looking at Charles.

"Go to church," said Lenox.

"Must I? It's an awful lot of rot."

Lady Jane, who was still holding Lancelot by the shoulder, patted his cheek. "On a Sunday? For shame. I will walk you out. Charles, can I have that twenty pounds you promised by the end of the day?"

"I said ten, I thought."

"For the orphans, Charles." She cradled Lancelot's shoulder. "Take pity."

"Fine," he said moodily. "I'll send Graham across with a cheque."

A long Sunday morning loomed in front of him. He was to go see Bonden the next day and begin their search for the painting but didn't quite know how to occupy himself until then. There were two small errands he could do—first, see Sir Richard Mayne, who had sent word asking him to visit, and second, check in with a friend he had at the British Library to learn more about Shakespeare, and potentially the portrait.

Neither seemed particularly promising. Still, at around eleven o'clock he put on a tie. Before he went, he looked through the new batch of letters that had arrived. There were several of interest, so it

was some minutes before he saw, to his surprise, that one bore the
ducal seal of the Dorsets.

> *As it happens I require your further assistance.*
>   *You may call upon me at three o'clock.*
>   *Dorset*

Lenox felt himself flush, fury making his skin tingle. The nerve
of it!

Without a second thought he took up a pen and a piece of his
own writing paper, with its own proud seal, from the stand on the
front hall table. Why, his family had been on the same plot of land
since the Domesday Book. Longer than the duke's. There was no
man he need bow in humility before for reasons of birth. He wrote
his reply.

> *You may call upon me between five and six o'clock in the after-*
> *noon today.*
>   *If I am home I will see you. If you are willing to tell me what*
> *you actually know, I may choose to help.*
>   *Lenox*

He sealed the letter and pasted a twopence-blue to it, so that it
would reach the duke with all haste, then dropped it in the local
letterbox outside before he could reconsider his tone.

CHAPTER EIGHTEEN

In this particular mood it was harder than ever to keep the secret of the duke's kidnapping. But Lenox did so.

"He has *no* memory of it?" Mayne asked once more.

They were sitting in the spacious, well-lit office of the Commissioner of Scotland Yard, with its view of the long avenue to Parliament. In the distance, heavy hammers worked; some tremendous bell was going to be placed in a tower right by Parliament, they said, five or six years hence.

Lenox leaned down and rubbed his shin, wincing. "He says not."

"What is it?" asked Mayne, rather rudely.

"Oh—nothing. My young cousin is staying with me for a few weeks. He hit me in the shin with a cricket ball."

"I hope you gave him a hiding."

"Ah," said Lenox, abashed. "No. I'm afraid everyone is rather soft on him. His father died when he was six."

"Oh. Shame."

Lenox nodded. He could see Lancelot's small, confused face as he held Eustacia's hand by the grave. "Battle against the French."

Mayne nodded. "Stout fellow. Died well."

"Indeed."

"About the duke, then—you two have had a dispute? The Palace has been in touch with me. They want no hint of a scandal, and they are worried there is a political element, given his high rank and his service in the cabinet. The ivory buttons and all that."

A cabinet minister's servants were permitted to wear ivory buttons with the Queen's seal on their uniforms. "We are meeting this afternoon," said Lenox. "I am happy to reconcile with him should he apologize."

"Do it either way."

Lenox nodded ambiguously.

They sat there speaking for half an hour or so, first discussing Dorset but then moving on to more general subjects, including a number of cases under Mayne's purview. The commissioner consulted with Lenox in this fashion more often these days, which was gratifying.

"Tell me something," said Lenox, just before he left. He was standing with his hat in his hand. "What do you know about Shakespeare?"

"I once played Ophelia in *Hamlet*."

"Did you!"

"Yes." Mayne looked dismal at the recollection. "I was nine, and I was the smallest boy at school. I wouldn't do it again for a hundredweight of coal. I've never been able to tolerate Shakespeare since."

Lenox smiled. "How were the reviews?"

Mayne brightened. "Not bad, in fact, I would have you know! We had it come happy in the wash instead of tragical—they ended up married, I think, Hamlet and Ophelia. The new king died very bloody. Gertrude, too. People liked that. I was a fair soprano then, if I say so."

Sir Richard smiled at himself, Lenox laughed, and they shook hands.

Mayne kept his grip, though, and added, "Keep me close on Dorset."

"Yes, Sir Richard."

"Good chap. Be safe."

"And yourself."

Nobody had betrayed to Lenox any reaction on his stray mentions of the name Shakespeare.

At a little after one o'clock, he stopped by the British Library. It was closed on Sundays, but Lenox's friend there, like Sir Richard, worked seven days a week. Lenox presented his card at a side door, and soon Duncan Jones came down to fetch him—a friend of long standing.

"Mr. Lenox! This is a pleasant and unexpected surprise."

"How do you do, Mr. Jones?"

"Summer could be kinder on my knees. Come in, come in—thank you, Hillhurst," he said to the library's guard, who touched his hat. Duncan Jones counted for a great deal in these noble halls.

He was a fellow of perhaps eighty-five, Jones, with short white hair and a deeply creased face. His father had been a Yorkshire farmworker. Neither of his parents had been able to read. But from an early age he had shown such brilliance in the year or two of school that was expected of him that he had simply kept advancing in his education, every year intended to be his last so that he could quit and help his family on the farm, until at last he found his way to Cambridge through the generosity of a Yorkshire squire.

Now he was perhaps the world's foremost scholar of incunabula, and the chief curator of the great library's collection of manuscripts. He still had a very heavy accent. Lenox could not quite remember whether he had been knighted; he suspected so. Nevertheless, there was no pomposity to him whatsoever. They had struck up a friend-ship once when Lenox requested a very old map of the Kingdom of Dalmatia, on Europe's southeastern coastline, and it had been in Jones's carrel.

"What brings you?" asked Jones, as they proceeded slowly down a long, dim hallway, striped at even intervals with shafts of sunlight from outside.

"I was hoping I could buy you a cup of tea as the price of your expertise."

"Of course. I was pottering—inexcusable, but at my age perhaps inevitable."

The tea was free, in a small room covered in eccentric portraits of old noblemen and women, ranging in size from a tenpence coin to twice Lenox's height.

They took cups, Jones's a proper Yorkshire cup, black with five lumps of sugar, and then retreated to a comfortable nook piled with odd cushions.

"What I was curious about was Shakespeare," Lenox said as they sat.

Jones squinted at him. "Who, now?"

"I—he was—oh, but I see now, you are having fun at my expense. Very good." Jones was laughing his wheezing laugh, which came from deep within his gentle soul. "Do you make sport of all your inferi-ors?"

"Do go on, Charles, do go on," said Jones, still smiling. "I apolo-gize."

Lenox smiled, too. "What I really hoped to learn about was the portraits of him that we know to exist."

Jones brightened. "Ah. An interesting question!"

"Is it?"

"Yes, because really there is only one. That is your answer. It is the black-and-white etching that appeared in the First Folio. You would recognize it instantly. He has a very high bald forehead in it, a white ruff, and a mustache. Not a good portrait—stiff—but his friends are recorded as saying it looked very like him. The artist was Martin Droeshout, who never did a single thing of interest with the rest of his mortal hours."

"Just one picture!" Lenox said wonderingly.

"There are dozens of imitations. But only one other candidate that *could* be real. The Chandos."

Here was a name that Lenox knew well. Just at that instant, perhaps the most famous man in England was Richard Plantagenet Temple-Nugent-Brydges-Chandos-Grenville—the 2nd Duke of Buckingham and Chandos. Some decades before, he had inherited one of the world's largest fortunes. Now he was bankrupt. Indeed, they said he owed a million pounds in debt.

"The same family?"

"The very same. In the sell-off of his belongings the current duke sold it to Ellesmere last year, who to his credit immediately donated it to the nation. It is an intriguing picture. Its sitter is dressed in open collar, with a gold earring, and he has a very bright, humorous face. That makes it nice to think it is him."

"But it is not certain."

"No, it is very far from certain."

"What would a certain oil of Shakespeare be worth?"

"Worth!" Jones smiled a private smile, a librarian's smile, full of dusty secrets and happy solitudes. He thought for a moment. "I often think of Thomas De Quincey saying that the plays are not works of art—they are phenomena of nature, like the sun and the sea, the stars and the flowers. But that was not your question."

"It was still a good answer."

Jones took a sip of his tea. "There is no price that could be too high, Charles. Imagine looking into Shakespeare's eyes! The most peerie little oval of his face would be worth the moon."

"What about twenty thousand pounds?"

Jones smiled, conceding to reality. "Yes. That sounds like a decent first approximation. Twenty thousand pounds. More if there were two buyers competing for it. These Americans are getting rather rich. Gold and railroads, I'm told."

CHAPTER NINETEEN

Lenox returned home at four o'clock and went to the small sitting room across the hall from his study, to wait for the duke. He wanted the advantage of Dorset—to make him wait—and asked Mrs. Huggins to show the Duke into the study and offer him a drink if he came.

At the stroke of five the doorbell rang. The estimable housekeeper did exactly as she was asked, telling Dorset that Lenox would be there shortly. About five minutes later the detective was just preparing to go across the hall when he saw, through the cracked door of the small sitting room, something that chilled his heart: Lancelot was approaching the study.

He watched, helpless as a fly in a spider's web, as Lancelot shoved the study door open and went up to the duke.

"Hello!" he said.

"Hello," said the lean, handsome duke, looking around, a bit baffled.

The conversation halted. They stared at each other across the length of carpet that lay between them, exactly like two Parliamentary leaders negotiating a bill, except that one of them happened to have mud all over the back of his jacket; not the duke.

Lenox was just going to cross the hall to intervene when Lance-

lot said, in a tone that was more anthropological than anything—
scientific—"You've got a perfectly enormous mouth."

The duke looked startled. "Excuse me?"

"You've got a huge mouth!" Lancelot bellowed. Then he added, with
sympathy, "My great-grandfather is deaf, too."

The duke reddened to the roots of his hair. "I'm not deaf. And I'm
fifty-seven."

"Oh, so it's age. Rotten luck. Well, swings and roundabouts."

"No, I—"

"Have you ever seen how many grapes you could put in there?"

"What?"

"In your mouth. Do keep up."

"Of course I haven't," he said. Dorset's hand went involuntarily
to his mouth. "It's a normal-sized mouth."

"Are you that duke?"

"I am the Fifteenth Duke of—"

"I bet you could get ten grapes in there without any problem at
all. After that it would be tricky."

"We could nev—"

"It's a once-in-a-lifetime opportunity. We'd simply be throwing
it away not to try," said Lancelot. "Shall I ring and ask for some
grapes?"

The duke, who had existed for many years without the encum-
brance of a living soul disobeying his wishes, looked truly bewildered.

"Who are you?"

"Who am I? I'm Lancelot."

"Lancelot."

"Yes, *Lancelot.*"

"I am not deaf!"

"Lancelot," said Lancelot, in a soft sort of whisper. Then he said,
"I go to Eton. Did you go there?"

"I was at Winchester," said the duke stiffly.

"Hadn't you the money to go to Eton?"

"The—my family has been going to Winchester for generations. Winchester and Cambridge."

Lancelot nodded encouragingly. "My father's vet went to Winchester. He had his whole arm up a cow once."

"No, he didn't."

"Well, up to his elbow."

The duke was leaning forward on his chair, irate. "No! I mean he didn't go to Winchester! Your father's veterinarian!"

Lancelot frowned. "I'm quite sure he did."

"Who *are* you? Why are you in this house?" said Dorset finally, trying to regain command of the conversation. "My God, it's like an asylum."

"They've got you in an asylum?" said Lancelot.

Lenox, in the doorway, was watching with a sort of rapt, immobilized fascination.

"No, they've not got me in an—"

"It's hard when they started you at Winchester, I guess."

"No, they've—"

"It's a lot to overcome."

"Winchester is—"

"The father is the child of the man, they say," interrupted Lancelot, benevolently. "That's what my headmaster tells us."

The duke, perhaps at last realizing that his role in this bewildering conversation was voluntary, stood up. "Where is your uncle?"

"In Surrey," Lancelot said instantly.

"In *Surrey*? I was told to meet him here at five o'clock! What is he doing in Surrey?"

"He collects fragments from Anglo-Saxon times."

"What are you talking about?"

"Is it hard, at your age, to keep everything straight?"

"What are you talking about?"

"My uncle Chips. In Surrey?"

"Your uncle—no, your uncle *Lenox*, you damned fool boy, *Charles Lenox*."

"Oh, he's my cousin," said Lancelot immediately. He chuckled. "Not my uncle. Dear old duke."

"Where is *he?* Charles Lenox?"

"He said he would be back in ten minutes."

"And he left you in charge here to greet me?"

"Oh! No, I was just bored."

The duke glared at Lancelot. "Bored! When I was your age—"

"Long, long, long ago," said Lancelot. "Yes?"

"When I was your age, not that long ago, as it happens, I would have received a caning for the way you're speaking to me. I've half a mind to give you one myself."

"I'm so sorry," Lancelot said simply and instantly. "I hadn't meant to be disrespectful."

"But you—"

"They tell me I'm very curious. That's all."

"Hm."

Dorset looked as if he could have come up with several hundred adjectives he would have used to describe Lancelot before he reached *curious*. He sat back down in his chair, staring at the boy with distaste.

"So you really are a duke?"

"Yes."

"What duke?"

"I am the Fifteenth Duke of Dorset," said the duke with fierce assertiveness, as if he had never been more pleased to declare it. "What does your father do?"

"Have you met the Queen?"

Lenox saw the duke relax, just minutely. "Of course."

"How many times?"

"More than you could count."

"Twice?"

"No! Dozens! She is my third cousin, and my wife's third cousin once removed!"

Lancelot looked at him pityingly. "Third cousin, is that it. So she wouldn't *remember* you."

"Of course she would remember me! Her Majesty is an intimate—a close—she is of course the sovereign, and never stoops to—she—"

Lancelot took advantage of the duke's flustered tact to say, "Perhaps she would remember your face."

"Of course she knows my face!"

"Perhaps she thinks you're a footman, or something like that."

"The Queen does not think I am a footman!" thundered the duke.

"No?"

"Of course not!"

"I was always taught—by my father—that it would be the greatest honor to serve as the Queen's humblest servant. That no Englishman would hesitate to lay down his life so that she might not besmirch her gown."

"Well, of course, that is quite true!" said the duke, confused.

"Then why do you seem angry about being her footman?"

"I am not her footman!"

"Sorry, about her thinking that you were her footman?"

The duke's face was so full of anger that he stood up again, and quick as a flash Lenox realized he had to move. He crossed the hall and entered with a pointed clatter of the door.

"Your Grace," he said, bowing slightly as he came in, "I am sorry to have kept you. It was unavoidable."

The duke looked irate. "Who is this child?"

Lenox glanced at the other chair, pretending surprise. "Oh, this is my mother's young cousin, Lancelot."

"He has been speaking to me in the most—in the most—"

"I said our veterinarian went to Winchester," Lancelot told Lenox apologetically. "I'm very sorry."

"Oh." Lenox looked at Dorset. "It must have been an error, Your Grace. He is only twelve, after all."

"And he's a dashed good vet, too," said Lancelot joyfully. Lenox thought he had never seen anyone quite so intensely happy. "I'll tell you what it is, Duke, I'll write to Father. I'll bet you ten pence he went to Winchester after all! That'll please you. A distinguished alumnus for Winchester at last."

"He did not!" said Dorset angrily.

Lenox intervened. "Lancelot, excuse yourself this instant. Your Grace, I apologize."

Lancelot, who to his credit moved fast for someone who loved eating so passionately, was on his feet quickly. "Good-bye!" he said.

And as he darted cheerfully away, he winked at Lenox.

It was only then that the penny dropped: Lancelot hadn't been making random mischief. He had been exacting a specific revenge for the duke's rudeness to Lenox; he had, despite every previous piece of evidence that existed, some kind of instinctive loyalty to Charles.

Could it even be love! Just possibly. How very astonishing that would be.

"Tell Mrs. Huggins you need your tea, please."

"I will. Cheerio, Duke. We'll talk about the grapes later!"

As Lancelot left, Lenox looked at Dorset, whose face remained taut with anger. "Grapes?" he said.

CHAPTER TWENTY

A further apology ("the boy grew up quite unworldly, living in Cornwall") mollified the duke a bit, and a few moments later they were seated in the same two chairs, the duke again in some possession of himself.

"You asked to meet, Your Grace," Lenox said. The reversion to this formal address was intentional. It would be delicate work to rebalance their relationship. "I thank you for coming here. I know it must have been an inconvenience."

This gave the duke a chance to be majestic, humbly. "Ah," he said. "Well."

"May I ask why you wished to meet?"

The duke hesitated and then said, very grandly, "You may have your terms, Mr. Lenox. I will disclose to you everything I know. After that, you may help me or not as you see fit."

Lenox nodded. But his reply was noncommittal. "You can perhaps conceive why I am disinclined to do so."

The duke looked at him warily. "I can."

Indeed, Lenox was tempted to say no. The humiliation of the duke's speech to him at White's lingered—would chase him down for a long ways yet, if he knew London, like hounds to a fox.

But he also knew that he had no choice but to accept. Curiosity: a bedeviling vice, a staunch ally.

"Why have you changed your mind?" asked Lenox.

The duke, economical of motion always, tilted his head very slightly. "You caught me when Scotland Yard did not. Though that was not a happy moment, clearly you possess some skill."

"I see."

The duke looked at him hard. At last, he said, "On my honor as a gentleman, then, I apologize to you for the harsh words I spoke at White's."

They stared at each other. A duke's apology was as rare as a winter swallow. But Lenox had been humiliated publicly, and this was an apology in private.

"Thank you," Lenox said.

He left it there and stared back at the older man. Finally, the duke said, in a voice that choked on its own concession, not out of any specific anger toward Lenox, but more for the abasement of his position, "I would be delighted if you would be my guest at luncheon at White's tomorrow."

"That is extremely kind of you, Your Grace, and I accept," said Lenox. "Let us move forward."

The duke nodded. "Yes."

There was a long pause. "Have you learned or observed anything new?" Lenox asked.

To his complete surprise, this question released a torrential reply. Within thirty seconds the duke had stood up and was striding back and forth along the carpet, excoriating the thief of the painting, muttering dark imprecations against his own family and staff again, who he claimed were not taking the problem seriously enough, and repeatedly expressing despair at the situation.

It was clear that he had kept his emotions in check for the past day. To Lenox he suddenly seemed unwell.

"Your Grace," he said at last.

The duke, hands behind his back, stopped. "Yes."

"Tomorrow I think that with some luck I may be able to discover where the painting has gone." He was referring to his plan with Bonden. "But I cannot help but suspect that my job would be substantially easier if I knew the full story of Shakespeare's portrait."

The duke stared at Lenox as if he were not quite real—a ghost—until finally he said, "You are right that I have been concealing a few important facts from you. I will retrieve the papers that tell the story from my personal safe."

"Shall we go now?"

"Come to my house tomorrow at lunchtime—if you don't mind. The safe is in Buckingham Palace."

Lenox nodded. "I see. Very good. In the meanwhile, Your Grace, could I recommend a glass of brandy and supper with your family?"

The duke regained a measure of his composure. "Yes. Yes, of course. I shall expect you tomorrow at noon."

"I apologize again for my cousin's words," Lenox said.

He watched the duke step into his carriage and depart. Almost at the same instant, Lady Jane flew down her steps and up Charles's.

"What was that!" she said when Lenox had gone to the front door and let her in.

"He's apologized."

"Ha!" she crowed. "Everyone in Hampden Lane saw his carriage in front of your house and knew he'd come to apologize. I'm going to tell Lady Helton as quickly as can be."

"He's in a dark place, poor fellow."

Lady Jane was giddy, though. "Let him be. We've won!"

He heard that word, "we," and though he smiled, something pierced him.

It had been nearly two years since he had made the enormous error of telling Lady Jane that he was in love with her. For six months afterward they had existed in a state of tense amity, the secret always between them, and at times he had wondered if their true friendship was permanently corrupted.

Then had come something surprising. For a three-month period, Jane's oft-absent husband, James Deere, had returned for an extended stay in London with his regiment.

Lenox had never known the man well. When Jane had married him, it had seemed quite within the cosmic order, she being the daughter of an earl, he the son of another. He was a tall, fair man, with thin nostrils, kind blue eyes, and a handsome forehead. The world thought him better-looking than Jane, and he was certainly more at home in London, having been raised primarily there.

All of this had rather predisposed Lenox to look upon him as a cavalier, one of those soldiers who marries and then never, much as they are glad it exists, off in the distance, waiting for them, thinks of their home as very real.

Yet upon Deere's return, Lenox discovered that he had been wrong. The soldier might have looked that way to the world, but as they had grown haltingly close over his three-month spell at home, at Jane's insistence really, for she would push them together—saying that Charles and Edmund Lenox were brothers to her—he had realized Deere was not at all the man he'd imagined.

His great pleasure in life was his own curiosity, Deere. He met all other human beings with a totally open interest, almost as an artist or a novelist might. When he learned Lenox—whom he had probably not spared much thought for, one of his wife's Sussex people—was a detective, he evinced no disapproval at all, but on the contrary was all delight, pressing upon him the most delicate but apposite questions, fascinated by every detail.

He was the same in all situations. He took like a duck to the culture of each place his army visited—not true, to put it mildly, of most army officers, who ate Yorkshire puddings on Sunday whether they were in New Delhi or Kabul or Yorkshire itself—and always brought home great troves of incidental objects, which he studied and collected at a high amateur level. He could name the grasses of the field, the trees of the meadow, the constellations; he had a taste for port wine and had read it up until he could describe its journey from grape to glass in the most charming, least self-serious terms; he cared deeply for dogs, knew the ancient legends about every breed, and would happily spend hours in conversation about the Clumber Spaniel with a stranger in the street.

At the end of the three months of his return to Hampden Lane, Deere hadn't merely won Lenox's affection—he had won Lenox's love, as he had once won Jane's.

This was both painful and a relief. Deere was a man of great parts, worthy of Jane's heart. One day he would make a very fine, fair, and kindhearted landowner. He loved his duty—but lightly, which was just as Lenox thought proper. He loved his wife—and dearly, which was also just as Lenox thought proper.

After he was gone, Lenox's friendship with Lady Jane had returned to its state of initial purity. He even called her Jane again; for a while she had been Lady Elizabeth, still her name at court. For instance, they could stand here, celebrating his victory over a duke, as if they really were a shadow kind of couple.

But it was still painful to him that they were not, he realized.

"Incidentally, what do you make of my Effie Somers, upon reflection?" she said.

"What do you mean?"

"Will you marry her?"

"She hasn't asked me yet."

"I believe the custom is that you should ask her."

Lenox frowned. "That doesn't sound right."

Lady Jane laughed. "It's true that Victoria asked Prince Albert. Then again, she was queen."

"Is Miss Somers not a queen? I call that a disappointment."

"What an oldster I shall be at your wedding. Too old even for a bridesmaid."

It was an ironclad rule that the bride's bridesmaids be younger than she. "You could stand best man."

"Edmund might be put out," said Lady Jane. "Listen, I had better go. My aunt Elyssa is over for tea."

"Have you left her this whole time!"

"Don't waste your pity—she is looking through my letters right now."

Lenox spent the rest of the day reading quite an interesting book about Shakespeare that Duncan Jones had lent him—there was a theory that he had been a secret Catholic, among other things—before dining out at the Athenaeum, where several men approached him and said they were bloody glad the duke had apologized, and it was a disgrace that he had caught Lenox unawares in White's.

He slept well that night. Early the next morning he was awake, dressed, brushed, and fed by seven o'clock, waiting with the papers. He would leave soon to meet Bonden on the east side of the city, at the Dovecote.

Just as he was in the hallway preparing to leave, however, he heard the door ring.

He opened up: Bonden.

"Oh, hello," said Lenox. "I was meant to come see you, I thought."

"Hello," said Bonden. Then, after allowing himself a leisurely draw on his pipe, he said, placidly—perhaps in coming, as he did, from the watery world, where death could descend from above or below or crossways at any instant—"Your duke has shot and killed someone overnight. His manservant, Craig. You had better get there quickly, I suppose."

CHAPTER TWENTY-ONE

Lenox had begun to carry the little soft leather book of quotations from Shakespeare with him everywhere, and as his hansom cab drove toward Dorset House, he opened it.

> Lord, what fools these mortals be.
> —A Midsummer Night's Dream

Well, even he knew that one. He closed the tiny oracle and placed it back into his breast pocket.

Bonden had been in possession of only the most basic facts. The fatal shot had been fired at five in the morning, before first light, and though Dorset had called a doctor instantly, Craig had died after an hour's struggle. Bonden had come west to tell Lenox—he was apparently an early riser—and ask if he wanted to meet the next day or cancel altogether.

"Tomorrow will do, or sooner if I can get free," said Lenox. His feeling was that finding the missing painting might yet be very important.

"I will be at the Dovecote tomorrow morning," Bonden said. "I may be there later today, though I'm not sure."

"Very good."

Now Lenox rode in solitary silence toward the river, contemplating this strange case. The streets on a Monday morning were crowded with carriages, and passage was slow—so slow that innumerable vendors had time to approach Lenox's open window. Whelks, spice cakes, jellied eel, lemonade, plum duff: He declined all of these as politely as he could. Such carts were the cafés of perhaps a third of London's population, who lived quite poor, and even the remaining two-thirds, up in all likelihood to the Duke of Dorset, partook of their wares at least occasionally.

At last, Lenox assented to a small boy who was selling ginger beer, and whose clothes told against his business being very successful, poor lad. He paid and tipped, then took the stone bottle and drank it—refreshing, actually, sparkly and bittersweet. The boy followed the carriage at a slow trot and took the bottle back with his thanks when Lenox was done.

They pulled clear of a traffic mixup (a "jam," as the younger constables sometimes called it, because it was so sticky) involving two hansom cabs that had locked axles, and soon enough they were at the great palatial house of Dorset, overlooking the Thames, whose austerely beautiful alabaster front now seemed a marmoreal sepulcher, ghostly and hant.

What could Lenox recall of Craig? He was of middling height; very strong; a faded Scottish accent; curt, never even marginally ingratiating. Shot! He recalled the duke's tense, nervy state the day before.

There were two unmarked police carts in front of the house, a far cry from most crime scenes, no doubt out of deference to the augustness of this one. Near one of them was Sir Richard Mayne, who had the grim and forbidding look of a powerful man in the last place he wishes to be.

He saw Lenox first and came to the hansom as Lenox was paying the driver. "Exeter would call you a bad penny."

"What would he call Dorset?"

Mayne jerked his head. "The duke is expecting you. I've never seen anything less like an arrest, I must tell you."

In the entranceway they met Ward, who was ashen. "Hullo, Ward," Lenox said sympathetically.

"I don't know what to make of it," said Ward, shaking his head. "Truly I don't. They were as thick as could be, Craig and the duke. One soul in two bodies, I sometimes thought."

"I wondered if it was an accident?" Lenox said. "The duke seemed wound tight."

Ward shook his head. "We don't know. Last night the duke had had all the portraits in his study screwed into the wall by one of the footmen. Then he hid in his closet, sleeping on a chair. Craig was in the process of unscrewing one when the duke woke up."

"Craig!" Lenox said.

In a way this attempted theft was a bigger surprise than the valet being dead. But Mayne nodded, the three of them in a tight circle just inside the front door. "The duke says he took Craig for a thief. Shot him right away."

This changed the complexion of the case completely. "Good heavens."

Just before he had come here, Lenox had quickly charged Graham with the task of finding out whatever he could about Craig—Alexander Arnold Craig, as Lenox had made note of his name when he had asked for details about all of the duke's staff.

Now he was doubly curious what Graham would uncover.

"The duke is distraught," Ward said, "though I cannot tell whether he is more upset about the betrayal or the death."

Lenox kept a dark thought to himself; it was the second time the Duke of Dorset had shot someone accidentally—or "accidentally." Pendleton's son had been first.

"Where is the duke now?" Lenox asked.

Sir Richard, leading them through a vast and beautiful drawing room, answered. "In the family's private drawing room, with his wife and his children. We are taking him into custody shortly, but we permitted him time to shave and dress."

"Good of you," said Lenox.

"Nice to be a duke," said Mayne. "He has also asked for a private word with you should you come. Which you have."

Lenox glanced around the room, filled with delicate porcelain, medieval tapestries, satinwood side tables, and example after example of fine old Louis XIV furniture—a thin-boned Mazarin desk, just for example, of ebony and copper, inlaid with the most beautiful pattern Lenox could remember seeing in such a desk, and he had been in no few houses with pretensions to attractiveness of interior design.

Not a house for a murder.

The Dorset family was congregated in the smaller drawing room Mayne had mentioned, and they proceeded there.

"His Grace's son, Lord Vere, is still fragile, but he has risen for this occasion," Ward said just before they entered, as if they were discussing a lunch party.

Lenox nodded. This was Corfe, whose fever had kept the family in London, in a way beginning this chain of tragic events. "Understood."

The family was arranged along two sofas. The duke rose as they entered. His son and daughter remained seated, as did his wife. "Lenox," said the duke. "I requested the courtesy that they wait to arrest me until I could hand you this letter."

"Letter, Your Grace?"

From the breast pocket of his handsome black suit, he withdrew a thin sheaf of papers, tied with string. Lenox saw that the reddish string was just to the left of a rust-colored stain it must have previously made on the outside of the papers—evidently it had sat somewhere for a very long while undisturbed until recently being reopened.

"After reading this there is little you will not know. Work as quickly as you can, please. Find out what Craig knew. I have instructed the servants to give you all access to the house that you wish. Ward will help as far you both see fit."

Despite their conciliatory meeting the night before, Lenox was surprised at this act of faith. "Thank you, Your Grace."

The duke looked more serene now than he had before he killed Craig, oddly. "You are my best hope. Protect it—and find it."

"Protect what?" said the duchess.

The duke ignored her. "I will be in the Tower of London if you wish to speak to me." He smiled ruefully. "My schedule there will be clear from as early as this afternoon, I understand."

As a member of Britain's nobility, it was his right to be imprisoned in the Tower. (Certain tourists from the continent would no doubt have paid a fortune to spend a night in the Tower—so long as they were allowed to leave in the morning.) He would pass his incarceration in very great luxury, that was a given. It was also the case that no common court would try him, only, if it came to trial at all, the House of Lords.

Goodness, the papers, Lenox thought for the first time. A former cabinet member; more significantly still, for circulation numbers, a Duke of Dorset.

"Very good, Your Grace."

"My daughter has agreed to act as my go-between—she will see my solicitor, call upon my friends. The duchess has a great deal of responsibility in her own right, so please call upon Violet should you need assistance that Ward cannot provide."

Lenox bowed to Lady Violet, who was sitting with great composure next to her brother. "Lady Vere," he said.

"Mr. Lenox."

Lenox watched the constables come to stand at either side of the duke. Time to go, one of them said, and the duke nodded. He looked at Lenox and said once again, to the mystification of all there except the detective, "Protect it." The fervor in his voice was remarkable; it was easy to believe that he had shot Craig without vacillation.

"I will do my level best," Lenox said.

"Thank you," said Dorset.

The elaborate process of arresting the duke commenced. The heir, Corfe, handsomely dressed, stood unsteadily, watching. As for the duke's daughter, she was full of solicitous suggestions, in a sort of ceaseless soothing chatter, telling her father about the meals that Fortnum would be delivering, naming all the ways they would be sure he was comfortable, asking which books he needed from his study, that sort of thing. None of this prevented the constables on charge from doing their duty, and locking the fifth-highest-ranking nobleman in Great Britain in a pair of scarred steel handcuffs.

CHAPTER TWENTY-TWO

He asked Ward if he could sit in some private place for twenty minutes, and the young secretary guided him to a sitting room with heavy velvet draping over the window, in the fashion of the moment. It felt stifling; when Ward had gone, Lenox opened the curtain and the window, and then at least a little breeze came in.

Lenox opened the papers cautiously. They were foxed with age, though the paper was of such quality that they had not grown brittle. The hand was legible, indeed elegant, and belonged very obviously to an earlier age.

On top was a hastily scrawled note from the Duke, written on one of the very cream-colored notecards that had given away his farcical kidnapping scheme to Lenox.

Lenox: The poem is on the portrait of S.—Dorset.

That was all it said, and Lenox frowned, not sure he understood, then riffled through the pages of the older letter beneath the notecard. He saw that there were seven in all. There was a heading at the top of the first:

> Dorset House, London
> 22 April 1771

And on the bottom of the last, a signature:

> Your father, Thomas,
> 13th Duke of Dorset

So this letter had been written, eighty-two years before, by the man in the stolen portrait.

In this very room, for all Lenox knew; certainly in this house. He sat down and read.

> Dorset House, London
> 22 April 1771

My dear Clarence,

I was pleased at the sincere curiosity with which you treated our conversation this morning. I wish to elaborate upon it in this letter, which, I flatter myself, might also serve as a guide to your heir some day when you have a similar conversation with him. Even should that not be the case, I hope you will permit your father this one circuitous story. It is indeed half-expected of men who reach my age; and I have never been voluble with you, so it may be that I can draw on that particular line of credit.

(I do not recall my own father saying more than a word or two before I first went to school. His advice when he left me there at 8 was "Don't peach, don't gamble more than your pocket money, don't cry when you're beaten, and don't be top of your class.")

To begin the story long ago:

In a lively market town in Warwickshire around the year

1570, a leather merchant and glovemaker, once very prosperous, was edging toward financial ruin.

Previously he had been one of the town's leading citizens—afeeror (here we run into a word I have watched pass out of existence in my own lifetime—an afeeror, in your great-great-grandfather's day, was the official in charge of assessing fines for which no specifically predetermined fine existed) bailiff, burgess, chief magistrate, and eventually mayor. A prominent person, you'll agree.

But on the heels of his rise came his fall. It began when the courts prosecuted him for two separate crimes, first the illegal trade of large quantities of wool, and second, usury. (This may be the crime I most abhor, as it preys on the poor and the credulous. A murderer may at least be said to have lost his ability to calculate right and wrong. Usury is done as coolly as shearing a sheep.) By 1576, this man had to forfeit his public office. There is almost no trace of him in the town records after that until his death.

This may seem like a dreary biography, with its minor apogee and depressing sequel. Certainly it would have been forgotten wholly, and I would not be recounting it to you, were it not for one of the man's children. Not Gilbert, not Mary, not Joan. No; you will have likely guessed this child's name; William. The market town was Stratford-upon-Avon, the glovemaker was John Shakespeare, and the son, our nation's greatest artist, William Shakespeare.

Even Malone knows very little (and as you know, in my modest way I have contributed to the scholarship on this subject) of the playwright's youth. Most famously, there is no record of his so-called "lost years," between 1582, when he was married at the age of 18, and 1592, when he began to make a name for himself in London. It is traditional to say that he fled to London to escape charges of poaching. I could go further into this notion (the *family of Sir Thomas Lucy cling to it). But here instead I will begin a second strand of our story.*

~

The title that I am humbled to bear, and which will one day pass to you, originated, as you know, during the reign of Queen Elizabeth, a crucial figure in this tale. I have personally never cared all that much about the schism between England and Rome. In our ancestor's time, however, religion was a choice with consequences of life and death.

You will remember the saga of Henry VIII from your schooldays. He left Catholicism and founded the Protestant church, that he might obtain a divorce. Then his daughter Mary restored the crown to the Catholic cause, before finally Elizabeth, during her long rule, made it Protestant again, a decision that her successor, King James, who gives his name to our Bible, helped finally to consecrate.

During the reign of that awful Mary, our family remained Protestant. We were rewarded for it with the title you will inherit, an extension of our lands, and a place in history's, and, we may hope, God's, graces.

Conversely, during the reigns of Elizabeth and James many men remained, at great personal risk, members of the Catholic faith.

Their reward has been more doubtful than ours. (The everlasting fires of hell, in the first place, if you wish to believe the curate at Dorset Chapel.) Foremost among these men was the rather romantic figure of Sir Edmund Campion, who took his life in his hands by returning to England from abroad with pamphlets preaching the Roman faith, dodging in and out of inlets along the coast in order to deposit them with members of the faith. He was finally caught by priest hunters—these were a cruel band of men, even we must own—and, after turning down the chance to be

Archbishop of Canterbury if he would only convert, was hanged, then drawn and quartered, at Tyburn.

When Elizabeth died, in 1603, there was hope for the Catholics that they might have more freedom, but in fact Elizabeth's successor, James, took a very hard line with non-conformists. Some lived in peace; some conformed; some were banished and reprieved; some, alas, were executed.

And it is here, with hopes that I retain your patience through these twisting lanes, that my stories merge.

John Shakespeare's household was broken up and sold upon his death, two years before his Queen's, in 1601. This father had regained some of his position with his son's success, and both were, in all outward respects, good Protestants.

What is known only to a few people, however, now including you, is a truth that has long been rumored but never confirmed: The Shakespeares remained Catholic.

One hundred and fifty years ago, five years after William Shakespeare's death, there was a raid upon the house. Anti-Catholic sentiment was high in London, and they had word from an informant.

That informant, I am at once chagrined and proud to say, was an emissary from that age's Duke of Dorset, my great-great-grandfather. He was a man of iron will. He ordered and supervised the raid, and the bailiffs who conducted it found, cleverly bricked away behind the hearth, a chest full of all the markers of the secret sacrament: vestments, a chalice, the wafers and wine that papists to this day believe constitute the body and blood of Christ. Most deadly of all, they found a bundle of Campion's pamphlets.

The owner of the house could have been executed for the possession of any of those. At a minimum, his property would have been forfeit and he might have been banished.

Your ancestor was merciful, however—because he had his

own motives. The Protestant church's lower officers were rude, rough men, who would have been contented to have found evidence of secret Catholicism. It was the duke who suppressed their record-keeping, because of his alternative purpose, which is a secret to this day. He was a benefactor of the theater; and discovered, as he had thought he might, more than simply artifacts of the Catholic faith: his men found the painting that I showed you this morning.

And with it, among the dusty odds and ends stored in the small bricked-off keep, a letter. It described a single hidden play.

CHAPTER TWENTY-THREE

Lenox stopped reading.

If what the letter said was true, all this had just increased dramatically in significance. He had been involved in cases of murder, and to be sure, nothing could matter more than those. But this was an issue of public magnitude upon a different order. If a lost play by Shakespeare were discovered, England would stop; the portrait would be a footnote to it. No greater treasure, shy of King Arthur's sword, could be discovered within the isle.

Protect it—the Duke had said, with a meaningful look—*protect it and find it.*

He may have meant in these last words not the portrait, but the play.

There was a knock at the door. He didn't know how much time he had passed in contemplation, but even as he rose he saw that the duke's daughter, Lady Violet, was entering the room. He turned the letter facedown.

Even at this moment, her posture and bearing were unmistakably aristocratic. She wore a plain blue house dress, and a row of dazzling emeralds pinned back her hair—though even this lightly worn fortune could not, alas, make her beautiful.

"May I have a word, Mr. Lenox?" she asked.

"Of course, Lady Violet," he said. "I am at your service."

She sat upon a plush settee near the window, so soft that she sank into it as if into a meringue. Outside there was the brisk sound of a horse passing, and Lenox remembered that there was a world beyond these walls.

"How may I help you?" he asked.

"We have just been informed by one of the constables that in fact my father will not be allowed visitors until he is processed into the Tower by the Keeper of Her Majesty's Jewels, Charles Wyndham, who has been called from a hunt in the country. Absurd, of course. But it is tradition. I myself am not allowed to see him. He will be free to receive visitors from tomorrow morning."

"You have spared me a trip this afternoon, then—thank you."

She put her hands together and looked down at them. "You can imagine that Corfe and I are exceedingly worried."

She didn't mention her composed and icy mother, Lenox noted. "Is your brother's health improving?"

"He is still low. But steady."

"Your father mentioned that he has refused to see a doctor. I know a very discreet one."

An odd, troubled look passed over her features. "He goes on refusing. But then he has always been stubborn as a rock. I thank you for the offer—I will pass it on to him."

"Of course."

"Above all, both he and I are mourning Craig, and despondent at our father's misapprehension."

Lenox nodded. "Yes."

"You know better than most that he had been acting erratically. Sleeping in the study, carryings his pistol to meals. Corfe and I have heard that he was rude to you at White's."

"That is forgotten, anyhow."

"Be that as it may, it is a behavior most unlike him."

She had a melodic voice, Lady Violet, its syllables as distinct as the facets of a crystal glass; the lone beautiful thing about her, perhaps, poor soul. Sitting here, fingers worrying at the scuffed silver ring on a gold chain around her neck, she reminded Lenox of a character from Shakespeare herself—wise older sister to a dashing younger brother (still abed somewhere nearby), devoted daughter to a capricious father.

There was a reason Dorset had left her in charge of his affairs, not Corfe, Lenox realized.

"And how may I help, Your Ladyship?"

"You are working upon the . . . mystery, I suppose you would call it?"

"Yes, I am."

"Have you made progress?"

"Incrementally, Your Ladyship."

She gave him an even look. "When my father said *Protect it*— what was he referring to, Mr. Lenox?"

"There I must refer you to him, I am sorry to say."

"It is a secret?"

"I suppose you could call it that."

She accepted this calmly, little knowing what lay in the letter on the table. "Very well."

Lenox filled the silence, sensing that she wanted to discuss all of this further, this tremendous explosion of incident, but didn't quite know how. "Is there anyone you can think of who might have stolen the painting?" he asked.

She shook her head. "No."

Lenox was quiet for a moment and then said, "Anyone who might wish harm to your father?"

She looked him directly in the eye but did not speak, returning his silence. At last, she said, "Corfe wonders about . . . someone."

"If it helps you to feel more free to speak, I will not whisper a word of it to anyone."

She hesitated. "What about Lady Jane Grey?"

"No."

He was not surprised that she asked, for they were known to be close. But he was surprised when she said, next, "Is it true she is having a garden party in two Saturdays?"

"It is, yes."

"Oh! I am sure it will be lovely." She looked down, knowing perhaps that she had given herself away. "I hope for her that the weather will hold as fair as it is now."

"Would you care to come as my guest?" Lenox asked.

She looked at him. "You are very kind. May I consider it?"

He bowed his head. "Of course."

Very suddenly she said, "Corfe thinks that it's General Pendleton. I do not know whether I agree. But that is what he thinks."

"Why?" asked Lenox, just as quickly, for admissions like this one had momentum.

"It is a long story."

"No, I know the story. Why now? Why the painting?"

"Corfe doesn't say—but he . . . he feels so sure! Perhaps he knows something I do not. I thought I would tell you. In fact—" She halted.

"Yes?"

"Corfe thinks that Pendleton shot Craig in a fit of madness—grieving madness—and that our father is covering up his crime."

"Goodness me. That is an extraordinary suspicion."

"I know. Yet he has one piece of evidence," said Lady Violet.

"What is that?"

"General Pendleton is in London. He is almost never here, but he has been here for the past week."

Lenox took this in. "That is valuable information, Lady Violet. I thank you."

She nodded unhappily. "Yes."

"Is there anything else?"

"There is one thing, though I am sure it is unrelated. A servant of ours disappeared yesterday."

His eyebrows rose. "Disappeared!"

"No—that puts it too strongly, I should not have used that word. Did not come to work, I should have said. She didn't come this morning, either."

"Who is the servant?"

"Her name is Maggie McNeal. She has been a day-maid with us here for about three months. She lives in the East End, in the large boardinghouse on Garnet Street. I only know that because she took the bed of a girl who returned to Ireland. She was homesick. The previous girl, not Maggie."

"I'm amazed your father didn't tell me."

"I doubt he knows," said Lady Violet.

"Oh, I see."

"She always struck me as very reliable and obedient, Maggie. I have no reason to think ill of her. But I thought I should tell you."

"Quite. Is there anything else?"

"Nothing." She shook her head, as if she wished there were. "If you are able to bring our father home and this matter to a conclusion, you and your family will have the gratitude of our family and all its descendants. I do not say that lightly."

He nodded. "I believe you. I shall certainly try."

She rose. "Thank you, Mr. Lenox. Use the room for as long as you please. Though I suppose my father has already granted you that permission. Excuse me—I am not myself."

"I think you are far more composed than anyone would expect of you under the circumstances, Lady Violet."

She smiled. All human beings are beautiful when they smile, for however infinitesimal a passage of time, and Lenox saw the ephemeral beauty in this deeply fortunate, deeply unfortunate young woman. "Thank you for your time, Mr. Lenox," she said, and left.

CHAPTER TWENTY-FOUR

When she had closed the door, he turned the letter the duke had given him over and continued reading.

. . . . *a hidden play.*

The portrait is firm evidence of Shakespeare's religion, the only firm evidence we have, though of course it lets in very little light upon his actual beliefs, which may have been, for all we know, atheistic. It has been observed that his work does not read as that of a zealously pious man.

The passion of my recent years has been to find the play that accompanies the portrait. The letter was destroyed by my great-great-grandfather, but we still have the portrait. Should I fail, you know now from our extensive conversation this morning all that I know: foremost, that the answer lies in my picture, which will of course be yours. In it rests, as you know, the part of the riddle that I have yet to solve. I hope that you have committed it to memory.

I make two requests of you as I pass on this knowledge, Clarence. The first is that you keep it as private as conceivably possible. Nobody—in short—must know of the existence of this

portrait. We are its protectors. Because of the clue it contains to
the whereabouts of the play, it must not become public until after
the play is found. Once the play is found, obviously, it would be
our honor to present the picture to the King; or to keep it, but
allow it to be publicly displayed, as befits its subject.

Why does all of this matter so much to me? Because I gaze upon
a portrait of William Shakespeare—a real oil portrait. Nobody can
stand prouder than you in his position, after I am gone, but others
may be equally proud; this, on the other hand, is ours alone, and
we must treasure it, and guard it, if need be, with our lives.

Your father, Thomas,
13th Duke of Dorset

Beneath this was the stamp of a signet ring with the Dorset arms
on it, and after that a lengthy postscript.

To add a word, Clarence: I would be well and truly ashamed if a
son of mine, or a son or daughter of his, were to subscribe to the
heresy that Shakespeare did not write his own plays. He did.
Every word I have read, every ancient widow I have spoken to in
Stratford-upon-Avon in my travels, every document I have traced
with my fingertips, every fact I have collected, confirms as much.

As you know, the primary contender for the authorship of the
plays after Shakespeare is the Earl of Oxford, whose absurd
family is insistent upon their forebear having "secretly" written
the plays. Their argument is that Shakespeare could not have had
the range of education to have composed the plays. This is a
demonstrable inaccuracy. Malone tells us very clearly that
Shakespeare's elementary education in Latin and religion would
have been as good as yours or mine. Consider, too, that among
Shakespeare's contemporaries, Spenser was the son of a cloth-
maker, Middleton a bricklayer, and Kyd a scrivener. Nashe was

a sizar at Cambridge—a servant to the other students—and never recovered from the ignominy of it. Class was not an obstacle to literary greatness in the Elizabethan world.

As for the Oxford case—that the earl was a secret genius—it conveniently leaves out that he died in 1604, meaning that in addition to his extensive courtly and baronial duties, he would have had to pre-write plays such as Macbeth, King Lear, and The Tempest. Which ran out, conveniently, just when the real William Shakespeare died.

It also relies on the idea that he would have written a great deal of mediocre poetry under his own name to further the concealment, while under his pseudonym becoming the greatest genius of his or any age. An idiotic thought. Dismiss it forever, if you respect your father's opinion.

This was the end of the letter. Lenox smoothed down the creases of the pages carefully against the table. Then he read it again, this time much more slowly.

At the end of the reading he felt strangely stirred. This wasn't simply because of the long-dead duke's pride, nor because of the present duke's fanatical faith in it, which had convinced him to do no less than feign his own kidnapping and shoot a man.

It was because he thought he had found two clues. The first was in this house itself.

He rang the bell, and Ward appeared. "Ringing for me now, are you?" said his old schoolmate.

Lenox smiled. "Sorry. I didn't want to venture out of the room and get lost."

Ward looked at a fine portrait of a woman, gazing with now immortal distaste upon all she surveyed, above a nearby sideboard. His thumbs were hooked in his waistcoat. "Wish I'd never taken this bloody job," he said.

"It'll turn out for you. Listen, Theo, could I have a moment in the duke's study?"

Ward turned back to him. "By all means. His Grace said we should accommodate you however possible. I warn you that there is still blood there—and three footmen the duke has ordered to stay in the room at all times, on rotations like a ship's. The largest footmen, blast them."

"I understand."

Lenox pocketed the letter and they went up by a back staircase he didn't know. Soon they were inside the duke's study.

Lenox approached the painting, briefly attracting the attention of the three immensely tall, cow-eyed footmen standing in the middle of the room, their numerousness apparently the duke's final idea of a defense for the portrait. But Ward waved them off, and Lenox, leaning in close to the portrait, for the first time read the poem that floated in an extremely fine serif hand next to the head of William Shakespeare. How foolish of him not to have looked at it more closely to begin with. He would add that to the notebook he kept of the errors he made—a document that gave him great joy.

Ward watched him curiously, though he betrayed no particular interest in what Lenox was doing. As for the young detective, his hazel eyes were just inches from the elegant gold scroll. He read the words:

> Forty miles from Charing Cross,
> then back one further apple's toss,
> under fields of wheat-grown gold,
> doth laze a buried story told.

Lenox read the poem twice more, committing it to memory.

Beneath it was a confused squall of black ink, like the elaborate scrolled marks that sometimes appeared at the bottom of poems in fine old books.

He stepped back, so that he was nearly leaning against the duke's desk chair, and turned his attention to Shakespeare's face. It was very difficult not to see brilliance in the little daubs of brown, specked with white, that were his eyes. The genius of his and every age.

Only now, though, did he notice that in Shakespeare's right hand, held carelessly, was a lily. In faint handwriting beside it were the words *Nomen Mariae, BV.*

He wrote these words down in his notebook.

There were brand-new braces at the corners of each portrait's frame and also on each side, six in total, bolted into the wall. Anyone who wanted to remove this painting would either have to spend a great deal of time on the task or cut the canvas out. It was no longer a matter of simply removing it from a hook, as it had been with the missing portrait.

What exactly had Alexander Arnold Craig been doing?

Lenox saw that there were indeed two screws gone from the new brace. He looked to the ground, stooped, and picked them up, next to the great roped-off stain of blood. Tiny brass things, the screws. They weighed close to nothing in his palm; had cost Craig his life.

He went into the hall and wrote several pages in his notebook at a rapid rate—he was bursting with ideas—then closed it with a satisfied snap.

"I will visit the duke in the morning, if you don't mind," he told Ward.

"Not at all. In fact I could pick you up—I have to bring some papers to him. Eight?"

"Perfect," said Lenox. They shook hands. "Chin up. You'll still be Prime Minister one day."

The fastest path to a high place in Parliament, should you be unlucky enough not to have a close relative with a seat to give away, was the kind of job Ward had now, secretary to a great gentleman.

"Ha. Chancellor of the Exchequer would be enough for me," Ward said. "I've always liked numbers."

Lenox smiled. "I shall remember that if the selection is ever in my power. Actually, I once thought I would go into politics. Impossible, of course, now that I have embarked upon all this bother."

"But you have Edmund just by," said Ward.

"True enough. I can always lean on him if I have a mind to invade France. And in the meanwhile"—he was allowing himself to feel just slightly pleased, because he was sure he was on the right trail now—"being a detective isn't all bad."

CHAPTER TWENTY-FIVE

Lenox departed into the bright heat of the June day. Even on this quiet street there were carriages trotting by, and he knew that a trip to the East End, where he wished to go, would take the better part of two hours right now. He squinted into the sunlight, wondering what to do.

Then he had an idea. Straight across the street from Dorset House was a high stone rail overlooking the Thames. He leaned over it to see what was beneath him. On the quay, he saw, there were two or three small craft floating.

He cupped his hands and called out, "Down there!"

The men, in conversation, craned their necks up. "Aye?" one replied.

"How much to drop me near Whitechapel? Tower Bridge, say?"

They conferred for a brief moment, until one looked up and said, "These are junk boats, sir."

"I don't mind."

They put their heads together again, this time for longer, until the same man said, "Half-sovereign?"

It was not much more than a hansom cab would cost, and would take a fraction of the time. "It's a bargain," Lenox said.

"How will you get down, though, sir?"

But Lenox had already begun to answer that question. There was a black ladder hammered into the sides of the wall, which was thirty-odd feet in height, and he had swung himself over, to a loud, startled buzz of protest from the men below. No matter—he was climbing down. With the sublime and silly confidence of youth he felt pleasure in the lark of it, the danger, knowing that he wouldn't lose his grip.

At the bottom there was a drop-off of about his own height, and his newly hired chauffeur came and caught him with an "oof" as he came down. The half-sovereign was already in Lenox's hand.

The boat was small. It smelled of fish, but Lenox, perched on a gunwale opposite Smiley (that was the fellow's name), only noticed for a moment, because soon they were zipping down the Thames, Smiley with the rudder and the string that controlled his one small, patched sail in a single hand, manipulating them together expertly. The wind happened to be theirs, and he moved among the larger ships with ease.

Along the way he touched his cap to perhaps two dozen people, and Lenox, who loved nothing more than being on the water, partook secondhand in the glories of these associations, touching his own hat, too. The Thames seemed its own waterborne city.

"Never done this before," Smiley commented when they were halfway. "An easy payday, with due respect, sir."

"An easy and enjoyable conveyance for me, Mr. Smiley," said Lenox.

He tipped an extra shilling when they arrived, and in a quarter of the time it would have taken by cab, Lenox was walking up the street to the Dovecote.

He had two reasons for wanting to be in this part of town. One of them was Maggie McNeal, but Bonden must come first.

Unfortunately, none of the fifteen or so men inside the pub was he, despite his remark that he might be here. Lenox went to the bar, disappointed.

The same angular man was standing behind it. He asked Lenox if he wanted ale again. Lenox said why not and, when he received it, asked if Bonden had been into the Dovecote that morning.

"Thaddeus Bonden? Why, he's directly behind you, sir," said the barman, with a look of surprise. "If he were a tiger he'd bite."

Lenox turned around.

And there he was, too, sitting at a small table with his pipe in his mouth. Lenox had passed him twice, and both times taken him for a stranger.

"How in heaven's name do you do that?" he asked angrily, lifting his tankard and taking the stool opposite Bonden.

"Sometimes at sea it pays to be very still."

"What a delightfully informative thing to know," said Lenox. "Thank you. Truly."

Bonden almost smiled. "Are we going picture hunting?"

"I hoped you would have the time."

Bonden finished off his drink. "I do. But if we wait fifteen minutes or so, we might hear a bit of information to our advantage first."

"Then we shall wait. Do they have food here?"

"I cannot recommend it." That was a serious statement coming from someone accustomed to ship's rations. "But," Bonden added, "there is a woman around the corner who makes a very decent vinegar chicken with hot potatoes and mashed turnips. One of the navvies will run round to fetch it for you if you give him a penny."

A boy of ten or so did just that, and soon Lenox was drinking his cool ale and eating a delicious plate of food, which had come under a cloth napkin with a crust of warm bread. He ate heartily, Bonden watching, and when he was done sat back, contented.

Now he felt braced for their expedition. He had heard so much about his companion's magical sense for where things were hidden, concealed, misplaced that he was eager to see him in action. But they waited patiently, and after thirty minutes a man came in who spotted Bonden right away.

He had a broad belly and a heavy beard and clattered his way to their table with no pretense toward stealth, saying hello to everyone whether he knew them or not. He looked and sounded roaring drunk.

"Bonden," he bellowed. He asked if someone named Bosun was there. (But weren't there hundreds of Bosuns? thought Lenox.)

Bonden shook his head and said no, Bosun wasn't there.

"Good," the man said. He went to the bar and ordered two pints of bitter. "He knows I'd kill him where he stood if he came in here." He said this so plainly that Lenox felt a wave of alarm. When he came and sat, the man chucked a nod at Lenox. "Mutton shunter?"

"No," Bonden and Lenox both said.

"Join a choir and save our ears, boys," the man said mildly at this simultaneous reply.

A mutton shunter, in these parts, was a police constable—so-called since they were known for wearing long muttonchop whiskers. "What news?" said Bonden.

The man drank the first pint in one draft, set it down empty, and shook his head. "Nothing," he said.

Bonden nodded. "Fair enough."

The man stood up. "If anything changes about that you'll know it first." He glanced at Lenox. "Good day, gentlemen."

As the man retreated to the back of the pub with his second pint of bitter, Bonden stood up. He left his sealskin coat there—it was a warm day—in, apparently, the full faith that it would be there upon his return.

"The painting is not for sale in London, according to Mr. Berendo, who you just met," said Bonden, leading Lenox out of the Dovecote. "So we may begin to look for it."

"Very well," said Lenox. "Where to go?"

Bonden looked at him warily. "You asked to stick by me today," he said. "But you must follow me and pay attention, and that's all, if you please."

"Whatever you like," said Lenox. "Lead the way."

And what followed was, in fairness, one of the most interesting mornings that Lenox had ever spent in London.

The first thing they did was board an omnibus bound straight westward, the direction from which Lenox had come. Only toward the end of the trip did he realize that they were going to the duke's house. For an alarming moment Lenox thought Bonden was going to knock on the door—but they debarked the omnibus at the end of the street, just next to Parliament. It was here that Bonden's investigation began.

Almost immediately, Lenox came to understand how Bonden had followed them so subtly, and how he had disguised himself at the Dovecote.

He had a gift for slipping his body into small areas where a person would never look twice. The overwhelming part of it was his use of the landscape, which he treated in a way that Lenox had never seen anyone do, not even pickpockets. (He had once paid three shillings to follow a pickpocket for the day. A highly illuminating experience.) He had an uncanny gift for standing just athwart of a tree, Bonden, or a quarter step inside a doorway.

This was harder with two of them, but the sailor often gestured to Lenox, primarily with his elbows, where he ought to stand. His hands stayed in his pockets, and soon Lenox's did, too.

Was this learned shipboard? In port? On some distant island where he had been marooned?

What was certain was that Lenox could not learn these tricks quickly. Perhaps the most remarkable gift Bonden had was for silence; not the silence that comes from not speaking, but some strange deeper silence that created a cocoon around them.

They began by staring for a good hour at the duke's house, from various angles. Bonden's eyes, alert, hawklike, mostly still, seemed to take in every stone of the building one by one. Occasionally he moved five or ten feet. On the pavement, people passed them without—though they were an unlikely pair—so much as a glance.

At long length, Bonden strode west away from the house, then switched directions, making a loop so that he could see it clearly from the rear.

In that hour, the only thing he said was, in a low voice, "I doubt very much that anybody went through that window."

"How do you know?" Lenox asked.

For he thought the same. But Bonden did not reply.

They spent the next hours in the streets around the duke's house. At first Lenox was baffled as to why. He was also glad that he was fairly tall, for Bonden could consume great yards of pavement when he wished, until he would stop suddenly but unnoticeably, light his pipe, then remain where he'd stopped for as long as he liked, unseen.

Only slowly did Lenox see the pattern that Bonden was tracing: He was examining every street near the duke's house in detail.

Was this wise? Was it foolish? Lenox had time to think it over, as they stood and stared at, seemingly, nothing, until eventually he realized Bonden's method: to start at the very center of the object's existence and then make slow circles away from it, considering each place the object might be.

In a way this was ludicrous. The painting could be halfway to Indochina by now. Yet on the other hand, Lenox almost believed that Bonden would ultimately make his way even to that outermost circle if it happened to be in Indochina—there was something so dogged, so unrelenting, in his method.

He wondered, in one of the many silent moments they had, if you could do the same thing with a dead body: retreat from it in the most careful concentric circles, gathering impressions. He was making a note of the idea in the notebook he kept in his breast pocket when a low motion from Bonden, barely visible, asked him not to do it.

At five o'clock, he said they had done enough for the day. They had done scarcely anything that Lenox could discern.

Yet Lenox's faith was intact, and just before they parted Bonden seemed to confirm it. "I think I know where it might be," he said.

"Do you!"

"I think—I do not know. I may well be wrong. There are two things to check. Could we meet tomorrow?"

"Of course, though I am not free until the afternoon."

Bonden nodded. "I will call on you then."

CHAPTER TWENTY-SIX

They parted not far from the duke's house. Outside, the summer sun was just beginning to dip, filling the old streets with dusty golden light. He checked his watch. It was half past six. At this hour the city would be overcrowded in every direction between here and the east side, yet he very much wished to go there again—this time to inquire about Miss Maggie McNeal, the maid who had disappeared the day before from the Dorset household, with either suspicious or grievously unfortunate timing.

He took a chance and looked over the stone rail again. His man Smiley was there, and he called down.

"Ahoy," the riverman cried up, grinning, when he saw Lenox's face.

"Any chance of another ride? I need to go to Whitechapel, so somewhere near Katharine Pier. Same rate."

Smiley looked at the clock on the shipping tower across the Thames. "At this hour?"

Lenox was, for better or worse, unafraid of Whitechapel at night, possessing as he did a sturdy pair of fists and a quick sprint. "Yes."

Smiley shouted, "All right. If you can go now."

Lenox again scaled nimbly down the wall leading to the dock, then crossed the pebbly strand along the Thames. Smiley asked again if he was sure and, when Lenox said he was, helped him into the boat—it was mostly full of cockles now—to travel down the river, this time nearer to the city's poorest, most thickly populated environs.

There was no more beautiful way to watch the sunset than from the river, and Lenox enjoyed the ride, the wind stinging his eyes. By the time they had reached their destination, it was nearly dark. "Are you sure you're all right here, guv?" said Smiley, tying on.

"I'll manage. Cheers," said Lenox.

He hopped off the boat in the East End with thanks, flipping the coin to Smiley, who caught it in his hat, saying he was happy to make a sovereign any day Mr. Lenox chose, then turned back upriver to sell his day's haul of cockles.

Lenox strode up a gangway and was soon in the busy weave of close-crossed lanes here. Before long he had reached Garnet Street—a rough-and-tumble but brightly lit thoroughfare, doing all sorts of busy trade even at the dinner hour, full of horses, boys, men, shopkeepers, bill stickers, newspaper criers.

"Excuse me," he said to a lad who was sprinting by.

The boy stopped. "'S'it?"

"Is there a large boardinghouse for single maids on Garnet Street?"

The boy gave him a lascivious look. "Yes."

Lenox sighed and handed him a halfpenny. "Where?"

The boy pointed up. "Not on Garnet proper, like—on Blossom, your second right, can't miss it."

"Thanks."

"Tell the misses I said hello."

"I certainly shan't," said Lenox, but the boy was gone already.

He went to the tiny Blossom Street, and there, indeed, he found a small respectable-looking brick house, which had posted on its door a severe malediction against any male visitors who might be coming in the evening. He knocked, and was answered by a broad-shouldered, ruddy woman, holding a broom, who looked as if she had probably had fifteen children, seen five husbands into the ground, and could still put away more rum than most of the punters in the Dovecote.

Evidently it was her boardinghouse. She was impressed enough by Lenox's clothing and accent to allow him a word, and he said he had come to ask whether Miss Maggie McNeal was present.

She wasn't, the woman said.

"When was she last here?" asked Lenox, curiously.

"Never."

"Never?"

"It's not a name I've ever heard. And I know all my girls."

Lenox asked her a series of questions then. Had there been any recent turnover in the rooms? Had anyone disappeared? Gone off without paying the rent? She might have gone by any name, Lenox said.

The woman shook her head authoritatively. No. Not for several months; it was the best establishment of its kind in London for day-maids—he could believe that—and if she wanted she could fill every bed again twice over. Nobody had left since at least January, and she had seen, herself, every one of the place's girls, twenty-four of them in twelve rooms, no later than that morning, for she fed them breakfast at 5:00 A.M.

She would swear it on any Bible, or *Pilgrim's Progress* if he preferred—or a jar of jam, *she* didn't care.

He thanked her and said that none of that would be necessary, then walked off, hands in pockets, eyes ahead of him—for now it was really nighttime—confused, very confused.

Walking through this neighborhood, it paid to keep one's eyes open. Lenox must have cut a strange figure—dressed in subdued, expensive clothes, with his tall hat and a gold watch chain that he tucked away as he came back onto Garnet Street—and he stayed alert as he turned up Milk Lane. He passed a yard where two men in their shirtsleeves were splitting the chunks of an immense tree into first logs and then kindling, which would be sold up toward Lenox's end of town.

No doubt they had overpaid the country laborer who shipped the tree into London. So it went—the vast, dimly visible economy of this capital, as complex and inextricable as the vascular system of a man, crisscrossing itself a thousand times.

He caught the omnibus at the corner, kept to himself in one corner until it reached the Strand, then hopped out and took a cab the rest of the way.

When he pulled up to his own house on Hampden Lane, Lady Jane's door opened and she came out. "There you are!"

"Did I do something wrong?"

"What on earth has that duke done?" she asked.

Lenox shook his head. He lived in several overlapping versions of this city; one had to do with crime, and he sometimes forgot that word of that London could be sent back, by the passenger pigeons of society, to this one, his own.

"Shot someone."

"My goodness, so it's true." She sighed. "The papers are being very cautious, libel. So he's shot someone! Will he go to prison?"

She was leaning against the railing of her own house. He paid the driver and walked toward her. The lime tree that grew between their houses was in full leaf now, casting a dancing shadow under the gaslight.

"I would be shocked," Lenox said.

"Hm." She wore a white dress with eyelets at the neckline, and looked like summer to him. "Yes, the Lords will hush it up. They always do."

"How is your reading of Marx and Engels going?"

She laughed gaily. "I am not converted yet."

Lenox noticed that she was holding a letter and said, "What news?"

"Oh!" She folded it and tucked it into the pocket of her dress. "It is sad news, in fact—well, sad, but happy. James and his company have been dispatched to India for six months. He only has time to stop home in London for a single evening before he goes."

"I'm awfully sorry to hear that," said Lenox. She had been anticipating a long visit. "It's wicked luck."

She smiled. "No, on the contrary, he says that he hopes to be home by Christmas, and what's better still, that he will have six months in London then—for he has just been promoted."

"I say, that's something."

"Yes—there's nothing I like better than Christmas, you know." She touched her stomach, not consciously, Lenox thought. "The best thing about having a child will be Christmas morning, I sometimes think."

"Your child will be lucky in its mother and father."

"We'll see, I suppose—he'll be a spoiler, James, dear one that he is, especially if it's a girl, and I think I shall have to be the harsh and exacting disciplinarian. Girls get such a bad hand in this world that they need toughening up from the start."

"Feel free to practice on Lancelot."

She laughed. "By the way, would you like to come to supper in two nights? There will be twelve of us. I have been counting on you. Effie will be there."

"Will she? Then I must accept, I suppose."

"Good. Until then, if not before, in that case. Keep the duke from shooting anyone else in the meanwhile."

He felt particularly alone walking into his study; particularly unmarried. He reached into his pocket and opened the book at random.

The barge she sat in, like a burnish'd throne, burn'd on the water.

—Antony and Cleopatra

What on earth was that supposed to mean? He closed the book in disgust, sick of Shakespeare. Nevertheless, he spent the rest of the evening painstakingly making notes for himself about every element of the case, from Maggie McNeal to John Shakespeare. Graham was out, which meant that he was still investigating Alexander Arnold Craig. Finally, Lenox poured himself a glass of red wine, took down his old Latin dictionary from school, and rang for dinner to be brought up to him whenever was convenient.

CHAPTER TWENTY-SEVEN

It was raining again the next morning, a thin drizzle that was still steady enough to leave the pavement darker and absolve the city of the previous day's accumulated dust, to the delight of maids everywhere. With the streets hushed, one could hear the songbirds of London very clearly, Lenox noticed as he read the papers.

At eight o'clock, Ward appeared in the duke's carriage to pick him up.

He was alone. "Hello," he said. "Ready?"

"Is anyone else visiting the duke?" Lenox asked.

"Lady Violet plans to take him lunch."

"And the duchess?"

Ward screwed his mouth to one side and raised his eyebrows. But all he said was that he didn't know Her Grace's plans. Lenox nodded—he understood the implication. She must be a cold sort, he thought.

Ward neatened a few papers he was holding as the carriage started away. "I must say, he has been very decent to me. He wrote and released me from my position. He has offered me my pick of spots in the Lords or the Commons to go to. Says his friends will of course honor their debts to him."

"That was honorable," said Lenox.

"I declined. I will stick here for now, anyway. Though the papers are getting uglier hour by hour."

Lenox nodded. He had read the articles that morning, which were still just skirting the word "murderer." "Ward—about Craig. Will you answer me something? Who was he close to?"

Ward frowned. "Close to? I'm really not quite sure. The duke. He got on well with Lord Vere, I think—Corfe, His Grace's son."

"Below stairs, though, I mean."

Ward shook his head. "I don't know."

"Fair enough," said Lenox.

They rode through the steady rainfall. They started chatting about nothing much—bygone cricket matches and housemasters, old friends—which was rather a relief, as it happened.

That lasted until they turned onto Tower Bridge.

Then both of them fell silent, staring at the hulking dark Tower of London itself, sitting heavily on its foundation across the Thames.

A strange chill ran through Lenox. They could see its two enormous concentric defensive walls, and rising above these, the White Tower, the center of the compound, a square building with the flag of the St. George's cross flying at each of its corners.

"There's the Traitors' Gate," said Ward quietly, pointing.

Lenox looked at the waterline of the Thames and saw it—a huge arched medieval gate cut into the very stonework of one wall and plunging directly into the water. This was where barges transported the worst prisoners into the Tower. Anne Boleyn had gone through the Traitors' Gate.

"The Duke of Wellington is still the constable, you know," Lenox murmured.

Wellington, the immortal hero of Waterloo, commanded every motion in the tower unless the monarch was present. To be constable was a position of huge prestige. "Yes," said Ward.

"I would bet you that he came to see Dorset in."

"Wellington? He's eighty-one!"

Lenox nodded. "Yes. But we are wading into very old customs here. The forms must never be broken—the ravens leaving and all that. A Duke of Dorset must be received as a Duke of Dorset. We might as easily be in 1550 as 1850 once we cross this bridge."

There were always at least six ravens in the Tower of London; terrifying huge black birds with strangely human eyes. If there were ever fewer—every child knew—the Crown would fall, and with it England.

Lenox and Ward, both twenty-six, were still just within fingertips' reach of that old schoolboy awe of Albion, Henry the Eighth, Sir Walter Raleigh, Oliver Cromwell. Poor Prince Edward and poor Prince Richard with their curling blond locks. Guy Fawkes had been tortured here. Such a great number of the country's most deeply etched mythologies had emerged from within these formidable walls.

They circled halfway around the castle once they had crossed the river, to a postern gate where two tall soldiers in bright red uniform stood sentry. Ward told them they were there to see the duke, and once the yeoman guards had been informed the two old Harrovians were ushered into the austere palace where much of England's long history since 1066 had, in one murderous way or another, taken place.

"Deep breath, old fellow," said Lenox.

"Deep breath yourself," said the short, solid Ward, shoving his taller friend over on the path.

Lenox laughed.

They climbed dim, circling stone stairs, each one worn down in the middle from centuries of use.

"Here you are," the guard said, and opened a wooden door.

The suite of rooms in which they found the Duke of Dorset could not have been more eligible, except that it locked from the outside. Its stone walls were damp, true, and there were bars over the window, old, strong, thin black ones crosshatching a sweeping view of the Thames and the city. But the Savoy could not have imagined finer niceties. There was a bowl of cut flowers, a handsome desk, a pen and inkstand, books, a plush settee, every comfort. Lady Violet had arranged it all very quickly, no doubt—or who knew, the Duke of Wellington himself.

Dorset rose, a pouch of tobacco in hand. "Good morning, gentlemen."

Mysteriously, he looked better to Lenox's eye than he had two days before. Perhaps it was that he had shaved, or perhaps it was that he had made some internal decision that this was an ordeal he would conquer through attitude. His soft crimson tie was knotted impeccably. A great deal could be got out of an aristocrat in a jam, Lenox knew. It was their lone teaching (Lord knew they couldn't muster much maths) from the cradle, stiffness of spine. It did lend them a certain glory at moments of embattlement.

Ward handed the duke the papers he was carrying. "Here you are, Your Grace," he said.

"Thank you, thank you." He looked around the room, papers in hand. "Not so bad, is it? They tell me Thomas Cromwell had these rooms."

"Indeed, Your Grace?" said Ward.

Dorset smiled at Lenox, bringing him into the conversation as naturally as any host could have. "I am not sure that is as reassuring as they believe it to be when they tell you. Anyway, perhaps while you are here you may solve the mystery of the Princes in the Tower, Mr. Lenox."

Lenox laughed politely. "It may be so, Your Grace."

"Has the press put their oar in yet?" the duke asked.

"Not that we have seen," said Ward.

"The jailers will bring me the papers. A shilling goes quite a way here."

"That reminds me—Lady Violet sends some ready money, in notes and coin, Your Grace, and also a kidney pie for your supper. That has gone straight to the kitchens."

Ward handed over a leather billfold. "Give my thanks to my daughter, if you would," said Dorset. "She is a sound one."

"With pleasure, Your Grace."

Lenox again noticed the strange absence of the duchess from these proceedings, this conversation.

"I wonder if you would leave me and Lenox for a moment, Ward?" said the duke. "They will make you comfortable. A cup of tea, perhaps."

The secretary seemed relieved. "Yes, of course."

As Ward left, the duke walked to one of the small windows and stared through it, hands clasped behind his back. There was no glass in them, only bars; Lenox could feel the cold gusting of the rainy wind.

Dorset was silent for some time, even after Ward had gone. Finally, he turned back to his visitor. "I had never imagined that I would kill a man," he said. "Much less someone I respected so highly as Mr. Craig. He was a person of the utmost character. I am grieved, I find—fiercely grieved."

"I am told that he died painlessly, Your Grace."

Dorset, hands still behind his back, said, "My emotions are complicated by the fact that he was attempting to steal from me, I fear."

"Could you describe the events of the morning to me, Your Grace?"

The duke shook his head and shrugged, as if he were wonderstruck himself. "It was so extremely quick."

"Anything you remember."

"I had fallen asleep in the armchair. The one I moved to the closet at the east end of my study. I woke because of a noise. I stepped out and saw a figure with a paraffin lamp set on the desk beside him, unscrewing the portrait of—well, you know what portrait it is. He seemed to charge at me. It was a confused moment. I fired my pistol. I hit him square in the chest, of course."

Lenox nodded. "Seemed to charge you? Was he on the other side of the desk?"

"He came around the desk. He was holding a screwdriver. I couldn't make him out—I wouldn't have shot had I seen it was Craig, that's sure."

"You thought it was merely another intruder."

"Yes. I went over and looked at his face by the light of his own paraffin lamp, and when I saw that it was Craig I was shocked to my bones."

"You sent for the police."

"For a doctor, and the police, immediately. But he was clearly dying." A muscle flickered in Dorset's jaw. "I shall never forget it."

Lenox paused. Then he said, "I have read your great-grandfather's letter, Your Grace, if you wish to discuss the portrait. And I have read the poem; and I have an idea."

CHAPTER TWENTY-EIGHT

He drew the duke's undivided attention with this comment. Indeed, there was a hunger in his look, an avidity—he had traveled many years alone with this secret.

"An idea."

"Yes, Your Grace."

"No man who has seen the clue has yet solved it. Perhaps you may be the one to do so. Nothing would relieve me more."

Lenox removed the ancient letter from his breast pocket and returned it to the duke. "Perhaps the first thing you could do is to tell me something about your great-grandfather. In particular I am confused as to the order of succession. He was the thirteenth duke, yet you are the fifteenth."

Dorset nodded. "It is a sad story. My grandfather, Clarence, to whom this letter was addressed, died of scarlet fever at the age of just thirty-one. His wife died at the same time. And in fact the author of the letter—my great-grandfather—followed them quickly to the grave. Of grief, I have sometimes fancied, for he was only sixty-three. He had no other children and was a widower."

"But he had a grandson."

"Yes, my own father. He was only three months old at the time his parents contracted the fever, but was quarantined. Needless to say, he survived."

"An orphan."

"He was raised well loved and well tended by his mother's parents at Stowe Lodge and lived to a healthy old age himself, long enough even to become close with Corfe and Violet. They often went to stay with him at Dorset Castle. We only lost him four years ago. I think that very good of God, after his own parents died so young."

Lenox did some quick math and calculated that the duke's father must have been seventy-seven or seventy-eight. This explained why there had been four sons but only three dukes within the family in the past seventy years.

"I see."

"When my father turned eighteen, our family solicitor gave him this letter, along with several important family possessions of traditional value, in a sealed box."

"But he never heard the story of the portrait firsthand."

Dorset shook his head regretfully. "No. He was scarcely a year old when he was passed into the care of his grandparents. It would have saved us an immense amount of trouble."

"So when your great-grandfather refers to himself and his son knowing the secret that he will not spell out . . ."

"A secret lost to history."

Lenox nodded. "And your father? What happened when he eventually received the letter?"

"He was eighteen. He was at Gonville and Caius then." This was one of the colleges of Cambridge. "Shakespeare became a deep interest of his, as it has of mine. You see our position: If we make the portrait public, given that it contains a clue—"

"Yes. If the riddle were public, any unscrupulous gold hunter in Christendom might find the play, and hold it hostage for whatever sum they chose."

They were standing about five feet apart, and Dorset nodded. "Exactly. I take it as a sacred trust that this should not happen."

Lenox wanted to return to the clue, momentarily. First, he said, "Your great-grandfather's papers of research—have they been preserved?"

The duke nodded. "Yes. My father spent much time organizing and examining them. I have done the same when I had respite from my public duties."

"And what do they reveal?"

"There is no clue either to the origin of the portrait or the specific play that was found. He was too canny to commit either to print, I suppose. As to the play, there are rumors, of course."

Lenox knew these from the reading Duncan Jones had given him. The legends of lost Shakespeare plays were ten-a-penny—to begin with, those that had very definitely been performed by Shakespeare's company, the King's Men, but of which no text existed. (For instance, *Love's Labors Won*—a sequel to *Love's Labors Lost*.) Others were only rumors. The tradition had it that there was a play about Queen Elizabeth herself, as well as a variety of plays with tantalizing names: *Cardenio, Double Falsehood, Fair Em, Lancelot, Lord Cromwell*. Men spent their lives in dusty bookshops and forgotten libraries hoping to unearth one of them. Thus far none had succeeded.

Lenox nodded. "And so now we come to the poem."

The duke smiled. "Yes, the poem. A trifle that I have spent many years of my life contemplating. A rhyme scheme of AABB, one of the simplest possible. Iambic tetrameter. Seven syllables, eight, seven, eight."

"Forty miles from Charing Cross," Lenox said.

"Forty miles from Charing Cross," the duke said, and nodded.

"I take it that you or your forebears have followed the instructions."

The Duke nodded again. "Yes. With a very considerable margin of error built in."

"What do you mean?"

"In 1822, my father used a compass to draw a forty-mile radius around Charing Cross. Then he spent a month traveling the terrain by horse himself, allowing two miles on either side—anything thirty-eight to forty-two miles from Charing Cross."

"He did not forget the apple's toss, then," said Lenox.

The duke shook his head. "Believe me, we have not."

"And what did he find?"

"There were around fifty fields that matched the description in the poem. He took his steward, Crawford, under his advisement, for he was a methodical man, and together they made a search, though my father never told him for what."

"What did they do?"

"First, they looked for markers. Wherever there was anything resembling a marker, they dug—my father spending very freely on local laborers and on the men to whom the land belonged, explaining that he was chasing an old Dorset cross, not especially valuable in itself but of great worth to our family."

"I wonder that they believed that."

"Perhaps they did not," said the duke.

There was a knock on the door, and then it opened, which, since the duke had not answered, was rather surprising—until Lenox remembered they were in a prison.

It was a middle-aged maid in a coarse dress, bearing a tea tray. Behind her was the bailiff, holding the keys. "Mr. Ward sent tea through, from the Port of Whitby downstairs."

"Ah, good of him, thank you," said the duke. The maid came in and set the tea tray with its small sandwiches and scones down on a table. "That reminds me that I have not asked you to sit, Mr. Lenox. Will you join me? It is not quite White's."

The young detective smiled. "It is more interesting."

By the time they were alone again, the door shut behind them, each had a cup of tea. The wind whistled through the stone turrets.

"To return to my story: They found nothing, my father and his steward. Nothing at all. My father once told me that he had not once ever felt even close."

"Was he bitter about it?"

"Oh, no. But he was certainly determined that I should continue to look."

Lenox nodded. "And the painting itself? Have you had it inspected?"

Dorset nodded. "Numerous times. Inside, outside, backside, frontside, framed, out of frame, the frame itself."

"And?"

"No clue about the play has come from it. It is obviously of the right age—various experts have attested to that. They have also noted that its sitter—"

"Is Catholic," said Lenox.

Dorset smiled faintly. "Well done. Yes. That is why the picture was hidden in John Shakespeare's house."

In his Latin dictionary, Lenox had looked up the phrase *Nomen Mariae, BV*. "In the name of Mary, Blessed Virgin," he said.

"Yes. The lily in the painting is her emblem. They are Catholic references that anyone of Shakespeare's own time would have known instantly."

Lenox nodded. He put down his teacup. "Very good, Your Grace."

The duke looked alarmed. "Are you leaving?"

"I have a solid idea of what we're working from now," said Lenox. "But I still must find that picture."

"Why? You know about the play."

Lenox was tempted to elaborate—but nothing good could come of talking before he fully knew what he was saying. "Your Grace," he said, "I wonder still whether your initial call upon my services began with an error."

"How is that?"

"Does it not strike you as implausible," said Lenox, "that someone would know of the existence of this portrait and then steal the *wrong picture?*"

Dorset frowned. "I assumed they sent a thief, who bungled the job."

Lenox tilted his head. "It is possible. Anyhow, I am very eager to learn more about your valet, and I am stubbornly still hopeful that finding the portrait will help us. If you excuse me, I promise to send you word of my progress this evening."

CHAPTER TWENTY-NINE

At home Lenox found waiting for him Graham, neat as a pin as usual in his laurel-gray suit, sandy hair combed right.

"Hello," said the detective. "Have a look at this."

He handed over the copy of the poem he had jotted down, and Graham took it and read it carefully. "New clues," he said, looking up.

"Yes, indeed," said Lenox.

They took two chairs in the front hall—this was too urgent a conference for them to make it any farther into the house—and Lenox enumerated all his discoveries of the past twenty-four hours, including the second clue he believed he had found in the letter, the one that led him to the notion of why the missing portrait had been stolen instead of Shakespeare's.

Graham listened carefully, occasionally intervening with a question. At the end of the explanation, Lenox felt obscurely relieved. It was always better to have Graham in possession of the facts of a case—always.

Meanwhile, the quiet, competent valet had himself been busy. "I have amassed the information you asked me to about Craig."

"Thank you. Anything interesting?"

"I hope so. I stopped into the Junior Ganymede, sir."

"You didn't!"

"I did, sir."

The Junior Ganymede Club was a gentlemen's club located just off of Berkeley Square, exclusively for the valets and butlers of the aristocracy. (This sort of specificity in a city with hundreds of gentlemen's clubs was not unusual—next door to White's was a very comfortable club for trout anglers, the Salmo.) Graham had joined the year before.

"I thought the first rule at the Junior Ganymede was the privacy of their masters?"

"In general it is, yes, sir. But I thought this likely would not touch on the Duke of Dorset's secrets. And more significantly, in this case there may be the chance that one of the membership has been murdered."

"Craig was a member!"

Graham nodded. "I approached a steward that I trust, sir. An Oxfordshire boy." Graham's rare smile appeared. He was himself an Oxfordshire boy. "He works the last shift. Hence my late return last night. I wanted to wait until most members had departed."

"That was clever. But I say, a servant in a servants' club. No putting anything by his masters."

"He is a stalwart fellow."

"What did you learn?"

Graham pulled a piece of club stationery from his pocket. "Alexander Arnold Craig, sir," he began. "Born in Dumferline on the fifth of November, 1810, making him forty-two at the time of his death yesterday morning."

"Too young."

"Craig joined the Scots Guards at sixteen as a private, sir, and mustered out with distinction at twenty-three. He went straight into service in the duke's household; he noted, in the Members'

Book, that he had a very strong recommendation from his commanding officer, Lieutenant Pinney-May, who is a cousin of the duke's."

"Do you know why he left the military?"

"He preferred a domestic situation, sir." Graham looked down at his notes. "He went into the duke's service as a footman, but soon thereafter became a valet, upon the retirement of his predecessor to the Sussex Downs."

"They spent nineteen years together," Lenox said.

"Yes, sir. Virtually Craig's entire adult life, and much of His Grace's. Before and after he ascended to the title. No criminal record in London—the Junior Ganymede does not permit it."

"For, say, stealing," said Lenox.

"Sir?"

"If that is why he was shot, I mean."

"Yes, that sounds out of character, sir."

"Does it?"

"Craig was by universal consent a model servant, sir, at least according to the Junior Ganymede's membership. Those who had worked in the Dorset household said he was precise and rigorous in his habits."

"The military."

"Exactly, sir."

"Debts? Family?"

"He paid his bill as soon as he received it each month, sir—"

"Well done, Graham."

"Thank you, sir. That includes this month, on the first. No family listed except a cousin, Walter Craig, who is a corresponding member of the club based in Essex, with the family of Mr. Peregrine Tarrant, a landowner of means there."

Lenox crossed his legs and leaned back in his chair, studying the matter from all sides, hand across the lower half of his face. He looked up. "Did you ever see him there?"

"No, sir. But I understand that he was a regular card player on Tuesday evenings—his afternoon off—and frequently lunched in the dining room, sometimes up to four or five times a week."

"I see."

"He was not a drinker, sir."

"Never?"

"Not according to my acquaintance, sir."

Alexander Craig. Nineteen years in service to one gentleman, then shot by him in the early hours of the morning. It was both a damnable and bizarre situation, no matter what he'd been trying to steal. And he sounded a conscientious servant, if anything perhaps even too austere in his habits, which matched Lenox's few personal impressions of him. The farthest thing from a thief imaginable.

"I wonder if I could ask you a favor, Graham. Could you try to get in amongst the servants at Dorset's house and ask about someone named Maggie McNeal?"

"Not Craig, sir?"

"If they have any information about Craig I would be curious to hear it. But Maggie McNeal is a person I am also curious about. She departed without notice from the duke's household two days ago."

Graham raised his eyebrows. "I see. Yes, sir. Of course."

Lenox glanced up at the carriage clock on the table near the door. "If you have time after you've done that, I would be grateful if you could run a General Arthur Pendleton to ground. It shouldn't be hard. He is staying in London at the moment, I would imagine at the Army and Navy. If not there, one of the usual places."

Graham—the quickest of studies—knew the world of London clubs as accurately as any man in the West End. "Very good, sir. Before you leave, you have a note from Thaddeus Bonden, sir."

"Do I? Let me see it, please."

Graham passed him a rough piece of paper folded in half.

Will be there at 3:37. No need to come east. Bonden.

It was just around noon. "Where is Lancelot?" he asked.

"Out with the curate, Mr. Templeton, sir, upon an educational trip to the museum of zoology."

"Ah, he'll hate that," Lenox said with satisfaction. "And meanwhile I can sit in my study, thinking, without a single person bothering me until—well, three thirty-seven. I wonder how he decided upon that hour?"

Graham took the note and read it. "I cannot say, sir."

"One of the things Willoughby Clark told me about Bonden is that he can multiply any two numbers in his head, just like that, faster than you could do it by hand. Large numbers."

"Interesting, sir."

"Clark called him a misfit, I think. An oddball? But I wonder if it has something to do with his gift. After all, there are all sorts of mad geniuses in painting, and that kind of thing."

"Indisputably, sir."

"Yes, laugh at me, but it's true. Perhaps Bonden is only . . . different. I don't know what I mean, I'm tired. Anyway, Lord, how I hope he has found that stupid painting. We are one piece away from knowing everything now. I'm positive."

CHAPTER THIRTY

At 3:38 P.M., Lenox and Bonden had been sitting in Lenox's library for one minute. Bonden had declined the offer of coffee or tea.

"You look different," Lenox said. "What have you been doing?"

Bonden was in a suit, a proper suit. "I broke into the duke's private study."

"You what!"

"It was necessary."

"The last man who did that was shot."

"On the other hand I was not."

Lenox frowned. "If he finds out, he'll rain every police officer in London down on you. And half the Coldstream Guards."

"I have no plans to tell him," said Bonden.

He was smoking. Lenox was torn between admiration and annoyance at his phlegmatic manner.

"Why did you do that?"

Bonden drew on his pipe and exhaled a thin river of smoke. "I wanted to see if it was possible to get in through the window."

"Was it?" asked Lenox.

Bonden shook his head. "I did it in the end. But no, it is not—practically speaking. I wouldn't care to come down with a painting, either. Even with a ladder, which nobody would dare use in plain view of the street. It would be difficult to gain entry through the window. The small hedge in front of the building makes for a sharp angle upward."

"What did you do after that?"

"Stood and watched the house for four hours."

"Four hours!"

"I wanted to see it."

"I should say you had the chance." And now Lenox felt his heart quicken, for they were coming to the point. "Do you know where the painting is?"

"Yes, I do."

"You've seen it?"

"No."

"Then how can you know its location?"

"Because I know that it's not anywhere else."

Lenox had to stop himself from scoffing. It could be in Indochina, he thought once more. "Then where is it?"

"In Lord Vere's bedroom."

The young detective was so taken aback that he just stared for a moment. "Lord Vere's bedroom."

"Yes."

Lenox took out his billfold. "Here is your payment," he said.

Bonden took half of the money Lenox held out. "For my time. See if the painting is there. If it's not, you owe me nothing more."

Lenox took the bills back and said cautiously, "You are that confident?"

"I am that confident."

"But it could be in Yorkshire now, or Florence. It could be ash."

"Yet it is not." Bonden stared at him impassively. "You hired me, Mr. Lenox. Go see for yourself if you like."

Lenox thought of what he knew of Corfe. He had seen him, sickly but dressed, on the morning of the duke's arrest.

"How can you be so arrogant!"

Bonden shook his head. "No."

"What do you mean, 'No'?"

"The person who stole the painting did not climb through the window—and they are not in Yorkshire now, or Florence. Nor do I think even Lord Vere would be stupid enough to start a fire in the dead of summer when he has a fever, so it has not been burned." Bonden paused and stood up. "Once I knew it was in the house, I paid a servant to give me the full layout of the place. There are new servants there every day, more or less. There were only four places in the house it could have been. She checked three of them for me."

It was obvious that Bonden hated speaking this much. "And that's all I'm to know," Lenox said.

"That's quite enough," Bonden replied shortly. "You may send the remainder of my payment to the Dovecote. Good afternoon, Mr. Lenox."

Lenox watched him walk down the hall and let himself out.

Magical, they had all said of Bonden. But this was the most obvious trouble with magic. It always turned out to be fake.

Still, what if it wasn't?

At seven o'clock, beneath vast gray rainclouds undercoating a heartache shade of evening, Lenox went to Dorset House. He was hoping that he would arrive in time to catch the family dining, and he did.

He was led to wait in a massive drawing room—yet another that Lenox had not seen—and nearby was a flawless Holbein (even he could recognize that much), a noblewoman against a background of pure yellow. This one was nearly priceless, he supposed. It convinced him more than ever of the significance he knew he alone suspected the missing portrait from the duke's study held—otherwise why not grab this Holbein and sell it to some unscrupulous upjumped American?

Ward entered, greeting him with an admirably friendly hello given how much of his time Lenox had demanded recently.

"What brings you here?" he asked. "News?"

"Tell me," said Lenox in a low voice. "What do you make of Vere?"

Ward frowned. "That is what you want to know about? Corfe?"

"For the moment."

"You don't suspect him of—"

"No, no."

Ward glanced over his shoulder. The cavernous room was empty. "A show-off. Not much account. At school they would have bullied him."

"Where was he?"

"Eton."

"Figures," said Lenox.

Ward smiled; Eton was the great rival to their own school, Harrow, and they both knew it to be, as an article of faith, a place full of weak-kneed, small-beer, mutton-headed coxcombs.

"D'you know who he reminds me of?" said Ward.

"Who?" asked Lenox.

"Wimple."

That said a great deal. Lord Wimple had been in Ward's form at Harrow and was widely despised. He played at the sportsman but had no physical courage; often mentioned his family, though of course every Harrovian's family was of distinction in one variety or other; and boasted incessantly about the lands he would inherit one day.

Lenox had once had a darting realization that Wimple *needed* to brag, he needed those lands to his name—there was some wound inside he was protecting with his self-importance. Thereafter Lenox had stopped quite hating him. Still, he could never abide his company.

"That bad?" asked Lenox.

"Perhaps not quite. Civil enough to me. I've run across him so-cially once or twice. I've no doubt you have as well."

"Who are his crowd?"

"Horse people," said Ward immediately.

"Tell me something, would Craig ever have gone into his room? Lord Vere's?"

"Oh, yes, he usually acted as go-between for His Grace and Corfe."

"What about this past week?"

"Especially then. Corfe has been ill—his health is the reason we stayed behind, which seems a bitter irony in retrospect for poor Craig—and the duke asked for regular reports as to his condition."

Lenox had been writing in his notebook before he arrived, and he tapped his pencil against the table. The sound echoed in the huge room. "And Dorset—he seemed broken up that morning, after he had shot Craig?"

Ward looked at him curiously. "Yes, half mad. He couldn't believe it was Craig. He said that over and over."

"Has Dorset been unhappy before now, in your experience?"

"Never for a day, I would have said, before that painting went missing."

Lenox leaned forward. "I need to ask you a very great favor."

Ward looked at him. "Do you think you've solved it, Charlie?"

"I'm not sure."

Ward stared at him. "All right," he said at last.

"Is Lord Vere dining with the family?"

"Yes."

"I need you to look for the painting in his room, if you could."

"In *Corfe's*?" Ward said in a tone of disbelief so pure that Lenox experienced a sense of discouragement.

"My man, Graham, can go with you. If you need an excuse you can say that I sent him to look for some papers the duke requested."

Ward checked his watch. "It's a pretty thin alibi."

"Could you try?"

"You have a good reason for it, I take?"

"I think so."

Ward nodded. "Fine then. But dinner should only be another thirty minutes. We must go now if we're to go. Where is Graham?"

"In the anteroom."

They got him, and Ward and Graham went. Lenox waited for them with a horrible sense of dread.

When he heard a footstep in the hall, he stood bolt upright. It was only Lady Violet, however, coming to see if he needed anything.

"No!" he called very brightly and loudly. "All's well!"

She looked bemused. "Can I help you?"

"No! No! Is your supper over?"

He was still shouting; she was too well bred to point it out. "Yes," she said. "Under the circumstances we have dined *en famille*."

"Of course! A short supper!" Lenox shouted.

She took her leave—no doubt thinking him insane—and his heartbeat slowed to something like normal. Not an instant later, Ward and Graham walked back into the room.

Their faces told the story. On the way home, Lenox and Graham stopped into the telegram office and sent a message to Bonden, care of the Dovecote.

Not there STOP Very bad loss of credibility STOP Lenox

CHAPTER THIRTY-ONE

How vital it would have been to find the painting—if his suspicion about the thirteenth duke's portrait, based on that old letter, was correct.

Fool's gold, Bonden had been, fool's gold.

As the carriage pulled away from the telegram office, he took out his watch, which was made of real gold, a present from his father given on his twentieth birthday.

Nearly nine o'clock. Graham sat quietly next to him. Neither spoke—the moment was tense—and Lenox coiled and uncoiled his watch chain around his finger.

This distracted habit of his with the watch chain always made him think of Theseus in the maze of the Minotaur, the story in old books from the nursery. There were different versions. In the one Lenox knew, just before Theseus entered the maze, Ariadne, the daughter of the king, had given him a ball of yarn, so that he could track where he had been as he hunted the monster.

In the oldest tellings of the story that ball was called a clew, the name for a ball of yarn in the 1300s. It was from this word Lenox and his kind had inherited perhaps the most important word in their own vocabulary: clue.

He wished desperately that he had just one more clue now, to guide him through the maze.

For what did he know? So little, really. He placed the thief in one of three categories: a) a person who wanted the painting; b) per Dorset's original theory, a person who wanted the painting of Shakespeare and had made a mistake; c) a person who wanted the lost play.

It was the third category that alarmed him.

"You ought to turn in," Lenox said when they reached Hampden Lane. "There will be more of this nonsense tomorrow."

They both seemed to feel defeated. "Are you sure, sir?"

"I'm sure. Lord, I wish I had never heard of the Duke of Dorset."

He went to his study, loosening his tie, and poured himself a brandy and soda. Lancelot, thank the angels, was out on an "evening of astronomy" with Templeton. As an inducement for good behavior, Mrs. Huggins had entrusted to the curate a bag of licorice allsorts, despite Lancelot's vehement insistence that they would be securest in his own hands.

He almost missed the boy. He smiled, reclining in his chair and putting his feet up on the coffee table. Almost. Outside it was still quietly raining. There was a low, rumbling, dark orange fire in the fireplace, on this cold summer evening.

He missed his father.

He must have fallen asleep, because it was only the dim consciousness of a distant noise within the house that brought him to his senses. His brandy and soda, he saw, had tumbled to the carpet, and clumsily he picked up the glass and set it on the table, still half asleep. He rubbed his eyes and stretched his shoulders back. The clock on his desk told the time—past midnight.

He stood up, aching a bit, and went out into the hall.

The noise was coming from the servants' quarters downstairs, and at that moment a young footman, Fitzwilliam, came upstairs. He had hastily donned his tie and jacket.

"Hello, sir," he said. "There is a Mr. Bonden who—he has insisted that he had business with you. He brought a large parcel."

Lenox was wholly awake now. "Where is he?"

"In the servants' dining room."

Poor Mrs. Huggins. Life was hard enough for his housekeeper, and now she would have to clean whale-oil stains out of the cambric on the chairs she kept so neatly in the room where the servants took their meals. "I'm coming down."

Bonden was sitting at the enormous scarred table that dominated the room. Fitzwilliam had lit a candle, but it was dark, and Lenox asked him for more. He returned with a candelabra that held six, and the room brightened.

There, leaning against the wall, next to a table with a quarter of a kidney pie left on it, was the picture—the 13th Duke of Dorset.

For a moment Lenox just stared. He was a ruddy, weighty fellow, very different from the present duke. The picture portrayed him on a marble balcony. There was a broad verdure behind him and a chapel in the distance.

He wore a jerkin.

"Where was it?"

At that moment Graham came in, dressed for all the world as if it were noon on a Sunday. "Good evening, sir," he said.

Bonden glanced at him. "It was in Lord Vere's room, sir. He is out for the night. Recovered from his fever, apparently."

"We searched that room top to bottom," said Graham, more curious than defiant.

"Not bottom. It was nailed to the underside of the bedframe."

"*Nailed?*" said Lenox.

"Yes. There's some writing on the back."

Lenox's heart started to thump. He turned the painting around. Its cloth backing had been roughly and recently removed. He saw what Bonden meant: four lines, written in thin white ink, one along each side of the wooden picture frame. A single splash of water could have wiped them away.

"I owe you an apology, Mr. Bonden," he said. "If you would consent to it, I would like to learn more of your craft. I could pay you for your time."

Bonden stared at him. "Maybe," he said, putting on his cap. "For now I'll take the rest of my pay."

When Bonden had gone, paid, Lenox stood there and looked at the words on the back of the painting for a long, long time.

It was what he had anticipated.

The next morning dawned sunny. Lenox's carriage was ready at six, by his orders. On the ride across town he ignored the stack of newspapers on the seat beside him, with their increasingly frenzied questions about the duke. Instead he watched the waking city through the window, occasionally checking his breast pocket for the piece of paper he had brought.

The duke was awake, shaved, and dressed, which surprised Lenox. Even since the day before, Lady Violet (presumably not the duchess) had brought over more from home to make him comfortable. He had a sterling silver coffee set—a beautiful ancient one, covered in intricate scrollwork, upon a gleaming tray—and offered the detective a blue Wedgewood cup.

"Thank you," said Lenox.

"There are jam rolls, too," said the duke.

Lenox took one and set it beside his coffee. They were in a small nook near the corner of this large sitting room, the door to the bedroom closed. "I have new information."

"You do?" said Dorset, with a hint of suspicion.

"I do. It is about the poem."

"The poem."

"Yes. The poem as you know it is obviously tantalizing. But from the moment I read your great-grandfather's letter, I have suspected something else very strongly: that it *is incomplete. It is a phrase he uses toward the end. The answer*, he says in the letter, lies *in my picture.*"

The duke was leaning forward, tense, confused. "Yes? What of it?"

"My picture. Then he says, '*In it is the part of the riddle that I have yet to solve. I hope that you have committed it to memory.*'"

The duke looked dangerously frustrated. "What are you saying, Mr. Lenox?"

"Everywhere else he calls the picture of Shakespeare 'the portrait' or something similar. But then he says 'in *my* picture,' though it is so clear, elsewhere, that he considers himself only a steward of the portrait."

"Lenox, for pity's sake—"

"My suspicion has been that you only have the first half of the poem, written on the portrait of Shakespeare. *That* is why there is all that black paint underneath the poem—to conceal its second half. Your great-grandfather scrawled out the second stanza himself, dividing the poem for safety. Then he put the second half of it somewhere in *his* picture, as he kept referring to it. That is why he hoped his son would commit it to memory."

The effect of this idea on the duke was electric. "Of course," he said, eyes shining. "Of course. That is why the thief stole the wrong painting. It was exactly the painting he wanted."

Lenox nodded. "I think so."

The duke's face had slowly assumed a look of nearly pure grief. "And now it is lost, and the thief has the complete poem to himself. I have failed."

"No, Your Grace," said Lenox. "I have recovered the painting."

The duke stood up. "You haven't."

Lenox took the piece of paper from his breast pocket. The night before, he had reached for a piece of his cook Ellie's scratch paper and a bit of charcoal, written out the first stanza from memory, then transcribed the second, sitting opposite the silent Bonden, tilting his head to read.

It was tricky—the letter *s*, for instance, looked like the letter *f*—but he managed it quickly. He had committed the lines to memory, but he had kept the paper, too.

"The lines were written on the reverse of the painting, underneath its backing. If I am not mistaken, for the first time in nearly a century we have the whole poem."

The duke took the poem and stared at it, the whole poem, complete.

> *Forty miles from Charing Cross,*
> *then back one further apple's toss,*
> *under fields of wheat-grown gold,*
> *doth laze a buried story told.*
>
> *Kent for they who wish it found,*
> *and dig beneath the churchyard ground*
> *behind the name my portrait gloss,*
> *forty miles from Charing Cross.*

CHAPTER THIRTY-TWO

The duke read and reread the poem for so long that Lenox almost interrupted him. It must have been a full ten minutes that he expended studying those sixty syllables.

At last he looked at Lenox. "I am in your debt," he said.

Lenox shrugged. "It is my work."

"No. I am in your debt. What do you make of the poem?"

"I'm not sure," he replied cautiously. "Obviously knowing the play is in Kent helps."

"Mm."

"And the churchyard ground. It also makes your concern that the place might have been built over seem less likely. They don't often get rid of churches."

The duke nodded. He looked around at the walls, irritated. "I must get out of here as soon as possible—as soon as possible." He studied the paper again, as if the poem would give up more on a hundredth reading. "The third line is the one that puzzles me. *Behind the name my portrait gloss.*"

"I have a theory there." Lenox was waiting for the other shoe to drop, as young folks slanged it these days—but for now he was happy to discuss the poem. "I suspect it puzzled the thief, too, for a while."

"What's your theory?"

"If I had to guess, I would hazard that it is a pun. That would be very much in the spirit of Shakespeare, whether he wrote the poem or one of his friends did. One of his siblings, even. A fellow Stratford artist, perhaps the portraitist himself."

"A pun?"

"The gloss is the topcoat of a painting, as you know. But as I'm sure you also know there is another common sense to the word, even more common in Shakespeare's day—a gloss, from *glossa*, Latin. An explanation of a word. There is only one name 'glossed' in the portrait. In its gloss, if you will," Lenox said.

"Mary," said Dorset. "*Nomen Mariae*."

Lenox nodded. "When we find the right churchyard, I would bet anything that the play is buried at the grave of a woman named Mary."

"A Catholic's joke," said the duke, smiling faintly. There was a beatific relief in his face. Prison was a strange place to see such a thing, but it was there. "You must be correct."

"Yes, Your Grace. A Catholic's joke."

But here it came—the other shoe, the question Lenox had been dreading. The duke, still standing, paper in his hands, said, "I have forgotten to ask you how you found the picture."

Lenox hedged. "It is a long story, and I would like to amass a bit more information. To begin with, may I ask, Your Grace, whether Mr. Craig's own financial position was secure?"

There was a river breeze in the cell, carrying on it the faint damp smell—cordage, closed spaces, open waters, salt, hardtack—of seagoing.

"I do not know to any exactitude, but I paid him well. He was unmarried and without financial obligation. He could have called on me for a loan of any size. I mean that literally."

"He knew that?"

"Yes. A Dorset is a loyal friend. What's more, I made over a par-

cel of land in our possession—six acres—to him. He planned to retire there. But he could have sold it for a few hundred pounds at any
time, as I made clear to him. He had the deed, free and clear."

Lenox nodded quietly. "As I thought, then. With the motive of
money excluded, it becomes easier."

"Easier?"

"I am still lacking information myself, Your Grace," said Lenox.
"Permit me to return this afternoon. I hope to have a fuller explanation then."

The duke didn't look happy, but he was still too preoccupied with
the poem—the quarry of a lifetime, that much closer to being cap-
tured—to care. "Fine," he said. "In the meanwhile I'm going to tell
Lord Aston that I must leave this place as quickly as possible. He
will accelerate matters. There is a play to be found now."

Lenox stood and buttoned his jacket. "Thank you for the coffee,
Duke."

The duke put out a hand. "Thank you for the poem, Mr. Lenox.
I owe you more than a lunch now."

"As I said, it is only my job."

Soon he was outside the Tower and in his carriage, heading back
to Hampden Lane.

In all of these early cases in his career, Lenox could look back
and identify some vital mistake he had made. He was still learning. For instance, the Thames Ophelia had taught him to look as
carefully as he could at faces; the majority of people let faces pass
before them like clouds in the sky, unremarked, without separable
identities.

On Dorset's case, he had made at least this one error: He had not
studied the inhabitants of the household closely enough. He knew
next to nothing about Corfe, Lord Vere, who if all went to plan
would some day become the 16th Duke of Dorset—just as powerful
as his father.

Nor did he have any grasp of the duchess. His thoughts ran to her supercilious cousin, Sir Japheth Miles, standing with her at the scene of the "kidnapping."

Back at Hampden Lane, the young detective heard a thumping on the staircase when he opened the door and found himself waylaid by Lancelot.

"Could I have ten pounds?" the boy asked.

"Ten pounds! What? Have you lost your mind?"

"*Please* could I though?"

"What in all the fires of hell are you talking about? That is a month of Clarissa's wages!"

Clarissa was one of the chambermaids. Lancelot nodded, his thin face as sincere as Lenox had ever seen it, to indicate that he understood this. "But Mr. Templeton knows about a horse than cannot lose in the fifth race at Anglesey. Cannot possibly lose."

"Mr. Templeton the *curate?*"

"Yes."

"MRS. HUGGINS," Lenox shouted.

"You can have some of the winnings."

"Shut up, Lancelot. Mrs. *Huggins!*"

"I would need it this morning."

"You would, would you?" said Lenox. "In that case let me go find my billfold."

"Oh, lovely, really?"

"No! Not really! You could stand here until the end of time and you wouldn't have ten pounds out of me." He paused for a second. "Why did you settle on ten pounds anyway?"

"The horse is ten to one, and I want a hundred pounds."

Lancelot explained that as if it had a Euclidean clarity of premise. Who wouldn't want a hundred pounds? "Oh, a long shot, perfect. What could go wrong. Mrs. *Huggins, would you—*"

Finally the housekeeper appeared, and Lenox told her about the curate's apparent plan to introduce his three boys to the pleasures of the turf. He asked if he could rely upon her to find Lancelot a minder who wouldn't actually take the boy to a casino, until he could find someone at the prison to take over the job.

"You don't mean that," said Lancelot.

"I can take the three boys to the zoo today, sir," said Mrs. Huggins worriedly.

"Fine. They'll fit in marvelously. You know where the other boys are?"

"Yes, sir."

"You know where I keep my ready money. Take whatever you need. Tell Templeton he is fired, unless he can prove to me that Lancelot is lying. Actually—Lancelot, are you lying?"

"No."

"You're sure?"

"Yes."

Lenox stared at him. "Well, then fire Templeton, and watch the three boys even if you have to tie them together. One of them must have a mother in London, or something similar. I am trying to solve a murder."

"Very good, sir."

"If Templeton comes to fetch Lancelot, tell him that I know every police officer in this city. Is he even a curate?"

"Oh, yes, he went to Cambridge, sir."

"That explains part of it, anyway," Lenox muttered—young and highly loyal to Oxford, he held Cantabrigians in roughly the same esteem as Etonians—and stamped out of the door into the gray day.

CHAPTER THIRTY-THREE

He took his carriage to Dorset House, studying his notes on the way. When he arrived, a servant led him into the small drawing room. She informed him that Lord Vere was just departing.

"Where is he going?" Lenox asked the housekeeper.

"To dine, sir," she said very bluntly, and she was well within her rights to be abrupt—it was an impertinent question.

"Where?" he said, pushing his luck.

When she replied, the "sir" was gone. "Out."

Lord Vere agreed to see him, however, and it was the job of this churlish housekeeper to lead Lenox to a large library that he had not seen before, on the east side of the house (it was a mansion of the sort that seemed to multiply with new rooms every day, as if breeding), where all the papers had been ironed and laid out upon an enormous oak table, just as usual it would seem—as if the oak table's owner were not in their headlines.

Lord Vere was waiting in a chair. He rose, buttoning his jacket. "Good morning," he said.

Lenox had not yet had the chance to study the young heir at close range. He was a fine specimen of his kind, perhaps four or five years the detective's senior. He wore a black frock coat; a brilliant white shirt; a paisley cravat; high-waisted checked trousers; a green waist-coat with gold buttons; and a signet ring with his seal on it. To his left was a black top hat, shining silkily under the lamplight. He was consummate: all that should be in a young gentleman.

The room was lined with shelf after shelf of books, stretching twelve feet high, a rolling ladder affixed to each wall. Dominating the center of the room was a marble of Christ and Mary Magdalene that Lenox could see was of the highest quality. He would have believed it was by Donatello.

"Lord Vere," he said, and dipped his head.

"Please, now, call me Corfe. I know your name."

"You are lunching out?" Lenox asked.

"Eh? Oh, yes. Good to get on one's feet again. Her Majesty has invited me to the Palace. To commiserate."

Good Lord, the Queen. For a moment there Lenox had nearly forgotten how high the altitude of this social sphere was, having moved into it so easily as an aide. "That is kind of her."

"Yes, she sent a considerate note. I thought after that I would tod-dle over to the Beargarden and scrounge up a drink."

"Ah, of course. I'm a member there myself."

"Are you! Well, we shall have to dine when this business is all over."

Lenox nodded at this queer politeness. "Of course. But for now, I wanted a quick word about your father and Mr. Craig."

Vere shook his head, face filled with consternation. He gestured for Lenox to sit. "Yes, a right collieshangie that."

Lenox, sitting and thinking of what to ask, had a fast feeling of displacement, as he sometimes did. What on earth was he doing here, playing at police like a child? But he persevered: He thought that probably everyone felt like a fraud now and then. Perhaps even the Queen.

"I wonder if you know a Maggie McNeal, Lord Vere?"

"Call me Corfe, as I said. No, I don't think I do."

"Perhaps just Maggie? She has been a servant here."

"Has she? No." He waved a hand around the room, which, though empty, did a fair job of making his point—that there were dozens of servants about. "Is she mixed up in this? Do you want her called in?"

"That won't be possible—your sister told me that the young woman hadn't been to work in a few days and hadn't given any notice."

"Oh, I see. Yes, that seems bad."

"But you don't recall her."

"Very sorry. No."

"Are there still footmen in your father's study?"

"No. It's locked inside and out now. New locks today. Only he has the keys, in the Tower. He entrusted an outside chap with the job. I hope it will make him feel better."

"So do I."

Corfe looked vaguely troubled to have said so much, as if he sensed that it was a bit unbecoming that his father had shot a man.

He leaned forward. "You don't care to tell me what's in there, do you? The Holy Grail, one would think, from the care he's taking."

"I don't have that information myself," Lenox said. He paused. Then he said, "I have something rather delicate to ask you."

"Anything."

"The missing painting—it was recovered last night by one of your father's servants."

"But that's splendid news!"

"It was recovered from your room."

Vere did an extremely credible—indeed, an almost unfakeable—show of surprise. "My room?" he said.

"Yes."

"But where? What on earth?"

"The underside of your bed."

"My bed? You're joking."

"No," said Lenox.

The handsome young lord sat back and studied the books. Then he turned to Lenox. "So it must have been Craig."

"The trouble there is opportunity," Lenox said. "You were in bed with fever. When would he have done it?"

Corfe frowned. "I was asleep much of the time. There was one morning I ventured out onto the terrace for a few minutes in a chair, hoping the sun would do me good."

Lenox nodded. "I see. Of course. Can I ask you about Craig, then? What do you make of him?"

For the first time something like human feeling came onto Corfe's face, which till now had been like his clothing—perfectly composed, a pose available for the world's scrutiny.

"Craig, poor chap," he said. "I hate that people will think of him as a thief. He was always very stern, but very kind to us."

"Us?"

"Violet and me, when we were small. It was always he who accompanied us to see our grandparents for Christmas. Our favorite time of the year, that, while our parents traveled to the continent."

"Can you imagine any reason for Craig's betrayal of your father?"

Corfe frowned. "Money, I suppose. It's usually money, isn't it?" He checked his watch. "Unfortunately I'll be late to meet my friend, Mr. Lenox. Could we possibly continue this conversation another time?"

Lenox hid his annoyance. The friend to whom he referred was— the Queen of England. "Of course," he said, and both rose from their seats.

He left Dorset House in a welter of emotions, confused and frustrated. He didn't know where he was going; he didn't know enough to know quite what he knew. All the facts were there. None of them would hang together in his mind. He walked in a terrible kind of anger for five blocks, then stopped.

"What have you to say for yourself," he muttered, pulling the little book of quotations from his pocket and letting it fall open to a random page.

We have seen better days.

—Timon of Athens

That was the quotation his eyes settled on. He stared at it for a long time. Then he felt something that he hadn't, in the eighteen months since his father died: tears coming into the backs of his eyes.

He blinked rapidly, and looked up at the dark gray clouds, letting his hand fall to his side. He felt a constriction inside. His face softened. Suddenly it all seemed full of meaning, the vast empty sky, its sorrowful leaden color, the world's inability to *answer* for itself.

He turned back toward the street and hailed a hansom cab. Though it was not in his plans, he directed it to a small boathouse by the side of the Thames.

Its keeper, Wilkins, greeted him with a nod. In thirty seconds he had Lenox's feather-light scull in the water, rain sprinkling the dock around them. Lenox changed in the small dark room off the boathouse, shook hands with Wilkins, and boarded the scull. Then, his back to the west, he eased into the Thames. Wilkins gave him a short salute of farewell, and he started a hard pull.

He had bought the scull four years earlier—from his and Ward's old school, Harrow—and it still pulled like a dream. For forty minutes he lost himself in the rhythm of the exercise, his mind emptied of all but the exertion.

At last, breathless, he glided onto the shore of an old hunk of rock in the middle of the Thames, Peanut Isle by name. A few trees stood high upon it, alone and old, undulating patiently in the soft wind. There was a tun of water here that the boathouses took turns filling, and Lenox pulled to, pried the lid off, took the ladle off the side of the barrel, and poured some of the fresh water gratefully over his body, the chill of chipped ice a glorious sensation on his reddened skin.

He pulled back steadily but more slowly, the rain heavier; he watched the city grow higher as he came nearer to Parliament.

Wilkins greeted him at the boathouse with a cold towel to wipe himself down with, a hot one to scrub off the sweat, and his pullover.

"Thank you," said Lenox.

"It had been a time."

"Work, you know."

"Aye," said Wilkins.

As he was changing back into his clothes, he saw the draw for the doubles race next month, a bracket of sixteen duos, eight on each side seeded by strength, thousands of possible outcomes among the matches.

It was at that moment—perhaps because the exercise had freed him from this terrible business of thinking—that everything clicked into place.

CHAPTER THIRTY-FOUR

It was a matter of numbers. Lenox had never been much of a fist at maths, but it would have looked something like $3 + x + y$, the equation he had in his mind.

He had taken on faith the duke's word that only three people knew about the painting of Shakespeare: in fact it was three plus the number those three people had told, and the number those people had told. $3 + x + y$: It might equal $3 + 0 + 0$, to be sure, as the duke was confident, but it might just as easily be $3 + 2 + 9$, or $3 + 1 + 600$. Who knew?

Or perhaps—and this was what he really suspected—the original number was not three at all. Perhaps it was four.

When he arrived at the duke's rooms this time, everything had a markedly different feel. There were numerous men in the hallways outside, and several inside as well, all of them solemn, and all of them very busy. Lord Aston's work.

The duke saw Lenox and dismissed them with a quick word; they looked at Lenox resentfully but left. The bailiff closed the door behind them.

"My apologies, Mr. Lenox," said the duke. "Solicitors, and men from the House of Lords, and the Palace, and all that."

And all that. "Of course, Your Grace."

They sat near the window again. The day wouldn't give in—still dark, still intermittently wet, and gusting with wind. They could see the ships rocking on the Thames, the taut flags on Tower Bridge.

"I have been contemplating the poem," said Dorset.

"I have been contemplating the missing picture," said Lenox.

"Yes, of course. Naturally. Where is it now?"

"In my house, Your Grace, safe under lock and key. I can have it sent back to you any time you choose."

"Where was it?" the duke asked curiously, as if it were a matter of academic significance to him, not germane to his primary interests.

Lenox took a deep breath. Here was where he felt his youth; he couldn't fluff this opportunity. "It was nailed to the underside of the bed of your son, Lord Vere."

The duke looked at him, taken aback. "Corfe? His bed?"

"Yes, sir."

The part of Lenox that had wondered whether the duke himself might be concealing something more gave way. No. His face now was unmasked and raw, his bafflement real.

"How strange that Craig would place it there. What can explain it?" said the duke.

Lenox held steady. "You mentioned to me, once, your gratitude that your own father lived to a good age, long enough to grow close to his grandchildren."

Corfe had said the same that morning: Christmases with the old duke. "Yes," said Dorset. "Why? Speak plain, Lenox."

"Very well, Your Grace. It is this way.

"When your great-grandfather's portrait was stolen, the windows in your study were open and it was locked. That led us to believe that it was a thief from outside who took the painting. I believe now that that was misdirection. It would have been nearly impossible to gain access from outside the house. Which means that the thief came from inside the house."

"Yes—Craig."

"The key was his, certainly. Was he loyal to Lord Vere?"

The duke put together what Lenox's questions implied. "Are you accusing my son of something?" he asked. "You had better be very sure of your facts if you are."

And so Lenox explained the facts as succinctly and linearly and impassively as he could to the duke, who sat opposite him, intimidatingly silent:

first, that he believed that Corfe had been feigning his fever; he had rejected doctor's visits more than once without any rational explanation, according to separate, equally exasperated accounts from Dorset and from Lady Violet;

second, that he believed Corfe had done so in the hope that he might be alone in the house, but had been thwarted when his parents had delayed their visit to the country to look after him;

third, that he had decided to attempt the theft of the portrait anyway;

fourth, that he was doing so because—and here was the crucial step in the chain of speculation—his grandfather, with whom he had been so close as a child, had told him the *whole truth about the Shakespeare*, old men being famously careless with their confidences, reckoners, totters-up of debt, and above all, among dukes, in love with their eldest grandsons;

fifth, that Craig had been Lord Vere's accomplice in all matters, first offering him the key to the study, then, apparently, going to fetch the second portrait, the Shakespeare, too;

and sixth, that his motive in this must be one of two things—either, Lenox said, a maniacal interest in Shakespeare, which he could not disclose to his father without betraying his grandfather's trust, or (and privately Lenox thought this much more likely) a matter of money.

The duke took each point as a blow, wincing slightly as Lenox spoke. When the detective was done, he stood and walked away across the cell.

When he turned back, something defiant remained in his face. "Corfe has all the money he could ever need—his allowance would put the full income of most households on your street to shame," he said, with, to Lenox, a remarkable lack of delicacy.

"No doubt that is true."

"Moreover, he and I are close. If it was the portrait of Shakespeare he wanted, he would have told me. You are wrong, Lenox. I don't doubt your good faith, but you are wrong. It must be Craig."

"Perhaps. There is one point I find telling."

"Well?"

"That Lord Vere was back on his feet the moment you were taken away. Fever gone."

The duke hesitated. "Fevers come and go."

"Then look at Craig, Your Grace. Is there anyone on earth for whom he would have betrayed you other than Corfe? Listen to me—I have been delirious with fever, as I imagine you have been. To me it seems implausible that even the deepest fever sleep could remain undisturbed by a painting being hammered to the underside of one's bed."

The duke looked at him for a long moment and then slumped back. "It's not possible," he muttered. He looked out through the window, thinking. "Did you know the last person executed here was a woman?"

Lenox had not. He did not especially want to know it now. "No, Your Grace."

"In 1780. Gordon Riots."

"Oh, right, yes."

"Gordon himself, of course, went free."

Another Etonian, Lenox almost muttered, thinking of Lancelot, who was probably leading a riot somewhere right now, and Corfe, too.

Lord Gordon had been a Protestant who stirred up a mob of sixty thousand or so because some very elementary rights had been restored to English Catholics. A fool. His timing could not have been worse: directly after the American revolution, and as the French one was simmering. The Gordon Riots had become a byword for brutality now; Lenox could recall his own father's anger at the stories of violence in London that year.

"I remember now," said Lenox. "The three traitors."

Dorset nodded. "They give you a ghastly kind of introduction when you come here. Or at least they did to me. Wellington was here, which I thought civilized in him. The first thing he mentioned was that there were a hundred and twenty-two executions here between 1388 and 1780. This poor woman apparently being the last."

"Mm."

The duke got up and strode around. Lenox noticed that he had the paper with the poem on it clutched tightly in one hand. "Ninety-three beheaded. Ninety-three! Twelve hanged. Three shot. Two burned at the stake. Eleven hanged, drawn, and quartered.

"And one, he told me, with a relish that I didn't quite like, who had his stomach cut open and his entrails thrown into a fire. After that they castrated him and threw *him* into the fire. Which must have been a mercy, all things told."

"Good Lord."

The duke nodded grimly. "Yes, quite."

"Well, they're not going to execute you, Your Grace."

Dorset waved an irritated hand. "I know that, of course." Still, he looked as if it weren't the worst of the options he faced at the present moment.

CHAPTER THIRTY-FIVE

Lenox measured his words. "My friend Cabot tells me that he thinks a hundred years hence all executions will have ceased. In his opinion we will be viewed as barbarians for having had them at all."

"By 1953. Lord Cabot?"

"Indeed, your Grace."

"A sound man, if a liberal." The duke wandered around his capacious cell. Outside, the hushed chattering of the black-cloaked men continued, just audible. But the duke was not concerned with them at the moment. "If we follow your theory," he said suddenly, "why was Craig unscrewing the portrait of Shakespeare?"

There was a gleam of hope in his eye—but Lenox had anticipated this question. "I think Lord Vere believed he needed it. The second stanza of the poem."

The duke read it over. "Well?"

"The third line: It would have been easy to mistake it, *behind the name my portrait gloss*, as an indication that there was another clue about the lost play behind Shakespeare's own portrait."

"Oh, I see," said the duke, pacing again. "Yes, that is possible, I suppose."

Then he muttered something to himself that sounded like "Kent."
Lenox wondered: Was everything Shakespearean in the end? Because
he looked like Lear now, certainly, this hopelessly rich and privileged
gentleman in his cell.

"Your Grace?"

"Kent, I said. Everybody knows Kent, don't they—apples, cherries,
hops, and women."

Lenox smiled politely. It was a famous line of Dickens's. "Not much
else."

"No. It must be a small churchyard."

"Yes," said Lenox.

The duke seemed to have accepted the detective's theory whole
cloth now. He read the poem again.

But then, all at once, he shook his head violently. "It still doesn't
make sense. I told you—Corfe has an allowance that a prince would
find generous. He is not a gambler—nor is there a woman I know
of—and in either case, there is no financial situation from which I
would be unable to extract him. We could afford ten ruinations over.
He is my heir."

Lenox nodded. "Perhaps he is embarrassed."

"No. He would never risk this embarrassment rather than coming to me. I told him when he was five that there was nothing I could
not get him out of."

Perhaps that was the problem, Lenox reflected. "Then it must be
that he is interested in Shakespeare."

The duke shook his head. "I know my son. He doesn't care a whit
about William Shakespeare."

That was curious. "Might he have been Craig's accomplice, then?"
he suggested.

The duke rejected that idea, too, though. "After all these years?"

"Perhaps he just learned of it."

"If Craig wanted money, there were a million things he could have
stolen without my even noticing. He has a key to the jewel room at

Dorset Castle, for pity's sake. Anyway, I trust him—trusted him—implicitly."

"And Shakespeare?"

"If there has ever been a person less interested in Shakespeare in all of Great Britain than Corfe, it was Alexander Craig. The only thing I ever knew him to read was the army gazette."

"I see."

And indeed Lenox was troubled by this assessment of the duke's household, by its head. His mind turned the facts over but could not quite make them add up. Something was missing.

Some*one*, too. The maid, Maggie McNeal.

The duke sighed. "Will you wait to dig until I am free? We may share the credit," he said. "It is just that it should be so, given that you have sleuthed out the poem."

Lenox was shocked at this offer. He admitted as much. "You surprise me, Your Grace."

The duke gave him a tired glance, but his voice was strong, unbowed. "Then we are both experiencing a day filled with surprise," he said drily.

"If you wish, Your Grace. Of course. I had planned to sit down with an atlas myself later today and begin investigating the churchyards of Kent. But I will naturally not dig without you."

Unless you are imprisoned for life, he thought to himself.

"Find out everything you can. Just keep going. As for Corfe—and Craig—all of that, leave in my hands."

"I have one request," Lenox said.

"Not money?"

"No," said Lenox coldly. "It is that if we should search for the play together, I may be allowed a friend to come along."

The 15th Duke of Dorset looked at him for a long while. This had been his own secret for many years. But he nodded. "As you please," he said.

Lenox returned to Hampden Lane not sure how to feel. What had he solved? Who had he helped? He ate lunch, a consoling cream of tomato soup, slices of cheese with hard biscuit, and a glass of ginger ale, the meal he asked for when he wanted sleep but before he knew he wanted sleep.

He napped once more before the low warm fire in the grate, this time with a novel on his chest. He dreamed that he was a child again.

When he woke this time, he could tell that it was midafternoon. There was a glimmer of yellow light in the branches of the trees, the sun at last showing itself. He heard a knock at the front door and realized it was this that had woken him.

The knock had apparently attracted Lancelot, too, because Lenox heard a noise like a large suitcase falling from a cliff on the stairs.

Lancelot and Lady Jane appeared in his study at once, her hand protectively on his head. She held a newspaper. Evidently it had been her at the door. "Hello, Charles," she said.

He stood up. "Hello. What are you reading?"

"The afternoon *Times*. I have missed the Dunmow Flitch again," she said.

"What is the Dunmow Flitch?" he asked, still blinking his way out of sleep.

She had walked over to the fire and was prodding it, paper in one hand. "Charles, really?" she said chidingly, looking up at him.

"Am I supposed to know?"

"The winners this year were a Mr. and Mrs. Herbert Cheese. Though numerous couples received the side of bacon, obviously."

"Jane, if you value my sanity, explain what you are talking about, or leave." He glanced over at his cousin, who was rooting through his desk. "Preferably with Lancelot."

She smiled and rose. "Every Whit Monday in Essex they award a handsome side of bacon to any couple that presents themselves and swears on a Bible that they have not broken their marriage vows or quarreled for at least the space of a year and a day. The *Times* has a full column on it."

"That is one of the silliest things I ever heard," said Lenox. He sat back down and suddenly realized that for the first time in days he was in a fair mood.

"Charles! Where is your sense of romance!"

"Anyhow it is not closely associated with slabs of dead pig."

"Think how easily James and I should win. We scarcely see each other three months a year, and I cannot recall quarreling with him during those. Poor Mr. and Mrs. Herbert Cheese would stand no chance against us."

"What did they do to win?"

"They wrote a poem. Would you like to hear it?"

"Less than anything."

"*Oh Mrs. Cheese*, it begins, *who brights when I awaken—*"

"Jane, I beg of you."

"*Celebrate our love with me, and with this side of bacon.*"

"What meter is that?"

"It's only fifty lines—shall I go on?"

"No."

"Almost all of it is bacon themed."

Lenox glared at her. "Leave me alone, I beg of you."

"Lancelot, come tell your cousin about the zoo. I know from my long friendship with him that he'll want to hear every last detail you can offer about the health of Obaysch the hippopotamus."

CHAPTER THIRTY-SIX

J ane had come in part to remind him that they were meant to dine that night; she had broken up her own party because there was to be a larger one at a friend's house. Would they ride over together? she asked. He said of course, promising to fetch her at quarter past eight.

Though his visit to Bedlam was some ways off, something had been nagging at him since his last trip. When Jane and Lancelot were gone he composed a wire to Dr. Hansel, his friend at the asylum.

Wondering if you have patient Belmont STOP alternatively Irvington STOP if so would like interview STOP warm regards STOP Lenox

He sent this out by a footman. He was thinking of the man who had approached him at the very end of his last visit, claiming to be falsely imprisoned—Irvington, he had called himself, before the guard called him Belmont.

It hadn't sat well with Lenox all week, and he was glad to have gotten the wire off. That done, he sat down and faithfully recorded the events of the day both for his own edification and to keep the facts straight in his mind. The Duke might be finished with the case, but he was not.

Graham returned just before six. "Hello, sir," he said.

"There you are. I was wondering."

"I have been searching for Maggie McNeal, sir, but unfortunately without luck."

Lenox frowned. It was very rare for Graham to fail. "No sign of her?"

"None, sir. Even within the household she is not remembered except perhaps hazily—that perhaps there was a Margaret employed there for a week or two some time ago. Yet it seems implausible that she should have had a more formal name below stairs than above."

"That is bizarre."

"I thought so, too, sir."

Lenox pondered this. There were often loose ends in his cases, false trails. He didn't like this one. "Thank you, Graham," he said. "I wondered if you wanted to tackle another job for me over the weekend. No rush."

"What is that, sir?"

Lenox smiled. "Don't get too excited. It is the churchyards of Kent I have in mind."

Soon the two were upstairs in their more traditional roles, Lenox shaving, Graham pressing his evening suit, a distracted chatter passing between them. By half past seven Lenox was dressed and his cheeks patted with sandalwood—a gentleman of London town.

Downstairs, he saw that a reply from Hansel had already arrived.

Odd you mention Belmont STOP transferred by family St Cs Edbrgh this week STOP no record Irv now or past STOP welcome any time STOP Hansel

Lenox was used to the doctor's economical style. He frowned as he read this over a second time. So that dark-eyed, dark-haired man, so urgent in his entreaties, had been pulled out of Bedlam after confiding in Lenox.

He would go to the asylum soon if he could.

But for now his duty was next door. On his way out he passed Lancelot and Mrs. Huggins playing checkers intently over an enormous supper. (Lancelot sat cross-legged on the floor across from the housekeeper, about eye level with the board, chin resting on his hand. He reported that she had won thirty-seven times in a row, but he had hopes of breaking through soon, and Lenox felt a quick involuntary burst of affection.) He decided to leave without even asking about Mr. Templeton, or the long shot in the fifth race.

He picked up Lady Jane, who was dressed in a lovely rose-colored gown with a blue taffeta shrug. Her hair was whipped into a high pile of curls.

"You look lovely, Your Ladyship," said Lenox, bowing.

"And you, Mr. Lenox," she said, curtsying.

Soon his carriage was on its way, headed toward the home of Mr. and Mrs. Caliban Edwards. Cal and his wife, Emily, lived in a rather shabby house near Bloomsbury. It was the envy of all their friends. Cal was the son of a very famous explorer and an equally famous beauty, she the daughter of two houses whose lineage dated to the Norman invasion.

They didn't have a penny between them. Cal rubbed along as a writer—a novel and some stories, the occasional tale of travel. Nevertheless, there was no house Lenox knew that was more full of happiness or of, because his father was always climbing some Himalaya or wading some Nile, interesting artifacts. A crocodile with its jaw wide open greeted you in the hallway. A walking stick carved with the symbols of the natives of America—it wouldn't have been out of place in Bergson's shop—was propped against it. The walls were covered with prints from Mr. Audubon's beautifully colorful book about birds. They had all 435 in frames, given them by the artist, and rotated the birds constantly; Audubon himself had been a dedicated visitor here until his death, two years before.

They dined cheaply but happily, all their friends having brought along additional viands and drinks, Lady Jane herself providing an excellent punch, sent over earlier in the day, which tasted of raspberries.

Lenox was seated next to Effie Somers—and the time flew away, as if it were on wings.

After dinner the men and women divided. Cal's father, a noble soul with a finely shaped head and a great coiffed sweep of gray hair, briefly back in London before he left for the interior of Africa, spent a great deal of time asking Lenox about his methods and his ideas.

At the end of it he offered a word of oblique praise. "They called me mad, too, you know," he said. "Perhaps they still do. I wouldn't trade a lifetime over again in the House of Lords for a single day of doing what I loved."

The two sexes rejoined in the drawing room, and Lenox moved into other conversations. But he was heartened by that one: He did love his work.

And he was improving, surely he was improving—or he was trying to improve, at least, which must matter in its own right.

He found Lady Jane and Effie Somers together on a couch as the hour neared midnight. "You look as if you've been brooding," said Lady Jane.

They were in the center of the small, comfortable drawing room, which was populated by a mix of generations, aging Explorers Club members and young society sorts.

"Only a bit."

"What about?" asked Miss Somers, accepting a glass of champagne from a footman with a graceful nod.

"Shakespeare!" said Lenox, and grinned. "How dull."

"Did you know he minded the horses for the theatergoers?" Effie said.

"I was always told he wrote the plays," Jane replied. "But then they never educate girls."

Her friend smiled, and in that instant Lenox almost loved her. "No, it was his first job in the business. When he was new in London."

"Was it!"

"I like to think of him standing there. He must have heard the laughs and groans from inside the theater and wondered what was prompting them."

"Every long silence," said Lenox.

"Exactly," she said.

Lady Jane excused herself. "Will you take care of Miss Somers for a moment?" she asked. "I have to ask Cal something."

Her motive in leaving them alone was transparent enough that when she had gone across the room, there was a slight humorous tension in the candid look Lenox and Effie Somers exchanged.

She wore a summer dress, yellow and white. Around her neck was a gold chain with a gold ring on it. She had pinned her thick golden-chestnut hair up, and Lenox could imagine, from the trace of scent he had caught when he said hello, what it would be like to stand before her as she unfurled it just for him.

A painful absence glanced through his insides. He thought, unbidden, how he wanted someone to love.

"How are you finding your return from America to England?" he asked.

"When I was last there everyone was reading *Uncle Tom's Cabin*. But I observe that it has followed me here."

"I haven't read it."

"No? It is quite wrenching. All of the people on the right side of things—the abolitionists—have high hopes for it."

"Did you not meet anyone on the wrong side of things?" Lenox asked.

She looked at him curiously. "You are not asking because you . . . you disagree with me?" she said.

"Never in life."

"Oh! Good. I did, though, to answer your question. The population is quite mixed. The pragmatists in Newport, where we passed last summer, have set a target date of 1900. The last slave shall be freed then, they say. Others are afire for it to happen tomorrow."

"What do you think?"

"I don't know—truly I don't."

"My second cousin went there, on my mother's side," said Lenox. "Fourth son. He is in South Carolina. He has land, and at least ten slaves. A very amiable person as I recall him—and yet I cannot imagine his life, how he justifies it in his mind! It beggars belief."

Miss Somers glanced across the room, and her hand went to her necklace nervously. "Mr. Lenox," she said quietly, touching her necklace, "may I confide in you?"

"Of course," he replied, surprised.

He did not know if it was going to be on the subject of slavery— did she need money?—but instead she said, "I am engaged to be married."

"Are you! My heartfelt congratulations. The chap is very fortunate, very."

"It is a secret. He lives in Philadelphia. My mother and father will—it is probably only half a step too far to say that they will disown me if I become an American, so we are waiting until he is on firmer footing there. He owns a printing shop for which he has high hopes."

"Like Franklin. I am sorry that you should be separated, though," said Lenox.

"I'm telling you this because Jane, in her foolish kindness—"

He put up a hand. "Miss Somers, say nothing more. I understand."

She looked at him gratefully. "Thank you, Mr. Lenox. You are a gentleman."

He smiled. "If your fellow has a printing shop, I imagine that means he is able to send you very handsome letters even from across the sea."

They talked quietly for some time, and Lenox, after the initial surprise and a pang of disappointment, found that his sadness was not attached to the particular personage of Miss Effie Somers, even with her beautiful hair. It was attached to the idea of a woman who might love him and give him children.

He had—in other words—learned something of himself that evening. That could never be all bad.

When he returned home it was to find the final edition of the late newspaper on his step. He picked it up and read its lead headline.

Duke of Dorset Released Home
Servant's death ruled self-inflicted
Coroner returns verdict of misadventure

CHAPTER THIRTY-SEVEN

Early the next morning—before six—his carriage was winding its way south. He was on his way to Bedlam after all. He couldn't abide seeing the duke ensconced again at Dorset House, master of all he surveyed; not yet, anyhow. There was more to be done about Alexander Craig's death, but he would not be doing it today.

He slept for some of the drive. The journey was quicker than usual because of the time, forty minutes perhaps. As it passed he read the papers by the light of the rising sun. Nobody challenged the narrative that it had been an unfortunate accident. A few made hay of the history of the Tower—the Princes, the nine-day Queen, Anne Boleyn—but that was it.

This was the power of being a duke, he supposed, folding the papers as they came to the gate of the asylum.

When he checked in at Bedlam, Dr. Hansel greeted him with mild surprise. "You are here." The old doctor smiled. They were in a small inner courtyard dominated by an ancient oak tree, putatively the preserve of the doctor since it lay just beside his office—but even here they could hear strange moans and screeches. "What brings you?"

"I wanted to ask in person about Belmont."

Hansel nodded. "Never a patient who attracted my notice. I had a look at his papers after you wired."

There were a thousand patients or more here. "What was his situation?"

"Committed for madness three years ago—delusions of grandeur, believed he was all sorts of people, the Empress of Austria, Beau Brummel, Alexander the Great."

Lenox asked if he could see the papers. "He approached me last week."

"What did he say?"

"That he was held here under false pretenses."

"I see." Hansel frowned. "You can examine his papers, yes. Strange timing. His sister wrote and asked that he be transferred to Edinburgh on the Monday after you left."

"Giving what reason?"

"She had recently married and moved there from London, wished him close."

"Is that sort of move unusual?"

"No, not in the least. In fact I didn't even hear of it—not a decision that would reach my desk. She sent the fees to have him go by post, though, which is rather luxurious."

It also meant two large bailiffs, Lenox imagined. Hansel signaled to a young assistant—brave lad, to work at Bedlam—and asked him to fetch the papers, spelling the name Belmont twice.

"Thank you," Lenox said.

"Of course. Tell me, do you have reason to believe him?"

"I don't know, in truth. But I didn't like how it felt not to come."

"I understand. But you must excuse me—I have patients to see, even early on a weekend."

"Of course," said Lenox.

He sat down in the courtyard. No matter what went on here, the birds in the trees sang their morning songs. He pulled the little

fortune-telling book of Shakespeare quotations from his pocket—
he felt he was getting the hang of the bard, a bit—and opened it at
random.

> *The abuse of greatness is when it disjoins remorse from*
> *power.*
>
> —Julius Caesar

Ten minutes or so later, the boy returned. "Here you are, sir."

"Thank you very much. Say, by chance do you keep the annual
naval gazette here? I can't imagine you do."

"Oh, yes. We have quite an extensive library, sir. Would you like
to see it?"

"Who uses it?"

"The inmates."

Lenox felt a trickle of panic at the idea of being in a room with
them—but he nodded. "If you don't mind, thank you."

The boy led him to a desk with a green banker's lamp. Lenox
glanced around nervously, but everyone there seemed absorbed in
scholarship. He could imagine what some of them must have done
to come to arrive at this station in life, yet all were calm now.

Belmont's file was a disappointment. The fellow had been here
for two years. His health was good. He had never caused trouble.
There were regular additional monies allotted to him for small lux-
uries: tobacco, newspapers, and so forth.

Lenox flipped through the pages twice but noticed nothing
else.

Then he turned to the long row of annual gazettes to which Hansel's assistant had guided him, bound in blue leather, with gold lettering on their spines. He tried the one from two years before. There
was no mention of a Captain Irvington in the index—the name Belmont had said was actually his own. He tried the year before and
after. Nothing.

But then he did find something. In the gazette for 1849, this short entry from November:

> *Captain T. Irvington, Hants, formerly HMS* Bella, Livia,
> Aurelie, *lost in solo hunting expedition from HMS* Victoria
> *near Storm Bay, Van Diemen's Land, Australia.*
> *Search fruitless; numerous inlets along "Tasmania," as*
> *locals call it; small parties gave up after several days;*
> *funeral services held at sea; Lt. Pilon breveted to Captain*
> *for remainder of voyage by Rear Adm. Weber.*

Lenox felt a rush of excitement. He looked through the previous years' gazettes methodically and found no mention of an Irvington except in the year 1842, when he had received his first captaincy aboard the *Aurelie.*

Was it possible that Irvington had been whisked away, his disappearance covered with this tale, and then pressed into his imprisonment here in England?

He turned back to Belmont's file. Something was bothering him.

Only after studying it carefully did he suddenly realize what it was: His visitor log for the past two years, despite his having this sister so eager to bring him with her to Edinburgh, was entirely empty.

He got up and went to the offices to send a few wires, one to a friend in the naval office, another to the asylum in Edinburgh, and a third to the sister there, return post paid, asking if Belmont had arrived safely.

He felt sure he was onto something. What had Belmont said? Never to let a member of the royal family fall in love with your wife. It seemed ridiculous to imagine an officer of the navy being interned here under a false name simply by royal fiat, but in the same thought he remembered the headline that had greeted him in the paper the night before, and all those clerks and solicitors in their efficient swarm around the duke in the Tower.

It was past nine o'clock by the time Lenox left, and he was hungry. They stopped at a coaching inn in Penge called the Sycamore, which his driver said was good—and though it was relatively quiet, he was right. They sat at a small knotted table together and fell ravenously upon eggs on toast, a piping hot Welsh rarebit, sausages, and strong dark tea, with a measure of whisky for the driver, to aid, he said, his concentration upon the roads.

"That works, does it?" said Lenox, ingenuously.

"Works a treat, sir—works a treat."

It was the first meal they had ever shared, but then there was something democratic about a coaching inn. It was different from a regular public house. A coaching inn was much larger, for a start, and generally located along a main road, since horses could be stabled there. All of them had private dining rooms and sleeping quarters for travelers; unlike a pub, a coaching inn never closed.

Some of the best memories of his childhood were of a coaching inn. When they were young, his and Edmund's father had taken them up to town by himself once a year for the start of Parliament, so they could sit among the spectators.

There had been something delightful about traveling without their mother, love her though they dearly did. It was more of an adventure with their father. He didn't have any particular rules, for one thing.

They had always stopped at the same inn halfway, the Admiral Nelson. It was a wonderful, uproarious place, full of the scent of beer and coffee and horses. Class vanished. Men of every stripe—he had never seen a woman there—traded stories, those coming from London, those headed there, over tankards of ale and the latest newspapers.

Most of all Charles remembered the food: His father, generally ascetic, had let the boys have whatever they wished.

Edmund's taste tended to mutton, but for Lenox the best sight was the huge black pot, trembling when there were footsteps nearby, that always hung over the fire, full of a delicious stew. It came in a tremendous bowl—what had seemed tremendous at the time, anyway—with hunks of bread and a pitcher of freshly chilled milk.

Edmund and Charles watched how their father handled himself, as they ate and their horses were watered and fed; he was civil to all, familiar with few, a figure, whether because of his clothes or because someone had whispered his name, of instant significance and respect.

He could so easily recall that awe.

Once he had told them—Lenox had never forgotten—about England's two most famous coaching inns, just a few hundred yards apart on the same road in Buckinghamshire.

Their father, eyes twinkling, said, "They are famous for their tall tales. Have been for centuries now. Nobody goes there expecting the truth—only for a good rattling yarn. And do you know what they're called?"

"What?" Charles and Edmund had said simultaneously.

He smiled. "The Cock and the Bull, lads," he had said. "That is why you shouldn't let anyone at school tell you a cock-and-bull story."

Lenox and his driver finished their breakfast and by ten had returned to Hampden Lane. Lenox had fallen deeply asleep again, full and tired, but apparently the driver was right—the whisky had kept him alert.

He woke up thinking of the dozens of words that he had been scrawling in his notebook before he fell asleep, trying to force his hand to generate what his mind could not: *Corfe, money, Craig, 20, Shakespeare, Vere, terrace*, a loose association. He read over them again as the carriage stood patiently in front of his house.

Something was still wrong. But what? The page wouldn't give it up to him, even after twenty minutes. At last he sighed and went inside.

CHAPTER THIRTY-EIGHT

Graham greeted him. "How was your journey, sir?"

"Puzzling. What have you been doing?"

"Housework, sir. But I have the maps of Kent laid out in the large drawing room, where with your permission I will consult them. Before that, if you have no need for me here, I thought I would find General Pendleton for you, and try one last trick to run Maggie McNeal to ground."

"Thank you, Graham," Lenox said. "If you have time, could you also do a bit of research for me? It would be on a sea captain, dead, by the name of Tankin Irvington. Only if you have time."

Graham was writing the name down. "Of course, sir."

"Thank you, Graham. Incidentally, where is Lancelot?"

"The junior curate at St. Michaels's, a Mr. Wilfrid, has agreed to superintend the three children for the next week, sir. Mr. Templeton has been reprimanded and placed on a month's involuntary leave. He is apparently somewhat susceptible as a gambler."

"Poor Mr. Wilfrid," said Lenox.

"Yes, sir," said Graham, with what amounted to fervent feeling for him—a slight rise of his eyebrows.

The confused state of Lenox's social status in London was clear from the table in his front hall: two more invitations stylishly withdrawn, but also a dinner invitation to White's from his father's old friend Lord Salisbury, a touching marker of good faith to which Lenox immediately replied in the affirmative.

A detective—and now bound up in the mess of Dorset. Before the summer of 1853 was out he would be an untouchable.

He riffled through the rest of his letters as he walked to his study. But perhaps Salisbury's loyalty stayed in his mind, for when he sat at his desk—through the windows it was turning into a clear, warm June day—he had a thought.

Wasn't it far more likely that Craig had died out of loyalty to the duke than anything else? It was the duke who had given him employment for close to two decades. He might have felt affection for the house's heir, but nobody so serious as Craig had been, both by appearance and by all accounts, would have risked everything for a silly young fool like Corfe.

And there was still the uneasy matter of Corfe's motive.

Solvitur ambulando. It had already been a long morning, but he decided that he would go out into the sunny morning and think it all through. He told Mrs. Huggins (coaxing a cat with milk, in the hallway) that he would be back shortly, then went out and headed in the direction of the river.

He kept a steady, unthinking pace, rather as he did when he rowed. For perhaps twenty minutes he didn't think of anything particular—only watched the city fold and unfold itself around him, the milkman delivering to a café, four boys playing skittles down an alley, an old woman walking with her spine very straight, and behind her a lady's maid holding a King Charles spaniel.

He stopped short at a bookshop on Bond Street and went inside and bought the first volume of *Uncle Tom's Cabin*, which was sold in separate parts.

"Flying off the shelves it is, sir," the lean young clerk told him.

"Is it any good?"

"Haven't read a word of it, sir. Here's threepence back. Enjoy the day."

He tucked the book into his jacket pocket and went on walking, thinking of Effie Somers and her secret engagement. He liked her. The night before she had told them amusing stories of her time in America, gently caricaturing her father, a diplomat who in his spare time was working on an apparently infinitely proliferating history of the American continent. (It was at nineteen planned volumes thus far—half of a quarter of the first one written.)

When he reached Pall Mall he leaned against a wall and lit his pipe, smoking and studying the comings and goings at the Reform Club. After a moment he reached into his pocket and took out the novel, and soon found himself consumed by its quick-moving story. He read for fifteen or twenty minutes, as long as it took his pipe to run cold.

Just up the street was the Army and Navy Club, and he had the idea that he would go in. In the carpeted front hall he was greeted by a smartly dressed majordomo, clearly ex-military himself, who asked if he could help. There were portraits of various generals running along the walls, and beneath them paintings of famous battle scenes.

"I was hoping to call on General Pendleton," he said.

"The general is not in town at present."

"No? When did he leave?"

"He was last here in April, sir."

Lenox raised his eyebrows. "Perhaps he is staying somewhere else."

The steward laughed. "Impossible, sir."

"I see. Well, thank you."

Lenox went outside, book tucked under his arm. The sand kept slipping through his fingers. He walked the beautiful green stretch of the mall in a deep study, the beds embanking it abloom with tens of thousands of yellow wallflowers and red tulips, tender sprays of purple salvia. The avenue was filled with prams, children, and couples—it was Saturday, a day to be outside.

Then, in the distance, he spotted a woman he momentarily thought was Effie Somers.

He saw when she turned that it wasn't, but it was this that caused him to reverse course, walking rapidly now, toward Dorset House.

He had it. He was all but sure—he had it. That glimpse had resolved all of his doubts.

One he reached Dorset House, he didn't approach it. Instead, he slouched back against the wall facing it, using the tricks that Bonden had taught him, or trying to, anyhow. It helped to be reading something, Bonden had said, and Lenox made it through a long stretch of *Uncle Tom's Cabin*; it helped to be eating something, so he bought some chestnuts from a passing woman; it helped to be smoking.

He moved fifteen feet here or there, and at least did not think he was observed. The same constable—one that he knew to say hello to, in fact, Sam Shepperton—passed by on his beat five times over the course of the next few hours without noticing Lenox once.

He observed the house's comings and goings. The duchess left and returned four times, three of them by carriage. The duke went out just once—for lunch, Lenox presumed—and returned after about ninety minutes. Lord Vere came out twice, once very quickly to run around the corner, returning with a bouquet of flowers, and then a second time to get into his carriage. Busiest of all was Ward, constantly in and out down the road to the Lords, though naturally various servants came and went too many times to count. They took deliveries from the butcher, the upholsterer, and the postman.

Staring at the house for such a long while, Lenox begin to grow almost fond of it. There were six majestic marble archways on its face forming an arcade that reached past the second floor. Above them were large Corinthian columns with rectangular windows between them. At the very height of the house were two enormous round windows, with a statue of the 1st Duke of Dorset standing between them, and statuary representing England and the county of Dorset around him.

Who made such a thing! It was glorious and absurd in equal measure; it belonged in the deepest woodlands of Pembrokeshire, not *here*, taking up a hundred feet on the river in the most densely populated city on earth.

But then, it always helped to have built in the year 1550—plenty of space back then, 250-odd years before they even conceived of Buckingham Palace.

He stood there as the long summer hours passed, watching. By the time the sun began to glow over the river he had finished the first third of *Uncle Tom's Cabin* and was desperate to eat something other than chestnuts—and he was very tired.

At four o'clock, he left. He knew it all now. It was just a matter of braiding the strings together. He felt exhausted, but triumphant.

He hailed a cab and went to Scotland Yard. Sir Richard Mayne, fortunately, worked seven days a week, was known for it.

He greeted Lenox warily, as if expecting to be criticized for the duke's release. "Well?" he said. "What is it?"

"I know what happened," Lenox said.

"What do you mean?"

"I mean that the coroner was right. The duke is innocent. Listen—will you travel down to Dorchester with me tomorrow morning? I do not feel equipped to go alone."

Mayne looked at him inquisitively. "Dorchester? Could one of the inspectors go? You may have your pick."

Lenox shrugged. "If you prefer," he said. "But it is the Duke of Dorset we are discussing. The Queen herself intervened in his release."

Mayne nodded. "Very well. Dorchester."

CHAPTER THIRTY-NINE

They consulted the timetable in Bradshaw's. There were thirty trains to Dorchester from London each day. They picked the earliest one, agreeing to meet on Platform 19 at Waterloo at five past six o'clock the next morning.

Lenox went home and had a quick dinner, doubtfully enlivened by a long monologue from Lancelot, which might, had he been presenting it to the Royal Academy, say, have been titled "A Schoolboy's Field Guide to the Practical Uses of Laxatives." From the sound of it there was not a beak at Eton who had gone unpunished by Lancelot and his two apparently likewise Luciferian friends, Mott and Wutherington-Fassett.

"Except the Head," said Lancelot, wistfully. "We can never get near his tea. He keeps it in a flask."

"That is how you get to be Head."

"They always say there must be something 'going the rounds,' which is awfully funny, don't you think? The way they bolt from their desks in the middle of a lesson."

"I do not think it is funny," said Lenox. He made a mental note not to drink anything whose decanting he had not personally supervised for the rest of his cousin's visit. "Did Templeton's horse win, by the way?"

"Dead last," said Lancelot cheerfully, and returned to his game pie with his customary gusto.

"I suppose the lesson there is not to gamble."

"The lesson," Lancelot corrected him, mouth full, "is not to trust a scrub like Templeton."

Lenox gave up. He finished his supper and soon was upstairs. Though it was barely eight o'clock, he fell immediately and deeply asleep.

The next morning he arrived at Waterloo early.

It was only five years old, this rail station, fresh and clean—it had replaced Nine Elms, though that superannuated terminus had remained open for the convenience of one cantankerous young person: Queen Victoria, who liked the privacy of traveling from a vacated station.

Lenox bought a cup of tea and a soft chocolate crescent roll, still warm, from a stallholder, then stood on Platform 19, watching through the enormous windows as the mist rose over London's uneven buildings.

Soon enough Mayne strode up the platform hailing Lenox, accompanied by his highly efficient secretary, Wilkinson. "You're sure of this?"

"Quite sure," said Lenox.

"On we go then."

The first-class carriage was comfortable; the trip took two hours and twenty minutes, during which time Lenox consumed much of the second volume of *Uncle Tom's Cabin*, which he had had a footman run out to buy for him. As they were pulling into Dorchester Station, he pulled his little leather book out for luck and let it fall open.

*In nature there's no blemish but the mind; none can be
call'd deform'd but the unkind.*

—Twelfth Night

He frowned. No idea what that one meant.

At the station they hired a carriage. They were in it for around forty minutes, until roughly twenty-five past nine, before they reached an immense black gate. They had arrived at Dorset Castle.

Except that it then took a long and winding drive down a tree-lined alley, ten minutes in its own right, to reach the building itself. Only at the last instant did it come into view—beautiful, isolated, a working wreck.

It was built as an extension from the partially ruined foundations of a very ancient castle. On one side there was a high turreted tower, but more recent architects had built behind it: two long sides in similar gray stone, around an open, grassy courtyard. It looked something like a college at Oxford, except the wrong color. To the west there were miles of wild gardens and forest—the opposite of the tamed and mown beauty at Lenox House, but immensely bigger, and impressive as only nature left to itself can be.

They knocked upon the heavy oak door. There was no answer. A quick sortie from Wilkinson revealed that the real front door was around the side (the private private door), where evidently the living quarters were situated.

A dignified, silver-haired butler answered. "May I help you?" he said with a face full of perfect incuriosity, though he must have heard the carriage coming for at least the last five minutes.

Mayne produced his royal seal. "We are with Scotland Yard. May we come in?"

The butler examined the identification and then surveyed the three of them unflappably—clothes, faces—before finally saying, "Excuse me for a moment."

They stood and watched the door close in front of them. They waited for about a minute, and then it swung open.

It was Lady Violet Vere. "Mr. Lenox?" she said.

"How do you do, Lady Violet," he said, bowing.

There was a moment of confusion upon her face, and after that—

she was a bright woman—a moment of realization, then one of res-
ignation.

That quickly! She had a rapid mind; she had outfoxed everyone
more than once.

"Come in," she said with poised courtesy. "Come in."

When Lenox had stood before Dorset House in London the day
before, he had watched every person who came and went—Corfe,
the Duke, the Duchess—but in that time he had not seen Lady
Violet once. This had been the confirmation of his suspicions that
he needed.

She led them into a dark room full of heavy old furniture, its
roughly coursed stone walls decorated with medieval hunting tapestries. It was cool here, by ancient design; the warmth of the day could
not penetrate the walls.

She offered them tea, which they accepted. When they had sat
down near the empty fireplace (there was a skeleton staff here, as
she told them, but you wouldn't have guessed—Lenox never saw the
same face twice as people tramped in and out of the room bearing
tea, scones, cakes, and sandwiches), she gathered her skirts under her.

Why was she not beautiful? The world was treacherous hard on
women, he thought. For Lenox, the whole impression was his only
means of judging these things, really. He knew, or did not know,
whether a person appeared attractive to his eye. If he focused he
could see that Lady Violet's eyes were too close together and too
small, her chin and nose too sharp, her cheeks low, her forehead
high.

He knew his own looks—he was about the average run of the
gentlemen of his class, he reckoned—and had the luxury of thinking about them rarely.

For Lady Violet Vere, by contrast, born to everything, absolutely
everything, *except* beauty, and in a world where even for an heiress
it must matter—he could only imagine how the fact had racked her
days, her weeks, her years with self-doubt and self-hatred.

At last the tea was all set before them, she having poured four cups and added sugar and cream as directed, an ideal host, and Lenox could speak.

"You shot Mr. Craig, I think, Lady Violet?" he said.

She took a careful sip of her tea and then set it down with its saucer, which had been in her left hand. "Yes, that's so," she said.

"Your father was not there?"

"He was not. Mr. Craig was sleeping in the closet, it would seem, to surprise intruders. I went to get the portrait. He surprised me."

"You know about the portrait, then."

She looked at Mayne, who was wide-eyed and silent. In much of the world he was a great man, but she was the daughter of a duke, and her glance toward him was dismissive. "Yes," she said.

"Why were you carrying a gun?" asked Lenox.

"I wasn't. Craig was. I shoved him and it went off, just like that."

Lenox nodded. It had been a detail of great uneasiness to him that the wound the duke had supposedly inflicted on Craig went *upward* through his chest, since the duke was the taller of the two men. But Craig would have had six inches or so on Lady Violet, and if the gun was between them, a stray bullet might easily have been fired upward.

For all that, he was not sure still that it was a stray bullet.

"Did he know it was you?"

"I don't think he did," said Lady Violet. "I did not know it was him. I thought it might be you, or a police officer my father had hired. I was scared."

"I'm very confused," said Mayne.

Lady Violet took a sip of tea. "I started out with a very simple plan. As it happens it has turned into a nightmare."

"You wanted to steal your father's portraits?" said Mayne.

Lenox intervened. "There is reason to believe that the two portraits, together, hold the clue to a very significant treasure."

"But you are—"

The commissioner did not finish his sentence, but his meaning was clear. She was privy to immense wealth. Hundreds of thousands of acres in any direction were rented to pay for the glories of her life, in immemorial custom. Out upon the heaths men raised crops and paid their duty out of them to the duke, and those sheaves of corn, those bushels of potatoes, transmuted magically into silver dinner plates, ruby necklaces, kid gloves, boxes at the opera. Ball gowns, taffeta, silk.

The tarnished ring on a gold chain that never left her neck.

It was in fact Miss Somers who had unwittingly forced upon Lenox the revelation that Lady Violet might be the prime mover behind the whole mystery. Lady Jane's friend had spoken of her American courtship, and her hand had gone unconsciously to the ring on a slim gold chain around her own neck—a ring not very different from Lady Violet's. When he had seen her doppelgänger the afternoon before, he had connected the two.

"I believe Lady Violet is engaged," Lenox said gently, "but that her parents will not approve the match. Thus it was that she needed money."

She looked at him. "Yes, that's the way it stands," she said, looking at him coldly, daring him to go on.

"Her grandfather had once told her of a treasure that might be had from the paintings she stole." Mayne looked puzzled and sat silent. The word "treasure" sounded foolish even to his ears, but Lenox pushed ahead. "The question now, as I see it, is whether Sir Richard will arrest you."

CHAPTER FORTY

The staircases in medieval castles were all identical—narrow and spiraling upward to the right. This design served two practical purposes. First, they were slower to ascend; second, they blocked the right arm on ascent but freed it on descent, meaning that only someone coming down from the keep had the use of his sword.

In the sieges of the very old days, they said, some unfortunate improvised troop of left-handers always had to make the first assault upon the stairs.

Lady Violet's rooms were in the castle's keep, she said, not in the modern wing. Sir Richard Mayne insisted that they had to accompany her as she gathered her things, to prevent some act of self-harm. She was to be taken in, Mayne said, and held until they consulted the duke.

They did not enter her actual bedchamber but lurked just outside, watching her consult with her maid. Lenox felt, to use Lancelot's words, a scrub, standing in the doorway.

Nor did he like Mayne's plan. "Are we to let her walk into the streets of London?"

Sir Richard turned full upon him. He had a great deal of authority he had suppressed in front of Lady Violet, and he let the store loose upon the young detective. "I suppose we are, Lenox, yes."

"That seems wrong."

"It certainly does."

They agreed then. The Queen made no intercessory requests about the fate of the prostitute who put a knife into the ribs of a man assaulting her. And it would take longer than they had now to ponder the father who would not allow his daughter to marry to suit her happiness, yet was willing to risk a trial for murder rather than let her come to public shame.

"I think of Craig," Lenox murmured.

"He will not wake up tomorrow morning either way."

Lenox could not let it go. "Is that the point of justice?"

"That is the reality of justice," said Mayne. "You would call upon it yourself if it were your brother or your nephew in question, I reckon."

And there he had Lenox. Every aristocrat with his politics wanted greater fairness, but they went on sending their sons to Oxford. How would any of it ever change?

Lenox fell silent and set to wondering about that tarnished ring around Violet's neck. What declarations had come with it, and how sincere they were. Most of all who had given it.

But she refused to say. After having packed, she was very becoming in following their instructions, in attending to their plans—she would be confined to Dorset House in London, with a constable— but would not add a word to what she had confessed.

She did ask how Lenox had known. "Was it just the ring? Such a minor error. Though I suppose it is out of keeping with my habits that it should be tarnished and made of nickel."

He shook his head. "You overplayed your hand, my lady. When I realized that I could find neither the maid Maggie McNeal nor General Pendleton anywhere in London, I knew that you had tried to misdirect me."

She looked at him. "I see."

"Nor could I, for the life of me, make any of it stick to Corfe."

"No, he is an innocent sort, my brother."

When they reached the gravel courtyard, Mayne asked if he might retire inside before their return trip, which they would take in her ladyship's carriage. Wilkinson was a little ways off, smoking.

Quickly, Lenox said, "The poem—you have misread it."

Lady Violet looked at him expressionlessly. "Is that so?"

"The clue is not in Shakespeare's portrait."

She studied him, then turned away in the gravel courtyard and touched the nose of one of her horses, feeding him a cube of sugar from her pocket. "What is the clue, then?"

"Were you planning to leave the country while your father was in the Tower?"

She turned back to him. "What a contemptible idea. Of course not."

"Yet you would have run away from him if you had found and sold the play."

"To the Americas or India, yes."

"Who is the young man?"

She ignored the question. "I could not live upon a single strand of pearls, like some heroine in a novelette. My own possessions are pretty but minor."

"But the play . . ."

She rubbed the horse's nose. "I consulted a friend who said that the bidding between Oxford and Cambridge and the British Library would be fierce. And there are these Americans, you know, coming pretty hardy into the fray. The Astor family has unlimited wealth, they say. Unlimited. Soon enough people like you will be marrying them."

"People like me," Lenox murmured, and smiled. "How much did you think you could fetch?"

"I was told I could be guaranteed a minimum of thirty thousand pounds in a private auction. My father need never have known."

"Your grandfather told you the legend?"

"He told us a great deal, yes. He was a wonderful person."

"Corfe was in on this scheme, then?"

"My brother?" she said. "No."

She turned away, walking a few steps to the third horse in her cortege of four. So much money around her! Each of these horses was flawless, twice the price of a house. Yet she needed her very own thousand pounds a year to live happily—even in love.

"What about Craig? He helped you?"

"He and I have always been friends."

"And now he is gone."

She brushed the remaining sugar off her hands. "Excuse me," she said, and stepped into the carriage.

They spent much of the ride back to London in silence, an unreadable silence on the young woman's part, a respectful one on Mayne's and Lenox's. Wilkinson rode on the box. The horses pulled them swiftly and surely—perfect beasts.

When they had arrived within the limits of London, Lenox begged Mayne to let him off at the Wilcombe Tavern. When asked why, he said he had some business to conduct here. He would meet them at Dorset House.

Receiving no farewell from Lady Violet, Lenox watched the carriage go.

Then he sprinted inside and asked for the hostler.

A grizzled old gentleman with squinting eyes met him. "I need a horse, your fastest."

"Three shillings and a five-pound bill of debt for collateral. Standard."

"Done."

Within a few minutes Lenox was in the saddle. He rode as hard as he could, aiming for the center of London.

It was a rough ride over uneven ground, and before long both man and horse were sweating. But they made excellent time—slipping through small spaces, easily outpacing the carriages that passed each other in a handsome, elegant trot along the road, carriages like the one carrying Mayne and Lady Violet.

His destination was Dorset House. He needed at least fifteen minutes, and when he pulled up in front, he thought he probably had it. He handed the reins of the horse, a fine youthful mare called Pepper, to one of Dorset's own stableboys.

Now it all depended on whether Lord Vere was home.

He was. He greeted Lenox, who was hot and sweaty, with some surprise and offered him a lemon ice, or a glass of water. The detective, though he was desperate for a sip of water, declined.

"Time is short," he said to Vere. They were in a drawing room, lined with oils of clouds by Constable. Yet another room new to him. Would this house never give up all its secrets! "Listen to me, Corfe. I admire you and Mr. Craig for helping your sister."

"Excuse me?"

"It may still be possible to ensure that her name is not brought before the public, which I imagine to be your wish, as it is your father's. But you must tell me all."

Corfe, who was again impeccably afternoonified, in black boots and a pink-and-white striped waistcoat under his navy suit, drew himself taller for a moment.

Then his face crumpled. He was not a very bright fellow. It was best, the thought flashed through Lenox's mind, that a king or a duke be either very stupid or very brilliant. No other kind of brain would admit for the paradoxical absurdities and dignities of the position. Corfe would pull it off well; his father was perhaps just a bit too clever.

"That damnable Walters," Corfe muttered, sinking back into a chair.

Walters. He knew that he had just learned the name of the gentleman who proposed to marry Lady Violet. That was worth the price of hiring Pepper on its own.

"You do not approve of the match?" Lenox asked.

"He is not a gentleman." Sometimes silence was best. Lenox let Corfe's troubled eyes turn away. "Little more than a decent shot. What a devilish thing that he should be so handsome!"

"Mm."

"We lost a good gamekeeper out of it, worse still."

A gamekeeper! That explained it. For a gamekeeper Lady Violet Vere was going to find and sell a lost play by William Shakespeare— her family's great imagined contribution to England, its great imagined treasure.

If Walters was indeed quite so handsome, though, Lenox could see why his appeals to Lady Violet had been irresistible, given that she was already up on the shelf, a spinster at age thirty.

It was also clear why the duke had forbidden the match.

Less clear to him was why Craig and Corfe had been persuaded to conspire against their father and benefactor, respectively.

"Hard on your sister," Lenox offered.

He was keenly aware of the time, but also keenly aware that he mustn't press Lord Vere. "Yes," the heir said. "Hard on her. Listen here—how did you discover I was involved?"

He hadn't. But it had struck him as simply too unlikely that Lord Vere's fever had coincided so exactly with the period of the thefts from the duke's study, and that the painting had ended up in his room. That was the sum of it. Still, he felt a bit of pride. His instincts must be improving.

He looked out through the window, expecting at any minute the carriage bearing Mayne and Lady Violet.

"That doesn't matter now. But I would like to know how the three of you devised this plot. Your grandfather told you about the play, of course. When did Lady Violet finally decide to take action?"

Corfe looked at him. "Two weeks ago. Walters is leaving for South Africa next month, if he cannot have Violet." He shook his head. "In the end we made a choice. It's a bad fare that Craig paid for it with his life."

Lenox nodded, still dreadfully thirsty, but aware that he was about to hear the whole story at last. "Go on," he said in a measured voice.

CHAPTER FORTY-ONE

Lord Vere looked down at the drink he had in his hand, a glass of amber something—perhaps brandy. "Pater was always devilishly awkward on Violet," he said.

Pater: Lenox was returned to his schooldays, when that was what the boys called their fathers, and he realized that in many ways Corfe, never touched by the world, remained a schoolboy still.

"How so?"

"It was a long seven years before I came along, you know. Hell for her, and everyone, that she wasn't a boy. The next in line for the dukedom is a distant cousin, the Earl of Coverdale, so it would have gone out of the family, essentially. Including the secret of the portrait—and you have seen how mad that has driven my father, a sane man. But then I came. I was something of a miracle."

"I see," said Lenox.

The window had fully half of his attention. Let them have been snarled in London traffic, Mayne and Lady Violet!

"It was my sister who loved me the most. My mother is a very responsible woman, her good works, the charities, a lady of great distinction of course, and . . ." He trailed off, looking to the side, and the unsaid opened up a whole vista onto the coldness of the mother's character. "Still, it was Violet who sent me packages when I went away to school at eight. And mended my trousers when I was home on hols. Wiped my tears."

He laughed scornfully at the boy he had been, after he said this, but to Lenox it was clear that the words carried deep feeling. "A very good sister," he said quietly.

"Oh yes, good as gold. Kind to Craig, too. Made him part of the family, you know. Had him play Father Christmas for me, which he claimed to hate, but you know. Pater is a bit of a tough nut, and Craig never had a family of his own. He loved her, too. We both loved her more because we knew nobody would marry her. Finally when it came down to it, we decided to do something for her, he and I. Craig thought of the ruse of my illness and putting the painting under my bed. Not just under my bed—he was very bright, old Craig. Christ. I still can't credit it that he's gone."

"And you had known about Mr. Walters."

"Oh, Walters! Yes. Yes. It was the subject of a great deal of discussion—within these walls. It will kill Father to hear it get out, if it does. He would rather hang in the Tower ten times over."

"That is why I am amazed that your sister decided to defy him."

"She felt she had a last chance at happiness. And she is such a sensible, engaging person—but she is . . . is thirty, you know."

Lenox nodded. His tone implied that she might just as profitably have been ninety. "Of course. Was—"

But at that moment there was a loud sound outside, four horses stopping at the door. Lenox rose and excused himself, saying that he would check to see if it was Sir Richard. But that was not his intention; he knew the house fairly well by this time, and he slipped back to the stables and fetched his horse. Once Lord Vere and his sister spoke, he knew, he would be unwelcome at Dorset House.

It was all clear to him now, regardless. Only two questions remained. One would never be answered—whether she had shot Craig on purpose. The other was whether they would find the lost play.

He rode home, gratefully took a sip from the barrel of water the servants kept just outside the back door, then asked his coachman to water and feed Pepper and return her to the Wilcombe.

He went inside, dusty and tired. Graham and Lancelot were both out, as was Mrs. Huggins, who was, according to the chambermaid Clarissa, who looked terrified at her temporary elevation in station, pricing cloth.

"Cloth? For what?" asked Lenox.

"I don't right know, sir," she said, trembling.

"I'm not mad," said Lenox carefully.

"Mad, sir!" she blushed to the roots of her hair.

She was a microscopically small and delicate person, holding a broom that as she shrank back came to be about twice her height.

He sometimes forgot that the staff must think his line of work very curious. "Angry, I mean!" he clarified quickly. "I am not angry."

"Oh."

"Nor am I mad."

"No, sir," she said, but looked unsure.

"Are you the Irish one?"

Mrs. Huggins suspected everyone of being Irish, and Lenox, in a fit of insubordination not long before, had insisted that she hire an Irish maid. That had been only a few weeks before, and he barely recognized this young person.

"Yes, sir."

"Well, you're doing capitally, from all I hear," he said. This wasn't strictly a lie, since he hadn't heard anything. "Just capitally. Carry on."

"Oh, thank you, sir," she said, with impossible gratitude, and went downstairs as if there were a fire to put out there.

Lenox, for his part, went into his study, where he removed his jacket. He sat down in his chair, looking out through the windows. The shop across Hampden Lane—what had been the cobbler's until that spring—had new lettering going up in its windows.

"Chaffanbrass," he read out loud to himself.

Sounded like a butcher—he hoped not, because of the smell. He was tired, but he began notes on the case, trying to write down all he could remember of his conversation with Corfe. Still, his eyes kept wandering to the window, the empty storefront, and he leaned back farther in his leather chair, and it was warm, and his eyes were so heavy . . .

What rest could do for a soul! When Lenox felt himself stirring half an hour or so later, lying comfortably tilted back in his thickly upholstered desk chair, he let himself linger in that half-state of sleep a little while longer, his eyes closed. He felt the coolness of the high-ceilinged room and the warmth of the day even each other out. He felt the air go in and out of his nostrils.

What a creature one was, after all, it turned out—thirsty, tired, and then to drink, to sleep, how joyful it was to be alive in a body sometimes.

He slowly let his eyes open. A noise had woken him. Something to do with the front door perhaps, but he could tell, through the innumerable small specks of comprehension that every person registers without naming, that it was nothing to do with him. He let himself turn to the street, body quiet, eyes heavy still, though open now. He watched the people pass, experiencing that dispassionate, affectionate, removed sensation of one who has just woken up. He had been to the other world; it was no bad thing to sit here, between ways, for another moment.

Finally he yawned, stretched his arms, shook his head, and stood up. He retrieved his notebook from the floor and went out into the hallway.

The noise had been a telegram, it turned out.

It was from the asylum in Edinburgh, and was quite to the point.

No patient of name Belmont received here STOP Nor Irvington STOP William Wellburn

He felt a chill run through him. Wellburn was the head physician there.

As he stood there, contemplating this telegram, trying to remember Belmont more vividly in his mind, Mrs. Huggins came in.

This was odd, as she would usually have entered by the servants' door. "Good evening, Mrs. Huggins," he said.

"Good evening, Mr. Lenox. Please excuse my intrusion. I had hoped to offer you some forewarning that—"

Behind her burst through Lancelot, who looked, first, thoroughly pleased with himself, indeed was whistling, and, second, a wreck, with two swollen red eyes, a split lip, and a gash across his cheek.

"What happened?" asked Lenox.

"I got in a fight!" said Lancelot excitedly.

"What, with a bear?"

"It was with Lord Decimus Spate, sir," said Mrs. Huggins. "He was riding in the park. Master Lancelot called him a name, I fear."

"*Decimus Spate?*"

"Yes, sir."

"But he's twenty-two! He did this to a child?"

"It was a very bad name," said Mrs. Huggins. "I have spoken to Lancelot about that."

Lancelot placed himself in front of Mrs. Huggins importantly. "Here's how it was. He shoved Wutherington-Fassett out of the way while we were playing skittles in Hyde Park—reckless as you like— and I called him a pompous fool—I thought that sounded good— and he said always to make way for horses—and I said I would, but he was a horse's *ass,* so I wouldn't—and he said well didn't I think I ought to apologize—and I said I did, to horse's asses, for confusing them with him—and that was a pretty good one to get off—and he said who was I—and I said who was *he* and why was he so fat—"

"Oh, Lancelot," said Mrs. Huggins despairingly, lovingly.

Lenox sighed. It was true that Decimus Spate had begun eating twenty-two years before and permitted himself only very brief cessations of the activity since—and was very sensitive about the results.

"Then he shoved Wutherington-Fassett again—and I called him the name—and he got down from the horse—and I caught him a lovely poke in the ribs before he knew what was on—and he set upon me—but altogether, Mrs. Huggins, wouldn't you say I got the best of it? How would you rank it?"

"For shame, Master Lancelot," she said.

"I thought *you* were pricing cloth," Lenox said.

The housekeeper's brow darkened. "Is that what the Irish girl said?"

Lenox threw up his hands. "I am going to my club to dine. Put ice and raw beef on this child's face—and you'd better wire Eustacia and say he's been in a fight, but he's all right. Lancelot, you'll write a letter of apology—"

"Never!"

"—tomorrow. Good-bye."

He left in a reasonable semblance of ire. But Lenox had always hated the Spates—Decimus himself was a great lump of unthinking brutish aristocratic matter—and before he went, he whispered to Mrs. Huggins to give him something soft to eat, like Italian pudding.

He wondered, as he walked briskly down Hampden Lane, if one day he would be a father after all, and the thought filled him with such terror that he almost forgot the telegram he had in his pocket.

CHAPTER FORTY-TWO

He dined at one of his clubs, the Beargarden. Arriving there, he found that his reputation went on pinging about like a bullet in a steel drum; now he was known to be Dorset's only confidant, privy to great secrets, engaged upon important missions—every variety of thing—and found himself once more in prestige.

He sat to eat a beefsteak, string beans, mashed potatoes, and gravy with a few of the people he actually liked, younger friends, sharing a jug of house claret with them.

At about nine o'clock, when he was in the midst of a hand of cards, the porter came in and said that a Mr. Graham attended upon his leisure in the servants' waiting room. Lenox went down to the basement straightaway.

It was a convivial and comfortably furnished chamber, the servants' waiting room, where the valets bided their time, many of them playing penny hands of whist and slanging their masters to each other, usually in varying states of progressive drunkenness. You saw every type of the genus here. There was a dull, burly, fish-eyed, suspicious boulder of a man, who served the very dull, burly, fish-eyed, and suspicious Lord Varling, a fellow not past thirty and exceedingly rich, who nonetheless lived his life in a state of continual ill temper. A lank, dusty chap named Pole—not below sixty-five in years—waited upon the sprightly Lucan Wells, one of the dandiest chaps in London. Half a dozen or so others were sprinkled about, none of them sober; in their midst sat Graham, legs crossed, arm along the back of the sofa, but alert. He rose when Lenox entered.

"Hello," said Lenox.

"Good evening, sir," said Graham.

"How did you find me?"

"Oh, I guessed, sir."

He said this casually, but Graham had an almost occult ability to predict where in London Lenox would be at a given moment. "You ought to guess the horses for Lancelot."

"Or Mr. Templeton, sir."

"Or Mr. Templeton! I wonder what they do with curates gone bad. Anyhow, come into the smoking room."

This was just up the front hall, a room to which members could invite their valets, or outside guests they wished to keep at arm's length. The upstairs was more restricted. As they crossed the lobby, Lenox nodded at the younger of the two doormen, who was about ninety-five.

The smoking room—a crimson-red chamber, encircled with sofas, hung with oils of various dead gentlemen—was empty. "There are two things, sir," said Graham. "First, this."

He handed Lenox a fresh copy of the *Times*, probably not more than twenty minutes from press. Lenox read its bold-faced lead article with care. Then he sighed. "It was to be expected," he said.

The *Times* reported more fully than earlier papers had that the Duke of Dorset had been cleared by an expedited coroner's report of any wrongdoing in the death of Mr. A. A. Craig, late of the Scots Guards. He would not stand trial.

No mention appeared of Lord Vere, Lady Violet, the duchess, a missing painting, or, of course, Shakespeare.

Lenox contemplated the article, which was reliable confirmation of what had seemed all but inevitable, and then told Graham about his long morning, culminating in his meeting with Corfe. The valet listened carefully, then said, "What will the young lady do, sir?"

"I cannot say."

"Are you not disturbed by her account of the night?"

Lenox looked at Graham wryly. "I am, as it happens. But what is the second piece of news?"

"Ah, yes, sir." He handed over two pages of handwritten notes. "In reference to Captain Tankin Irvington."

"Oh, thank you! That is useful. I have not told you why I asked."

Lenox explained this situation briefly to Graham, too, and the telegram he had received from Edinburgh earlier. Then he turned to the investigation Graham had done for him.

Irvington had been the only child of a prosperous seagoing family. He had cousins but no close relations. He had also had a wife: Mrs. Eliza Irvington. No issue. She had removed herself upon news of his death from the naval city of Portsmouth to Hampstead, in London.

"Was there an address for her?"

"Not in the naval archives, sir. Only a mention of Hampstead."

"No brothers, no sisters, no children, no living parents or grandparents, a cousin who is a lieutenant on a ship that is probably in the China Sea as we speak," muttered Lenox, more to himself than Graham. "His body was never even found."

The simplest identity to wipe off the face of the earth. Was it in fact Belmont's true one?

He and Graham walked home through the breezy summer evening, discussing both cases. What remained of Dorset's, of course, was the play. Lenox and Graham agreed that they would research the churchyards that evening—all those matching the geographical restrictions of the poem and dating back to at least the year 1600.

He would call on Dorset House the next morning, he thought, though he had no idea at all of the reception he would receive there.

At home they found Lancelot and Lady Jane playing checkers in the drawing room. "Look at this poor fellow!" said Lady Jane, rising and giving Lenox her hand to clasp. "Set upon by ruffians—and now losing very humiliatingly at checkers."

"I am not!" said Lancelot hotly.

"I count that nine games in a row this time."

"Have you ever won yet?" asked Lenox.

It was the wrong question—and even a hardened criminal of a twelve-year-old was still, after all, twelve. His eyes grew large and his face started to tremble.

"Oh, Charles! Shame!" said Lady Jane. "You're doing wonderfully, Lancelot. You almost won two games ago. And after the day you've had. Do you need more sherbet?"

"Yes, please," he said pitifully.

She went to the door to poke her head out for Mrs. Huggins. As soon as she was out of sight, Lancelot instantly reshaped his face into a sort of diabolical grin, and Lenox realized that he had been fooled once more.

He called to Jane to cancel the sherbet. "He's pretending!" Lenox said.

"Do be quiet, Charles," she said distractedly.

"Do," said Lancelot in a quiet voice, nodding solemnly at him.

"I'll get you for this," said Lenox.

"Get him for what?" said Lady Jane, who had come back into the room. "Leave him alone. Decimus Spate, that barrel of lard—I have half a mind to go and speak to his mother."

"You are only four years older than he!" said Lenox.

"I am a married and respectable person," said Lady Jane.

"That's true," said Lancelot.

"Shut up," said Lenox.

"Charles! You'll teach him the most ill-mannered kinds of—what would Eustacia say?"

Lady Jane waited until Lancelot's sherbet arrived. Then she asked

Lenox if they might have a word in his study—she would return to finish their game, she promised Lancelot. She and Lenox crossed the hall. He had a few telegrams and numerous letters on his desk, but none of them were of immediate interest; none related to either Dorset or Belmont.

"Is everything all right?" Lenox asked her.

"I have led you up a garden path," said Jane, full of regret. "It is not Violet's fault at all, nor yours, obviously, but mine. She is engaged to be married. It's a secret."

"Oh! I see."

"Are you terribly disappointed?"

Lenox let a chivalrous amount of time pass. "Perhaps a bit. But it will be a quick recovery. We were not so very close."

She grabbed his hand, so firmly that it almost hurt. "I will find you someone."

He laughed. "Unfortunately I have very little doubt of it, knowing you."

"I promise."

"Is your aunt Moggs through her twelve and one?"

This was a recently widowed relative of Jane's, aged about seventy, and among the most unpleasant people alive; her primary pastime was sitting at the window of her cottage in Hampshire with a shotgun and firing it into the air when anyone came close, up to and including her ill-starred postman. (Lenox's question was whether her husband—whose grave must have felt a merciful place—had been dead for the twelve months and one day that a widow was required to dress in full mourning.)

"Oh, be quiet," said Lady Jane. "No, I have in mind—don't dismiss it out of hand—Miss Auburn, who will come out in the fall. She is young, but she is so lovely, Charles! And so accomplished, mature beyond her years."

It was no use at all to tell her that it was no use. In fact he had not even quite formed that knowledge into something he actively knew. It merely lived somewhere within him, forgotten. So he consented to hear more about Miss Auburn and her accomplishments, and eventually they recrossed the hall in full and fluid conversation.

CHAPTER FORTY-THREE

The Duke of Dorset was ensconced once more in his private private study. What could be more appropriate? The front hall of Dorset House was as busy as a village square on Saturday night, everyone either leaving a card (the Prime Minister's stood at the top of the gleaming sterling rack) or, in the case of a few select friends, the Earl of Cadogan for instance, accepting an escort into the library, where they could smoke and read the ironed papers while they waited to see His Grace.

Ward greeted Lenox. "He asked that you be seen straight up."

"This is quite a palaver," Lenox said, as they walked up the stairs, leaving numerous people behind them.

"Yes." He leaned confidentially close. "He has gotten me a place as the Prime Minister's second secretary. As thanks for sticking with him, he said."

"That's a coup for you, Theo," said Lenox. "Congratulations."

He had leapfrogged several intervals on his way to a seat in Parliament. Lenox was glad on his behalf. "Kind of him, yes," said Ward with satisfaction.

The duke's door was open, and Lenox caught a glimpse of him

before he knew they were there. He was bent over his desk, reading intently.

Dorset looked up at their entry. "Ah, hello. Thank you, Ward. Please give us a few minutes."

"Of course, Your Grace."

Lenox sat down after the duke had gestured at a chair. There were now once again eight paintings on the wall behind him. Lenox had sent the missing one back that morning.

"All resolved, then, Your Grace," he said to Dorset. "Mostly."

The duke's handsome, middle-aged face again bore a distinctive superiority. Lenox bridled against it; he disliked the whole thing.

The duke did not respond for quite a while. When he did, it was to say, "You are now aware of several very closely guarded facts about my family."

"You ought to have hired a worse detective if you didn't wish it so."

"You are the only one I know of."

"I could find you a worse."

"Ha."

The duke was in no mood for banter. He fell silent, but his imperious stare had lost some of its power over Lenox. "May I ask where Lady Violet is?" Lenox asked.

"You took advantage of my son's open nature yesterday, Mr. Lenox."

"I thought for all our sakes that it was best I learn the full details of the matter, Your Grace. I still do not feel sure that I have them."

"What do you mean?"

Lenox shrugged. "There is a great deal of talk in all these accounts, Your Grace, of a scuffle with Mr. Craig. There is also the presence of a pistol, something I find more surprising still. Need I elaborate?"

"Perhaps you had better."

He didn't want to. So he asked again where Lady Violet was, and Mr. Walters. "I wonder if perhaps they are bound for some foreign shore together."

"In asking that question you go beyond your brief, Mr. Lenox."

"Well?" said Lenox.

He was in a hard-hearted mood, and he met the duke's stare with cold eyes.

What he suspected was this: that Craig had not been in league with Corfe and Violet at all, but that his loyalty had remained to the duke all along; and that he had died for it. How? Only those who had been in the room knew. Perhaps there had been a set-to. Perhaps Violet had shot him in cold blood when he tried to stop her from taking the painting, and she and Corfe had agreed to claim that Craig was part of it all along. Perhaps the truth lay somewhere between these possibilities.

But Lenox knew in his bones that something closer to murder than manslaughter had occurred, and he also knew that nobody would be punished for it.

"My daughter is traveling to the Continent."

"To be married?" Lenox asked.

"Stop pushing me."

"Or what?" said Lenox angrily. "Where is your loyalty to Craig, I ask you? If someone shot my valet—my friend—Graham, I would damn well push to find out who had done it."

"You are not a father."

"Nor am I a liar."

The duke stood up. "What did you say?"

"You heard me."

Lenox remained seated, and they stayed in that position, staring at each other. The duke had, on his side, the immutable social laws of their society. On his, Lenox had the truth—the truth about Lady Violet, about Shakespeare. Even about Corfe, who was dim but sharp enough to lie for his sister about Craig's involvement.

The duke at last tore his gaze away from Lenox and said, "Give yourself thirty years. Have a daughter whom no amount of money can persuade someone of her birth to marry—who is a daily shame to her mother—to both their discredit—watch her fall in love with a gamekeeper, a young woman with Plantagenet blood in her veins, with a gamekeeper!—and learn, after all of that, that she is the person who has been attempting to steal your most precious possession. Then see how you react, Charles Lenox."

"A fine speech. Craig is dead."

"Craig would have died for me."

"Presumably he would have preferred the chance to volunteer for that task rather than be volunteered for it," said Lenox. "Would you have died for him, I wonder?"

"Stay here for a moment," said the duke, and in three long strides he had left the room.

He was absent for some time. It gave Lenox a chance to examine the river through the window—it was a bright day, lovely and soft—and to contemplate the string of stupidities that had led to all this.

First was Lady Violet's attempt on the painting. (And of course, it occurred to him, if Craig had really been in league with her, she could have had all the time she wanted in the duke's study without stealing it. That ought to have told him from the start that Craig wasn't involved.)

Then came Dorset's idiotic attempt at kidnapping. The tragic attempt to steal the second painting—whoever had been in the room. Corfe's defense and alliance with his sister, though that was hardly surprising, if, as it seemed, reading between the lines, neither of them had had a very kind mother.

And finally, the system clicking irreproachably into motion to exculpate the duke and Lady Violet.

It galled Lenox that Lady Violet should get what she wanted—money, marriage—even though the week before he would have called the duke cruel in the extreme for denying it to her.

At last Dorset returned. He was clutching a white piece of paper. "Here," he said.

"What is it?"

"The codicils to my will, last updated in January."

"And?"

"You will see on the second page that upon either my death or his retirement, Craig was to receive ten thousand pounds and an extension of the lands already given him, and that his nephews' schooling was to be paid for, age eight through university. That, naturally, will still be the case. They will be set on the path toward becoming gentlemen."

"I see."

"This is how I behave to one who has earned my loyalty."

High talk, high talk. Lenox leafed through the pages, and what the duke said was true. "Generous," Lenox replied, indifferently.

"I am as unhappy as you imagine me to be relieved, Mr. Lenox. Perhaps that will give you some peace. Craig was my brother and my confidant. I hoped that we would both live out our old age in Dorset Castle. My daughter has robbed me of half of all I ever loved. Including herself."

In bitter retaliation against his own autocratic ways, however, Lenox thought. Wasn't this what Shakespeare's readers called by the name of tragedy? A man destroyed by his own qualities.

He looked at the painting of the writer—the sly, amused, sorrowful eyes.

"I am sorry about that," said Lenox, handing the pages back.

He wished he had never taken the case. "Thank you, I suppose," said Dorset.

"And your daughter? Where has she gone?"

"Corfe will accompany her to Biarritz. From there she will make her way in the world as she sees fit. I have settled a sum on her, if you want to know the crude details of the matter."

"I always do, I am afraid."

Dorset looked at him with a flash of revulsion, and Lenox realized how different their codes were—to the duke, Lenox had sullied himself; to Lenox, the duke.

"She is independent now. She is welcome to return here as a single woman. As Mrs. Walters I will not receive her."

"The blacksmith in Markethouse disapproved of his daughter's marriage, when I was a child. On his deathbed she was the only person he wanted to see. But she could not be fetched back in time before he died."

"A fascinating anecdote," the duke said.

Lenox shrugged. "Your pleasure, Your Grace."

His Grace sat down, looking Lenox in the eye yet again, wearily, warily. "I suppose the question now is whether we shall try to find this play."

"I see no reason why we should not," said Lenox, though he felt equally tired. "When would it be convenient for you to go to Kent?"

"I can leave tomorrow morning."

Lenox stood up. "So be it. Good day, Duke."

CHAPTER FORTY-FOUR

When he left Dorset House, Lenox saw a young man in a summer suit lounging by the front steps, a foot propped back against the railing. One of Corfe's friends, from the look of him. Lenox touched his hat and went on his way, mind back on Captain Irvington, lost at sea.

"Sir," the fellow said when Lenox had gone about ten paces.

He turned back and, after a moment of what felt like an intense dislodgement from his own senses, realized that it was *Bonden*, of all people. "Bonden!" he said.

"How do you do?"

"Fairly well. You—you surprised me."

Bonden fell into step with him. They continued in the direction Lenox had been going. "I read this morning that your duke had returned. I wanted to see if his painting had followed him."

"It did."

"Yes, I saw. The matter is concluded, then?"

"It is."

"To your satisfaction?"

That was a more difficult question. "I don't know that I would say that."

"Mm."

Bonden raised his cigar again, and Lenox thought that perhaps it was this prop that allowed his astonishing concealment (for the younger man had looked the older straight in the face when he touched his hat, and Lenox would have sworn him to be no more than thirty or so). That, and the suit of clothes, and a fresh-shaven cheek.

"You spent all morning here, then?" Lenox asked.

"I often find that it pays to be careless with my time. In this instance I was curious." They turned into the park (Lenox, at least, was walking automatically toward his home), and Bonden went on. "I observe that it was the butler who died. Not the duke, or one of the duke's children."

"Yes."

"They used to sing a shanty at sea. There was always some tuneful soul who passed the third watch in song, quiet, you know, since it was after midnight, but keeping those on watch awake." Bonden tossed his cigar into the cobblestones of the street, then sang, in a quiet and surprisingly mellifluous voice, "*Same the world over, ain't it a shame—the rich what gets the pleasure, the poor what gets the blame . . .* That's the part I remember, anyway."

So, then, Bonden had sniffed out what Lenox had taken until today to piece together: that Craig's death had not been accidental.

"True too often, I fear," said Lenox.

"I wonder if you would give me an hour of your time? Not more."

They were on one of the pathways in Green Park, and before answering Lenox nodded to a gentleman he knew, Sir Thomas Clapton, and wished him a good day. Clapton was walking toward Parliament, where he was greatly concerned with foreign affairs, cane under his arm. The year before he had written a long report on currency reform that nobody had read, and with whose ideas nearly every reasonable person in England vehemently disagreed; naturally he was knighted in the next honors list, and now considered in all the papers as a wide-ranging authority.

Passing Clapton suddenly made Lenox rue every one of his decisions. Each single one. Clapton was only six years his elder! He was not very remarkably smart, not even amiable. He would be in the next cabinet.

Meanwhile, Lenox was bound for God knew where with an old sailor who wouldn't tell him anything straight, and the career he had chosen as a detective had already cut off, permanently, his path to Parliament, the other vague dream of his youth.

Without showing any of this feeling—he hoped—he turned to Bonden. "Lead the way," he said.

They boarded an omnibus bound east. They passed the trip in silence, until at last Bonden signaled, when they were in Eastcheap Street, that they should disembark.

It was an insalubrious, swarming stretch of London, families stacked too close together, pawnbrokers next to rag shops, prostitutes out in plain sight even at this early hour. Unaccompanied children ran to and fro.

They turned off Eastcheap and into Pudding Lane. This was the heart of where the Great Fire had raged in 1666, and all the buildings were of the last hundred years or so, some of them tilting oddly, jury-rigged, no doubt unsafe.

The fire had incinerated thirteen thousand buildings, Lenox knew—all slums, skirting up only toward the edge of Mayfair.

"Do you know how many people died in the fire, out of curiosity?" Bonden asked.

"I do, as a matter of fact," said Lenox. "Six."

"Ha! Yes, that's what they say up Parliament way. More like six hundred, they'll tell you here. The bodies weren't found, that's all."

Lenox was about to answer that he doubted that when they stopped. Bonden acted out his usual small performance—leaning against a building, producing his tobacco, acting busy—and Lenox followed his example.

They were opposite a small yard, mostly in disuse. In it was a lone woman. She looked up at them, without recognition, for a beat— large, faded eyes, strong cheekbones, hair in a bonnet. Then she turned back to the yard, where a small row of lettuce plants grew; she was plucking paltry leaves from them, brushing away dirt. She put what she had retrieved in her apron and then went with a small pail of water to some kind of bare-limbed tree that Lenox could have told her from this distance would never flower or fruit again.

"That is Mrs. Lila Wallace, relict of the late Alec Wallace, a cart-horse driver. Two children. He was murdered seven months ago."

"Why?"

"Nobody knows."

"Money? A bar fight?"

"Not money, not a bar fight. He was shot in his own rooms."

Lenox crossed his arms. "Does she need money?"

"No, she manages."

"What point are you making, then, Mr. Bonden?"

"None at all, Mr. Lenox. I had it in mind to offer you a trade."

"What sort of trade?"

"I will teach you what I know if you help me find out who killed her husband. It is a matter of some interest to me. She is my cousin."

"She didn't recognize you."

"Nor did you."

Lenox looked across the way again. "Yes, true. But why don't you solve the case?"

"I don't have your gift."

"You!"

Bonden nodded, pipe now in his mouth, in place of the West End cigar. "I can find things; I can watch. But you can ask questions— and your name, your face, your manner, gain you admission where I could well be denied."

"This is a genuine offer?"

"It is. You know how to be active. I can teach you how to be . . . perhaps not passive, but certainly quiet. There is a great deal of power in quietness, Mr. Lenox. And not only quietness of voice but of body, of posture."

"I see."

"And together perhaps we may give my cousin some peace."

At that moment something overcame Lenox. The lesson was there, whether Bonden intended it or otherwise: that crime happened indiscriminately, or if with discrimination, then with discrimination against the poor. He must redouble his efforts. No more dukes for a while; the Yard could help him or it could not.

But there was the potential all around him to do something useful in the world, just what his father had always emphasized, and Bonden had articulated something that Lenox had known but never conceded to himself, or even considered especially.

It was that he had a gift for this. What was he thinking? He wouldn't have traded places with Sir Thomas Clapton.

"You have a bargain," Lenox said. "Thank you for taking me on as a pupil. I am full of effort, even if I am a slow fist sometimes."

Bonden nodded. "Good."

"You will have to wait two days to begin, however. Perhaps three." He didn't like to say that Lady Jane's garden party was to take place in two mornings. "I must go to Kent to see to a few remaining pieces of business."

They shook hands—and it was left to Lenox, as Bonden strode off, to determine how to return, handkerchief across his nose, to his own part of London. In any event he had his next case. He was already wondering if he and Graham had clipped anything from the newspapers about Mr. Alec Wallace, or whether the Yard had made any headway on the matter at all.

CHAPTER FORTY-FIVE

The duke's carriage was so large that it took up a lane and a half of most roads, a marked inconvenience when passing anyone other than perhaps an exceptionally thin adolescent on a donkey. Lenox would have preferred the train but had to admit, by the third church they visited, that it was a comfortable conveyance, four seats wide, well ventilated, with a compartment beneath their feet where a large slab of ice cooled the carriage, leaving a trail of water droplets in the dust behind them, fairy-tale fashion.

It was a company motley enough for Shakespeare's own enjoyment. There were the duke, Lenox, and Graham, of course, but with them as well were two learned gentlemen. One was Sir Charles Locke Eastlake, the only person other than Queen Victoria whom Dorset had told about the portrait. He was a middle-aged fellow with lank, curled brown hair who had, for reasons known only to himself and his valet, worn a heavy flannel suit and was now perspiring at rates of almost indescribable speed and volume. Lenox tired of him after, oh, five minutes of travel—he was pomposity itself—but fortunately the near closeness of apoplexy quieted him somewhat.

That left old Duncan Jones, quiet and benevolent, whom Lenox had coaxed from the British Library with some of the story.

Dorset hadn't been happy, but Lenox had asked for and received the favor several days before, the permission to bring a friend. A duke could not go back on his word.

They had been to three of the five churches that Lenox and Graham's research had turned up: St. Wistan's, St. Aethelstan's, and St. Bartholomew's. The first churchyard had been tiny and offered no probable candidate; the second was large, but the rector informed them that nobody had been interred there until the 1790s. The last was middle-sized, and they had gone tombstone by tombstone and found nothing except a Mary Swindle, buried in 1844 beside her husband, Samuel Swindle.

This left two churches, St. John's-upon-Wold and St. James's.

They were headed now for the latter, having stopped at an inn to order food. Eastlake had drunk so much water that he looked half drunk when they were again seated in the carriage, his eyes closed. The duke, meanwhile, was equanimity itself. One would never have guessed that the week before he'd been locked in the Tower of London.

The general conversation had been only polite until now. Lenox and Jones had been seated next to each other, and talked a great deal privately.

As they had reseated themselves, though, they had ended up in opposite corners, and Lenox said, hoping to make the last few hours of this task more pleasant, "Do you believe that Shakespeare was a Catholic, Mr. Jones?"

The old Yorkshireman considered the idea carefully. He was a pleasure to have brought, Lenox was glad to observe, slow but certain in his motions, deferential to the duke but his own man, polite to Graham.

"It's a vexed question, I fear," he replied. "The—"

"OPINION IS DIVIDED."

Eastlake managed to eject this judgment before sinking back into the cushions. He wasn't a large or overweight gentleman—it was surprising that he should be quite so red—but the effort of a day out of the dim corridors of his museum seemed too much for him.

"Sir Charles is quite correct," Jones said politely. He waited a beat to see if the other man would go on, but it wasn't even clear that he was conscious. The duke looked at him with disgust. "My personal belief is that Shakespeare was irreligious. Coleridge says it well: 'Shakespeare is of no age—nor of any religion, or party, or profession. The body and substance of his works came out of the unfathomable depths of his own oceanic mind.' There is certainly a great quarrel with God running through the plays.

"On the other hand, it seems definite that John Shakespeare was Catholic, and I think it would have appealed to William in more than one way to remain a Catholic."

"How's that?" asked the duke.

"Well, Your Grace, he was mischievous, for a start. He was not Marlowe, who lost his life in a cheap tavern over spying—"

"CHRISTOPHER MARLOWE," said Eastlake forcefully.

"I am quite aware of him," said Dorset with irritation.

"He was Shakespeare's only real peer," said Jones, "but died at twenty-nine. Shakespeare's rebellions were much subtler, as befits a country boy. Marlowe had been at Cambridge."

"What was the other reason?" asked Lenox.

"Ah! Well, his father, you know, the great life force that never left Shakespeare. Evidently a man of tremendous charm. Long after his father's disgrace, William paid an immense amount of money to buy back all his father's lands in Stratford and more. And he finally obtained a coat of arms for the family, something his father had fought in vain to accomplish for many years. It meant that they were a family of gentlemen at last."

"You think he would have been as loyal to his father's religion as to his aspirations, then," Lenox said.

"ROT," said Sir Charles.

They all looked at him expectantly.

"How so, Eastlake? Speak up," said the duke, his scorn undisguised.

"HATED HIS FATHER."

Jones tilted his head. "There may be something in what Sir Charles says. I have always thought it curious—and this is a personal theory, not an academic one," he added, though his clear blue eyes, buried in crow's-feet, sparkled, "—that Falstaff might have been based on John Shakespeare."

Probably no character was closer to the hearts of Englishmen than Falstaff, the witty, obese, drunken, zestful, devious, cowardly best friend of Prince Hal.

Indeed, it was Graham, now, who said, "Falstaff!"

The democratizing effect of their hours in the carriage could be seen—nobody thought twice about Lenox's valet interjecting. "Yes," said Jones. "To begin with there is his name—Sir John Falstaff. John! Can we consider that an accident? After William's son, Hamnet, died, he wrote his saddest play, *Hamlet*. He obviously cared about names.

"Then there is that 'Sir,' a title no character in all of Shakespeare deserves less. If John Shakespeare was a chaser after titles and coats of arms, it might be a mockery of his father, that. But what I like best of all is the name—*shake, speare; false, staff*." He looked around hopefully. "Do you see the echo?"

"Yes," said Dorset, unexpectedly.

"Shakespeare was highly conscious of his own name. Sometimes he was called Shakeshaft. Falstaff! It seems more than a coincidence to me. And his father was a drunk, made great sums of money and lost them, beloved, loathed—a man not unlike Falstaff. Is there a more conflicted portrait in Shakespeare?"

They all glanced simultaneously at Eastlake, but he had gone as pale as Banquo's ghost and, as if sensing their gaze, finally loosened his tie. His relief was palpable. "Ah," he said. "Good God. That is better."

"It is an interesting argument," said the duke.

Jones nodded his thanks. "I have considered sometimes that Falstaff makes more direct Catholic references than almost any other character—the catechism, the *ecce signum* . . ."

He would have gone on, but at that moment the carriage drew to a stop.

And Lenox knew before he had set a second foot on the ground that this was it.

St. James's was a tiny crumbling church with a peaceful grassy churchyard next to it, shaded by an enormous flowering oak. The sun struck the tree in different places, so that it was dark green in some, golden in others. There was a deep feeling of serenity here, of eternity. Perhaps of God.

"Sir," said Graham, and pointed.

One of the few dozen tombstones in the churchyard had recently had its dirt turned over. Dorset glanced at the grave and then broke into a hard walk. Lenox followed him. Behind them, Graham—good soul—stayed with Jones, who trailed more slowly, using a silver-capped cane.

The duke fell to his knees at the tombstone. "Mary!" he cried, and indeed the name was there on the tombstone, faint but legible: Mary Pike.

He dug with his hands, though the driver had gotten down from the box with the trowel, spade, and shovel the duke had specifically ordered brought.

After only a short time the duke brought up a dark mahogany box, battered and scored. He brushed the dirt off the top.

But why was it still here, Lenox wondered, if it had been dug up so recently?

The answer came: The duke pulled from the box, which was lined with some sort of crude tin, a single aged sheet of paper and a letter on fresh blue paper.

He studied the sheet, as Lenox looked over his shoulder.

Campion
As it hath on two occasions beene publicly acted, by
the Right Honourable the Lord Chamberlain,
his servants
Written by Wm. Shakespere
Printed by Iames Roberts, 1599

"The authentic title page of a quarto, or the best imitation I have ever seen," Jones said softly. Both Dorset and Lenox looked back. The old scholar looked like a man gazing into the face of an angel. "Campion. A Catholic martyr. Roberts would have happily printed off five or ten copies for a playwright who had given him so much worse. He was a broad-minded man. They performed it, I would guess, for highly select audiences."

"But where is the *play?*" asked Dorset.

Lenox pointed at the letter in his hand and said, cursing himself for having told her she got the clue wrong, "Your daughter has it."

The duke looked confused; then realization dawned on him. He opened the letter.

> *9 June 1853*
>
> *Father,*
> *Here is the title sheet. The remainder of the play will be yours when you receive, with her husband, at a ball of the usual sort at Dorset House,*
>
> *your loving daughter,*
> *Mrs. Isaac Walters*

So the play was with Lady Violet.

All of them reacted differently. The duke looked stunned, there on his knees, unmoving. Lenox himself felt a kind of stupor. She had pieced together the clues; he had been beaten.

He gazed at the ground. Shakespeare's own hands must have turned over this earth once. Only after a moment, because of that stupor, did he appreciate the final trick of the thing, whether it was intentional or not: *pike*, Mary Pike's last name, was another word for staff; or spear.

CHAPTER FORTY-SIX

After they had all returned to the carriage—it was Graham, good fellow, who thought to smooth the earth above Mary Pike's mortal remains back into tidy order—the duke asked if they would do him the favor of a few minutes' silence.

The few minutes extended past an hour. Sir Charles Eastlake fell into a peaceful sleep, his face a less alarming color now that he had removed his tie and jacket. Jones watched the golden evening light, as old men will; Lenox read on in *Uncle Tom's Cabin*.

Occasionally he looked up and thought about *Campion*. A hundred years hence, would the play be performed on the great stages of the world, between runs of *Macbeth* and *A Midsummer Night's Dream*? It was this that they were all no doubt wondering: the immortal preciousness of what Lady Violet Walters, as she must now be called, had carried away so fecklessly, tearing a title sheet from it as if it were a common newspaper. Sublime arrogance.

Just after the carriage had stopped to let Jones off in Bloomsbury (Dorset had the grace to take each of them directly home) and the driver had opened the door, he said, "Lenox has not confided your circumstances in me, Your Grace. But I hope we may see the play. Fifteen ninety-nine! He never had a year when his genius reached a higher pitch—and if it was only performed twice, this may be the only copy, fair or foul, we have any chance of seeing."

The duke only nodded. "Thank you for your knowledge and your civility today, Mr. Jones. You have been an admirable addition to the party."

The scholar touched his hat. "Your Grace."

Now only Lenox, Graham, and the duke remained. (They had dropped Sir Charles off first; one could only imagine that it would take him weeks to recover from his bid at fashion.) Lenox was about to speak when the duke asked him abruptly if he was free to dine at White's on Monday, three days hence. Lenox said he was. The duke then tapped the carriage door with his cane.

"Take these gentlemen home," he said to the driver. "I shall walk."

They watched him go in the gloaming, spine stiff, hands clasped around the cane behind his back, his top hat adding a foot to his imposing height, his swallowtail jacket lending a formality to his passage through the throngs. Nobody glanced at him: the third man in all the land, probably; and now a witness to his own death, father-in-law of a gamekeeper, father of a murderer and her accomplice, husband to a wife indifferent on all accounts, and accidental traitor to his family's great secret pride and duty.

It was possible to have sympathy even for a duke.

"Rum day," said Lenox as the carriage stirred into motion.

"Among the rummest, sir," said Graham.

Lenox laughed. "Three years ago I thought a case such as this one would reach its conclusion and every last string would be tied off. As if I were delivering a fruitcake in brown paper on Christmas. But what do we have now? A lost play still lost, a death unpunished, a father and son who have lied to each other, a father and daughter who may never speak again. It is thoroughly unsatisfying."

"People have remarked that life is unsatisfying, sir," said Graham.

Lenox smiled. He knew his immense good fortune, and felt a guilt shadowing it—perceived it even in comments like this, which he knew were not personal. "Indeed," he said. "Indeed."

When they pulled up at Lenox's house in Hampden Lane, he saw that an arrangement of flowers was visible along every sill of his house. They hadn't been there that morning. He pointed them out to Graham.

"Peculiar, sir," said the valet.

"You see what it means?"

"No, sir."

"My mother is here. The only person whose opinion Mrs. Huggins truly cares for in my family."

Graham raised his eyebrows. "Do you think so?"

"I'll bet you Mr. Templeton's tenner."

"I shall have to respectfully decline the offer, sir. I see that the lights are on in the lower drawing room—and I smell gingerbread, Mrs. Huggins's specialty. I think you must be right."

And he was. Seated comfortably in his study were Lady Emma Lenox, along with Edmund. They both rose when Charles came in.

"Hello, Mother," he said. It was so ingrained in him not to ask a direct question of a woman that he said, first, "I hope you are doing well," before adding, more directly, "How are you? What brings you here? Am I being shipped to the colonies?"

"Where have you been all day?" his mother asked.

"Kent."

"Kent! Apples, hops, cherries, and women? For shame, Charles. And I hear you have murdered a duke, or something of the sort."

"Mother," said Edmund chidingly.

She gave Charles the kind of hug only a mother can give, in which part of her love passes into a person, truly and physically, a press of the body holding in its few seconds a history of tenderness that dates to the time when the two of you were one.

Lenox hugged her back, suddenly exhausted and feeling very, very young, where just twenty minutes before, staring at Dorset's back, he had felt old and wise.

"If you don't mind giving me a minute, I will wash and change. It has been a long day."

"Of course," said his mother.

In the hallway he met Mrs. Huggins. *"Your mother is here,"* the housekeeper hissed, forgetting all formalities.

"Yes, I know. You just saw me leave the room in which she's sitting."

"What are we supposed to *do?*"

"Do?"

"About it, sir?"

Lenox looked at her with genuine bafflement. Of all the people to pick in his family, Lancelot and his mother. After them came the cats, and then Charles a very distant sixth, probably. "I'm not sure I see it as quite the emergency you do, Mrs. Huggins. Has she tried to steal something? What's wrong?"

She looked at him with a face full of despair and betrayal and stormed away, off toward some task only she understood.

Edmund caught up with Charles in the hallway as Mrs. Huggins was going. "A quick word?" he said.

"Yes, is everything all right?"

"Of course it is. But what on earth are you doing with Thaddeus Bonden? Thomas Clapton almost fell to the ground when he saw you, Charles. You must be more careful."

Lenox was bewildered. "What?"

"Have you involved yourself in politics?"

"Politics! No. He was helping me with Dorset. Politics?"

"Oh." Edmund looked relieved. "That's all right, then."

"What does Bonden have to do with politics?"

Edmund shook his head. "I cannot say much. Only that he is our side's greatest spy against the French. If we fight a war with them again and win it, he will be the cause."

"*Bonden?* At the Dovecote?"

"Yes. Why? How did you hear of him?"

"About, I suppose. He is an expert in finding things."

"Oh, that. Right. He refuses a government salary above his naval pension."

"Good Lord."

"I'm going back to Mother. Be discreet if you wander around with him again, and don't mention what I've told you. Clapton will be comforted."

"I am so pleased to be able to comfort him," said Charles, but Edmund had never done very well with catching sarcasm, and only nodded.

Lenox went upstairs and washed. Looking into the mirror, he saw that his face was tired, sun-beaten. He realized that he had needed his mother. How did she always know?

Since his father had died, Charles and Lady Emma—who had always been closer than she and Edmund—had stuck close, but she had also transferred a great deal of her attention to her elder son. He was the baronet, and though Lenox House was hers, its ways, its history, its custodianship, its people would all slowly have to become his. It was perhaps in this that she had found consolation from her grief at being widowed—she had observed firsthand her husband discharging his duties for forty years, and nobody could be better positioned to help pass those duties between generations.

But the oceans could dry, the sky fall into darkness, Charles knew, and she would find him, one way or another.

He went downstairs, where he was immediately asked if he was going to marry Miss Auburn; he coughed into his brandy with alarm, and when he had recovered said no, not just at that moment, it had been a long day; his mother told him he mustn't be facetious; he told her not to gossip so much with Lady Jane—and all in all, to both parties, the visit had thus commenced satisfactorily.

CHAPTER FORTY-SEVEN

The two brothers and their mother stayed up late that night, talking over local matters from their hometown of Markethouse. Every name that came up was as familiar as their own; when Edmund and Charles heard that Mrs. Carter was marrying yet again they rolled their eyes at the same instant.

At long length, when the last bits of cheese, fruit, and biscuit on the tray had been eaten, when the teapot was empty and all three were yawning, and Mrs. Huggins seemed at last satisfied that she had discharged her responsibilities toward Lady Emma, Sir Edmund rose and said he ought to be getting home, and that he would drop their mother at the Savoy—where she always stayed when she didn't want to open her own London house. She added before she left that she would be by in the morning to inspect Lancelot.

"You won't like what you see," Charles warned.

"Neither of you were as angelic as you seem to believe."

"I was," said Edmund.

"Ha!" said Charles.

"Charles!" said their mother. She gave him a kiss on the cheek. "I wish you wouldn't tease your brother."

"Well, you may go on wishing if it pleases you," Lenox said in a grumbling way, and saw them to the door, closing it after they were in a carriage with a tremendous yawn.

Before he turned in, he decided to quickly check his desk. It was piled with notes and telegrams. He sifted through these until he saw one that attracted his attention.

It was a letter from a woman named Mrs. Anderson Withering, posted at Cowgate, Scotland. That was, if Lenox recalled correctly, the long thoroughfare that lay between the old town and the university in Edinburgh.

7 June

Dear Mr. Lenox,

Thank you for your solicitous concern about my brother. He is here at Mrs. Walsh's House for the Incurably Mad. (It is not a name I like, but offered the best care that was recommended to my husband, who sought several medical opinions.) He has a private room there and I visit him twice a week. He is a lovely companion—but as you have apparently witnessed, erratic in his behavior. He had known for some time that we were to resituate him in Scotland, and he was displeased with that. Perhaps it was this that motivated him to approach you.

The name Captain Tankin Irvington means nothing to me, and my brother has no naval background, nor has he spent any time in Australia—to answer your three questions. You are welcome to visit either him or me should you happen to be in Edinburgh.

Best wishes,
Kitty (Belmont) Withering

PS: I write this having just seen your second telegram. I was never required to sign a visitor log at Bedlam. I do not know why.

Lenox quickly dug through the rest of the letters on the desk. He checked the previous wire—the Edinburgh Asylum. He had written to the wrong institution. A creeping feeling of dread, just the initial stage of comprehension, crept up the back of his neck.

He knew he must act or he would sleep badly; he wrote out a few questions for Dr. Hansel and sent a sleepy footman out to send the telegram and pay for return post, so that Hansel could write as voluminously and as quickly as he wished.

This done, Lenox sat in his chair, holding the letter and thinking about Belmont. He fell asleep there—and it was long after two in the morning when he woke, stumbled heavily upstairs, and, a cool breeze running in from the windows, took with gratitude to his bed.

A reply from Hansel awaited him when he woke, just after seven. It was tucked under a glass of apple juice with chips of ice in it, next to his teacup. Lenox slid into a dressing gown and, picking up a piece of bacon with his fingers simultaneously, tore open the wire.

Dear Lenox STOP received your wire and shall endeavor to answer all questions STOP in first place families have not for some seven hundred years been required to sign in STOP shame of association STOP only medical visitors and so forth STOP in second place Belmont was indeed billeted with a former member of the navy for a time STOP full name Carleton Wexford unsure rank STOP standard lunacy STOP finally Mrs Walsh an excellent home by all accounts STOP smaller and more discreet STOP in hopes this helps STOP Hansel

This was a tremendously expensive number of words, but Lenox didn't care a fig. He flattened it on the table, running over its folds with the side of his hand, and read it once more.

"Graham," he called.

The valet appeared, already dressed in his crisp gray suit, hair newly clipped. When did he find time to go to the barber? Before Lenox awoke, obviously. There was an old man who walked from house to house with scissors and mirror. "Sir?"

"Will you fetch me the naval register from the study—the big blue one on the upper shelf near the windows—and then come and join me?"

Lenox ate his eggs and pondered Belmont until Graham returned a moment later. Lenox leafed through the oversized book until he came to the name Wexford. There were two of them.

Only one he needed: "Midshipman Carleton Wexford, sometime officer of Her Majesty's ships *Isabelle, Livia, Victory, Roseanna, Julia, Victoria*, retired Her Majesty's service 1844, living Cable Street, Portsmouth."

And later Bedlam, it would appear.

Lenox saw immediately that Wexford had been on at least two ships upon which Captain Irvington had also served, the *Livia* and the *Victoria*.

"That settles it, Graham," he said.

"What's that, sir?"

Lenox sighed. "I have been made a goose of—by an inmate."

"Belmont, sir?"

"The same."

They sat and picked over the news as Lenox picked over his eggs. Obviously Belmont had picked up Irvington's name from his bunkmate; obviously he was no more unfairly asylumed than most men at Bedlam; obviously his sister cared for him greatly.

Lenox felt very, very stupid. It was unlike him to be so credulous. He said so to Graham.

"Perhaps there is a lesson in it, sir," said Graham.

"Not to trust the passing comments of insane people? Most people learn that lesson some time before the age of twenty-six."

Graham smiled. "That sometimes there are simple, unsuspicious reasons behind a mystery, sir, I would venture. The profession you have chosen cannot always be portraits of Shakespeare."

Lenox speared a sausage moodily. "I suppose. It's not as if even that was very satisfying." He considered his lunch with the duke on Monday. "I wonder if we shall ever see that play in England again."

At that moment Lenox felt, out of absolutely nowhere, a sharp pain on his chin, like a bee sting. It took him a bewildered second to realize what had happened, and then he stood bolt upright.

"*Lancelot,*" he shouted, as the boy, with his peashooter, sped away upstairs to his hideous den.

"Shall I fetch him, sir?" Graham asked.

Lenox sat down, rubbing his face. "No. I deserve it for falling for Belmont."

"You are done with him, then?"

"I shall ask a friend in Edinburgh to verify what the letter says. But I have no doubt it will all prove out." Lenox grimaced, rubbing his chin. "It really does hurt, that little hellion."

"I can fetch ice, sir."

"Oh, sit down, bother you, pour yourself some tea." Lenox thought for a moment. "Do you know, of the numerous arguments that I have seen London make that the world is a cruel and meaningless place—murder, theft, fraud—none is more profound than that Mrs. Huggins should love that boy."

"She is childless, sir."

"And that is the child to make her regret it? No—mark my words, I will never have children, Graham. Poison my soup one supper if I ever tell you otherwise."

"Very good, sir."

"Make it some quick and painless poison, if you wouldn't mind."

"To be sure, sir."

CHAPTER FORTY-EIGHT

There was a table at White's that belonged exclusively to the duke, one of just three members accorded the honor, and was otherwise kept empty. The headwaiter led them to it—the center of the most important room at the most exclusive club in the British Empire.

By leading him here, the duke had discharged a certain duty; Lenox was a gentleman who could be respectably met in the highest echelon of London society, up to Buckingham Palace. There would be new invitations on his hall table when he returned home that afternoon, some so brazen as to be given again after an earlier withdrawal, he reflected as they looked at the menus.

They ate salmon, pheasant, mashed potatoes, and long beans, with the house popovers, light and eggy, serving as sauce-pushers, per tradition. Lenox was a member at White's, and when the check came with coffee and brandy, he offered to sign it. But the duke gave him a look somewhere between contempt and amusement, and just waved it away, unsigned.

They had spoken so far only of neutral matters. The duke reminisced about Lenox's father in kind terms, and they spoke at some length about how Edmund was managing his new responsibilities.

"Please tell him that he is welcome to call on me if he should need any advice," Dorset said, sipping his coffee black.

"It is very kind of you, Your Grace."

"Meanwhile I wonder if you would join me in nominating Ward for membership here. It is perhaps slightly above his station, but he has been loyal to me, and he is well educated and very sound."

Lenox looked down at the petit fours. "Of course," he said.

It was remarkable how rapidly the duke had returned, unstained, to his previous sphere of social activity. That night, he mentioned in passing, he would be dining with the Queen, and the next week he planned to do some stag shooting at his friend Lord Mountjoy's estate.

Lenox thought of General Pendleton.

"Tell me," Lenox said at last, "only because I am inveterately curious. Will you seek the play?"

The duke's expression flattened. When he spoke, it seemed to pain him; he did not even say his daughter's name, merely, "She has married one of my cotters."

"I know," said Lenox.

This was an ancient race of farm laborers, many of their families on the small parcels of land just as long as the dukes and earls who rented to them had been on theirs. Their dwellings, over time, had taken their names—cottages.

"You went to Harrow and Oxford. Your father was a traditionalist. You must have some comprehension of my position. Imagine your own position, but magnified a thousand times."

It was exhausting, this arrogance. He was only a man, the fellow across the table, with his lined face, his smooth gray hair, his gold ring, his cup of coffee. One day the last person who had ever loved him would die, just as was true for everyone within these convivial walls. What lay beyond this earth they none of them knew—but nobody could believe there would be dukes there.

Or perhaps they could. "I can see the difficulty, Your Grace," said Lenox. "But it is Shakespeare."

"Yes, Shakespeare," said the duke, turning his eyes to the windows. "William Shakespeare. I think it is time for that portrait to be stored in the vault at Dorset Castle, and perhaps in three or four generations someone will take it out, and read my letter. But not till then."

So *Campion* would not be coming back to England! Could that be? Lenox felt a shiver of rage—but knew he might just as profitably yell at the crashing shore as at the Duke of Dorset.

To his credit, the duke, before they left, invited him to play a few games of billiards, doubles. The message was clear: that it was a social luncheon, this one, a friendship. He was loud in his proclamations of affection for Lenox, free in his teasing, before half a dozen men who would each tell another half a dozen about it. 6+x+y.

They went to the cloakroom together and fetched their hats at a little past two o'clock. Emerging into the lobby, Lenox saw his brother.

"Edmund!"

"Oh, hello, Charles." He bowed to the duke. "Edmund Lenox, Your Grace."

The duke inclined his head in response. "A pleasure to make your acquaintance. I have been telling your brother that you ought to call upon me if you need any advice about that small estate of yours."

Only someone who had known Edmund exceedingly well over the course of many years would have discerned the anger in his voice when he said, "I will be sure to do so at the first possible chance, Your Grace. Thank you."

"Well!" The duke slapped his gloves against his palm. "I will bid you both good day."

"Good day, Your Grace," said Charles, with the peculiar consciousness that they were passing out of each other's lives. "I will write Ward's letter this evening."

"Capital." The duke looked briefly troubled. "And you will be . . . discreet."

"That goes without saying."

"My apologies. Yes. Good day, gentlemen."

The whole lobby watched him leave, that figure of greatness, and step into his gilt carriage. Charles, for his part, preferred the more modest company in which the duke had left him.

"Why are you here?" he asked Edmund.

"Lunch with the American ambassador, Streeter. Very civil fellow, you know. Lovely daughters."

"Surely you can't be trying to marry me off, too."

They had spent much of the weekend fending off Lenox's mother's suggestions, abetted by Lady Jane, of whom he ought to marry.

"No, no," said Edmund.

They turned into the card room off the lobby and ordered two cups of coffee. When it arrived, Lenox reached into his pocket. He had his little book. He finally felt, for the first time in his life, having glanced into it forty or fifty times in the past week, that he was starting to understand something about why people loved Shakespeare. He had flapped down a tiny corner above one quotation that very morning, struck at how it described his feelings for the person who had given him the book: *This earth that bears thee dead bears not alive so stout a gentleman.*

He showed the little volume to Edmund. "Did Father give you one of these when you went to school?"

Edmund looked at the title page and smiled. "No. He gave me Hesiod's *Days*. Great lot of rot about farming. Did he write in it?"

Lenox showed him the front page. "No."

Edmund looked at him queerly. "Charles, you must remember that Father always wrote at the *back* of the books he gave. It was a quirk."

"I don't remember that at all. Why?"

"He said it would be rude to speak before the author." Edmund smiled. "Excuse me for a moment, would you? I need a quick word with Chalmers there about the Irish bill, damn him. Only a moment."

Lenox watched him go, frowning—the Irish bill wouldn't come up this session—until he realized, dolt that he was, that his brother had been exercising tact, leaving him alone to look and see if his father had written in the book.

He flicked through the pages slowly.

And there, at the back, was his father's infinitely familiar handwriting, so disposable while he was alive but now so precious-seeming.

Charles,

It took me a long while to love Shakespeare. In school I preferred Donne. For a long time my main knowledge about Shakespeare was that his name was an anagram for I am a weakish speller, a trick which occasionally impressed my schoolmates, and which now that you are going to school may impress yours.

But eventually I did love Shakespeare, for his wisdom, his wit, and above all for his clear-seeing love of his fellow man. I hope you, too, will have the pleasure of this discovery, whether it is now or much later in your life. Please know that whenever that time comes, if it does, I will be with you here, in the pages of this book, both now and then.

the proudest of all fathers, yours,
Thomas Lenox

CHAPTER FORTY-NINE

The next day, the time had finally come for Lancelot to depart.

"Well, it's flown by, hasn't it!" said Mrs. Huggins at breakfast, as she poured cream over Lancelot's porridge.

The lad was kicking steadily away at the legs of the dining table. "No," said Lenox.

"Oh, come now, Mr. Lenox!"

Lancelot, looking serious, said, "Do you think they'll believe me at school if I say I fought a duel in France with Spate?"

This was the huge brute he had argued with in the park; France where duels were still legal. "No," said Lenox.

"And you mustn't lie, of course," said Mrs. Huggins.

"Right, of course," said Lancelot, without, seemingly, any sense of irony. He looked at his cousin. "What if I just say I challenged him to a duel?"

"No," said Lenox, who was quite pleased that his lines were so easy.

"The story is interesting enough on its own," said Mrs. Huggins pacifyingly.

"Interesting!" Lenox said. "Mrs. Huggins, are you endorsing that kind of common low-down scrabble-hearted run-amok fistfight! You!"

The housekeeper went pink. "No!" she said. "Not at all!"

"It *is* a good story," said Lancelot, looking pleased. "He must weigh twenty stone."

"Yes, a regular David and Goliath story," said Lenox, "if they had both been imbeciles."

At around eleven o'clock, Edmund and Lady Jane came to say good-bye. (Graham, as usual the most intelligent of them all, had cleared off after a firm handshake before breakfast. No risk for him of getting caught in a last peashooter crossfire.) Lancelot was upstairs with Mrs. Huggins, shoving things into his trunk. Lenox's mother—who loved train stations dearly and irrationally—had gone to pick Eustacia up at Charing Cross. It had taken Charles some restraint not to mention the apple's toss.

He was entertaining Lady Jane and Edmund with the story of his misguided attempt to save Belmont; a comical story now, though for several days it had plagued him. But error could always lead to growth—and even as he and Edmund and Lady Jane laughed, he resolved that he would do better, in the future, at looking through appearances to the nuance that any plain-told story inevitably missed.

"Ed," said Charles, "did you know they give away a side of bacon to a couple in Essex every year that can prove they haven't quarreled in thirteen months?"

"Yes, I read the *Times*," said Edmund.

Lady Jane laughed. "Stout fellow."

"I bet you didn't know that they roll a tremendous wheel of cheese down a hill in Gloucester every year and the first person to catch it gets to keep it."

"Who told you that?" said Charles.

"Fotheringay-Phipps."

"A known liar."

Edmund shook his head gravely. "No, he had it on absolute eyeball account from his brother Waller, who's as honest as the day is long."

Charles acknowledged that Waller was a good source. "You should try to get it next year."

"I don't like cheese that much."

"What a thing to say," Lady Jane replied. "In my own house."

"This is my house," said Charles.

"In as good as my own house," she said, scowling at him and picking up the cane he used to knock on her wall.

"I don't! I prefer potatoes," said Edmund.

"Nobody's making you choose, you dunderhead," said Lady Jane. "In fact there is a reasonable argument to be made that cheese and potatoes are best together."

"I like plain buttered potatoes," said Charles, for one had to draw one's lines.

"I only said a reasonable argument."

The front door opened, and all three got up. Lenox's cousin Eustacia, a pretty, lively person, very small, with endless tea table conversation and endless goodwill toward the world, gave him a tight squeeze.

"You must tell me," she said, gripping him by his shoulders and looking up at him. "Has he been a bother?"

"My housekeeper isn't even willing to let him leave," said Charles.

She squeezed. "Good. I worry that he can be a bit high spirited."

"A bit, perhaps, at times," said Charles thoughtfully. "But I think he's turned out splendidly. You've done such good work with him."

"So he didn't bring his peashooter?"

"Well . . . he did bring it."

"Oh, Lancelot," she muttered. "Well, thank you anyway, Charles. He needed this."

At that moment there was a noise on the stairwell, and Lenox flinched, fully expecting to be shot one last time.

But his young cousin was looking almost bashful, if anything. He accepted a long hug from his mother, then said very polite good-byes to his cousin Edmund and to Lady Jane, each of whom tipped him. (Lenox could have told them the money would be spent on mischief, but what was the point?) Finally Mrs. Huggins enclosed him in a tight embrace, which he wriggled out of.

To Lenox's astonishment, he saw that she had tears in her eyes. "Please visit again sometime very soon, Master Lancelot," she said.

The boy looked at Lenox, whom he had been studiously ignoring until then. "Is that . . . do you think so, too, cousin Charles?"

Lenox realized that it was a sincere question. "Why, of course," he said. "You are welcome in any home I have, as long as I have one, Lancelot."

"I am?" he said, as if looking for a catch.

"Of course you are. When you are expelled from school I hope you will come directly here." All of them laughed, even Eustacia—except Lancelot, who, without warning, got his cousin into a tight squash around the midsection, burying his head in Lenox's waistcoat. "Well, well," said Lenox, taken aback. "You know, you are family."

Lancelot let go and, refusing to look his cousin in the eyes, went outside with Lenox's own mother and waited for Eustacia—who said her own quick good-byes, for they were due on a train to Eton soon—and departed without another word.

Lenox stared after their carriage in a sort of shock. What strange creatures children were!

"That was very sweet, after all," said Lady Jane.

"Yes," he said, "it was."

He felt a vibration of happiness inside, something in between hope, sorrow, and life. He realized that he had accidentally done something *good*, having Lancelot here.

He watched the carriage all the way to the corner, where it disappeared into the great smoky city. Finally he turned back inside and checked his watch. "Blast," he said. "I'll be late. I'm going to the East End."

"You can give me a ride partway," said Lady Jane. "I'm having my tea with Duch. But open my present first."

She had brought it earlier, and it stood by the door, about the size of a footstool. "I will, thank you, though I don't know the occasion."

He unwrapped the parcel and saw, after a moment's confusion, what it was: a gleaming brass and satinwood barometer, fit for an admiral's cabin, with a delicate pendulum and beautiful workings.

"Jane!" he said, astonished.

She smiled at him. "For putting up with Lancelot. You can thank me in all the boring detail later—tell me how it works. For now I'll pop next door and get my things, then we can go. Let's meet soon, Edmund. There's much to discuss about Molly's party."

After she had left, Edmund said, "Why are you going?"

"I'm meeting Bonden and Graham. A case down there, a murder."

"Cor! What a life, Charles."

Lenox smiled at his brother, a radiant smile. "And yet here you are, in Parliament, titled, with Molly and two lovely sons. That is what I call a life."

"We'll swap for a day sometime. I have to go listen to them drone on in the Commons all afternoon."

"You have a deal. Good-bye till then."

Edmund watched as Charles walked outside to his cab. The baronet remained in the doorway, waving good-bye.

His secret, as he stood there, was that there had been no lunch with an American diplomat the day before; he had gone in case his younger brother were subject to another one of the duke's attacks.

Edmund watched Lenox and Lady Jane leave in the carriage. After a little time had passed, he buttoned his own jacket, a little more deliberately, and shut the door behind him after calling out his good-bye to Mrs. Huggins. He stood on the house's steps for some time, gazing out at the distant spires, the square countinghouses in the middle distance, the smoke rising from a hundred buildings into the clear summer sky, and wondered to which hidden, mysterious, thrilling corner, in the great city spread before him now like a world of marvels, his brother's new case would take him.

TURN THE PAGE FOR A SNEAK PEEK AT
CHARLES FINCH'S NEW NOVEL

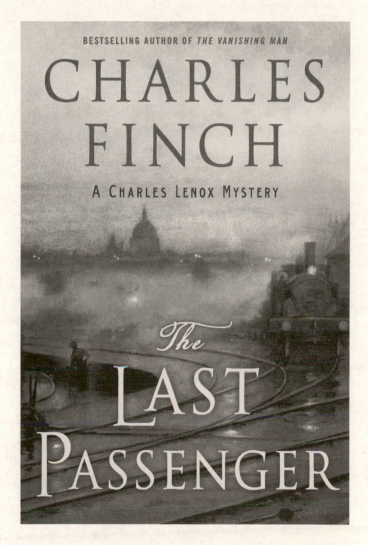

BESTSELLING AUTHOR OF *THE VANISHING MAN*

CHARLES FINCH

A CHARLES LENOX MYSTERY

The
LAST
PASSENGER

AVAILABLE FEBRUARY 2020

CHAPTER ONE

O
n or about the first day of October 1855, the city of London, England, decided it was time once and for all that Charles Lenox be married.

Lenox himself didn't even necessarily disagree. He lived a happy life as a bachelor in the passage through Mayfair known as Hampden Lane, but for the first time had reached a stage when he could admit that a wife might settle his days into a still more contented rhythm. Nevertheless, the city's vehemence in its new convictions about his future came as a surprise.

On the second Tuesday of the month, at an evening salon at Lady Sattle's, a footman discreetly handed him a note:

Mary Elizabeth Sharples
Throw into fire

He studied this epistle for a moment. He knew the handwriting. He looked over at Mary Elizabeth Sharples, holding a tiny glass of almond brandy across the room, a violet shawl around her shoulders.

She was a handsome woman in her third London season, Kentish, immensely rich, and also a fair four or even five inches above six feet tall—and, of greater significance than any of that, was help-lessly in love with the gentleman standing next to her at just this moment, Mark Blake. It seemed doubtful that Blake himself knew anything about it. Lenox had been familiar with him at Oxford. He was a virtually penniless fellow of good birth, so short in stat-ure that there were carnival rides to which his successful admission would be an uncertain matter, and whose only subject of conversa-tion, whose exclusive interest, was Dutch silver.

He did have a fine head of gleaming black hair, however; that had to be owned.

Lenox glanced across the room toward his friend Lady Jane. It was she who had passed the note by the footman. She was now in the midst of an animated conversation with her husband, James, and two gentlemen from his regiment in the Coldstream Guards.

He managed to catch her eye, however, and she returned his gaze queryingly.

Lady Jane and Lenox had known each other since they were children. She was perhaps a year younger than Mary Elizabeth Sharples, and a good ten inches shorter. She was a plain but pretty person, with dimpled cheeks, kind gray eyes, and hair that fell in soft dark curls. This evening she wore a wide blue crinoline.

He crossed the room toward her, an icy pewter cup of punch in hand.

When she was just loose from the group's conversation, Lenox said, "Hello, Jane."

"Ah! Hello, Charles," she said innocently.

Lenox leaned close. "Shall I really throw her into the fire?"

"Excuse me?"

"I will do it if you insist, but I feel people would notice. I am almost sure."

Lady Jane looked at him crossly. "What are you talking about?"

He consulted the note. "You write, *Mary Elizabeth Sharples*," he said in a quiet voice, though the lady in question was some thirty feet away. "*Throw into fire.*"

A look of wrath came onto Jane's face. "The note, you fool. You're to throw the note into the fire."

"Oh, the note!"

"Yes, the note, as you very well know."

"I was going to eat the note," he said.

She shook her head. "How I hate you."

He smiled. "I could ask her to marry me in front of all these people and it wouldn't make a whit of difference, Jane. She is going to marry Blake, whenever he stops talking about sterling cow creamers long enough to notice that it is possible. I imagine they will be transported to the church in a carriage of Dutch silver."

"I think her a very agreeable person," said Jane stiffly, not just yet prepared to laugh at her suggestion. "And I am not at all convinced that her affections are as settled as you say. But you may suit yourself."

Lenox held up the note. "I must go to the hearth, now that I understand your meaning. Be good enough to watch my back, please. For enemy action."

"I hope you fall into the fire," she said, and turned back to her husband and his friends.

So it had been for weeks, mysteriously. Ancient, distant, respectable cousins had dropped in on Lenox after years of silence, mentioning their friends' grandnieces. Peers from his schooldays delicately proffered their sisters. Even his close friends, Lady Jane, for instance, and his brother, Edmund, seemed to think he was in desperate want of a wife.

Part of it was no doubt that the season had just begun. After the long summer, in which those who could mostly retreated from the city into the clearer air of the countryside, all had returned, and every night there was a different salon or ball. The next night these same people would be crowded into Mrs. Wilcott's immense ballroom in the guise of either "lions" or "lambs," however they chose to interpret that directive. (Lenox hadn't chosen. He dreaded it.)

Still, this was his sixth autumn in London, and the assaults upon his liberty had never been this concerted or numerous.

He was, after all, an unusual match. It was true that he had a good deal to recommend him. He was a slim, eligible young man of twenty-seven, always well dressed, with a thoughtful face, hazel eyes, a short hazel beard, and an easy smile. In his manner there was a simplicity that perhaps derived from his background in the Sussex countryside. He had been born the second son of a baronet there—sometimes a tricky position—but was fortunate enough to have means of his own. He had a good character, lively, happy friendships, and a family respected on both sides.

What's more—though perhaps he did not see this for himself, bound like all men and women in the intense, confused impressions of his own inner world—he was an appealing young fellow. It was hard to say precisely why. Perhaps primarily because he was that most fortunate creature, from whatever class one might pick: the child of two parents who loved him.

"Lenox!"

He had just tossed Lady Jane's note into the fire, and now turned. It took him an instant to place Robert Dudding, a fashionable clubman of roughly forty-five.

They only knew each other remotely. "How do you do, Dudding?" said Lenox, surprised at the enthusiastic greeting.

"Oh, fine, fine. I had a bad Goodwood, you know. After that I stayed off the turf. Dull without gambling, life. But a decent summer still. See here, though—I particularly want to introduce you to my sister's ward. Miss Louise Pierce, this is Charles Lenox."

Only then did Lenox notice a young woman standing next to Dudding. He bowed to her.

"How do you do?" she asked, curtsying.

How indeed?

Many hours later, as he rode home in his carriage alone, it occurred to Lenox that Dudding's friendliness was the best representation yet of this unexpected new element in his life.

He would have felt by no means sure of the man's handshake even three months before. Dudding was a snob, and Lenox, though he had nothing to be shy of concerning his parentage, was something of an odd figure, ever since, upon his graduation, he had come to London and taken the unexpected step of becoming a private detective.

It was a decision that had, whatever his connections, immediately disqualified him from certain parts of the best society. Bad enough that he should work in some field other than the clergy or the military, traditional realms of the younger son—but outrageous that he should become . . . well, what? Nobody seemed sure. At times, Lenox himself was least sure of all. It was a profession he was designing on the fly, like a railroad thrown down a few desperate ties at a time ahead of the train.

His motivations had been complex. A mingled desire to do right and to do something unique, a sense of adventure, and an unbecoming kind of inquisitiveness to be sure—all alongside, crucially, a fundamental and irresistible fascination with crime. Murder was his own version of Dutch silver. His interest in it was intense and long-lasting, galvanized when he was a boy by penny magazines and consolidated, since he had arrived in London, by a serious and comprehensive study of all the endless, multifarious crimes that occurred here.

He was convinced that it was a subject worth close attention. Most people were not. Men and women who would have eagerly solicited his good opinion had he chosen to remain utterly idle, living off his income and staring at a few hundred hands of whist a week, had cut him again and again in the past few years, some even going so far as to bar him from their doors.

Their stance wasn't universal. His friends remained staunch, and the great majority of people didn't have the energy to care much, viewing him more as eccentric than ruined. But men like Dudding, conscious at every moment of status . . .

The only thing Lenox could think was that there must be some shortfall of unmarried men this year.

As he stepped out of his carriage at home, he sighed. At times he wondered whether this profession was even worth his time. The fact was that his progress as a detective had been halting: one or two notable successes, but also long periods of stagnation, and the derision of his class and of Scotland Yard. A less stubborn person might have given the folly up.

But if he kept at it—would it not be nice to return to a comfortable hearth, bedecked with a lady of sweet disposition and aspect, and perhaps even one or two small humans, playing blocks in that mood of intense concentration he had noticed in the visages of his friends' children?

"Graham?" he called, entering the house.

"Good evening, sir," said Graham, the house's butler, standing up from a chair in the small alcove in the front hall, which served as his version of an office. "A pleasant evening?"

Graham was, though a servant, one of Lenox's closest confidants, a compact, sandy-haired, gentlemanly person of about Lenox's own age, attired in a subtly faultless suit of clothes.

"I was married off twenty times or so. Other than that it wasn't so bad."

"I'm glad to hear it, sir," said Graham, taking Lenox's cane and hat.

Lenox looked at the grandfather clock. It was past midnight. "I know you must be tired, but what do you say to ten minutes on the Claxton case?"

This was a peculiar death in Nottingham that they had been studying.

"With pleasure, sir," Graham said. "Mrs. Huggins has left tea on the warming plate. And there are cheese-and-pickle sandwiches at your desk, sir, in case you didn't have supper."

CHAPTER TWO

Two nights later, Lenox sat in his study, playing chess with his next-door neighbor, Lord Deere.

This study was a large, high-ceilinged, rectangular room that overlooked the street from just a few feet above it. At the other end of the chamber a fire burned in the grate; books and small paintings lined the walls.

It was a rare night away from the social round, made possible by a thunderstorm—and not just any thunderstorm, but a hard one, almost moralizing in its intensity. A whipping rain was falling across the ancient gray stones of London; water flushed days of autumn grime from every narrow fissure and channel in the cobblestone streets, eddying around clots of fallen leaves until it loosened them all at once. An October storm. The last stale heaviness of summer heat being rinsed clean away.

"One of the troubles with cinnamon toast is that the edges never have much cinnamon on them," said Lord Deere.

Lenox glanced over the board, irritated. He liked Deere, and loved Deere's wife, Jane. But he was about to lose, and it had been extremely close this time, too. "*One* of the troubles? What are the others?"

"Where to begin. It doesn't dunk well."

"Doesn't dunk well."

Deere grinned. "In tea."

"Doesn't dunk well in tea."

"No, it falls to bits immediately." He gestured at the board. "Rather like the little triangle of pawns you set up around your king."

"That's a very dishonorable comment, if you ask me," Lenox replied darkly, staring at the board.

"I am detestable in victory. Everyone must have his flaws," said Lord Deere in a cheerily philosophical tone, munching a piece of the cinnamon toast with what appeared, despite his objections, like great relish. In his other hand was a cup of tea, steam drifting upward from it in a loose coil. "Listen, why don't we start over?"

Lenox was not prouder than the typical young man of good education, ample means, and a strong intelligence. Alas, even the average pride of such a specimen of person must be very high.

"That is the most cowardly offer I ever heard."

Deere was a tall, thin man with fair hair and striking blue eyes. Somehow, in whatever the circumstances, he always looked crisp and tidily arranged.

He protested. "I was only hoping we might fit in another game!"

Lenox glanced at the gold carriage clock on his desk. After a hostile pause, he knocked over his king. "Fine," he said.

"There you are, see?"

"Hm."

They began setting up the pieces, or rather Deere did, because Lenox had started hungrily eating toast and sipping his own tea.

He had never been a soul to hold a grudge, even in childhood, and before the pieces were up the last game was forgotten, replaced in their conversation with Lenox's frank admiration for his opponent's skill. Somehow he always managed to slip through the narrowest slivers of logic when they played, Deere. He might be two important pieces down, yet invariably he found a way to recover his balance and best Lenox. Or so it seemed anyhow.

"Don't forget that I am in the army," he said, after Lenox pointed this out. "Much of our training is calculated for dire strategic situations."

"True. I wonder if chess in the military is played to a higher standard than among us civilians."

The young lord looked contemplative. "I could not promise you that. We have our share of dullards. I suppose all professions do."

"Of course."

"Indeed, I would wager many among the infantry would get the better of their officers. It's a great hobby—they all have pocket boards. Handy when you are stuck on some hillside for a week with nothing to do."

When Lenox had learned that Lady Jane had married a military man, he had been predisposed to look upon the gentleman as something of a cavalier, one of those soldiers who marry and then return home but rarely, glad as they may be when there.

But of course Jane—always the smartest person he had known—would never have married for less than true love, and Deere, as Lenox had very slowly and somewhat reluctantly learned, was a special sort of person.

He was entirely open with others, entirely generous; wanted to see only the best in them; above all, wanted to learn what they were like, what they loved, who they were. For instance, he delighted in Lenox's profession, pressing questions upon him about it in a way almost no one else did. When he did travel, he brought home innumerable local objects, which he studied and collected with careful attention. He knew the names of flowers, grasses, trees, and stars. He especially loved dogs: He knew every breed, and though an earl, and thus entitled to be extremely haughty, would stop with anybody in the street who happened to be walking one for a long chin wag.

He was commissioned as a captain in the Coldstream Guards, a demanding position. He was away from home more often than not, but hoped that he would be here for a decent stretch now. (He was still awaiting new orders.) It was commonly agreed that he had a very bright future.

Halfway through the next game that he and Lenox played, there was a sharp knock at the front door.

The young detective frowned. He wasn't expecting anybody. Lady Jane—whom he would normally have suspected—was at the bedside of a friend in South Kensington, who had just been delivered prematurely of a son.

"I wonder who could be abroad in this weather," Lenox said.

"The devil knows."

After a beat, Graham appeared at the door of the study. "Inspector Hemstock wishes to call upon you, sir."

"Hemstock!" Standing up, Lenox glanced at his friend. "You'll have to forgive me, Deere. Graham, would you ask Elliott to get the horses warmed, please?"

This was the groom. "Of course, sir."

Lenox held up a hand. "No. On second thought, don't. But please show Hemstock in."

"Very good, sir."

He didn't need to go out on a rainy night at Thomas Hemstock's whim.

Deere knew something of Lenox's business—indeed, it sometimes seemed to Lenox that all of London did. "Not in the mood for a case?" Deere asked.

"No. I have rarely been busier."

It was true. After long stretches of idleness in previous years—though he tried his best to stay busy during these, through an improvised course of self-instruction—at present Lenox had two cases, besides his conjectures from afar about the Claxton murder. Both were minor. Still, he was pleased to be occupied.

Graham returned with Hemstock, who had left his hat and his cloak in the hall but was nevertheless dripping wet.

As usual, he was in a state that you might certainly call jolly, if you wished to be polite—outright drunk, if you were blunter.

"Hullo!" he cried. "What's this? Chess? Sport of kings, chess."

That was horse racing. No matter. "How are you, Mr. Hemstock?" Lenox said, putting out his hand. He liked the inspector, taken all in all. "Much occupied this evening?"

"Yes! Thought you might want to come round with me, learn a trick or two. It's a murder."

"Whereabouts?"

"Paddington Station."

Some piece of ha'penny violence, Lenox supposed. A burglar, a gang member, a sailor. The motive probably petty vengeance or drunken ire.

"Unfortunately I don't think I can. I have a guest, as you see."

Hemstock looked surprised. It was the first time Lenox had refused such an offer.

An affable, short, solid fellow, about forty, with a squashed face and an infectious gaiety, Hemstock was the worst detective Scotland Yard had. Indeed, the job belonged to him only because his late father had been one of the original Peelers, a figure of legend and lore, revered at the Yard. The son did little harm in his sinecure— if not, unfortunately, much good either. Lately, however, he had been allowing Lenox to solve his cases, under the guise of his "helping" the young squire, showing him "a trick or two." Most men at the Yard despised the idea of Lenox's amateur involvement in their work, but Hemstock had noticed that he could be useful.

"It's a strange one," the inspector said.

"Perhaps I could come in the morning and see you about it then," said Lenox.

"Of course. Until the morning."

"The morning. And I say, I am sorry. Thank you for stopping by."

Hemstock had recovered from his surprise. "May be dry by then, eh? Or else we'll soon be boarding the animals two by two. Any time after ten o'clock."

He accepted a drink to see him on his way—a brandy, which vanished quickly—and left.

Deere, surprised, watched Lenox take his chair again. They were not quite close enough that he could ask why Lenox had declined. (If Jane were here, she would have done so without hesitation.) Instead they played out their muddled, unsatisfying third game.

The instant it was clear that Deere had won, the detective stood up.

"I'm sorry, Deere," he said.

He called for Graham. "Sir?" said the valet—somewhere between a butler and a valet, really—appearing at the door.

"I'm sorry, Graham," said Lenox, who was handing out apologies this evening at such a rate that he would soon run short of them, "but could you get the horses warmed after all? I think I must go to Paddington Station, or I won't rest."

"They are ready in front, sir."

Lenox gave a look of surprise, then a rueful smile. "Thank you, Graham," he said. "I suppose I am predictable after all this time under the same roof."

"Not at all, sir."

"Just give me my hat and my cane then, if you don't mind. I bet I can beat him there."

Timothy Greenfield-Sanders

Charles Finch is the *USA Today* bestselling author of the Charles Lenox mysteries, including *The Woman in the Water*. His first contemporary novel, *The Last Enchantments*, is also available from St. Martin's Press. Finch received the 2017 Nona Balakian Citation Award, for excellence in reviewing, from the National Book Critics Circle. His essays and criticism have appeared in *The New York Times*, *Slate*, *The Washington Post*, and elsewhere. He lives in Los Angeles.

Find him online at www.facebook.com/ charlesfinchauthor and on Twitter @CharlesFinch

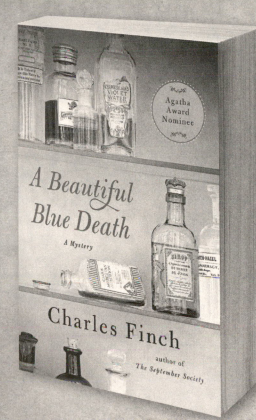

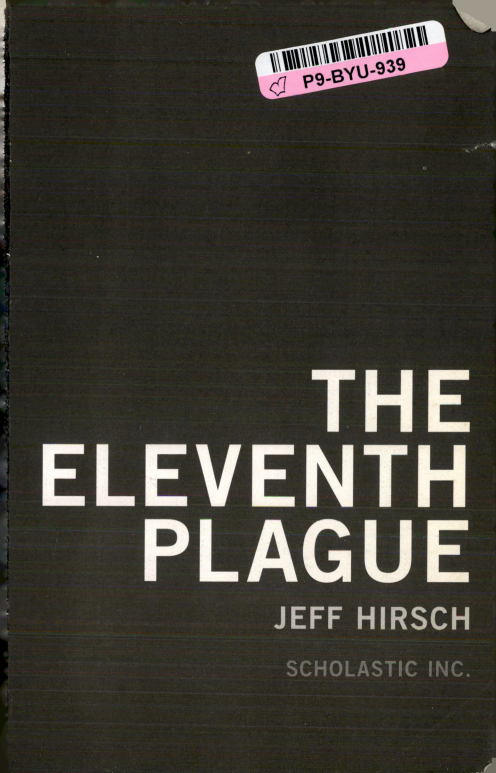

THE ELEVENTH PLAGUE

JEFF HIRSCH

SCHOLASTIC INC.

No part of this publication may be reproduced, stored in a retrieval system, or transmitted in any form or by any means, electronic, mechanical, photocopying, recording, or otherwise, without written permission of the publisher. For information regarding permission, write to Scholastic Inc., Attention: Permissions Department, 557 Broadway, New York, NY 10012.

This book was originally published in hardcover by Scholastic Press in 2011.

ISBN 978-0-545-29015-9

Copyright © 2011 by Jeff Hirsch. All rights reserved. Published by Scholastic Inc. SCHOLASTIC and associated logos are trademarks and/or registered trademarks of Scholastic Inc.

12 11 10 9 8 7 6 5 4 3 2 1   12 13 14 15 16 17/0
Printed in the U.S.A.   40

First paperback printing, September 2012

Book design by Phil Falco

To Gretchen.
You never stop changing my world for the better.

PART ONE

ONE

I was sitting at the edge of the clearing, trying not to stare at the body on the ground in front of me. Dad had said we'd be done before dark, but it had been hours since the sun went down and he was still only waist deep in the hole, throwing shovelfuls of dirt over his shoulder.

Even though it was covered in the burlap shroud I could see how wasted Grandpa's body was. He'd always been thin, but the infection had taken another ten pounds off him before he went. His hand fell out from a tear in the burlap. Shadowed from the moonlight, it was a desert plain, the tracks of the veins like dry riverbeds winding up the crags of his knuckles. A gold Marine Corps ring sat on one finger, but it barely fit anymore.

Dad's shovel chewed through rocks and clay with an awful scrape. Finally I couldn't stand it anymore and escaped into the thicket of trees that surrounded us, stumbling through the darkness until I came to the edge of the hill we were camped on.

Far below were the slouching ruins of an old mall. Rows of cars, rusting in the moist air, sat in the parking lot, still waiting for the doors to open. Beyond the mall, the arches of a McDonald's sign hovered like a ghost.

I remembered seeing it for the first time, ten years ago. I was five and then the sign had towered in its red and gold plastic. It seemed gigantic and beautiful. One trillion served. Now fingers of vines crept up its base, slowly consuming more and more of the rusty metal.

I wondered how long it would be until they made it to the top and the whole thing finally collapsed. Ten years? Twenty? Would I be Dad's age? Grandpa's?

I took a breath of the cool air, but the image of Grandpa's hand lying there on the ground loomed in the back of my mind. How could it be so still?

Grandpa's hand only made sense in motion, rearing back, the gold ring flashing as it crashed into my cheek. He had so many rules. I could never remember them all. The simple act of setting up camp was a minefield of mistakes, and Dad and I both seemed to trip over every one. I could still feel the sting of the metal and the rasp of his calloused skin.

But that's over, I told myself. *We're on our own now.* Grandpa's fist was just another bit of wreckage we were leaving behind.

"Stephen!"

My chest tightened. It wasn't cold enough for a fire, but I didn't want to go back with nothing to do so I collected an armful of wood and brush on the way. I dropped it all between our sleeping bags, then leaned over the tinder, scraping the two pieces of my fire starter together until a spark caught. Once I had a proper campfire, I sat back on my heels to watch it burn.

"Think it's deep enough yet?"

Dad was leaning against the wall of the grave, his body slick with sweat and dirt. I nodded.

"Come on, then. Bring the ropes."

Once I helped Dad out of the hole, we knelt on either side of Grandpa's body and drew lengths of rope under his knees and back. Dad started to lift him, but I didn't move. Grandpa's hand, one finger crowned with gold, was only inches from me.

"What about his ring?"

The ends of the ropes went limp in Dad's hands. The ring glinted in the firelight. I knew he stung from it just like I did.

"There's gotta be a half ounce of solid gold there," I said. "If not more."

"Let's just do this."

"But don't we have to — ?"

"Stephen, now," Dad snapped.

We lowered Grandpa into the grave and then, before I could even pull the ropes out, Dad began filling it in again. I knew I should stop him. We could have traded Grandpa's ring for food, new clothes, even bullets. Dad knew that as well as I did.

When the grave was filled, the shovel slipped from Dad's hands and he fell to his knees, doubling over with his arms around his stomach. His body seized with small tremors.

Oh God. Don't let him be sick too.

I reached out to him. "Dad?"

When he turned, the light caught tears cutting channels through the dirt on his face. I turned toward the woods as he sobbed, giving him what privacy I could, a knot twisting tighter and tighter inside me. When he was done I laid his favorite flannel shirt over his shoulders. Dad drew it around him with a shaky breath, then searched the stars through red, swollen eyes.

"I swear," he exhaled. "That man was a purebred son of a bitch."

"Maybe we should put that on his tombstone."

Dad surprised me with a short, explosive laugh. I sat beside him, edging my body alongside the steady in and out of his breath. He draped his arm, exhausted, over my shoulder. It felt good, but still the knot in my stomach refused to unravel.

"Dad?"

"Yeah, Steve?"

"We'll be okay, won't we? Without him?" When Dad said nothing I moved out from under his arm and looked up at him.

"I mean . . . nothing's going to change. Right?"

Dad fixed his eyes past me and onto the dark trail we would start down the next morning.

"No," he said, his words rising up like ghosts, thin and pale and empty. "Nothing's ever going to change."

TWO

We clawed our way out of our sleeping bags just before sunrise, greeted each other with sleepy-eyed grumbles, and got to work.

I dealt with Dad's backpack first, making sure the waterproof bag inside was intact before loading in our first-aid kit and the few matches we had left. I did it carefully, still half expecting to hear Grandpa's voice explode behind me as he wrenched the bag out of my hand and showed me how to do it right. I paused. Breathed. *He's gone,* I told myself. I reached back in and felt for our one photograph, making sure it was still there, like I did every morning, and then moved on.

As I arranged the clothes in my pack, my hand hit the spine of one of my books. *The Lord of the Rings.* I had found it years before in a Walmart, buried underneath a pile of torn baby clothes and the dry leaves that had blown in when the walls had fallen. I'd read it start to finish six times, always waiting until after Grandpa went to sleep. He'd said the only thing books were good for was kindling.

I flipped through the book's crinkled pages and placed it at the very top of the bag so it would be the first thing my fingers touched when I reached inside. Doing this gave me a rebel thrill. I didn't have to worry about Grandpa finding it now.

When I went to water our donkey, Paolo, I found Dad staring down at something in the back of the wagon — Grandpa's hunting rifle. It was lying right where he'd left it two days earlier, when he'd become too weak to lift it anymore.

Dad reached down and ran the tips of his fingers along the rifle's scarred body.

"So . . . this is mine now."

He lifted the rifle into his arms and slid the bolt back. One silver round lay there, sleek and deadly.

"Guess so," I said.

Dad forced a little smile as he hung the rifle from his shoulder. "I'll have to figure out how to work it, then, huh?" he joked, a dim twinkle in his eye. "Come on, pal. Let's get out of here."

As Dad started down the trail, I turned for a last look at Grandpa's grave. How many such mounds had we seen as we walked from one end of the country to the other, year after year? Sometimes it was one or two at a time, scattered like things misplaced. Sometimes there were clusters of hundreds, even thousands, littering the outskirts of dead cities.

It was still hard to believe his death could have come so quickly. After all that he had survived — the war, the Collapse, the chaos that followed — to be taken by . . . what? An infection? Pneumonia? The flu? We had no idea. He was like a thousand-year-old oak, scarred and twisted, that was somehow chopped down in a day. It made me feel sick inside, but some part of me was glad. Like we had been freed.

I was about to ask if Dad wanted to make some kind of marker before we left, but he had already moved down the trail.

"Come on, P," I said, tugging on Paolo's lead and guiding him away.

The sun rose as we moved off the hill, pushing some of the chill out of the air. We passed the mall and crossed a highway. On the other side there was a church with the blackened wreck of an army truck sitting in front of it. Beside that were tracts of abandoned houses, their crumbling walls and smashed windows reminding me of row after row of skulls.

It was almost impossible to imagine the lives of the people who'd lived and worked in these places before the Collapse. The war had started five years before I was born, and over nothing, really. Dad said a couple of American students backpacking in China were caught where they shouldn't have been and mistaken for spies. He said it wouldn't have been that big a deal, except that at around the same time the oil was running out, and the Earth was getting warmer, and a hundred other things were going wrong. Dad said everyone was scared and that fear had made the world into a huge pile of dried-out tinder — all it needed was a spark. Once the fire caught it didn't take more than a couple years to reduce everything to ruins. All that survived were a few stubborn stragglers like us, holding on by our fingernails.

We made it through what was left of the town, then came to a wide run of grass, framed by trees with leaves that had begun to turn from vivid shades of orange and red to muddy brown. We shifted east, then dropped into the steady pace we'd maintain until it was time to jog south for the final leg.

"We're gonna be fine," Dad said, finally breaking the silence of the morning. "You know that, right?"

The knot from the previous night tightened in my throat. I swallowed it away and said that I did.

"The haul isn't too bad," Dad continued, glancing back at the wagon, which was filled with a few pieces of glass and some rusted scrap metal. "And hey, who knows? Remember the time we came across that stash of Star Wars stuff in — where was it? Columbus? Maybe we'll wake up tomorrow morning and find, I don't know, a helicopter. In perfect working order! Gassed up and ready to go!"

"Casey'd probably like that more than a bunch of old Star Wars toys."

"Well, who knew the little nerd preferred Battlestar Galactica?"

Casey, or General Casey as he liked to call himself, was the king of the Southern Gathering. His operation sat at the top of what was once called Florida and was where Dad and I traded whatever salvage we could find for things like clothes and medicine and bullets.

"We still got ten pairs of socks out of it," I said. "How many do you think we could get for a helicopter?"

"What? Are you kidding? We wouldn't trade it!"

"Not even for socks?"

"Hell no. We'd become freelance helicopter pilots! Imagine what people would give us to take a ride in the thing." Dad shot his fist in the air. "It'd be a gold mine, I tell ya!"

Dad laughed and so did I. It was a little forced, but I thought maybe it was like a promise, a way to remind ourselves that things would be okay again soon.

It grew warmer as the morning passed. Around noon we settled onto a dilapidated park bench and pulled out our lunch of venison jerky and hardtack. Paolo munched nearby, the metal bits of his harness tinkling gently.

Dad grew quiet. He took a few bites and then stared west, into the woods. Once I was done eating I pulled a needle and thread out of my pack and set to fixing a tear in the elbow of my sweatshirt.

"You should eat," I said, drawing the needle through the greasy fabric and pulling it tight.

"Not hungry, I guess."

A flock of birds swarmed across the sky, cawing loudly before settling on the power lines that ran like a seam down our path. I wondered if they had been able to do that before the Collapse, back when electricity had actually moved through the wires. And if not, which brave bird had been the first one to give it a shot once the lights had all gone out?

Distracted, I let the needle lance into my fingertip. I recoiled and sucked on it until the blood stopped. I heard Grandpa's raspy voice. *Pay attention to what you're doing, Stephen. It doesn't take a genius to concentrate.* I leaned back over the sleeve, trying to keep the stitches tight like Mom had taught me.

"I keep expecting to see him," Dad said. "Hear him."

I pulled the thread to a stop and looked over my shoulder at Dad.

"Was he different?" I asked. "Before?"

Dad leaned his head back and peered up into the sky.

"On the weekends he'd take me to the movies. He worked a lot so that was our time together. We'd see everything. Didn't matter what. Stupid things. It wasn't about the movie, it was about us being there. But then everything fell apart and your grandma died . . . I guess he didn't want to live through that pain again so he became what he thought he had to become to keep the rest of us alive."

Even though it was still fairly warm out, Dad shivered. He wrapped his coat and his arms tight around his body, then stared at the ground and shook his head.

"I'm so sorry, Steve," he said, a tired quiver in his voice. "I'm sorry I ever let him —"

"It's okay," I said.

I snapped the thread with my teeth and yanked on the fabric. It held. Good enough. I slipped the sweatshirt on and zipped it up. "You ready?"

Dad didn't move. He was focused on a stand of reedy trees across the way, almost as though he recognized something in the deep swirl of twigs and dry leaves. When I looked all I saw was a rough path, barely wide enough for our wagon.

"You find that helicopter?"

Dad's shoulders rose and fell and he let out a little puff of breath, the empty shape of a laugh.

"Better get going then, huh? We can start south here."

There were heavy shadows, like smears of ash, under Dad's red-rimmed eyes as he turned to me. For a second it was like he was looking at a stranger, but then he pulled his lips into a grin and slapped me on the knee.

"Reckon so, pardner," he said as he lumbered up off the bench and hung the rifle on his shoulder once again. "Reckon it's time to get on down the road."

I took Paolo's lead and gave it a pull. Dad hovered by the bench, staring back at the path west, almost hungrily, his thumb tucked under the rifle's strap.

I stayed Paolo and waited. What was he doing?

But then, in a flash, it was gone, and Dad shook his head, pulling himself away from that other path and joining me. He ruffled my hair as he passed by, and we began what would be the last leg of our yearly trip south.

"Hey! Look at that."

We were moving across a grass-covered plain. Dad was out front, facing west, shading his eyes from the glare. I stepped up next to him, but all I saw was a dark hill. It seemed out of place in the middle of the flat plain, but was otherwise unremarkable.

"What is it?" I asked.

Dad raised the rifle's scope to his eye. "Well, it ain't a helicopter," he said as he handed me the rifle. "Looks like a bomber."

"No. Really?" I lifted the rifle and peered through the scope. That's what it was, all right. About forty feet tall. Whole, it probably would have been over a hundred and fifty feet long, but it was broken up into two sections at the wing, with a long section in back and a shorter one up front. The whole thing was covered in dirt, vines, and a mantle of rust.

The remnants of a cleared stand of trees lay between us and the plane. It looked like it had been cut down only a year or so ago. I figured that must have been why we hadn't seen the plane the last time we'd come this way. How long had it been sitting there? Fifteen years? More?

I drew the scope down along the length of the plane, marveling at its size, until I came to the tail where I could make out a big white star.

"It's American," I said, lowering the rifle.

Dad nodded. "B-88," he said. "Probably heading to Atlanta. Or Memphis. I don't think it crashed, though — it's pretty intact. Looks like it tried to land and failed. Must have been forced down somehow."

I waited for him to make the next move, but he went silent after that, staring at it. Adults were always weird when it came to talking about the Collapse. Embarrassed, I thought, like kids caught breaking something that wasn't theirs.

"Well . . . we better check it out. Right?"

"Guess we better. Come on."

We got to the plane about an hour later. The two halves sat just feet from each other, like pieces of a cracked egg. The plane's wings were hunched over and crumpled. A bright bloom of flowers had grown up around them, taking root and shining purple in the sun.

I led Paolo over to where he could munch on some flowers and followed Dad to the opening. The plane had split in two just behind the cockpit, which was closed off with loads of twisted metal. To our right was the empty bomb bay. I leaned in, squinting past the wreckage. It was bright at the mouth of the steel cave, but toward the back it grew dark enough that I could only make out a jumble of broken metal covered with dirt and vines and weeds.

"I don't know," I said. "Doesn't look like there's anything here. Maybe we should —"

"It's gonna be fine," Dad said. "We'll make it quick. In and out, okay?"

"We'll need the flashlight."

Dad tugged at the end of his beard, then nodded. I pulled the light off the back of the wagon and rejoined him. There was a narrow

14

catwalk that led alongside the bomb bay to the back of the plane. Dad stepped up onto it and shuffled crablike down its length. I crept along behind him until we came to the remains of a steel bulkhead separating the compartments. It had been mostly torn away, but we still had to crouch down low to get through it.

It was humid inside, and musty smelling. I slapped the flashlight on its side until its beam ran down the length of the plane.

The back section was lined with a series of workstations, alcoves where I imagined soldiers performing their various duties. All that was left of them were welded-in steel shelves and short partitions. All the chairs, electronics, and wiring had been ripped out long ago by people like us. Vines crept up the walls and hung from the ceiling. Every so often some rusty metal lump emerged from underneath the plants, like the face of someone drowning.

"Why would it have been going to Atlanta?" I asked, hoping to drive the eerie silence out of the air. Dad's answer didn't help.

"P Eleven."

I shivered as he said it.

"We tried to quarantine the big cities, but the people inside didn't want to be cooped up with the sick, so the government decided to burn them out."

"They bombed their own people?"

"Didn't see any other choice, I guess. If it got out . . . 'Course, in the end it didn't matter. Got out anyway."

After that first spark the war escalated fast. It was only a few months before the United States launched some of its nukes at China and its allies. P11H3 was what China came back with. Everybody just called it P11 or the Eleventh Plague. It was nothing more than a souped-up strain of the flu, but it ate through the country like wildfire, infecting and then killing nearly everyone it touched. The last reliable news anyone heard before the stations went off the air said it had killed hundreds of millions in the United States alone.

I cleared my throat to chase out the shakes. We had to stay focused on the task. The faster we got done, the faster we'd be on our way. "See anything worthwhile?" I called out.

Dad appeared in the beam of my flashlight, blocking the light out of his eyes with his hand. "Looks like it's been pretty picked over already. Let's check farther back."

We rummaged through the rubble but only found the remains of some seats and a few crumbling logbooks. There were lockers along the walls but they were rusted shut or empty. Useless. It was as though we were wandering through the remains of a dinosaur, picking through its bones.

"Last of its kind," Dad said, patting the wall. "These things went into production right before the Collapse."

The Collapse followed in the wake of P11. With so few people left alive, everything just shut down. Factories. Hospitals. The government. The military crumbled. Power stations blew one by one until the electricity went out countrywide. It was like America had been wired up to one big switch and the Eleventh Plague was the hand that reached up and clicked it all off. Millions more must have died in the darkness and neglect that followed.

"See anything?" Dad asked.

I shook my head. "Nah. Let's get out of here, okay?"

"All right, all right." Dad patted my shoulder as we started back for the bulkhead. "Hey, what's that?"

"What?"

Dad knelt down by a metal locker at my feet. It was partially hidden under the overhang of one of the workstations, right by a small crack in the plane's skin that let in a finger of sunlight. Dad pushed a cover of weeds and dirt out of the way.

"It's just an old locker," I said. "If there was anything in it, someone would have taken it already."

"Maybe they didn't see it. Come here and give me a hand."

I looked up through the bulkhead to the open air outside. We were so close. "It's rusted shut. We'll never get it open."

"We can't get careless when it comes to salvage, Stephen," Dad snapped. "Now come on. Pull on it when I do, okay? On three. One. Two. Pull!"

We threw our backs into it and, surprising both of us, the lid screeched loudly and popped off, throwing us on our butts with a heavy thud.

"Ha! See? Me and you, kid, we can do anything!" Dad pulled himself back up and leaned over the open locker, rubbing his palms together. "So, what've we got here?"

At first glance it wasn't much. Dad handed back a thick blue blanket that was worth keeping. There was a moment of excitement when he found stacks of prepackaged military rations, but they were torn up and past their prime. Worthless.

"Okay. Can we go now?"

"In a second. We —" Dad froze, his eyes going wide. "Oh my God."

I scrambled to join him. "What? What is it?"

He reached deep into the locker and struggled with something I couldn't see.

"Dad?"

His back flexed and he managed to lift whatever it was into the light.

"What is —"

It was a metal can. Not one of the little ones we used to find lining the shelves of abandoned grocery stores, but a big one. Forty-eight ounces at least. Dad turned it around so that the light shone on the label. It read, simply, in black letters: PEARS.

"Fruit," Dad said, his voice thick with awe. "Good Lord, it's canned fruit. Jesus, how long has it been?"

Two years at least. Dad had saved a can of pears for my thirteenth birthday. Since then if we had fruit, it was a runty crab apple or a nearly juiceless orange. My stomach cramped and my mouth watered at the memory of those pears and the sweet juice they sat in.

Dad set the can down between us, then scrambled into his back pocket for the can opener. He was about to crack it open when my hand shot out and snatched his wrist.

He looked up at me, his eyes looking almost crazed. "Steve —"

"We can't."

"What do you mean, we can't?"

"What would Casey give us for this?"

"Stephen," Dad laughed. "Look, I don't know, but —"

"We have *nothing* in that wagon out there. Could we get bullets? New clothes? Batteries for the flashlight?"

"But . . ." Dad scrambled for a defense, but nothing came. His eyes dropped to the can opener, considering it a moment before his hand went limp and it clattered onto the floor.

"I mean . . . we have to be smart," I said. "Right?"

Dad nodded once, looking exhausted.

"You're just like your grandfather," he said.

It hit me like a hammer in the chest. Before I knew what I was doing, I grabbed the can opener and stabbed its blade into the can, working it around. Dad tried to stop me, but before he could, I had the lid off and was tossing it aside. I dug my hand in and pulled out a fat slice of pear, holding it up into the narrow beam of light. It glistened like a jewel. Perfect and impossible.

I paused, my heart pounding.

"Go ahead," Dad urged. "Take it."

The flesh of the pear snapped in my mouth when my teeth hit it. There was an explosion of juice, so much of it and so sweet. I chewed slowly, savoring it, then dug my hand in the can and shoved a slice at Dad before taking another for myself. We devoured them, all of them, grunting with pleasure. There was still some part of me, some tiny voice in the back of my head, screaming that it was wrong, but I kept stuffing pears into my mouth until the mean, raspy voice receded.

We ate all the pears and split the juice inside, then we lay back, our bellies full and our mouths and hands sticky with sweet juice. Dad had this happy, dazed look on his face, and I was sure that he, like me, was replaying the moment over and over again in his head, committing the feel of the fruit in his mouth and its sweetness to memory.

I lifted the empty can into the flashlight beam. Its dusty sides were splattered with congealing syrup. Stray pieces of flesh clung to the insides. Empty, it was as light as air. The dazed excitement of the pears began to fade, and some dark, clammy thing took its place, creeping through me. The sweetness of the pears turned bitter. My mouth ached. In an hour or two we'd be hungry again, the memory of the fruit would fade, and we'd still need clothes, bullets, batteries, and food. Winter would still be coming. I could hear Grandpa's voice as clearly as if he was sitting right next to me.

Stupid. Wasteful.

I wished I could smash the can to pieces on the floor, tear it apart, the metal shards slicing up my hands as punishment for being so thoughtless.

"Where are you going?"

I had climbed out of the plane and was walking down to the end of one flower-covered wing. It had grown darker while we were inside. A curtain of dirty gray clouds blocked out the sun and there was a thick tingling in the air.

"Stephen?"

I picked one of the flowers off the wing's edge and rolled it around in my hand. It left a purple smear of blood on my fingertips.

"We should get moving," I said.

The rusty skin of the plane flexed as Dad leaned against it behind me.

"You ever wonder what's out there?" he asked.

When I turned around, he had his hands stuffed in his pockets and was looking over his shoulder to the west, just as casual as you please. A small range of mountains hung over the woods, gray and misty-looking in the distance.

"I always think maybe there's, like, some quiet place. Somewhere you could build a little house. Hunt. Fish." A dreamy grin drifted across his face. "Maybe even somewhere we could find other people like us."

I kicked at the dirt. "Find slavers maybe. Red Army. US Army. Bandits."

"We've stayed out of their way before."

I shot a sharp look across the space between us. Was he really talking about this? Leaving the trail? I tossed the flower into the grass and worked it into the ground with the toe of my boot.

"We should get going," I said, "and cover some more ground before dark." I tried to push past him so I could gather Paolo, but Dad stopped me, his palm flat in the center of my chest. I looked straight across at him. Now that I was fifteen, I was nearly as tall as he was.

"Listen, it's just you and me now, Steve. Maybe this is our chance."

"Our chance for what?"

"A life. A home."

Our nearly empty wagon and all the miles we still had to cover that day loomed just over Dad's shoulder. I heard Grandpa's voice, the ice-cold rasp of it, clear as day.

"This *is* our home."

I knocked Dad's hand off my chest and pushed past him, ducking back into the plane and through the bulkhead. My knees slammed into the dirt and rust, and I dug around for the flashlight and the can and its lid.

A quiet place. A home. It was a fantasy, same as the helicopter. Dad knew that as well as I did, so why would he even bring it up? What was he thinking? First it was the ring, then the pears, and now this.

I paused, feeling the bitterness of the words turning through my head. Was it true what he said? Was I like Grandpa? Part of me cringed at the thought, but who had kept us alive all these years?

"Stephen!"

What now? I hauled myself up and out of the plane to find Dad squinting off in the direction we'd come from. There was a puff of smoke rising into the air a few miles back.

"What's going — ?"

"Rifle," he commanded. "Now!"

I snatched the rifle off the wagon. Dad raised the scope to his eye and tracked it north across the horizon until he found what he was looking for.

"People coming this way. With a vehicle."

He was trying to be calm, but I knew the hitch he got in his voice when he was scared. No announcement could possibly have been worse. One of Grandpa's absolute, unbreakable rules was that if we saw other people, people we didn't know, we were to avoid them at all costs. Other people meant trouble. Other people with a working vehicle meant even more trouble.

"What do we do?" I asked, my heart pounding in my ears. "Run?"

"We're on foot. They'd be on us in a second."

"So what, then?"

In answer, Dad grabbed Paolo by his reins and drew him around to the opposite side of the plane, out of sight. He tied his lead to a jutting piece of metal and told me to get our backpacks. I grabbed them and followed Dad into the plane.

"All the way to the back," he said, pushing us past the bomb bay and again through the bulkhead. We stumbled into the last of the stripped workstations and crouched down. We were hidden but still had a straight view through the bulkhead and to the rent in the plane ahead.

"We'll wait them out," Dad said, stuffing our packs behind us. "They'll probably do just what we did — look around and head on their way."

"But what if they don't?"

"They will," he insisted.

My chest seized with nerves. I knew he was only trying to make me feel better, but he was no surer than I was.

I swallowed hard. "You're right," I said. "You're right. They will. They'll just go right on by."

But then it started to rain.

THREE

It came lightly at first, finger taps, barely noticeable, but within minutes it was a real storm. Rain slammed against the roof of the plane. Wind howled through it. We were crouched down behind the workstation, legs cramping and hearts pounding.

"Maybe they rode by us," I said.

"Would you? In this?"

There was a flash of lightning and thunder that made both of us jump, and the rain seemed to double in power in an instant. Back where we were a steady but light spray of water squeezed through the tiny cracks in the airframe, but it was a waterfall up by the opening. Water crashed down in a bright curtain and coursed down the floor of the plane, pooling at our feet and surrounding us in a cold, oily muck. I peeked over the edge of the partition, pushing a wet strand of hair out of my face. My eyes had adjusted to the dimness and I could see the entrance to the plane clearly. Nothing there.

"It's okay," Dad said. "I think they really did go —"

The waterfall split in two as the barrel of a black rifle pushed through and scanned the interior. I jerked back but Dad took my elbow, steadying me. We were about a hundred feet back and hidden. With the dark and the rain, it was a safe bet they couldn't see or hear us. Still, my hands quaked as the rifle eased forward and two men came in behind it. One man held the rifle while the other followed with what I first thought were horse's reins. As he stepped farther inside, I saw what was really at the other end.

The reins ran from the man's hand to cuffs around the wrists of a boy and a woman, and then up to thick collars on their necks. The two captives moved with the fearful slowness of people who expected to be beaten.

"Slavers." Dad spat it out, like the word itself was foul.

If there was any group we avoided the most, it was them. Some were ex-military, some were just brutal scum. We saw them skulking around the edges of the trade gatherings like a bad disease. They mostly kept to themselves, but as far as we knew, they ranged throughout the country taking whoever they could and selling them to scattered militia groups, the few surviving plantation owners down south, or even the Chinese.

The man with the reins pointed for them to go sit up against one wall, then tied the reins to the edge of the bomb bay. The woman and the boy never raised their heads to face him, never spoke, just shuffled to their places like broken animals. The slavers situated themselves in a dry spot in the bomb bay. One of the men pulled the cap off a flare and the entire plane exploded in a flash of red light. Dad and I ducked down behind the partition until the light lowered and we smelled the smoke of a small fire.

It was still dark where we were, so I took a chance and peeked around the edge of the partition. The men were gathered around their fire with a deck of cards and a bottle of liquor. Their clothes looked military to me. One was black with long dreadlocks and a thin beard.

The other was white and immense, with bull-like shoulders and a jagged scar that ran from his temple down his cheek, disappearing at his jaw. It glowed pale in the firelight.

Dad was up on his knees beside me. His eyes were narrowed and his lips were a tense line, but it wasn't the slavers he was watching.

The woman and the boy were illuminated by the ragged edge of the fire. It magnified the hollows of their eye sockets and the cruel thinness of their birdlike arms. The woman had scraggly hair and was wearing a short white dress that clung to her. She was so thin I could see the shadows of her ribs. The boy was smaller than me, barefoot, and wearing torn-up jeans and a filthy T-shirt. Across from them, the men drank and played cards, their laughter mixing with the driving rain and peals of thunder.

Dad was holding the rifle just below the edge of the partition, gripping it so tightly his knuckles were white as bone. His finger was on the trigger.

I grabbed his wrist. "We don't get involved," I whispered. "Grandpa said —"

"Grandpa is gone," he hissed.

I glared down into the cold muck, my arms wound tightly around my chest. We needed to stay right there, still and quiet, until the rain passed and they were all gone. The woman. The boy. We didn't know them. They weren't our responsibility.

Dad pulled the rifle back and huddled behind the partition with me. "I'm not saying we fight them," he whispered. "They're drinking. We give them time to get drunk and pass out. When they do, we untie the woman and boy on our way out and let them go. That's all."

Dad's hand fell on my shoulder, but I pushed it away.

"I know what Grandpa would say," Dad said. "But we don't have to be like him. Not if we don't want to."

I peeked around the dripping edge of the partition. The boy tried to squirm his way deeper into the crook of the woman's arm, but since her hands were tied, she couldn't comfort him. She let her head fall back against the wall. Her mouth hung open and she stared upward, blankly. The boy fell across his own knees, his spine sticking out like a range of knobby mountains.

A spark of anger flared inside me. If we had ignored the plane, or if we had just taken that can and gone, we would have been setting up camp miles from here. Dad would be cooking dinner and I'd be brushing Paolo, getting ready for the next day's hike.

"Stephen . . ."

Anger was a compact burning thing in my stomach. I prayed he knew what he was doing.

I nodded. I couldn't bring myself to speak.

After that, all we could do was wait.

FOUR

Once the men fell asleep Dad and I slipped on our packs, then unfolded ourselves from behind the panel. It helped that the rain hadn't slacked off. The constant thrumming echoed through the metal coffin of the plane, helping mask our movements.

We crept across the uneven floor, squeezed through the bulkhead, and emerged on the other side. As we moved into the firelight, the woman nearly gasped, but Dad held up his hands to show we were no harm. She glanced over at the sleeping men. For a second I thought she was going to warn them, but then she sat back and watched us through narrowed eyes. Dad slipped his hunting knife out of its sheath and handed it to me. Then he turned and leveled his rifle at the sleeping men.

As I approached, knife in hand, the boy woke with a start. His eyes were as big as lily pads. I put my finger to my lips to quiet him, then slipped the blade under his bonds and cut them. He rubbed his wrists and stared up at me blankly.

"They won't let you get away with this," the woman hissed. "They won't let you take us."

"We're not taking you," I said, sawing through the leather reins that bound them to the plane. "We're freeing you."

The woman actually laughed. It was a dreadful, breathy thing. "What do you expect us to do? Just run out into this storm? And then what?"

I glanced out the opening. The whole world was a gray mass of pounding rain and wind. She was right. They wouldn't get far. And as weak as they looked, even if the slavers never caught up to them again, they were as good as dead. I turned to Dad. His brows furrowed as he searched the muck at his feet for an answer.

"But if we had their jeep . . ."

I turned. The woman was pointing to where the black man lay sprawled out by the dwindling fire. A ring of keys was clipped to one of his belt loops.

"If you really want to help us," she said, "we need the keys."

I shook my head. If she thought we were getting any closer to those men than we already were, she was insane. I was about to signal that we should go, but by the time I did, Dad was already slipping the rifle over his shoulder and crouching down into the mud.

"Dad, no."

He waved me off. There was nothing else I could do. Any more and I'd wake them. I had to stand there and watch as Dad crept closer to the sleeping men. The black man's chest rose and fell as he snored. The fire crackled. Dad halved the distance between them before his foot hit some debris and he pitched forward. I gasped, but he got his hand up on the wall just in time to stop himself.

Dad took a shaky breath, then another painstaking step forward. He was less than a foot away now. The fire was bright red on his face, and his wrinkled forehead glistened with sweat. Slowly, painfully, he knelt down. Thunder boomed overhead and he froze for a second, looking at the man's face, studying it for any hint of consciousness. When he saw none, he reached his hand out little by little until the tips of his fingers brushed the metal keys, then crawled up their length toward the clasp. My stomach was a knot. Dad pinched the clasp open gently and then slowly, achingly slowly, he pulled the keys away and they fell into his palm. My heart leapt.

"Put the keys down."

The man with the scar was up on his knees. An enormous gun grew out of his hand and was pointed directly at Dad's head.

"Now."

Everything was deadly still for a split second, but then Dad jerked to one side, tossing the keys at me as he did it.

"Run!" he shouted.

I scrambled to catch them but the woman sprang up behind me and pushed me down, snatching the keys out of the air. There was a *boom*, deafening in the steel walls of the plane, as the man's gun rang out. Thank God he was drunk. The bullet missed Dad by inches and slammed into the ground.

Dad scrambled toward me as the black man woke and pulled his own gun out of its holster. The slavers slid out of their places, weaving in their still-drunk state. Dad didn't say a word. He leveled the rifle and fired, its report pounding at my ears. The bullet went high, ricocheting with a wet-sounding *ping*. The men stumbled backward, surprised.

"We don't want any trouble," Dad announced.

"They're ours," the man with the scar slurred in a deep Southern accent.

Dad kept his voice level. "Not anymore."

The slaver laughed. It sounded like a landslide, boulders tumbling together. He slapped his partner in the chest and they got on their feet and came toward us.

"Get back," Dad commanded, backing up and jutting the rifle out in front of him, but the men just laughed and kept coming. They must have heard the fear that had crept into his voice. They saw us for what we were. We were no heroes.

I backed out of the plane. The woman and the boy were already gone. As I stepped outside the slavers' jeep was revving up and pulling away.

"Wait!" I screamed, but the woman didn't even look back as she took off with the boy beside her. Red taillights glowed in their wake.

Dad tumbled out of the plane and fired two more shots over the men's heads, sending them ducking inside. Then he turned and headed toward me.

"Run," he called. "Go!"

The two slavers emerged from the plane behind him.

"Dad! Look out!"

Drunk or not, the man with the scar moved fast. He was on Dad in a second, grabbing the top of his backpack and yanking him backward. Dad lost the rifle and his pack, but he whipped around and threw a punch that glanced off the man's head. It didn't do much damage but it knocked him back, into the mud. The black man came at him now.

Dad turned and screamed, "Just go!" as the man slammed into his back and they hit the ground, grappling in the mud. The man with the scar was coming at Dad from behind so I scooped up the rifle and swung it by the barrel like a club. The heavy stock struck him on the back of the head and sent him down again.

Dad reared back and threw a solid punch to the black man's face, dropping him into the mud with his partner.

"Run!" Dad yelled again.

We took off, blind from the pounding rain that turned the world around us a featureless gray. Paolo brayed as we passed him. There was no other choice. We'd have to come back for him. We'd never escape with him in tow.

I couldn't tell if the men were chasing us or the woman, so I just ran, cradling the mud-covered rifle in my arms, desperately trying to keep up with Dad, who was little more than a flickering shadow darting ahead of me. The thunder pounded constantly, atomic blasts of it, following blue-white flares of lightning. Every time, I ducked instinctively, like I was expecting a shower of shrapnel to follow.

Who knows how long we ran, or how far. At some point I crashed into what felt like an oak tree. I tried to dodge around it, but then I looked up and saw it was Dad.

"Do you see them?" He had to lean right down by my ear and shout for me to hear him at all.

"I can't see anything!"

Dad turned all around, sheets of water coursing off his head and shoulders. I wanted to scream that it was pointless, that we needed to keep running, but then there was another flash of lightning and a *crack*, and for a second it seemed like there might be a ridge of some kind out ahead of us. Dad grabbed my elbow and pulled us toward it.

"Come on! Maybe there's shelter!"

By then, the ground had turned to a slurry of mud and rocks and wrecked grass. Every few steps my feet would sink into it and I'd have to pull myself out one foot at a time, terrified that I'd lose sight of Dad and be lost out in that gray nothing, forever.

As we ran, the ridge ahead of us became more and more solid, a looming black wall. I prayed for a cave, but even a good notch in the rock wall would have been enough to get us out of the rain and hide until morning. We were only about fifty feet from it when Dad came to an abrupt halt.

"Why are we stopping?!"

Dad didn't say anything, he simply pointed.

Between us and the ridge there was an immense gash in the earth, a gorge some thirty feet across and another thirty deep, with steep, muddy walls on our side and the ridge on the opposite. A boiling mess of muddy water, tree stumps, and trash raged at the bottom.

Dad searched left and right for a crossing, but there wasn't any. His shoulders slumped. Even through the curtain of rain I could see the sunken hollow of his eyes, deep red-lined pits that sat in skin as gray as the air around us.

"I'm sorry, Stephen. I swear to God, I'm so sorry."

I reached out for his arm, to tell him it was going to be okay, that we'd be fine, but before my fingers could even graze his soaked coat, the ground beneath his feet disappeared. What was solid ground turned to mud in an instant and he went flailing, flying backward. There was a flash of lightning as he fell, arms pinwheeling, his mouth open in a shocked O. There was nothing at his back but thirty feet of open air and, beyond that, the bared fangs of a raging river.

When the lightning subsided, he was gone.

FIVE

I didn't think, I just jumped, sliding down the muddy wall, then tumbling end over end when it collapsed beneath me. I hit a small piece of ground at the bottom, a tiny shore, and pulled myself up out of the mud.

"Dad!" I screamed, searching the river and the opposite shore for some sign of him, but it was useless. "Dad!"

Another lightning flash and I caught a glimpse of something large in the water, moving fast downstream. I tugged off my pack, stripped down to my shorts and T-shirt, and dove in.

The icy water ripped the breath out of me as soon as I hit it. I had to struggle to move and get my blood flowing again. It took all my strength to stay focused on the big shadow in the water downstream and avoid the outcroppings of rock and the logs that shot by. I knew it could have been anything — a tree, or a clot of mud and rock — but I dug my arms hard into the cold water, praying, pulling for it.

I was only a few feet away when a flash of something dark and a thrashing arm shot up out of the churn. *Yes!* I stabbed my arms into the water and managed to get ahold of the collar of his coat. I pulled him to me but only had him for a second before we slammed sideways into a rock jutting out of the water. Dad shot away again headfirst down the river. He wasn't moving. His body was limp, tossed about and swept away by the current.

The cold sank deeper into my body, seizing on my muscles, paralyzing them. I let out a scream and pushed off the rock I was stuck on, thrashing through the water. A surge in the current rocketed me forward. I was almost on him. I reached, missed, then reached again, feeling the barest whisper of his coat against my fingertips. The third time I caught him.

I scrambled forward, catching hold of his shoulder, hooking my arm under his armpit, and dragging him to me. Soaked with water, he was incredibly heavy. The current tried to suck him away and under, but I managed to draw him to my chest and kick off toward a shallow area at the edge of the river. I kicked and kicked, dragging us toward the shore, pushing Dad ahead of me and then climbing out after him.

I turned him over onto his stomach and leaned over him, putting all of my weight into his back, hoping to push out whatever water was in his lungs. He was bleeding from the back of his head. Thick clots of blood pooled at the base of his neck and then washed away, misty red in the rain. I was pretty sure his right arm was broken in more than one place, maybe a leg too. I turned him over onto his back. His skin was a ghastly blue-gray in the low light. His mouth was hanging open. A voice in my head, Grandpa's sandpaper rasp, told me he was dead.

I laid my ear up against his mouth and listened as hard as I could, clapping my hand over my other ear to block out the rain. At first there was nothing, just empty silence, but then there was a flutter, and the slightest rise in his chest. He was alive!

I pulled him farther from the edge of the water, his waterlogged clothes adding twenty pounds or more. The muscles in my arms and back and legs howled, but I made it to the ridge and found a deep depression in the rock. It wasn't as good as a cave, but it would have to do.

I dragged Dad in and laid him on his side in case he started throwing up water. I thought about trying to go back for our stuff. There were some medical supplies on the wagon — bandages, antiseptic — but God knew how far away it was, and the storm, if anything, was getting worse. Instead, I pushed myself into the hollow beside him.

Blood was pouring out of the gash on his head. I tore off my T-shirt and ripped it into strips with my teeth and used them to pack off and bind the wound, trying my best to ignore the soft broken feel at the back of his skull. My breath froze in my chest as the blood advanced through the cloth, eating through several layers before finally stopping and holding still. I breathed again.

I wanted to do something about his arm and leg, but what they needed was some sort of splint. That clearly wasn't possible, so I had to let it go. They looked bad, but not life threatening.

My biggest problem was the cold. The depression we were in only gave us a bit of shelter from the wind and the rain. There was no brush to pack around us and no possibility of a fire. I wasn't sure if it was cold enough to kill us, though I suspected if it fell another five to ten degrees during the night, it might be. I strained, trying to think of some other option, but finally had to admit that there was none.

I sat up with Dad all that night, clutching him to my chest and fighting the waves of exhaustion that threatened to drag me under. I couldn't sleep. I couldn't leave him alone. As the lightning slashed the dark and the rain poured around us, all I could think about was the bear.

I was seven. We were camped in dense forest way up north at the Canadian border, a day or two from the Northern Gathering. The trees in Canada were the biggest I had ever seen, standing close together in impenetrable ranks with thick, nut-brown hides and a tangle of branches and leaves that nearly blotted out the sun.

I didn't plan to wander off, but when we got to our campsite and Mom, Dad, and Grandpa began setting up, I saw a robin at the edge of the clearing. It flew off as I approached it but I kept on going, drawn toward a pile of smooth rocks or a splash of sunlight on the pine needle–covered ground. It was a beautiful morning, cool and misty, with only the first stirrings of animals to keep me company. Before I knew it the forest had closed behind me and I was alone. I wasn't scared. It was thrilling being off the path. I dodged through the trees, down a hill, and deeper into the woods. It grew dim and hushed all around, the air full with the smell of decaying things.

It wasn't long before I found the video game. It was one of the big stand-up ones that Dad said they used to have in arcades when he was a kid. It was sitting at an odd canted angle, half on, half off a thick tree root that had sprung out of the ground. It said MORTAL KOMBAT on its side and was covered with colorful pictures of gigantic men and women in masks grappling with one another. The paint was peeling off in places, revealing a rusty metal surface underneath. Who knew how it got there? We ran into things like it, strange misplaced relics, from time to time.

I crunched through fallen leaves and up onto a little metal step at the bottom that raised me higher so I was face-to-face with the machine. Mom said she had played these constantly when she was a kid, before her parents finally broke down and bought her a home system. Down by my knees were two slots for coins. I reached into my pocket and mimed dropping two in, then started jerking the hand controls around, imagining the characters fighting it out at my command, making the sounds of punches and kicks with my mouth.

Bam. Bam. Baf. Crash. Ugh!

Leaves crunched behind me.

A twig snapped.

My hands froze on the controls.

I saw his outline first, a great looming thing reflected in the glass of the game. When I turned, the bear was maybe fifteen feet away, staring at me through the low tree branches, his mouth hanging open, teeth glistening. I guessed he had to weigh five hundred pounds or more. The bear's head was lowered, his brown muzzle thrust out at me, sniffing. His blank black eyes were fixed at the center of my chest.

I thought my heart would crack a rib the way it was pounding. The thing lumbered forward, slow and awkward as a nightmare, until he halved the distance between us.

He was close enough now that his breath, smelling like the humid rot of a swamp, struck my chest like an open palm. His black-spotted tongue lolled around in his mouth and over the peaks of his fangs. The bear reared back, then opened his maw and roared. It went on and on and the sound of it, so close, dropped me to my knees in the grass. Everything inside me, everything I had ever felt, or thought, or hoped for, was pushed aside like a river tearing away soil and grass and trees, leaving only bedrock.

The bear raised one paw to close the remaining distance between us when an explosion rocked the air. The bear flinched, whipped its head backward, and roared, but then there was another explosion and the bear crumpled into a heap at my feet. His lungs filled once and then collapsed with a slow whine.

Someone was racing through the woods toward me, but I couldn't look away from the bear. I had never been so close to something so wild, yet so still. I reached out, brushed my hand along the rough grain of his fur, and started to cry.

Dad dropped to his knees beside me. The barrel of Grandpa's rifle was still smoking as he wrapped his arms around me, pulling me tight to his chest. I could feel his own heart pounding.

"You're safe," he said over and over, rocking me back and forth and crying too. "I'm here, Stephen, and you're safe. You're safe."

Safe.

The war of rain and lightning and thunder hammered on throughout the night. I looked up at the gorge's edge high above us, but I knew that no rescuer would appear. There was no one left.

There was only me.

I wrapped my arms around Dad as tight as I could, shivering, hoping our little bit of body heat would be enough to keep us alive until the rain stopped and the sun rose.

It had only been twenty-four hours since Grandpa died.

SIX

When morning came, the storm had passed. In its place was a bright day with a blue sky. Dad's eyes were closed and his mouth was hanging slightly open. I put my ear down to his mouth and waited. At first there was nothing, but then I made out his slow, ragged breathing. I sat back, relieved.

His lips were horribly dry and cracked, so I went down to the river and brought back as much water as I could in my cupped hands. It was dark and silty and I knew it could be polluted, but what choice did I have? I knelt down next to him, awkwardly trying to keep the water from spilling, then leaned forward to trickle some of the water down into his mouth. I stopped before the first drop fell.

Can he swallow? Or will the water just make him choke?

My hands and back cramped as I leaned over him, indecisive. It was too much of a chance. I splashed the water onto the rocks, then sat down with my back to him, facing the river, stewing with frustration.

Grandpa always said that a good plan will get you out of anything. But what plan could I make? I was at the bottom of a gorge with thirty-foot walls. Even if I could get out, where would I go? Back to the plane?

Certainly the slavers would have taken anything worthwhile that we left.

If Grandpa had been alive, or if Dad had been awake, then maybe we would have had a chance. They were the ones who came up with the plans. They were the ones who knew what to do. I just did what I was told. I ached for things to be the way they were.

I lifted my head out of my hands and watched the river course by, carrying with it leaves, trash, and shattered logs. A current of broken bones and tattered skin. I thought again of that day with the bear and the crack of Grandpa's rifle.

No one is coming. If I do nothing, we die.

I managed to push Dad to the back of the little cave, out of the glare of the sun. Then I knelt down beside him.

"I have to go," I told him, clinging to his arm. "But I'll be back, okay?"

I found my clothes, backpack, and the rifle at the base of the gorge and waded across the river to get them. After I washed the mud off my clothes, I put them back on. The rifle was caked with grit, useless. If I could find the cleaning kit back in our wagon, then maybe I could get it working again. I dug inside my soaked pack and lifted out my three books. Each was swollen to nearly double its size. Just touching the waterlogged paper caused it to slough off like dead skin.

My eyes burned, but I wouldn't cry. Not over that.

I threw the books aside, located my fire starter at the bottom of the pack, and stuck it in my back pocket. The wall was higher than I remembered, its face made of mud and half-dried dirt. Outcroppings of rock and tree roots sprouted here and there. It was so steep I got dizzy just looking at it.

I jammed my hands and feet into the mud and started, painstakingly, to pull myself up. For every two feet of progress I made, I'd slide at least a foot, but I didn't give up. I kept one of Grandpa's commandments running in my head the whole time. Food. Water. Shelter. Fire. That was all that was important. Find these things and live. Don't, and die.

Panting, I clawed my way to the top, then pulled myself over.

The land we had crossed the day before, with its carpet of sparkling grass and flowers, was now a plain of mud strewn with branches, rocks, and dead leaves. It was like the end of the world had returned, eager to finish its work.

I didn't know how far we had come or in what direction. The plane could have been anywhere. I started by walking directly away from the gorge and then, pretty sure that the ridge we saw the night before had always been on our right, turned so it was on my left and kept going. The sun dried my clothes until they became stiff and scratchy. I walked until I wanted more than anything to sit down and never move again, but there was something in me that kept going, no matter how much I wanted to stop.

Finally a dark shape appeared far up ahead. Through the rifle's scope I could see what I was sure was a wing emerging from the mud. It was still a mile or so off. I dropped my head and pushed on, trudging toward whatever small salvation might be there.

When I reached the plane, the first thing I did was check for Paolo. He was gone, of course. Only a few scrap pieces of leather and brass from his tack remained.

I squatted and held his reins in my hand, rubbing my finger over the rough surface. Mom had found him on an abandoned horse farm and we'd nursed him back to health. I wondered if the slavers had taken him or if he'd freed himself in the storm somehow and had gone looking for us. That idea of Paolo lost, wandering about in the storm hoping to find me and Dad, made me feel like I was drowning.

Our wagon was smashed to pieces. All that remained of our things were a few useless pieces of metal and a big water jug I knew would be too heavy to take back to camp. I took a long drink, then stepped carefully inside the plane, where, after digging around for a few moments, I found Dad's knife and slipped it underneath my belt.

Dad's pack was half buried in the mud outside. Luckily the waterproof bag where we kept our first-aid kit, water purifying tablets, and extra rounds for the rifle was intact. I pulled all of them out along with some beef jerky and the gun-cleaning kit. I tore off a hunk of jerky and muscled it down my throat. Even though it hit my empty stomach like a ball of lead, it made me feel solid and awake for the first time that day.

Before I closed up Dad's pack, I reached down to the bottom and hunted around until my fingers closed around the only photograph we owned. I pulled it out into the sun.

It was of me and Mom and Dad. There was a stand of trees behind us and, towering above it, the bright red tracks of a roller coaster, twisting like the unearthed skeleton of a dinosaur, and a sign that said WELCOME TO SIX FLAGS GREAT ADVENTURE! We were all grinning. I was maybe seven or eight, leaning against Mom's legs, her small hands resting lightly on my shoulders. She was caught mid-laugh, pretty and young-looking in her blue coat, her tree-bark curls poking out from the big straw hat she sometimes wore. Her cheeks were bright and rosy from the cold. Dad was next to Mom giving a goofy double thumbs-up to the camera.

The way the shot was framed, you could barely tell that the roller coaster was half covered in rust, only a few years away from collapsing, or that the rest of the amusement park was a no-man's-land filled with wild, rabid dogs.

It was taken as we'd traveled toward the Northern Gathering. This seedy little guy had been wandering around with an old camera, one of those automatic ones, the kind that develop the pictures themselves. He was making a small living trading pictures for food and supplies, trying to make as much as he could before the batteries or the film ran out and he'd be unable to replace them.

I traced my finger around Mom's face and then around the outline of us standing together, a cloudless blue sky behind us. I liked to imagine that the picture had been taken before the Collapse, that we were just a family taking a trip out to the amusement park where we would ride rides and eat popcorn, our laughter rising into the sky like balloons. At the end of the day we'd drive home in the gathering dark and I'd fall asleep, my head cradled in Mom's lap, her fingers lightly brushing the hair back from my forehead.

But then, as always, I looked down, just to Mom's left under the Six Flags sign. A couple years later, Dad and Grandpa would dig two graves there, one large and one small, while I watched.

There was a sudden, sharp pain in my left hand. When I opened it, a line of blood trickled down my wrist and dripped onto the ground. In the center of my palm there were four half-moon-shaped cuts from where my nails had dug into the flesh. I wiped the blood on my jeans and put the picture safely back in the pack. As I walked away from the plane, I stuffed my left hand deep down into my pocket, as though I was scared someone might see.

It was late afternoon by the time I got back to the gorge, loaded down with supplies and whatever little bits of wood I could find for a fire. Dad hadn't changed much. His breathing was shallow but regular. The first thing I did was unwind the T-shirt bandage around his head and check on his wound. The gash along the back of his skull still seeped blood, but slower than it had last night. I pulled some antiseptic out of the first-aid kit and smeared it over the wound, then packed it off and bound it with some clean bandages. Again I felt the shifting, broken feel at the back of his head, the bone plates sliding against each other, but there was nothing I could do about that.

I arranged the bits of wood and kindling I'd found but paused before lighting them up. We were on fairly open land. The smoke would go up like a beacon, visible to anyone for miles around, but I didn't see a choice. The wet and chill could kill us.

The fire I got going was smoky at first, but finally a decent flame started. I stripped off my clothes, then Dad's, and hung them from a crack in the rock wall by the fire to dry. I huddled up as close as I could to the flames. It was amazing how much difference being warm made. I cleaned and loaded the rifle until the stars emerged and spread across the sky.

It was quiet then, just the crackle of the fire and the soft ripple of the dwindling river below. The world felt enormous and as empty as a dry well. In my mind I ran through a picture show of campsites we had stayed in over the years: the mall in Virginia, the gas station in South Carolina. I finally settled on the cracked parking lot of a Kroger supermarket in Georgia. The last time we'd been there, years ago, daisies had begun to burst through the concrete. I imagined there were fields of them now. I saw myself unpacking our camp, laying out our bedrolls, and gathering wood for a fire while Dad fed Paolo and then got our dinner together, humming as he did it.

I sat for a while in that fantasy until darkness began to seep into the picture around the edges and I felt low and cold. My clothes were mostly dry by then so I dressed and turned to Dad, his clothes in hand. When I saw him there, still and broken on that rock, it was like a wave hit me out of nowhere.

Why did we have to help those people? You said nothing would change. You promised!

I snapped my left hand closed, urging my fingers deep into the half-moons. A sharp thrill of pain shot up my arm and chased the thoughts away, clearing my head. Blood ran down my hand, but I didn't care. The pain was a relief. It was easier.

My head fell back against the rock and my eyes closed. I was exhausted but I wouldn't let sleep come. *What now?* I thought. I had supplies. Dad seemed stable, but I couldn't feed him or give him water. I looked up at the gorge wall, black against the gray night sky, and my heart thrummed against my chest.

I have to get us out of here. But how?

After I got Dad dressed again I reached behind me and drew his arm over my head and down across my chest, holding on to it tightly, nestling my head into the crook of his elbow. I sat that way for a long time, shivering, until my eyes closed and I slipped off into sleep before I could stop it.

I don't know how long I slept, but it seemed like only minutes before I snapped awake to a soft shuffling sound from above us. I closed my eyes, trying to listen past the crackling of the fire.

Footsteps on the ridge above us.

Men. Four, maybe five, creeping along the shore of the river down-stream with one on the ridge. They were moving slowly and not talking.

My hand fell to the stock of the rifle.

Slavers.

SEVEN

Of course. Grandpa had told me a hundred times. Fuel was incredibly scarce so people who had vehicles never went far from the central place where they stored it. Dad and I had wandered right into the slavers' territory, stirred up a hornet's nest, and didn't even know it.

Seeing no other choice, I left Dad for an outcropping of rock a few feet upstream. I was too exposed with him. From where I was, I had a good view down the gorge and, since the fire was still going, anyone coming from downstream would be distracted by it and not see me. I pulled my boots on and checked the rifle. One round in the chamber and six more in the magazine. Despite the years of attempted training by Grandpa, I knew I wasn't a very good shot. I aimed the rifle downstream and waited, hoping that I could at least scare them off.

The men in the gorge materialized out of the darkness. Three of them. Creeping shadows, sweeping their guns back and forth. My hands grew slick on the rifle's stock. The cuts on my palm stung.

The man in the middle stepped into the outer circle of our firelight. He knelt down next to my backpack and started to go through it, balancing his shotgun on his knee, finger on the trigger. He wasn't one of the two from the plane. He was older, Dad's age maybe. The two others stayed hidden in the shadows behind him. After the man went through my bag, he looked to his left and that's when he saw Dad. He signaled to his friends, then brought his shotgun to his shoulder and crept toward the cave. The other two followed.

I brought my rifle over the lip of the outcropping. Icy sweat was pouring down my face and arms. The leader of the slavers set his gun down and reached out toward Dad. I had his back squarely in my sights, but I was paralyzed, too afraid, too uncertain, to act. I was seven years old again, on my knees before the great brown bulk of that bear, waiting for someone to appear and make it all go away.

But then there was a voice in the back of my head. Dad's.

You're not seven years old anymore, it said, *and you're not helpless.*

The pounding in my chest slowed. Suddenly everything seemed clear. I clicked the rifle's safety with my thumb, then stood up behind the rock and squeezed the trigger twice. My ears rang as the shots echoed off the canyon walls. The bullets slammed into the dirt inches from the leader's feet.

The three men jerked away from Dad, the man in the middle yelling at them all to run. He and one of the others scrambled into the shadows along the wall of the valley, but the third one, a tall skinny one with a flash of yellow hair, stepped forward and raised his rifle. I fired. I was sure I'd missed until I saw his leg buckle and he went down. Winged him. Just enough. He staggered back to the shadows but collapsed before he made it there, hitting the ground right behind the fire.

Shots came from my left, over by where the other two had ducked into the shadows. One bullet struck the wall behind me, sending a rain of gravel down over my head, and the other slammed into the dirt in front of me. I dropped down behind the rock.

"Jackson, no!"

I raised the rifle just as someone came out of the darkness downstream, running to the man on the ground, a rifle in his hand. I leveled the scope. His face was round, unlined, beardless, and framed in a tangle of reddish curls. The ground beneath me pulled away and I went icy inside.

My God. He's younger than me.

Sand crunched behind me.

I spun around. The last thing I saw was the wooden stock of a rifle flying toward the side of my head.

EIGHT

"I don't *care* what Caleb Henry would say."

"Marcus —"

"He's just a kid, Sam. He's not a damn spy."

I woke up the next morning to voices I didn't recognize. My head was pounding. My hands and feet were tied with lengths of rope. Three men were standing by the side of the stream with their heads down, talking low and passing around a bottle of water. My rifle was on the other side of the camp near Dad, who was in his place at the mouth of the cave, unmoved. I shifted my weight quietly and sat up, my head swimming as I did it.

"How do you know that?"

"We're half a day from home, Sam. If they're spies, they're the worst damn spies I've ever heard of. Besides, he could have killed Jackson and he didn't. He had him in his sights."

"That doesn't mean —"

"Look at them, Sam. What would Violet say? What would Maureen say, if she was still with us?"

They weren't slavers, I was fairly sure. Farmers maybe, traders, or — who knew? — maybe even salvagers like me and Dad. The man who'd gone through my backpack the night before stood in the center of the group. He was compact, bald with a band of messy black and gray hair around the sides. Next to him was the man he called Sam, a black man in his fifties who wore a sweat-stained New York Yankees ball cap and had a heavy belly and a thick mustache.

The kid I'd almost shot was next to him. He was heavyset with a pinched, worried-looking face. He kept his head down and his arms crossed over his chest, not meeting anyone's eye.

Whoever they were, I didn't know what they intended to do with me and, like Grandpa always said, if they weren't family, they were trouble. I scanned the ground around my feet and found a rock about the size of a small apple that came to a brutal point at one end. I leaned forward, slipped it into my palm, then pushed myself backward until I was up against the wall of the gorge.

The kid nudged the leader. "He's awake."

The bald man was about to step forward, but the one I had shot, a teenager with a shock of golden hair that fell over his eye, appeared out of nowhere.

"Who are you?" he spat. "What are you doing here?" I gripped the rock in my fist, ready to defend myself, but the bald man pushed him out of the way.

"He's just a kid, Will," he said. "Not much younger than you. Now step back and let me handle this."

"We oughta string him up, right here and now, Marcus."

The bald man, Marcus, looked around the bare walls of the crevasse. "String him up from *what*?"

"Marcus —"

"No one is getting strung up," Marcus said sternly, which only enraged Will more.

"He shot me!"

"He *grazed* you, Will," Sam said. "You were barely bleeding. You're not even limping."

Will ignored him and kept after Marcus. "He's a spy for Fort Leonard! They both are! When I get home, I'll tell my father. I'll tell everyone!"

Marcus took a step closer to Will until their chests were almost touching. Marcus was actually an inch or so shorter, but he had shoulders like a buffalo and something deep and forceful in him.

"Tell them anything you want, Will, but for right now, shut the hell up. You're giving me a headache."

The black man laughed at that, a booming "Ha!" that caused Will to shoot him a deadly look before he sneered and, with a chuckle, shook his head in a snotty attempt at saving face. In the end he skulked away downstream, kicking a charred log from the fire with his bad leg. Marcus turned his back on Will and squatted down in front of me. I jerked away instinctively.

Marcus held up his hands, palms out. "It's okay," he said. "Don't mean any harm. Will there's daddy owns a lot of cattle and things. Sometimes he thinks that means he's next in line to a throne we all keep trying to tell him doesn't exist."

Marcus smiled, obviously trying to put me at ease, but I just stared at him, turning the rock around in my palm.

"Looks like Sam gave you a hell of a knock there."

"Sorry," Sam said in a deep Northern accent. He dropped his paw of a hand on the kid's shoulder. "Couldn't let you shoot Jackson here. We've just gotten to like him."

Jackson shrugged out from under the man's hand, embarrassed. "Sam . . ."

"What do you people want?" I asked.

Marcus dropped his grin. "I'm Marcus Green," he said, then pointed to the kid who stood shyly in the background. "That's my son, Jackson. His highness there is Will Henry. Sam Turner's the man who gave you that tap on the head."

"Howdy," Sam said.

Marcus looked back at Sam. Something passed between them that ended with Sam looking off after Will, then nodding. Marcus slipped a hunting knife from a sheath on his belt.

I flinched backward, ready to swing the rock as best I could, but Marcus held his hands up again to steady me, then began sawing at the ropes around my wrists. I watched him carefully, even as the ropes popped open and he started on the ones at my feet.

"That your dad?"

Marcus waited, but I said nothing. Grandpa always said you should never tell anyone anything they didn't need to know.

"Well, whoever he is, he looks like he's hurt pretty bad."

Marcus looked up at me as he worked, like he was taking my measure. He was trying to talk himself into something, and the fight was going back and forth. When the ropes snapped under his knife, he glanced back at Sam again. Sam hesitated, then gave a reluctant nod.

"We can help you," Marcus said under his breath. "We have a town. It's not too far. My wife, Violet, is a doctor. Not one of those drunks running around claiming to be a doctor either — she's the real thing. Army doctor before the Collapse. We could bring you both back to town with us and she could take a look at your dad."

He was lying, of course. If they had medicine, why would they waste it on some guy they didn't even know? Still . . .

"I don't have anything to trade," I said.

"We're not asking for anything," Sam said. "Just offering our help."

I scanned their faces, searching for some sign of the deception I knew had to be there. But I wasn't Grandpa; I didn't have his eye. Whatever they wanted, whatever they were planning, I couldn't see what it was.

Not that it mattered. Small towns had begun to pop up in the last few years, but Grandpa had always kept us away from them. They were nothing but muddy collections of tumbledown shacks, he said, that stank of people living too close together and bred smallpox and dysentery. Besides that, they were targets for every slave trader, scavenger, or bandit around, like nails begging to be hammered down.

"We just want to be left alone," I said squarely to Marcus. "We can take care of ourselves."

"You sure?" Marcus asked.

I nodded. Marcus signaled to Jackson and he stepped forward, his eyes on the ground in front of me. He handed Marcus a small cardboard box, then retreated to the stream's edge.

"Looked like you were about out," Marcus said, handing me the box. "You take care of yourself now. Sorry for the trouble. We're heading west if you change your mind."

They gathered up their things and turned to head downstream. Jackson lagged behind them, and for the first time that morning, he raised his eyes to meet mine. His were light blue and big and, like a doe's, smart and skittish at the same time. He looked like he had something to say.

"What?"

Jackson shook his head. "Nothing. Sorry." Then he turned and followed the others out of our camp.

Only when they were out of sight did I reach for the cardboard box and open it up. Inside were four rows of five gleaming silver-jacketed bullets, set tip-down in a piece of white foam. I pulled one out and rolled the cold metal between my fingers. They were much newer than the ones we had, probably made right before the Collapse.

Footsteps clicked against the rock, echoing down the walls of the gorge, growing softer each second. It wouldn't be long until Dad and I were alone again.

With Dad the way he was, I'd never be able to get us out of there. I closed the box of bullets and struggled to my feet, my head pounding.

I knew that what I was doing was wrong. If Grandpa had been around, he'd have had a better answer, but he wasn't. It was just me.

"Marcus!" I called out as I ran down the shore. "Sam! Wait up!"

PART TWO

NINE

We headed west for the rest of that day, tumbling through the yellow grass just below a heavily cratered highway. A thin sheet of clouds, like dirty cotton, was smeared across the sky.

They had me wear a bandanna over my eyes all morning so I wouldn't know the path they were taking, but they let me take it off by the time the sun was halfway into the sky. Not that it mattered much. I had never been so far west in my life and had no clue where I was.

Marcus led the way with Jackson bringing up the rear. I was with Dad in their wood-slat wagon, sitting behind Sam and Will. Lying across from us was a buck Marcus said he'd shot earlier that morning. I tried not to look at it. Its stillness and empty, glasslike eyes caused something inside me to quake.

I scanned the area around us for salvage, eager for something familiar, but there was nothing useful on the path, just blowing trash and a few distant billboards and road signs.

I huddled down behind the front bench of the wagon and tended to Dad. He was lashed to a driftwood stretcher that Sam had improvised to get him out of the gorge. I raised his head into my lap and poured some water over his lips to wet them, careful that none of it went down his throat. I made sure Sam and Will were focused on the road, then took his arm in my hand and squeezed, praying that if some part of him was still awake he'd feel it and know I was there.

Jackson had abandoned his position as rear guard and was trailing along behind the wagon, his rifle too big for him and cradled awkwardly in his hands.

"You know, my mom's real good," he said. "Last year she fixed my friend Derrick's broken arm."

He waited for a response, but I ignored him, turning my attention back to Dad. I was relieved when Jackson finally let the wagon pull away. I couldn't seem to look at him without seeing his face framed in my scope the night before. The memory of my finger tensing on the trigger felt cold and dark inside me, like a stone at the bottom of a well.

"Hey, look at that!" Will called out, his golden hair fluttering in the wind. We were rolling past an island of gas stations and fast-food restaurants off the highway north of us. An Applebee's sat in the center of it all like a faded king, its red, white, and green striped awning in tatters. A pack of dogs, razor thin and rabid, was in the parking lot, snarling as they fought over bits of trash. "Looks like some friends of yours!"

"Will," Sam warned.

"No, seriously. Bet they even smell the same, like a mix of dead horse and an outhouse."

Will had raised holy hell when Marcus and Sam had told him I was coming, yelling about outsiders and spies and how I'd tell everyone where their town was.

"Guess they don't have bathtubs in Fort Leonard, huh, spy?"

I gritted my teeth. I didn't know what Fort Leonard was, or why he thought I was some sort of spy for them. I knew I should ignore him like

I'd ignored Jackson, but I found my fingers curling around the handle of Dad's knife instead.

Will was about to start up again when the wagon slammed to a halt, tossing him back into his place at the front. "Ow! Sam!"

"Oh gee, sorry, Will."

Sam turned and gave me a mischievous little grin as Will righted himself, cussing and spitting.

Marcus came striding back from his place at the head of the group, wiping sweat off his bald head with his sleeve. I hid the knife under my coat before he could see.

"It's time," Marcus said, and dropped a red bandanna on the wood rail at my shoulder — we must have been getting close. The whole thing seemed pretty ridiculous, but Marcus was nice enough about it, so I went along.

As I was about to tie on the bandanna again, I caught Jackson staring at me. He held his rifle tight to his chest, his arms straining, his finger along the trigger guard. His face had gone stony. Confused, I followed his eyes down to my lap and saw that my coat had brushed open, exposing the weapon in my hand. Our eyes met before his darted away, but in that second I saw that he was afraid. I eased the knife back into its sheath before tying the blindfold around my eyes, feeling strangely satisfied to be the one causing fear instead of the one feeling it.

The air grew steadily cooler and twilight settled around us. After a while, we came to a halt, and Sam and Will piled out of the wagon. There were shuffling footsteps and low voices up ahead, then the sound of something large brushing against the ground. I slipped the bandanna up over my eyes while their backs were turned and caught the four of them moving aside a group of small trees and brush to expose a rough path cutting into the woods ahead of us. Clever. I raced to pull the bandanna back down before they returned.

It was colder and darker in the woods. We were surrounded on all sides by creaking branches and animal calls. It was another hour or more of bouncing travel before we moved out onto open ground, where we flew downhill before coming to a stop.

There was a pause, then Sam loosened the knot of my blindfold so it fell to my shoulders.

We were at the bottom of a grass-covered valley, surrounded on all sides by deep forest. Ahead of us was a white stone wall that cut across the entire valley like a bright line of snow, with a heavy double iron gate at its center. Two words were engraved in deep letters on the white wall: SETTLER'S LANDING.

After Marcus opened the gates, Sam shook the reins and we rolled through. The gates made a rusty clank and then a deep final boom as they closed, hemming us in. A nervous flare bit through me. For a panicked moment, I wanted to leap out of the wagon and run. I took Dad's arm tight in my fist.

What have I gotten us into?

On the other side of the gates, the grass turned into black asphalt, not at all the cracked, bomb-ravaged stuff most highways had become, but smooth and neat, snaking away down the hill. The horses' hooves clicked as we followed it. The trees on either side of the road filtered the dying rays of sunlight so that they fell on us in shifting patterns of small shadows. It was achingly quiet. As we got farther in, I caught flashes of black and white and bright, unnatural colors peeking out through the trees.

I was about to ask what they were but before the breath could leave my lungs the first house emerged from the trees. It was set back about a hundred feet from the road, two stories, with bright yellow on top and brick on the bottom, the whole thing circled by a wide porch the color of beach sand. Glass glittered in the window frames and there were brass fixtures on the doors and casements. In front of the house, a man in a sweater and jeans was raking up leaves from the lawn. He waved as we passed.

"Better close your mouth before a bug flies in," Sam said to me as he waved back.

Will snickered. "It's like the spy's never seen a house before."

It was true. I hadn't. Not like this anyway. Grandpa said that in the days of P11, people tried to escape the disease by barricading themselves in their homes, praying it would pass them by like an ill wind but it rarely worked. Somehow the plague always slipped in, under the doorways or through the windows like a mist, and killed them as they lay in their beds or sat at their dinner tables. Grandpa said that people used to think their home was their castle, but the Eleventh Plague made them all tombs. Every house I had ever known stank of rot, desperation, and fear. I didn't go anywhere near them.

But these . . . They were like a nest full of bird's eggs, painted pale pink or blue or a green that was like the color of sun-bleached moss. Some even flew crisp-looking flags from their porches that fluttered and snapped in the breeze. I tried to find some flaw, some sign that this place had been through the same history that the rest of the country had, but I found, unbelievably, nothing. Part of me wondered if I was actually still lying with Dad at the bottom of that gorge, starved and delirious, imagining all of it.

"You all right back there, son?" Sam asked.

I nodded dumbly as he turned the wagon onto a side road where a green and white street sign said SETTLER'S LANDING TERRACE. The road led downhill to a two-pronged fork. Where the roads diverged was an open area like a park. It was grassy, with a few trees and low bushes scattered here and there. In the center were two large swing sets, a slide, and a big jungle gym made of multicolored lengths of steel tubing.

Sam pulled on the reins and brought the wagon to a halt in front of a white house north of the park. He looked around at the other houses and cleared his throat — nervously, I thought. Sam had agreed to bring me here, but he was worried about it, not as sure as Marcus that it was a good idea. It made me wonder again what I had gotten myself into.

"Okay," he said. "Here we are."

As soon as we stopped, Will jumped off the bench and leaned over the side of the wagon. "Don't get too comfortable, spy," he hissed. "They may be fooled, but I'm not. This is *our* town. I'll make sure you're not here long." He laughed, a self-satisfied little chuckle, then took off down the road.

"Will, you should let Violet look at that leg," Sam called, but Will didn't even turn back. His grievously wounded leg seemed to be causing him no trouble at all. Sam shook his head. "You ready?"

Sam offered me his hand but I ignored it and dropped onto the asphalt. Marcus had gone ahead into the house, so Sam and I lifted Dad out of the wagon before Jackson led the horses away. Dread settled over me as I followed Sam up the white house's stairs. The door seemed like a great set of jaws, ready to swallow me whole.

"You okay?" Sam asked.

"Fine," I said, sucking back the fear so he wouldn't see. "Let's go."

I held my breath as we stepped inside. I had never seen anything like the room we were in. It had clean white walls, a brick fireplace with an only slightly cracked marble mantel, and scuffed wood floors. All of it was lit with candles and small oil lamps that cast a dim amber glow. It smelled of sweet wood smoke and somewhere, faintly, what I thought was baking bread.

"Set him here."

Sam pointed to a cot just under a window beside the front door. We got Dad off the pallet and onto it just as Marcus hurried into the room from another part of the house, a small woman with curly black hair following him.

"This is Violet," Marcus said.

The woman pushed through us, snapping on a pair of latex gloves as she came. "What happened?" Her voice was sharp and flat as a shot.

"He fell," I said.

Violet dropped down by Dad's side. "How far?" When I didn't answer, she turned back. "How far?"

"I don't know. Ten, twenty feet? He was in the water and hit his head."

Violet gently slid her fingers behind Dad's head and closed her eyes, concentrating. "More like thirty feet, I think. He lost consciousness immediately?"

"I don't know. I think so."

Violet went to a wooden cabinet along the wall and pulled open one of about ten narrow drawers. Inside I saw rows of small glass bottles with white labels. Gleaming silver instruments lay beside them. I tried to get a better look, but Violet selected a few instruments, then snapped the drawer closed and came back to Dad's side.

She worked quietly, listening to Dad's heart, checking his temperature, pulling back his eyelids to stare into his eyes. Her movements were quick and precise but never rushed, as though she was moving methodically through some checklist in her head. Even when she unwrapped his head and the blood began to flow again, she didn't panic. Instead, she grabbed some clean bandages and went to work.

I couldn't watch. The way she poked and prodded at him made me feel sick and hot. I turned away; outside the window, I could see a group gathering in the park, a small assembly of women and children in old jeans and flannels. Some were tending the beginnings of a bonfire, while others set a collection of torches into the ground and opened up a large plastic folding table.

"It's Thanksgiving."

I turned to Marcus and Sam, standing behind me. "What?"

"Today," Marcus said. "At least we think it is. Anyway, that's what we got the deer for. Couldn't find a turkey. We're putting together a barbecue tonight out in the park. Why don't we all go? Violet will come get us when she's done."

I shook my head and turned back to Dad. If they thought I'd leave him alone so easily, they were crazy.

"Look, there's really nothing you can do here. Why don't we —"

"Marc, maybe it's better if he stays inside for the time being. Right?" Sam said it gently, but there was a trace of warning there.

"Why don't you go on ahead, Marcus?" Violet said. "You too, Sam. We'll be okay here."

"Vi —" Marcus started, then pulled back. "You sure?"

Violet examined me over her shoulder. Her lips lifted into a thin smile beneath her blue eyes and pink freckles.

"You're not going to be any trouble, are you?" she asked.

The way she was leaning over my father — was it a threat? His life was in her hands. I shook my head slowly but didn't speak.

"Okay," Marcus said, backing away from me. "Come on out if you get hungry."

Violet waved Marcus off over her shoulder, then the front door opened and shut again.

"Sit down if you like," she said.

I didn't move.

In the stillness of the room, I was aware every time Violet's instruments clanked together. I looked over to the mantel, where there were two rows of framed pictures. The frames were whole, but the pictures inside them were discolored, torn in places, and repaired. One showed a family, tanned and smiling and trim, posing on some tropical beach in front of a huge white boat, while another was of a mother and father sitting in lawn chairs out in front of a dilapidated trailer, a baby in an old stroller beside them.

"Those are our folks," Violet said as she worked. "The poor rednecks are mine. Marcus's are the ones with the yacht. I think they actually owned that island."

Looking at the faded pictures of their long-dead families, a chill moved through me.

"What's your name?" Violet asked, but I glared at the floor. "There's no harm in telling me your name. Unless you're Rumpelstiltskin, I guess. Are you Rumpelstiltskin?"

"Is he going to be okay?"

"Why don't you sit down? We can —"

"Just tell me when we can leave." My voice echoed in the small room, but Violet acted like she barely even heard me. Her flat expression never changed.

"Your dad's right arm and leg are broken in multiple places; so are a few ribs. He's dehydrated. He has what I think are infected cuts in various places. The worst of it is he took a pretty good blow to the head, enough to crack his skull. That put him in what people call a coma. That's when —"

"I know what a coma is. When will he wake up?"

Violet's eyes never wavered from mine.

"It could be five minutes from now," she said. "Or it could be five years. Or it could be never. I won't lie to you. In the old days there'd be more we could do. More tests so I could be sure. But now . . . it's serious. The head injury is bad, but those breaks could cause trouble too."

It was like she wasn't even speaking English, just voicing a twisted jumble of sounds. A dark weight settled on my chest, pressing down on my lungs. I felt sick. My head swam.

Violet took a breath, about to say more, but was interrupted by a pounding at the front door. She set her hand on my back as she passed by me and went to answer it. When the door opened, I caught a glimpse of an older man standing outside, tall and craggy looking with shining white hair.

"What were you two thinking?" he demanded as he tried to push his way in.

"Caleb, I don't have time to —"

"Where's Marcus?"

"He's getting the barbecue ready. I'm with a patient."

"That's exactly what I want to talk about. Will —"

The man started to force himself inside, but Violet planted her hand in the center of his chest and pushed him out onto the porch.

"If you want to talk, we talk outside."

Violet slammed the door behind her. The two of them were just outside the window, but I couldn't understand what they were saying. The man towered over her, beginning to shout, trying to intimidate her, but Violet didn't give an inch. She argued him down the stairs and out into their front yard.

I looked from the window down to Dad, and that's when what Violet said hit me. It was like I was in the middle of the ocean and my hands had slipped off the side of a lifeboat. I sucked in a deep breath. I had to be calm, like Grandpa. Strong, like Grandpa. This was reality, and I had to deal with it. How I felt wasn't important. My fingernails dug into my raw palm.

I stuffed my hand into my pocket as the door opened again. Violet swept in and went directly to the wooden cabinet. She drew something out that I couldn't see, then returned to Dad's side.

"That was Caleb," I said. "Will's father."

"That's right," she said.

"He doesn't want us here."

"I think that's putting it mildly."

"He's why Sam wasn't sure I should come here."

Violet looked at me steadily but said nothing.

"What did you tell him?"

"I told him that if my family wanted to share our home and food with you, it was our business." I watched as Violet lifted a needle into the candlelight and filled it with liquid from a small bottle. "But that I definitely, without a doubt, wouldn't use any of our medicines."

Once the needle was full, Violet flicked it with her finger, then slid it into Dad's arm and pushed the plunger. When she was done she turned back to me.

"What he doesn't know won't hurt him," she said with a wink. "These are antibiotics, in case there are infections and to protect against pneumonia." Her brow furrowed. "He needs blood thinners because of the breaks but . . . we ran out months ago."

"Why are you helping us?"

"When I was in med school," she explained, "one of my teachers told me that my only job was to treat the patient in front of me. He said I couldn't change the world, I could just treat what's in front of me."

Over the next hour or so, Violet fed Dad with a plastic tube threaded down his throat and then made some plaster and set his arm and leg in a cast, struggling to make the shattered bits of bone line up and lock into place.

I fell into a chair behind her, sinking into its deep cushions, while outside it slowly grew dark. A bright orange glow rose from the park. Maybe fifty men, women, and children converged around the bonfire. It had a large roasting spit built over it that Marcus and Sam were tending, turning the big deer around and around over the flame.

A string of about twenty small torches was set in the ground around the perimeter of the group, making flickering islands of light. The people milled around, laughing and talking, swimming in the glow.

"Who are you people?" My voice sounded strange and distant, like pieces of wreckage bobbing along on dark water. "What is this place?"

Violet smoothed a length of plaster-covered cloth across Dad's knee, then gave me a kind and soft smile over her shoulder.

"There'll be time for explanations later," she said. "I'll be done soon. When I am, we'll get you cleaned up, and then I should get you something to eat."

I shook my head. Violet persisted, but I didn't move. I wasn't being taken away from Dad.

Outside the window, people moved dreamily around the playground. Groups came together and apart, only to re-form again like beads of oil on water. All of them talking, hugging, throwing their heads back to laugh. All of it an eerie dumb show, silent to me in the house.

Violet continued working and I closed my eyes, surprised to find sleep overtaking me. I fought it for a moment, but it was too strong, too long in coming. I just prayed my dreams would find me back out on the trail with Dad, crashing through the grass with Paolo behind us, Dad talking a mile a minute, me bringing up the rear.

When I finally did sleep, though, I dreamed I was walking through the woods alone, late at night, my every step mirrored by an immense shadow with claws that lumbered by my side.

TEN

When I woke up, Violet was gone and there was a gnawing emptiness in my stomach. I couldn't even remember the last time I had eaten. As I sat up, I saw a note sitting on a table near Dad.

We're all at the barbecue. Come out and have something to eat when you get up. — Violet

Outside, the party had gotten smaller, but a group of twenty or so still milled around the fire.

There was some jerky in my pack, and maybe a few crumbs of hardtack had made it through. That would do. I looked around the room, but then remembered with a jolt that in my hurry to get Dad inside, I had left the pack outside. I could see it peeking over the lip of the wagon. Grandpa's rifle leaned against it. The realization that I had left them both sitting out there in the open made me forget my hunger for a moment. I could feel the sting of the beating Grandpa would have given me if he had seen. *Stupid.* I wished I could just make my bed on the floor next to Dad and go to sleep, but I couldn't leave my gear out there for anyone to take.

I struggled out of the chair, kneeling at Dad's bed on my way to the door. The dirt and splashes of blood that had lingered on his face were gone and his skin wasn't quite the waxy mask it had been. I tried to tell myself that he didn't look any different than he ordinarily did when he was asleep, but there was a stillness there, an absence that seemed vast. I squeezed his arm and leaned down next to his ear.

"I'll be right back," I whispered before stepping outside.

The hairs on my arm lifted in the cool air, and the spicy smell of wood smoke and roasted meat made my stomach roar, pushing the last remnants of sleep out of my head. I crept down the stairs and across the yard, easing up to the wagon, hoping not to be seen. When I got close enough, I drew my bag toward me. Unfortunately I forgot that Grandpa's rifle was leaning against it, so as soon as I pulled the pack away, the rifle fell with a clatter. My insides jumped.

"Hey."

I looked down. Jackson and two others were sitting near the wagon's tires, a litter of plates and half-eaten dinner all around them. There was a skinny kid with big glasses and another larger kid with thick curly hair. All of them were staring at me, three pairs of eyes burning in the dark.

"You get something to eat?" Jackson asked.

I clutched my pack to my chest. "I have food."

"We've got venison," Jackson said. "And some potatoes Derrick's mom made."

"They suck," the big kid, Derrick, said.

The kid with the glasses was sitting on the other side of Jackson. "My mom brought her blueberry pie," he said, which for some reason caused the big kid with curls to shoot him a leering grin.

"Oh, I *bet* she did, Martin," he said.

"Shut up, Derrick! That doesn't even make sense!"

"Oh yeah? You want to know what makes sense?"

"Oh, I don't know," Martin said. "My mom?"

Jackson pushed Derrick away and stood up by the wagon. "Ignore Derrick. He's obnoxious. You should stay and have some food."

"I'm fine."

I shouldered my pack and reached for the rifle, but before I could get away, Derrick leapt in front of me and started doing a spastic shuffle, jumping up and down and throwing his arms around at his sides like he was having a fit. I took a step backward.

"Uh . . . Derrick?" Jackson said, stepping up to my side. "What are you doing?"

"Well," Derrick said, panting, "I figured, uh, maybe the problem was that he didn't feel entirely at home yet, so I thought I'd perform the Settler's Landing Dance of Welcoming."

"You look like you're having a seizure," Martin said drily.

Derrick cackled and threw himself into the air, which I guessed was his big finish, since when he landed he swept his arms out in front of him and took a deep bow. Martin clapped sarcastically and Jackson laughed. When Derrick stood up again, he somehow had a plate of venison and potatoes in his hand. Where it came from, I had no idea, but when he held it out to me, the smell of it almost made me faint.

"Eat," he said. "Eat, my new and tiny little friend."

"What do you care if I eat or not?"

Derrick's grin froze.

"Just being friendly, man, that's all. You want it or not?"

I was about to turn and run back up the stairs into the Greens' house, but my hands moved before the rest of me could. Before I knew it, I had snatched the plate from him and dug my fingers into the pile of meat. It was rich and gamey and seeped into every part of my body.

I gulped it down, and when it was gone, I scooped up the potatoes and devoured those too, sucking the remains from my fingers. When I was done, I had to gasp for air. Jackson and the others stood there, jaws wide.

"Uh . . . you want us to go kill you something else?" Martin asked. "I think we have a horse that's lame."

Embarrassed, I pushed the plate at Derrick and grabbed the rifle out of the wagon. "Thanks," I mumbled.

"Hey, it's no problem, man. I'd do anything for the guy who shot Will Henry."

I turned, glaring at Jackson. "They know about that?"

Jackson flinched. "I—"

"Relax," Derrick said. "We just wish your aim had been a little better."

"Hey, you coming to school with us tomorrow?" Martin asked.

I looked at him, blank faced, sure I hadn't heard him correctly.

"School. You know. Teachers. Books." Derrick whacked Martin in the stomach. "Girls in tight sweaters."

"You all go to school?"

"Sure! How else are we going to get into a good college?"

The three of them laughed, but I didn't get it. The way they talked, like they were tossing a ball around in a game of keep-away, was confusing.

"So you wanna come?" Jackson asked.

I looked over my shoulder at Dad's window and shivered at the thought of him lying in that tomblike quiet. What if he woke up and I wasn't there? I shouldered the rifle and backed away from the three of them without a word.

Derrick called after me. "Okay! Take it easy. Come back anytime!"

Jackson pushed Derrick hard on the shoulder, knocking him off balance.

"What? I was being nice!"

"You were being a spaz."

I left them bickering, getting halfway across the road, when Marcus spoke up from behind me.

"Everyone? Everyone, can I have your attention please?"

Marcus was standing by the fire with Violet at his side, waving everyone closer together. Caleb Henry loomed in the background.

"Just for a second. Thanks, everybody. Um. I just wanted to say it's great that we could all be here like this tonight. It's Thanksgiving today, uh, we think, and I'm sure most of us remember that from back when we were kids. Every year we'd gather the whole family and spend the day together, eating and watching football and arguing."

"Was this back on the yacht, Green?" someone called, and a laugh rose up from the group.

Marcus chuckled. "Well, wherever it was, I don't remember ever feeling closer to my family than I did right then. And I don't think I've ever felt closer to all of you. We've done great work in the past year, haven't we?"

There was a general murmur of agreement from the assembled, a scattering of applause.

"New wells were dug, the crops came in a bit better than expected, and everybody's house is ready for the winter. But most of all, another summer has gone by and we're all still here, together and safe. We're lucky. Damn lucky, I think."

Just then Caleb edged Marcus out of the way and came forward. His face looked even rougher in the firelight, creased like an old map.

As soon as he stepped up, everyone went quiet. Caleb looked from person to person grimly, then began a prayer. Everyone lowered their heads as he spoke. His voice was dark and sharp.

"Lord, after the flood, many of us believed it would be the fire next time. All of us here saw that fire, and thanks to your grace we were among the few who found their way through it. As we struggle to please you, we are beset on all sides by those that would tear down all that we have built."

As Caleb spoke, his blue eyes searched the crowd. I wondered if he was looking for me.

"Today we give thanks and reaffirm that the price of your gift is vigilance and obedience to your will. Amen."

The crowd murmured "Amen" and then someone at the back of the group began singing a song that I didn't recognize at first. "Oh, say, can you see, by the dawn's early light . . ."

Even Jackson and his friends joined in. Some of the adults laid their hands over their hearts. I remembered it then from the few times Grandpa had sung it when he was drunk. The American national anthem. What were they singing that for?

"What so proudly we hail —"

"Leave me alone!" someone shouted.

The singing stopped and the group turned as one body to a mass of shadows that was swirling at the edge of the park.

"Oh no," Jackson said from behind me.

Derrick barked with laughter. "Here comes the show, ladies and gentlemen!"

As the group turned more into the light, I could make out a kid standing in the center of a circulating mob of five or six others, all of whom were jutting in and out at him like crows after a scattering of seed. The kid in the center was thrashing hard and had already put two kids on the ground, one clutching his knee to his chest, the other cradling his jaw. A third boy got up his courage and went in, only to get a kick between his legs that put him down howling.

"Nice one!" Derrick shouted.

"Stop it!" Marcus hollered as he rushed toward the scene. "Stop this right now! Jennifer!"

Jennifer?

Marcus grabbed the arm of the kid in the middle to pull him out of the melee. To my surprise, it wasn't a boy at all, but a black-haired girl of about sixteen, dressed in dirty jeans and a loose blue-and-red flannel shirt. As she stumbled closer to the firelight, her tan skin glowed like bronze. Marcus pulled her back just as she was going after one of the boys who was stupid enough to have gotten up off the ground.

"What have I told you?" Marcus yelled as he pulled her away. "What have I told you about fighting?"

The girl didn't argue with him, and instead took the time to kick one of the remaining boys firmly in the calf.

The group of adults broke up as Marcus came charging through with her in tow. Some of them went to pull their wounded sons off the ground and others gathered in a tight knot around Caleb Henry, sternly watching the proceedings and whispering among themselves.

As Marcus and the girl came closer, I got a better look at her. She had broad shoulders for a girl, inky black hair, and dark, almond-shaped eyes.

Chinese, I thought, gripping the stock of Grandpa's rifle. They were all supposed to be west of the Rockies. *What is she doing here? With them?*

"You could have walked away," Marcus said.

"And let them call me a murderer and a spy? Let them call me a Chink?"

"They're just words."

"They're just words to you!" she screamed, yanking her arm out of Marcus's grasp and stalking away. "I didn't start any damn war!"

I tensed up as she came toward me.

"Jenny!" Marcus called. "We'll say something. I'll talk to their parents!"

"Forget it. Just forget it!" Jenny stomped toward the wagon, her face screwed up in rage.

"Hey, Jenny, how's it goin'?"

"Shut up, Derrick!" she said, then whipped her head my way. "And what the hell are *you* looking at?!" she snapped as she shot past me.

Jenny tore across the park and into the Greens' house and returned several moments later with a big bag slung over her shoulder.

"Jenny!" Marcus barked. "Don't you just walk away! Jennifer Marie Green!"

She whirled around to face him. "It's Tan! My name is Jenny Tan!"

Jenny ran up the road, disappearing into the darkness. It was quiet then, like the aftermath of a storm. Most of the other parents had drifted off, injured sons in tow, leaving Caleb Henry and his grim circle.

"Beset on all sides," Caleb intoned, looking from the Greens to me. His blue eyes reflected the twisting fire. "Even from within."

Marcus was about to say something back, but Violet appeared at his shoulder and he swallowed whatever it was. Caleb grinned wolfishly, satisfied, and drifted out of the group, his followers trailing behind him like smoke.

Marcus stood in the middle of the road, his shoulders slumped, his hand clasped on the back of his neck. Violet rested her hand on his arm. He looked up wearily and nodded.

Jackson was sitting against the wagon. His knees were drawn up to his chest, head back, staring blankly up at the stars. I would have thought he was praying, except for how his hands were curled into bone-white fists. He saw me and forced a smile.

"Welcome to Settler's Landing."

Soon the park emptied and I followed the Greens inside.

"Jackets on the rack, everyone," Violet announced as we entered. Jackson and Marcus dutifully obeyed, stripping off their coats and hanging them just inside the door.

"If I don't keep at them, they're pigs," she said. Once Violet got me settled in the room with Dad, she disappeared into the kitchen with Marcus.

I stood by Dad's bed, pulling my thin blanket out of my backpack.

"Sorry for all that tonight," Jackson said from the doorway behind me. "You can pretty much bet that if Jenny sees calm water, she'll throw in the biggest rock she can."

"She's your . . . sister?" I asked, still amazed that a Chinese girl lived with them.

"Adopted, yeah. I was little, so I don't really remember, but Mom said we went through this town the day after some big fight and there she was, wrapped in this old Chinese army jacket she always wears. She was all cut up and bloody. Mom figured whoever her parents were must have left her, thinking she was a goner, or maybe they got killed themselves. Anyway, Mom fixed her up and took her along with us."

"So how does she know her real name is Tan?"

Jackson laughed. "She doesn't," he said. "That's the thing — she just made it up. Guess that's how much she didn't want to be one of us. Anyway, she'll go sleep it off in this old barn she goes to, out north of town. She'll be well rested and ready to embarrass us again soon enough."

I rolled my sweatshirt up into a pillow and laid it out on the blanket. Jackson stood behind me a little while longer, then stepped back into the hallway.

"Well . . . anyway, good night," he said.

Soon I heard the creaking of stairs and the soft shutting of a door. I blew out the candles scattered around the room and the house settled into darkness.

Even in the dark, Dad's skin was powdery and pale against his beard. His cheeks were sunken and there were hollows around his eyes. He looked like a stranger. An aching homesickness shot through me. There was so much that was new: these people, this place. I wished we could be back on the trail, just the two of us.

I closed my eyes, praying I'd drift off immediately, but of course I didn't. In fifteen years I had spent the night in tents and caves and abandoned buildings but never once in a house. I couldn't breathe. I wrestled the window over Dad's bed open, letting in the rhythmic chirp of crickets and the blow of the wind rustling through the trees.

Across the park, the other houses loomed in the moonlight, their unlit windows like blank, staring eyes. Looking at it all made me feel the whole Earth tilting underneath me. Every other time in my life when I felt like this, I would go to Dad and it seemed, with just a wave of his hand, he could make things right again.

Before I went to sleep, I leaned over his chest, straining to hear the soft pat of a heartbeat, but what was there was too soft and too far away to grasp.

I was on my own.

ELEVEN

I woke with a start before dawn, disoriented. But soon the memories of the day before fell into place and everything began to clear.

The house was quiet. Dad hadn't moved.

I pulled my blanket aside and rubbed the sleep out of my eyes, wondering what I was supposed to do next. No salvage to secure, no trail to start down. I felt like some great wheel was spinning inside me, but it had nowhere to go.

I slipped into my jeans and moved through the downstairs rooms, exploring. I found a sharpened stub of a pencil and an old nickel lying in a dusty corner and pocketed them. Other than that, there wasn't much I hadn't seen the night before. A few pieces of furniture. The pictures. The big wooden cabinet.

I froze, remembering the glass and shining metal, and how Violet had shut the drawer so quickly, like she didn't want me to see inside. I closed my eyes and listened to the house. Nothing. I slipped over to the cabinet and opened the top drawer. Inside there were gleaming rows of silver instruments: razors and scissors, picks and tweezers. I lifted out a large saw with brutal teeth. I set it down and moved to the next drawer.

There, lying on strips of green felt, were the rows of frosted glass bottles. They all had white labels, with words like MORPHINE and PENICILLIN written on them in precise black letters. Marcus said Violet had been an army doctor. I guessed maybe she had done a bit of salvaging too before the military broke up. Whatever the case, it was a gold mine. For a fraction of what was in that cabinet, we could get a new wagon and mule, maybe even a horse, and enough supplies to get us trading again.

A spring squeaked upstairs, followed by the sound of feet hitting the floor. I scrambled to make sure everything was in its place and then shut the drawers. When the Greens came downstairs, I was sitting innocently at Dad's side.

"How we doing this morning, Aloysius?" Marcus asked. He was standing in the doorway that led back to the kitchen, munching on a hard-boiled egg. He had a bowl of them in his hands.

"Who's Aloysius?"

"You are," Marcus said. "Well, at least until you tell us your real name." Marcus held the bowl out to me. "Egg?"

I hesitated for a second, but then the hunger took over.

"It's Stephen," I said as I plucked an egg from the bowl.

"You think about what you'd like to do today, Stephen?"

I glanced out the window. It was a bright fall morning, crisp. A full moon still hung in the sky, fading as the sun rose. Every part of me yearned to be out of the stifling closeness of the house.

"I should just stay here," I said. "With my dad."

"You sure?" Marcus asked. He gave me a moment, then turned back toward the kitchen. "Okay. Suit yourself." His boots echoed down the short hallway.

"Wait," I called before he could disappear. "Maybe . . ." My mind spun in place. Wouldn't Grandpa have given me a pounding if he knew

I was in a place like this and didn't take the time to do a little recon? I mean, who knew what else I'd find? "For all you've done for us . . . I can't pay you, but maybe I could work."

"I told you, there's no reason to —"

I turned my eyes from the window and set them on Marcus, unmoving. It was a look that, when Grandpa used it, said there would be no compromise, no discussion. To my surprise, it actually worked.

"Well, there's a little of the fall harvest left," Marcus conceded. "It's not much but —"

"It's fine," I said. A buzz of excitement lit through me. Just the idea of being out in the open air was a weight lifted off my shoulders.

"Vi!" Marcus called into the kitchen. "Gonna take Stephen out with me to the harvest."

"Who's Stephen?"

"Aloysius."

"Oh! He should rest!" she yelled back.

"Can't! Says he has to be our indentured servant."

"Okay, well, have him clean the gutters while you're out."

Marcus laughed. "Come on. I promise you, though, you'll regret this."

I pulled on my boots and coat and tucked a piece of jerky into my pocket for later. I started to follow Marcus but stopped at the foot of Dad's bed. Violet had removed the feeding tube from the night before, so he almost looked like he was just sleeping, his hands resting atop the clean white sheet. Could I really leave him here with these strangers? Then I remembered how Violet had cared for him, even defying Caleb to do it. I leaned down by Dad's ear quickly, so Marcus wouldn't see. "I'll be back," I whispered.

Marcus grabbed his coat off the rack by the door and then I followed him outside.

The second I stepped out the door I felt like I could breathe again. As we made our way deeper into the neighborhood, kids of all ages blew past us carrying salvaged backpacks and carpetbags. Groups of girls would meet up on the road and separate into age groups, the younger ones squealing and hugging, the older ones trying their best to seem unimpressed. The boys pushed one another, braying laughter loud as donkeys. I flinched as they thundered by and disappeared down a hill that dipped into the trees a few houses from Marcus's.

"Heading to school," Marcus said. "Welcome to join them, you know."

I shook my head at the thought of being shut up inside some room with the screeching horde. I could only imagine what Grandpa would say about running off to school when there was work to be done.

I cracked the egg Marcus had given me and ate it as I scanned the roadside and the yards along the way, looking for treasures like the ones in the Greens' house, but found little. The place was amazingly neat; only a few scattered toys lay about here and there, abandoned as kids raced to school. The houses, though . . . what was in all of these houses?

"Listen," Marcus said, stuffing his hands into the pockets of his jeans. "Sorry about Will and all. What are ya gonna do? Last month he accused Winona Lee of being a Fort Leonard spy. She's eighty-three."

"What is Fort Leonard anyway?" I asked. "Another town?"

"Barely. It's a little settlement that popped up to the north. The map says it's near a place called Fort Leonard. People have a bee in their bonnet since somebody saw a scout poking around east of here the other day. That's who we were out looking for when we spotted you and your dad."

I nodded, but didn't really get it. They brought me and Dad in, two complete strangers, when they were supposed to be out looking for a spy?

The houses thinned out and then the land opened up into five large fields that stretched out about as far as I could see. Most were barren at this point, but the closest one was still full of rows of thick green sprouts. A dozen or so adults circulated around them.

"Well, here we are," Marcus announced. "The land of plenty! Whole thing used to be the town golf course. Took us almost the whole first year to clear the ground. 'Bout killed us all, but it was worth it. We bring in a decent amount of wheat and corn and beans now. People mostly raise vegetables in their backyard gardens. Hey, Sam!"

Sam waved from where he was kneeling down in the rows of plants.

"We owe it all to Sam, actually. His people were farmers way back. He told us what was what."

Sam tipped his hat at the compliment. Marcus held out a handful of thin plastic bags to me. They said SAFEWAY in big red letters.

"Okay," he said. "You asked for it."

I took the bags and we picked two rows alongside Sam's. We were harvesting carrots and onions. I stripped off my coat and sweatshirt and got down on my knees. At first I worked just enough to cover my inspection of the area around me. There wasn't much to see though. A few farming implements, hoes and shovels mostly, sat nearby. I made a mental note of them.

I ranged out toward a fence that ran along the length of the fields. The branches of the brown-leaved trees squeezed through its narrow openings or surged over top like an advancing army. The fence was warped in places, bent inward from years of trying to hold the forest back. Farther east, the fence disappeared — torn down, I guessed, when they'd cleared the land.

"It used to be a gated community."

Sam was kneeling in the rows behind me, pushing his hands through the carrot leaves, picking and choosing. Marcus joined us from a few rows down.

"What's that?"

"Before the Collapse," Sam continued, "rich people like Marcus here's family liked to build these self-contained neighborhoods, surround them with fences and security and whatnot. You know, keep out the riffraff. Anyway, this whole place was built right before everything went bad. After that, the people living here closed themselves up. Cut access to the roads, let some of the forest grow back in. With so much going on, they were just forgotten."

I stopped my digging and sat back on my heels. "What happened to them?" I asked.

"P Eleven," Marcus said. "Sickness took all but the Henrys. You know? Your buddy Will? His family. They have this big house on the north side. They were here when all of us arrived. Had a hand in building the place, I think."

"Yeah," Sam said with a chuckle. "And they *still* think it's theirs."

The sun was out now in full. A flock of birds cut across the sky and landed on the field, pecking briefly at the earth before swarming away again. I looked around at the ten or fifteen people moving through the rows, pulling in a harvest like it was the most natural thing in the world.

It was sad in a way, standing there in the fields, watching them. They'd been lucky, incredibly lucky, but sooner or later I knew their luck would run out, just like it had for Dad and me. Just like it had for everybody. All it would take was one little mistake and they would be found and wiped out.

How could they not know how useless it all was?

"Lunch," Marcus announced a couple hours later, stretching his back. "You ready, Stephen? I bet Vi has something good for us."

"Maybe I'll keep going," I said, thinking of the house's awful stillness. "Is that okay?"

"You should come and eat."

"I'm fine, really. It's just . . . it's good to be *doing* something. You know?"

Marcus looked over at Sam, who just shrugged. "Kid wants to work."

"All right," Marcus said. "But not too much longer."

I handed Marcus my bags of carrots and he and Sam followed the others back toward the house. Once they were gone, I clapped the dirt off my hands, cut through the fields, and wound through the neighborhood's unfamiliar streets.

I ended up at the spur of a road leading down a hill, the same one the kids had streamed down earlier on their way to school. I looked over my shoulder: No one was around. I pulled the scrap of jerky from my pocket and chewed on it as I followed the road. Down at the bottom of the hill, there was a black parking lot, cut up into little slips with fading yellow paint. A low building, surrounded by a neatly trimmed yard that stretched behind it, was backed by a hill dotted with one large sycamore. Just behind a sidewalk that ringed the building there was an old sign that said in large black letters: SETTLER'S LANDING HIGH SCHOOL.

I kept close to the school's beige walls as I passed. Like all the buildings in the neighborhood, it was neat and well maintained, the brick foundation without a crack. The grass around it was short and free of weeds, and I found discarded kids' things here and there on the ground. A jump rope. A broken colored pencil. I took what I could and kept going.

I walked around the school, looking in the windows as I went. Inside there were empty classrooms filled with abandoned desks and chairs. I made it around to the back of the school, found a lone window, and peeked inside.

Desks and chairs sat in six neat rows far below. There was a kid at each desk, pencil in hand, leaning over a stack of papers and writing intently. The rows were broken up by age, the youngest in the front, oldest in the back. Jackson and his friends sat together toward the rear. Will Henry sat on the opposite side of the room behind them, dozing, surrounded by twins, two pale, greasy boys who reminded me of slugs, and a giant redheaded boy with a grove of acne covering his face.

All the rows faced a black chalkboard and a long wooden desk to my right. Sitting at the desk was a tall, thin man with steel-rimmed glasses, wearing a black suit that was a bit too tight and made him look like a scarecrow. He scanned the room, watching the quietly writing students.

"Freaky, huh?"

I whirled around, dropping my hand to the hilt of Dad's knife.

Jenny Tan lounged against the big sycamore behind me, wearing a green army jacket with a red star on the sleeve. She had a large pad of paper spread on her lap and a line of colored pencils in the grass next to her.

"You gonna stab me with that thing, or what?"

Suddenly feeling foolish, I jerked my hand away from the knife.

"So," she said. "You're the spy."

"I'm no spy," I said. "We're salvagers."

"Salvagers," she said, tilting her head against the tree trunk and studying me. "Never actually met one of you before. You travel around, right?" She nodded her head out toward the trees and the edge of town. "Out in the great beyond?"

I nodded. Jenny watched me a moment longer, then took a pencil off the ground and started drawing. She looked past me into the window of the school and then down again. I watched as she erased a line and redrew it, then smudged it with her thumb. Her eyebrows knitted together in concentration. Her hair, loose and tangled, framed her face like a deep shadow. I kept thinking of the hurricane she had been the night before, amazed at how she seemed like someone completely different now.

"How come you don't go to school with the rest of them?" I asked.

"And listen to Tuttle go blah-blah-blah-blah about history and math and the poetry of English guys who have been dead for a thousand years? No thanks. Only reason anybody goes is because it's what their parents remember doing when they were kids, so they're doomed to repeat it." Jenny looked up at me. Her eyes were deep brown and seemingly flecked with gold, like a hawk's. "Sounds kind of dumb, huh?"

I shrugged. "Guess so."

Jenny glanced down at my hand. "No dumber than reaching for a weapon every time you see a Chinese girl."

She sprang it like a bear trap. I scrambled for something to say, but when I opened my mouth, no words came.

"What? Your folks tell you to expect horns and a tail or something?"

"No. I —"

Jenny's grin grew wider, about to burst into a laugh. "Relax," she said. "I'm just messing with you. Hey, I'd probably reach for a knife if I saw me too."

A rumble came from inside the school. I turned to the window and saw the students were pushing back from their desks and stampeding toward the double doors at the back of the classroom.

"Uh-oh. Here comes the flood." Jenny tore the drawing out of her pad, crumpled it up, and tossed it to the ground. As she stood up and stretched, her Red Army jacket lifted, revealing a scar that was thick as a trench and curled across her middle and around her back.

"I don't know. Maybe I *will* go back to school on Monday," she said, letting the statement hang in the air for a moment before turning and giving me a quick look. "It's been a while since I annoyed Tuttle. Maybe I'll see ya around, tough guy."

Jenny gathered her things, then strode away on bare feet down the hill, just missing the torrent of bodies that roared into the playground outside the school. I turned to escape before they could reach me, stopping only to snatch Jenny's crumpled drawing off the ground, then dashing into the forest.

I tromped through the brush, not looking where I was going, simply trying to escape the strangeness of the day. She was right — I had never actually seen a Chinese person up close before, let alone talked to one. These were the people the United States had been at war with? The people who'd released P11 and killed millions? After the plague had passed and the Chinese troops had invaded, there'd been years of vicious fights between them and the survivors. My family had fled San Diego a year before I was born, though, so we mostly kept out of it. Still, we couldn't help but see the spreading aftermath.

Grandpa said the Chinese were subhuman. Savage, ugly, and vicious. *But if that's true,* I wondered, *how come when I look at Jenny, that's not what I see?*

I skimmed the edges of backyards as I went deeper into the woods. The neat lines of the houses were just visible through the trees, which were hanging over thick grass and vegetable patches. I thought again of the treasures Violet had laid out in that cabinet of hers. Drugs. Priceless medical instruments.

I wondered: *How is it possible that while we had nothing, these people are here with all of this?*

A twist of anger made me stop to catch my breath. The forest shifted around me in the wind. Something small skittered through dry leaves. Grandpa had told me a hundred times that life wasn't fair and that expecting it to be was for fools.

These people got lucky. That's all. It can't last. All that matters is that I have to be ready when Dad gets better so we can get on track again. We need supplies and things to trade.

But what?

I searched and searched for an answer, only to return to the same place each time.

There was only one thing to do.

I didn't like it, but the truth was we had never been in anywhere near this much trouble before and I was the only one who could save us.

A blackbird cawed loudly, startling me. The sun had dropped a couple degrees in the sky. I thought of Dad lying there all alone and started to go, but then I remembered Jenny's drawing still clenched in my hand. I turned the crumpled ball over, and before I knew it, my fingers were pulling it open. The paper crackled as I spread it open on the ground in front of me.

It wasn't what I expected at all. Inside was a nearly perfect sketch of the back of the school with the sky and drifting clouds in the background. The scrub and grass leading up to the brick wall were textured and deep. It all looked unbelievably real, like a photograph, except that on the other side of the window, instead of a class full of students, desks, and a teacher, there stood a lone, riderless horse.

Its head was bowed almost to the floor. It had no saddle or bridle, and its dark mane was long and tangled. The strangeness of it was overwhelming, but not in the same way that the town was. Looking at it made my pulse slow and my breathing run shallow and quiet for the first time since I'd arrived, like it was speaking to me in a language I could almost, but not quite, understand.

I traced the lines of the drawing with the tip of my finger, looping and slashing across the paper like Jenny had, trying to imagine what was in her head as she did it.

The blackbird cawed again, pulling me back into the world. *Waste of time*, I thought, and folded the paper up and shoved it in my pocket. I had no time to be looking at pictures.

I had work to do.

TWELVE

Late that night, once everyone had gone to sleep, I sat up in the darkness. I dressed as silently as I could, then gathered everything I needed — moving achingly slow to avoid making any sound — and crept out of town.

I followed the road up toward the white stone wall that seemed to glow in the moonlight. Luckily the gates had been left slightly open so I was able to slip past, avoiding the rusty creak that I was sure would have carried across the entire town. Once through, I headed for the woods on the other side of the grass plain.

It took me more than an hour to cross through the forest. When I stepped down onto the cracked remnant of the highway on the other side, my boots were caked in mud and my arms were raked with scratches from the thornbushes woven through the trees.

The land across the road was dark as slate. It seemed to stretch westward nearly forever, dotted with scattered families of trees, until it ran up against low mountains that loomed far off in the distance. Off to the north there were the remains of a casino called the Golden Acorn and a Starbucks. Their billboards stretched into the sky.

I made my way up the hill until I found an old lightning-struck tree. It was split down the middle with the very first showings of sprouts growing out of its charred interior. I stepped back into the cover of the woods behind it before I pulled the gauze-wrapped package from my coat pocket and opened it.

Two glass medicine bottles and a few stainless steel instruments, priceless at any trade gathering, glittered in my hand. A sharp stitch of guilt knotted in my chest. *I'm no thief,* I thought again. But the fact was that we were broke. No wagon. No supplies. Nothing to trade. I couldn't let that happen. With no one else around, it was my responsibility and mine alone.

I found a sharp, flat rock, pushed aside the leaves, and started digging into the soft ground until I had a wide hole cut about two feet deep into the earth. I set the gauze-wrapped medicines, along with the pencil and old nickel, carefully into the bottom. The way the gauze lay over the medicine bottles made them look like two bodies wrapped in a shroud.

I pushed the dirt over them quickly and sat back on the hill, leaning on my elbows, pulling in the cool air that tasted of wood smoke and decaying leaves. That pang of guilt hit me again. My hand moved around to my pocket and I laid Mom's picture out in a patch of moonlight.

Hours after we'd taken the picture and made it back to camp, I'd slipped into Mom and Dad's tent, squirming in between them. Mom lit a candle, opened one of our few books, and laid her arm across my back while Dad turned the pages. Mom would read a passage out loud and then I would read the next one, both of us quiet as could be, so as not to wake Grandpa.

I'd liked how, when I stumbled on words I didn't know or couldn't pronounce, Mom would reach for our battered dictionary and we'd go over the definition and sound it out, over and over until I had it down. It always felt to me like trudging up a tough and rocky hill, sweating and pushing until finally I made it up over the top to land that was flat and bright.

We made it through *Sounder*, *Charlie and the Chocolate Factory*, and *Great Expectations* that way, the words rolling from Mom's mouth in her high, clear voice that was like a bird's or a bell's. We'd read until my eyes drooped and the steady in and out of Mom's and Dad's breathing on either side would rock me to sleep.

Grandpa thought the idea of my learning to read was a waste of time, and in a way I'd agreed with him. I was going to be a trader like him and my dad — what use would reading really be?

Mom had said that maybe the world wouldn't always be like it was now. But even if it was, she said, sometimes it was important to do things there was no real use for. Like reading books and taking pictures.

She'd said we had to be more than what the world would make us.

A branch snapped and leaves rustled down to my left. I scanned the woods with my hand on the hilt of the knife, but everything was blurry, swirling like the forest was underwater. I reached my hand up to my eyes and it came back wet. I had been crying and didn't even realize it.

Stupid baby. I wiped the tears away with my dirty coat sleeve but still didn't see anything. *Probably nothing anyway. A deer. Maybe a stray dog.*

I swept leaves over the disturbed ground so it blended into the hillside, then marked the place by half burying the rock at the head of the hole. It didn't matter what Mom would have thought. Like Grandpa, she was gone, and I was here.

I surveyed the highway and the land beyond, all flat plains of black and gray. The stars, straining through the thick canopy above my head, shone like bits of broken glass.

As soon as Dad was better, all we'd have to do is stop here on the way out of town. Then we could trade for whatever supplies we needed. Everything would be back the way it was.

The only question was, what would I do until then?

THIRTEEN

"So what do they do down there?"

I was lingering by the window over Dad's bed a few days later, full from a breakfast of eggs and bacon and bread that Marcus had cooked and insisted I join them for. The sun was spread across the asphalt where it dipped into the woods a few houses down. Soon that road would be stocked with kids jostling and laughing on their way down to the school.

"Usual stuff. Math. English. Why? You want to —"

"No," I said quickly. "I was curious. I'll help you and Sam in the fields again."

"I bet we could do without you for a day or two."

Violet had changed Dad into a pair of Marcus's old pajamas that had white and blue stripes and a neat little collar. His face and beard were clean. There were shadows all along the white sheet that covered him. Dips and peaks. It was like he was buried under a drift of snow.

"What are you two talking about?" Violet appeared in the doorway behind us, drying her hands after doing the dishes in a wash bucket out on the porch.

"Stephen going to school this morning."

Violet glanced down at Dad and then fixed me with a no-nonsense gaze, her hands on her hips. "There's nothing you can do for your dad that I can't. I'm sorry, but that's the way it is. I'm sure he would want you to go to school if you could. Don't you think?"

"I —"

"Jackson," she called back into the kitchen. "You have some note-books and things to give Stephen if he wanted to come to school with you?"

"On my desk!"

"Upstairs to the left," Violet said to me, turning back toward the kitchen. "Better get moving. Don't want you two to be late."

I was about to argue, to insist that I would stay behind with Dad, but there was something about the swift sureness of Violet's command that had me falling into place behind her and following her through the kitchen. Besides, I had to admit I was curious.

The kitchen was wide and open with tall windows all along the back looking out onto a porch. Jackson was sitting at the end of the long table with a big book that said AMERICAN HISTORY on the spine. He peeked over it as I came in, then away again as soon as I caught him.

"Next to the bed," he said. "Take a couple pencils too."

I nodded and looked up the length of the dark staircase that sat behind him. I took the rail and climbed slowly, feeling a strange leg-shaking vertigo. Once I reached the landing at the top of the stairs I saw his open door, went through, and was instantly struck dumb. To my left there was a bed, an actual bed, neatly situated under a curtained window with a little nightstand next to it. The bed was crisply made with a bright red blanket and two pillows.

Standing there, I felt the same eerie sense as when I saw the pic-tures of their long-gone families. Everything they had was left over from the last inhabitants of the town. After they had died, the Greens and the others swept in, tidied up, and took their places. Slept in their beds. Cooked in their kitchens. Started their lives all over again.

I stepped farther in. Next to the bed was a shelf that, incredibly, held at least thirty paperback and hardcover books. I stepped closer and ran my finger along each book's cracked spine. The same hunger I felt when Marcus laid down that first plate of eggs and bacon that morning twisted inside of me. I felt a stab of jealousy again — How could they have so much? — so I made myself look away. That's when I noticed that there was a second room across the hall. From where I stood, I could just see the corner of a bed and a bureau with its drawers hanging open. Clothes, bits of paper, and nubs of pencils littered the floor.

Jenny's room?

I scooped up a notebook and a couple pencils from Jackson's desk and crossed the hall, lingering at Jenny's door and listening. Glass clinked together as Violet put the dishes away. Jackson talked low to Marcus downstairs. I slipped inside.

Light flooded in from the one bare window, harsh and glaring on the bone-white walls. Where Jackson's was clean and orderly and spare, hers was a junkyard. There was a bed stripped of its blanket with a couple coverless pillows and a balled-up sheet. Old clothes lay among dishes that were covered in congealed candle wax. A big hardback book was spread-eagled on the floor. It said CHEMISTRY in black letters.

Her mattress was small with thin blue pinstripes. I could imagine Jenny lying there, her hair spread out like a thick black cloud, staring up at the ceiling and waiting (like me?) for sleep that wouldn't come.

I remembered Jenny's body stretching in the sun, her heavy scar glowing white like a vein in marble, a sketch of a smile on her lips.

Violet's voice drifted up the stairs. "Stephen?"

As I pulled myself out of the room, I caught sight of a spot to one side of the door where the wall had been crushed inward. I stepped up for a closer look. The hole was in the shape of a small fist. Smeared traces of blood lay where knuckles would have bit into the plaster. I opened my own hand and looked at it.

In the center of my palm were the four half-moon slashes I had made the morning after Dad's accident. I reached my hand out, laid it over the hole in the wall, and closed my eyes.

"Stephen? You okay?"

It sounded like Violet was at the foot of the stairs now. Any second she'd come up to check on me.

"Coming!" I called, feeling strangely drained as I ran down the stairs to where Violet was waiting with two metal pails. I scrambled for an explanation for what I had been doing, but she handed one pail to Jackson and one to me. Puzzled, I peered inside and found a few big lumps wrapped in cloth.

"Your lunch," she said helpfully.

"Oh," I said and stood there awkwardly for a moment. Just over her shoulder I could almost see the edge of her big medicine cabinet. "Well . . . thanks."

Violet pulled at my collar, fussing with my clothes to get them straight. "If I had known you were going, I would have heated up enough water for a bath. Marcus, I don't know. . . ."

"He'll be fine."

Jackson was hovering by the door, impatient.

"I'll be fine," I said. As I started to go, Violet turned me around and pulled me into a warm hug. Close up, she smelled like baked bread and dried flowers.

She said nothing, just held on, her breath rising and falling, matching the swell of my own. The feeling was familiar, nice at first, but as it lingered it was like being embraced by a ghost and I had to push myself away.

"We better . . . we should go. Right, Jackson?" I blew past him, not waiting for a response, and threw myself into the front door, relieved to feel the blast of fresh air that hit me as soon as I was outside.

"God!" Jackson said when he caught up to me. "She's always doing stuff like that!"

I had my head down, watching my old boots slap against the asphalt, trying to swallow the thick lump in my throat and shake the warm feeling of Violet's arms around me.

"It's okay," I said. "Moms are like that, I guess."

Jackson and I fell in with a torrent of kids that pushed us faster toward the turn in the road that led to school. Jackson tried to explain the school day to me as we went, but I only caught bits of it. Six class periods broken up by lunch. Something about math. A buzzing nervousness had come over me. I craned my head toward the safety of the Greens' house, wondering if I could turn back before it was too late.

"Hey, look, there's Derrick and Martin!"

Martin looked half asleep. He stared blankly at the road in front of him, glasses slightly askew and shirt untucked, his chopped-up crew cut glistening wet. Derrick, on the other hand, reminded me of corn popping in a skillet. He bounced from toe to toe as though he could barely contain himself.

"Guys!" Derrick shouted. *"Compadres! Mis amigos! Como estás?"*

"Hey, Derrick," Jackson said.

"Well, if it isn't my little friend with the big appetite," Derrick said to me. "What's up, my man?"

Head cottony with nerves, I didn't know what to say. I hitched my shoulders noncommittally.

"Awesome. We all ready for a big day of learning?"

The double doors to the school loomed ahead of us, and the crowd swept us right toward them. Derrick knocked a few little ones out of the way. I took a deep breath, and in we went.

We were herded into a narrow hallway lined with metal lockers and doors to other rooms. I had never seen so many people my own age in one place before. I marveled at their clean clothes and the way they coursed through the hall, full of purpose. As with the houses the day I came to town, I searched for any sign that these people had grown up in the same world I did, but found nothing.

As I studied them, I was being watched too. When I caught them looking, they'd wrinkle their noses before turning away to whisper to their friends. A girl in a gray skirt pointed out my ratty old coat and giggled. I faked like I was cold and pulled it tight around me, hoping to hide the rest of my clothes.

Once we were inside the classroom, Jackson, Martin, and Derrick took desks about halfway back. Jackson pointed to an empty chair in front of him.

"Sit here," he said.

All around me, kids were writing in their notebooks, desperately trying to finish their homework, I guessed, like Jackson had done that morning. The ones who weren't working were talking. The roar of it came in waves, building and building until the entire room was shouting at once. It sounded to me like glass grinding against glass. *Why does everyone talk so much here?* I wondered. *What is there to say?* I almost put my head down on the desk and covered my ears, but the last thing I needed was to stand out even more. I looked up to my right. Above a set of tall bookshelves I could see the blue sky and the waving branches of the sycamore tree out of the window.

"What are *you* doing here?"

At first I didn't realize anyone was talking to me, but then someone's knee bumped roughly into my side.

"Hey! Spy! I'm talking to you."

I looked up. Will Henry. He was wearing a black T-shirt and a pair of jeans that bulged a bit around the thigh where I guessed a bandage was. He was with his three friends, the two sluggy twins and zit-covered mountain of a redhead.

"I said, what are you doing here?" Somehow Will's eyes glittered but were utterly blank at the same time. My hand fell beneath my coat and closed around the handle of my knife. When I didn't say anything, Will snatched the notebook out of my hands and held it up to Jackson.

"You give him this, Greeny? You and your folks? How many of these you think we have left? And you give one to some spy?"

Will planted his fists on my desk and leaned over me.

"These things are for us," he said. "Not you."

"Leave him alone, Will!"

I turned and was surprised to see that Jackson was up out of his seat. Derrick and Martin rose tentatively to join him.

"What are you going to do?" Will continued, leaning toward him. Even though he was a whole row of desks away, Jackson took one nervous step back, which clearly delighted Will. "You and your folks gonna save this stray too? What? Was the first one not pathetic enough for you?"

Every part of me tensed, desperate to shoot up out of my chair and knock Will into the wall behind him. I struggled to stay calm even as he leaned over me, his face inches from mine.

"How about you, spy? You gonna do something?"

My cheeks burned and the wounds on my hand throbbed as I gripped the rough leather of the knife's hilt.

The doors at the back of the classroom flew open and slammed against the wall.

"Class, settle down! Settle down, everyone!" the teacher called as he rushed in past us to the front of the room. "Mr. Henry, take your friends and sit."

"Mr. Tuttle —" Will began, pointing at me.

"No time, Mr. Henry," Tuttle said, distracted with papers at his desk. "Sit or find yourself in detention."

Will glanced at Tuttle. "You're lucky, spy," he said as he tossed the notebook over his shoulder to one of his friends. "Come on, guys. Kid's stinking up this side of the room anyway."

The redhead gave me a vacant, moist-eyed glare while one of the slug twins nudged my desk so my pencils fell to the ground with a clatter. I waited until they were back at their seats before bending to pick them up, but when I did, Jackson was already holding them out to me.

"Here you go."

"Thanks." I turned away from him and rearranged my things. It was odd how Jackson and the others had stood up for me the way they had. Getting backed up like that by people who weren't family didn't make sense. It felt good, but I couldn't afford to be careless. Nobody did anything for free.

"Class, I will need your attention . . . now."

Tuttle smacked his ruler across the desk and there was a rustle of bodies as everyone dropped into their seats and shot to attention. He surveyed the room, moving from face to face and making little marks on a sheet of paper until his eyes fell on me.

"And who is this?"

"Stephen," Jackson piped up from behind me. "Stephen, uh . . ." Jackson tapped my shoulder.

"Quinn," I said.

"Stephen Quinn. He's new."

Tuttle glanced at Jackson. "Yes, I can see that he's new, Mr. Green. If he wasn't, I would not have expressed surprise upon seeing him, would I?"

"Um —"

"Rhetorical question, Mr. Green. Now. Quinn. Stephen. I am Mr. Tuttle. Have you been in school before?"

I cleared my throat and tried to sit up straighter. "No sir."

"Can you read? Do you know your numbers?"

"Yes sir."

"The Pledge of Allegiance?"

"The pledge of allegiance to what?"

The class laughed all around me. I felt my cheeks go red and hot.

"Well, you'll have a lot of catching up to do, but I can't afford to slow down." Tuttle went back to marking his paper, then nodded toward Jackson and Martin. "Mr. Green and Mr. Stantz will help you."

"Hey, what about me?"

Tuttle glared at Derrick. "I think Mr. Quinn would do well to pay as little attention to you as possible on educational matters. Don't you agree, Mr. Waverly?"

"Yes! Absolutely!" Derrick said. "Good call, sir."

Tuttle gave him a withering look, then stepped back to the blackboard behind him. It was covered by some kind of pull-down screen. The class groaned as he reached for it.

"Yes, class," Tuttle said. "That's right. If you were able to better control yourselves, these little tests wouldn't be necessary. So take out your —"

Before Tuttle could finish, the doors behind us burst open again, smacking against the walls. The class turned as one body toward the sound as Jenny Tan strode barefoot into the classroom. She carried a tattered notebook. A nub of pencil was stuck behind one ear.

"Well, well, well, this is quite an honor," Tuttle deadpanned. "We haven't been graced with your presence in weeks. So nice of you to join us today, Miss Green."

"It's Tan," Jenny said as she plopped down into an open seat toward the back of the class and put her bare feet up on the chair in front of her. "And you're welcome."

A ripple of laughter went through the classroom. Jackson had his eyes closed tight and his head in his hands. Irritation pulsed off him in waves. Tuttle slapped his ruler down on the corner of his desk.

"I won't have any more disruptions."

Jenny raised her hands, palms up, as if to say he wouldn't get any from her. Tuttle considered her a moment, made a notation on his sheet, then stepped back to pull on the screen in front of the blackboard. It shot up toward the ceiling, revealing a long list of questions written in chalk. Jenny bent over her desk, laying her chin in the palm of one hand while she dug into the wood of her desk with her fingernail.

Jackson handed me a sheet of paper from his notebook as the rest of the class picked up their pencils and began writing. Jenny flicked her hair out of her face, turning just enough to catch me staring at her. It was like being stuck out in the open as lightning flashed all around me. I knew I should look away, and quickly, but I froze.

Jenny raised one eyebrow, and when I still didn't look away, she jutted her face out at me, bugging her big brown eyes and making a show of staring back. I looked away immediately, up at the test questions, trying to calm the thrill of nerves in my stomach.

I was surprised to find that the test was on *Great Expectations*, a book I had actually read and more or less remembered. I made a stab at the questions, but it was hard to concentrate. I could feel Jenny across the room. It was like her body had this gravity all its own and it was pulling at me, trying to make me turn. I thought of her drawing spread across that rumpled paper. The riderless horse, motionless but somehow pulsing with movement and life.

Jackson nudged the back of my shoulder. "Ten minutes, Steve," he whispered. "Come on."

I shook thoughts of Jenny out of my head and forced myself to focus. The test was a fill-in-the-blank thing and time was ticking down, but I rushed to fill in the last answer just as Tuttle pulled the screen back down in front of the questions.

"Now, class," Tuttle said as he collected papers. "We will continue our discussion of algebra. Turn to page two twenty-three. . . ."

Jackson nudged me again. When I turned, he was holding a folded piece of paper. He jerked his thumb over toward Jenny, who was bent over her notebook, drawing in the margins. I took the paper and unfolded it.

It was a short note, just two lines long, but when I was done reading, it felt like something had sucked every last wisp of breath out of my lungs.

Across the room, Jenny was smiling in a way that reminded me of a wolf.

The note said, in a jagged scrawl:

I saw what you buried in the woods Friday night.

You are a naughty naughty boy.

FOURTEEN

As soon as Tuttle dismissed us for the day, I jumped out of my seat and ran for the door.

"Hey!" Jackson cried. "Where are you going? We've got a game!"

I ignored him. Jenny had started to leave before "Class dismissed" had even left Tuttle's mouth. I raced down the hallway behind her, but by the time I made it through the school's front doors and outside she was gone.

The doors behind me opened again and someone rammed into my shoulder, pitching me forward. I turned around just in time to see a golden flash of blond and Will's grinning face.

"You oughta watch where you stand. I think some people are trying to walk this way."

Will and his friends laughed.

That's it.

I grabbed two handfuls of Will's shirt and spun him around, slamming him into the wall. An icy thrill went through me as his eyes bulged with surprise and fear. I was about to cock my fist when someone grabbed my elbow.

"Stephen, don't," a voice said. "Tuttle."

As soon as he said it, Tuttle appeared behind us like a pillar of black smoke. "Mr. Green, Mr. Quinn, Mr. Henry. What's going on here?"

"Nothing, sir," Jackson said quickly. "Right, Stephen?"

Jackson gave me a nudge and I managed to back away from Will and agree through gritted teeth that everything was fine.

"Good," Tuttle said. "Mr. Henry?"

Will jumped forward with barely disguised glee. "He's got a knife, sir," he said, pointing at my waist. "He keeps threatening us with it and it's making all of us feel really unsafe."

"That's not true! I didn't —"

Before I could say anything else, Tuttle pulled aside my coat and yanked the knife straight out of its sheath.

"I see," Tuttle said, turning the dark blade over in his hands. "Mr. Henry, you and your friends are dismissed."

"But —"

"You're dismissed."

Will's glare bloomed into a wide smile. He held up one finger and mouthed the words *strike one* behind Tuttle's back before he and his friends glided lazily up the hill and away from the school.

"You three may go as well," Tuttle said to Jackson, Martin, and Derrick. As they left, I caught Jackson's eye. He had a strange, worried look on his face but motioned that I should follow them toward the field east of the school when I was done.

"It's old," Tuttle said as he turned the leather-wrapped handle of the knife over in his hands. "Older than you. Your father's?"

I nodded.

"I thought as much," he said quietly. "He's hurt, I understand."

I nodded, struggling to swallow something bitter that had risen in my throat.

"I see," Tuttle said. He ran his finger gently along the knife's blade. "I will not have chaos in this place, Mr. Quinn. There's enough of that on the outside. To discourage it, there are a range of punishments I have for my students. Would you like to know what they are?"

I stood my ground, saying nothing.

"There is detention. There is extra homework and cleaning of the schoolhouse. If that doesn't work, there is brief but vigorous corporal punishment. Now, for someone such as yourself, someone who has no ties to this town, I believe there is another option, the one I hear that Caleb Henry and a few others are already eager to exercise. Expulsion. From school and, if needed, from the town. I believe that would be something you or your father could ill afford, would it not?"

Tuttle waited for an answer. An ember burned down in the pit of my stomach. My fingernails stabbed into my palms. For this man who I didn't know, had never met, to have that kind of power over me and my dad . . . it took every ounce of my strength to shake my head.

"I thought not. Luckily for you, there is another option."

Tuttle turned the knife's hilt back toward me.

"The stern warning. Take it home and do not bring it to my class again. Do you understand?"

I paused, expecting some sort of trick, then took the knife from him. Tuttle clasped his hands behind his back and stepped down to the concrete sidewalk.

"I'll be watching you, Mr. Quinn," he said over his shoulder. Then he was gone.

I fell against the brick wall behind me and clamped my eyes shut, grimacing from the spiky seed of a headache that was sprouting in the back of my skull. *What was I thinking? First Jenny sees me burying that stuff in the woods and now this?* Will said he'd make sure Dad and I weren't here long, and now it was pretty clear how he intended to make that happen. In coming to school, I couldn't have helped him any more if I had tried. I should have seen it. I let my head fall hard onto the brick behind me, relishing the dull shock of the pain.

"Well, *that* was kind of awesome."

I opened my eyes. Derrick was grinning madly and bouncing on the balls of his feet. Martin and Jackson were behind him.

"Just what we all needed before a little baseball game, right? Excitement!"

His voice was like broken glass in my head. I pushed off the brick wall and blew past the three of them without a word.

"Hey! Where you going?" Derrick cried as he jogged alongside me, trailed by the others. "We need you! You can even play second base!"

"Leave me alone, Derrick."

"But —"

"I don't want to play some stupid game, okay?"

"*Stupid* — are you kidding me? Have you ever played baseball before? I mean, what the hell have you been doing all these years?"

"Gee, Derrick, maybe he's been spending all his time looking for food and shelter and stuff."

"Valid point, Green!" Derrick said, and darted in closer to me, sticking his face right in mine. "But you don't have to look for food and shelter right now, do you?"

I glared at him, but he kept going.

"Okay, I get it. Crappy day for you. No question," Derrick went on. "And I know that most people would back off at this point and let you go and gather your thoughts or whatever, but I can't. My mom says it's 'cause I've got, like, this thing in my head that makes it so once I get on something I can't let it go, and I get kinda hyper about it. She said when she was a kid they'd have doped me to the gills on this stuff called Ritalin, but now — ha! — everyone has to just put up with me!"

"It's true," Jackson said. "He won't stop bothering you until you play or one of you dies."

"Ha! Nice one, Green. Steve, look, seriously —"

"I said leave me ALONE!" I planted my palms on Derrick's chest and pushed him so hard he stumbled and fell back into the grass.

Everything went quiet except the sound of blood pounding in my ears.

Derrick looked up at me with huge eyes. Jackson and Martin were motionless, just behind me, waiting.

"Steve," Jackson said, his voice tremulous. "Hey, come on, we were just trying to —"

I turned and shot him a hard glare. He staggered backward as I tore past Derrick and up the road.

The Greens were both gone when I got back to the house. I slammed the door behind me and threw my coat in a heap by Dad's bed, fuming.

How could I have been so stupid? School. What was I thinking?

My fingernails found the scabs on my palm and sank in. I gritted my teeth. I wanted to break something. The chair by the fireplace. The frames on the mantel filled with pictures of idiotic smiling boaters, tanned and lying about in the sun, with no idea that their world was about to come crashing down around them.

I wondered how it would feel if I put my hand through the window above Dad. The glass would tear through my skin and scrape along the bones, maybe shattering them. I flinched at the idea of it, but still my hand collapsed into a fist and drew back. Just then, there was a rattle next to me as Dad's chest rose slightly and then fell again.

My fist fell open. Will wanted me kicked out of here, and hadn't I helped him enough already?

I break something, maybe Marcus gets mad, maybe that's strike two. . . .

I sucked in an angry breath, and slowly the redness that clouded my vision flowed out of me, replaced by something cold and dark, something empty.

"You okay?"

Startled, I turned to see Violet standing in the doorway, a big medical book tucked under her arm. I found a nearby chair and pulled it up to Dad's bedside. I sat with my back to her as a tidal surge of guilt rocked through me. *This is where I should have been the whole time.* I took Dad's hand in mine. It was light as a handful of grass.

"I imagine they're getting a game started over there. I'm surprised you didn't join them."

I glanced over my shoulder. Violet was sitting in a chair just behind me. She had grabbed an old ball cap off a nearby table and had pulled it down over her hair. The book lay open in her lap.

"It *is* the national sport, you know."

"It *was* the national sport," I said. "I don't understand why you people talk about America like it still exists. My grandfather would say it was" — I searched for the phrase. I had heard it a thousand times growing up, generally whenever one of us suggested a slightly shorter hike or a little more sleep — "like square dancing on the *Titanic*."

Violet's book closed softly behind me. I didn't move. My eyelids felt heavy watching Dad's shallow breathing rise and fall.

Outside, the remaining leaves of fall swayed in the fading sun. Two kids, a boy and a girl with wide, bright faces, were playing out in the park. I looked away and my eye fell on Violet's cabinet, the cabinet that only I knew was lighter a few bottles.

"Why are you people helping us?"

"Why wouldn't we?"

"You don't know us," I said, surprised at the wave of disgust rising in me. "You're giving us medicine, food, your home, and you're just getting in trouble for it. It's stupid."

"You're what was put in front of us," she said.

"That's not an answer."

Violet crossed her arms and looked out the window over my shoulder. "Because there was a time when people helped each other," she said. "And that made the world a little bit better. Not perfect, but better. We'd like to think we can have that time back."

"But what if you're wrong?" I asked.

Violet shrugged. "Maybe we *are* on the deck of the *Titanic*," she said. "Maybe the Collapse isn't over and this will all be gone tomorrow. I don't know. What I *do* know is what it's like out there, we all do, and even if I can only have a little break from it, if I can be the kind of person I was before all this happened, then I'm going to take it. Even if it's just for a day."

Violet tossed the baseball cap into my lap.

"You know what I mean?"

She left without another word, entering the kitchen and leaving me alone.

I shifted in my chair. Outside, leaves swayed across the blue sky. Dad lay before me, as still as ever. I turned Violet's threadbare cap over and over in my hands.

There was a squeal of laughter and the two kids flew by the window. They were maybe six or seven years old, the girl with a long stream of golden hair. The boy was taller and thin as a sapling. They were both holding sticks that had colored streamers attached to the ends so as they went by they were a streak of red and purple and blond, like a flight of brightly colored birds. I pulled the cap down over my head and watched as they banked into the sunshine and disappeared into the park.

FIFTEEN

I skipped school the next day and spent it searching for Jenny but had no luck finding her. I ended up standing in the field east of the school, watching Jackson and the rest gather for their daily baseball game, choosing sides, lining up, swinging their bats through the crisp air.

I had never played baseball, but with how much Dad talked about it I almost felt like I had. He pitched throughout high school and was a passionate Padres fan. Sometimes to keep us entertained on the road, he'd recount major games he had seen in painstaking detail. I stuffed my hands in my pockets and let myself drift closer to the game, finally finding a spot to sit in the grass.

No harm in watching, I thought. *Just for a few minutes.*

Derrick and Jackson's team was lining up for the first at bat. Martin threw a battered plastic helmet to a broad-shouldered girl, and she took a few practice swings before making her way to the plate. She hunkered down, eyeing the tall pitcher sharply, and let the bat hover over her shoulder. She was ice-cold and didn't move an inch on his first two pitches but unloaded completely on his third and sent the ball rocketing into the blue sky. She made it to second, then stopped, cheating out toward third.

"Carrie V."

Jackson had strayed from the game and was standing just a few feet in front of me. I half expected him to tell me to beat it, given how I'd acted after school the previous day. But he just stood there and watched the game, his hands in the pockets of a worn pair of khaki pants. Soon he eased down next to me. I set my palms in the grass, ready to get up and walk away, but for some reason I didn't. I just sat there, watching.

"She's one of our best. The pitcher is her boyfriend, John Carter. She knows him inside and out. Almost always gets a hit off him."

Jackson turned to face me over his shoulder.

"You can play, you know. If you want."

"I gotta get back to my dad."

A shrimpy kid with long hair made his way nervously to home plate with the encouragement of his teammates. "Stan," Jackson said. "Not our best player. Hey, where were you today?"

"I was out," I said, quickly. "Just . . . looking around."

"So what did it say?" Jackson asked.

"What?"

"The note. The one Jenny made me give you that got you tearing out of school."

"Oh. Nothing. She was" — I scrambled for a lie that might sound even slightly convincing — "messing with me."

It sounded weak. Jackson gave me a little sideways look, then returned to watching the game. "Yeah," he said. "That's Jenny, all right. She can't leave well enough alone."

It was silent for a moment as Stan took a couple practice swings. I felt another twinge of guilt. Jackson didn't have to come over and talk to me, not after how much of a jerk I had been.

"I was looking at your books," I said. "The other day. It's a really good collection."

Jackson turned back. "Thanks. I do chores for people and they give me books in return. You like to read? You can borrow them anytime if you want."

"Thanks," I said. "That'd be great."

Jackson nodded and turned back as Stan took a couple practice swings, then lifted the bat over his shoulder. The ball came streaking toward him. For some reason Stan stepped closer to the base as he swung, bringing his right leg into the path of the oncoming ball. Jackson saw it just as I did.

"Oh, this is *not* going to be good."

The ball slammed into Stan's thigh and he went down cursing.

"Every other time," Jackson said. "I swear, the kid gets hit by the ball more than he hits it. Aw, man, now we're one man down. I better go. See ya, Steve."

Jackson hopped up and ran to his team, stopping to check in on Stan, who was sitting on the sidelines. I stripped off my coat and lay in the grass, watching as Jackson and Derrick conferred. They seemed to be having some kind of argument. Derrick was waving his arms and refusing some request of Jackson's, but Jackson kept at him until Derrick finally relented. He turned away and began waving to someone behind me to join the game. I looked back, but no one was there.

Oh no.

"Hey! Steve! Hey! Over here! Yoo-hoo!"

I tried to ignore him, but Derrick made it nearly impossible. Soon he was jumping up and down on his toes and calling in a high-pitched squeal. The whole team was watching now, and a rush of embarrassment hit me. I started to retreat back to the Greens', but something made me stop and look around.

The grass, holding on despite the coming of fall, was thick and green. There was the slightest chill and the smell of wood smoke in the air. Where was I going? Back inside the tomb? To my dad, who, no matter how much I wanted to, I couldn't help? It was true that soon all of this would be gone and we would rejoin the trail, but I was here now. This was my world. Would it really hurt to live in it, just for a day?

Before I knew it, the grass seemed to be moving under my feet. I trotted, head down, toward the game.

"It's okay, everybody!" Derrick shouted as I reached the edge of the field, hanging back from the team. "Our savior is here! Steve will fill in for Stan."

"Can he even play?" someone shouted from back in the lineup.

"Can he play?" Derrick repeated, dumbstruck. "He's a heckuva lot better than any of us. His dad was an actual New York Yankee before the Collapse. Taught him everything he knew."

The flash of embarrassment hit again as the team erupted into a chorus of *oohs* and *aahs*.

Derrick leaned in. "You, uh, do know how to play, right?" he whispered.

"In theory."

"Well, you're still one up on Stan," Derrick said. "Anyway, you're at bat!"

"Oh wait, maybe someone else should —"

But Derrick was already pushing the bat into my hand. He and the others were cheering me from behind the fence to home plate. I felt like I was being pushed onstage to star in a play I didn't know any of the words to.

"Hit and run!" Derrick shouted. "Just hit and run!"

"Tear the cover off it, Steve!" Jackson yelled.

"Don't suck," Stan called from the bench.

My stomach quivered, but I found myself raising the bat to my shoulder, readying myself for a fresh disaster. I took a deep breath and got into a slight crouch, eyes on the pitcher. He nodded at the catcher behind me, then started his windup. Before I could move an inch, the ball slapped into the catcher's glove.

"Well done," he said, smirking as he tossed the ball to the pitcher. "I think you're a natural."

"It's okay, Steve!" Jackson shouted. "That one wasn't yours!"

The pitcher turned back, a big grin on his face. I raised the bat and crouched, scowling. He wound up and threw, but this time it was like everything slowed down. I could see the white ball tumbling toward me. The voices behind me elongated. I brought the bat around in a quick arc, and as it connected with the ball there was a sweet, sharp *crack*. The ball sailed out into the field, over the head of the pitcher, into the outfield.

Dopey and amazed, I watched as the ball lifted into the sky and over the trees whose top branches moved in the wind like hands waving good-bye. I turned back to my team, bat dangling from my hand, eager to share this incredible triumph, but they were all standing on the tips of their toes, looks of terrified anticipation on their faces.

"Don't just stand there, you moron!" Carrie screamed from second, shattering the moment. "Run!"

Oh! Right! Now I run!

The bat clattered at my feet as I took off. I passed first base easily, then skidded in to second. The baseman there was pivoting toward the outfield and raising his glove, his eyes squinting to track the ball headed his way. In a second he'd have me, so as I got closer I threw my shoulder out and it connected with his right arm. It knocked him off balance enough to make him miss the throw. The ball bounced off his glove and bobbled into the outfield. While he was scrambling for it, I was leaving him behind and making for third base in a cloud of dust.

Carrie waved her hands wildly to get me to stop, but it was like there was this engine in me that was running nearly out of control and there was no way I could stop it even if I wanted to. It felt too good: my feet ripping into the soft dirt, my lungs and legs pumping madly, the distant sound of cheering. Finally Carrie was forced to abandon her base and run for home. Following her, I rounded third, digging in and pushing myself faster. I was halfway there when I caught some movement out of the corner of my eye — an arm reeling back to throw a ball.

"Dive!" Jackson shouted.

I threw my arms out in front of me without thinking, as though I was diving into a huge, clear lake, and I sailed across the next few feet, weightless, stretching for home. When the ground leapt up to meet me, it was like jumping headfirst into concrete. The impact rang through me and I got a face full of dirt, grass, and bits of rock. When I could move again, I rolled painfully to my side and saw the catcher standing there with the ball in his hand.

He dropped his arm to tag me, but stopped when he saw my outstretched fingers, straining, but definitely, without a doubt, touching the flat gray rock that was home.

We played until the sun sank behind the trees and cast gold-streaked shadows across the field, then we gathered up our equipment and started the walk back to town. I trailed behind the main pack with Jackson, Derrick, and the other side's pitcher, John Carter.

"You did good, Steve," Derrick said. "I mean, you kind of tanked after that first run, but —"

I surprised myself by giving Derrick a playful shove, knocking him into Jackson. He was right — after that first run, I had struck out three times in a row. When it was time for us to play defense, I was stuck safely way out in right field.

"So you really never played before?" John asked.

"No. Never."

"Not anything?"

I scooped up a pebble from the road and skipped it down the asphalt. "Dad found this old football once, out behind a Walmart. We'd play catch with that sometimes."

Up ahead, Carrie drifted toward the four of us, falling in next to John and taking his hand. "You guys up for going to the quarry?"

John said sure, but Derrick hedged. "I don't know. I really have to do my homework and then get right to bed."

"Shut up, Derrick," Carrie said. "What about you, Steve? It's just this place out to the east, like a manmade pond. We go there after games sometimes."

I looked over my shoulder, back to where Dad lay in a deep coma at the Greens' house, but the tug I felt toward him seemed fainter than it had before. I knew he was safe since Violet was with him. And hadn't she said he would have wanted me to go to school if I could? Well, maybe he would want this too. Me playing baseball. Me with people my own age. Having a life a little bit like he must have had back before the Collapse.

"Yo!" Carrie called out. "Everybody! Quarry!"

We continued up the hill and then moved out to the east of town, past the fields and into the trees as night began to settle around us. After a while the path opened up into a circular clearing, the ground at the center of it falling away in rocky steps, leading down to a pool of water that was dotted with the reflections of stars that were just beginning to appear.

Everyone scattered when we got there, breaking up into smaller groups of two or three or four and finding places around the pool. One kid, the third baseman from the other team, dipped his hand into the water and pulled out a net that was filled with mason jars. He unscrewed the top off one, took a long drink of whatever was inside, then passed it around the circle.

When it came to me I dipped my nose in and caught the smell of rotten fruit and a nose-singeing tang of alcohol. Home brew. Grandpa used to trade for it sometimes when we had some salvage to spare, and he would get blisteringly drunk on it after dinner. Mom would generally lead me into the tent for a reading lesson whenever he got going.

I took a small sip, then winced. "So, how did all of you end up here?" I asked.

"We were coming north from Georgia," Martin said from his place behind me. "And we ran into, like, this entire ex-US army regiment. Dad decided we'd go through these caves he found to get around them. Took us five days. Five days with no food. My brother" — Martin's voice hitched, then he continued — "he was really freaking out. Cried the whole time until we found our way out. We had no idea where we were, but a few weeks later, we found Derrick and his folks. And then Jackson and his. Now here we are."

As soon as he stopped talking, Martin stared down into the dark water, his face cloudy and distant. I knew why, of course, could tell from the millisecond stumble after he said "my brother." It was the same one I always made after saying "my mother." Somehow between that story and now, his brother was lost. I nudged Martin with the edge of the jar and held it out to him.

"Thanks," he said.

Others told their stories and as they did I looked around the group, noticing things I hadn't seen before. A long jagged scar along the fore-arm of the blond kid who played right field. A deep smudgelike burn mark peeking out from under the sweater of the redheaded girl sitting on the other side of me. The more I looked, the more I saw them, those telltale marks of lives lived after the Collapse. How had I not noticed them before? Was it possible that they all had lives like mine at some point until they came here?

What would have happened, I wondered, if Dad had stood up to Grandpa when I was little and insisted we leave the trail? Could we have ended up here? Would we be living in houses and going to school and cookouts and baseball games?

Would Mom still be alive?

The redheaded girl tapped my arm with a second jar of home brew that had made its way around the circle. I shook my head and she passed it along down the line.

"I'm Wendy, by the way," she said quietly, her small fingers grazing my arm. "You okay?"

"Yeah, I'm —"

"Cann-on-ball!"

There was a gigantic splash that soaked all of us. When I looked up, Derrick was shooting to the surface of the churning water, in his underwear, a dopey smile on his face. Two of the mason jars sat empty where he had been sitting. Jeers came from every corner of the quarry, but they were all mixed with laughter.

"Derrick!"

"Derrick, you jerk!"

"You got us all wet!"

Derrick laughed a deep stuttering laugh and floated lazily on his back.

Wendy shook her great head full of curls and chuckled. "Love, hate. Love, hate. That's all it ever is with him."

"Okay!" Carrie said, rising unsteadily from John's lap. "I think that's our cue, babe."

John offered me his hand. "Hey, man, good job today."

"Thanks. You too." Carrie dragged John up and the two of them said their good-byes and headed down the path to town with their arms around each other's waists. Soon, other couples emerged from the woods and drifted home.

"Well," Jackson said, "I guess we should go pull him out."

Martin and Jackson and I stripped off our shoes, rolled our pant legs up high, and went in after Derrick. Luckily by that time he was pretty tired, so it wasn't too hard to catch him. The trick was getting his bulk out of there and to shore while he mumbled over and over how much he loved us.

"Really, honestly, totally, you dudes are awesome. Just awesome," he said, struggling with his pants.

After we finally got Derrick up and dressed, but before we could get him moving down the path, he lurched forward and grabbed me up into a soggy bear hug, pushing us away from the others.

"This is what it's like, Steve," he whispered intently only inches from my ear. His breath was heavy with the sweet cherry smell of the home brew.

"What what's like, Derrick?"

He pulled back slightly and for a moment didn't seem drunk at all. His eyes were clear and focused.

"This is what it's like to have friends," he whispered.

I stood there in the silence as a grin grew across Derrick's face and then he fell into Wendy's and Martin's arms. "Home, friends! Take me to my home! And you! Wendy! Off with your pants! You too, Marty!"

He giggled as Wendy and Martin led him down the path back to town. I stood there motionless, surrounded in the rhythmic chatter of the grasshoppers and cicadas and the gentle lapping of the quarry's water. Everything seemed to hang in perfect balance, all of it strange and welcome at the same time.

This is what it's like to have friends.

"You okay?"

Jackson was standing in the shadows, waiting.

"Yeah," I said. "Sure."

We left the quarry and made our way through the woods to Jackson's house. Before we got there, though, we slowed without a word and stopped in the park across the street. Jackson sat on one of the swings and I climbed up onto the jungle gym next to him.

To our left, the road wound out of town and away like a ribbon. The pinpricks of candlelight in the windows around us gave the neighborhood the look of a constellation come to Earth.

"So how'd you guys end up here?" I asked. "You never said."

Jackson twisted the toe of his sneaker into the dirt. For a second I thought he hadn't heard me. "We were in, I don't know, Kentucky, I think, with some other families in a little tent city. Mom and Dad were out doing some hunting, and Jenny and I were by this stream downhill from the camp playing Go Fish with some cards she had made. The sun had just gone down and it was all orange and gold." Jackson's fingers curled tight around the swing's chain. "That's when we heard them coming. There were maybe fifteen of them. Twenty. They looked just like us. Maybe a little better off. They came into camp, all smiles, asking if they could have some water from the stream. Nice as could be.

"The man who I guess was their leader was walking with Mr. Simms. Mr. Simms was a friend of my dad's and was in charge of us when Mom and Dad were away. He was older than my folks and lost his whole family to P Eleven and kind of adopted all of us.

"Anyway, the new group's leader, this big hulk of a guy, put his arm around Mr. Simms's shoulder as they walked. After a few steps he pulled Mr. Simms close and said, 'Knock, knock,' which is the start to this old joke. When Mr. Simms said, 'Who's there?' the man reached into his jacket, pulled out a gun, and pressed the barrel right into Mr. Simms's temple."

Jackson's voice caught in his throat. His eyes were far away, remembering. "I saw him do it and I thought, 'Oh, this is a joke. It's a joke.' But then the man pulled the trigger and there was this explosion and Mr. Simms . . . dropped."

Jackson's Adam's apple rose and fell and his lips pressed into a tight line.

"Everyone froze. All of us. There wasn't a sound, just Mr. Simms hitting the ground. Jenny and I stood there watching this fan of blood spread out around his head. Then someone screamed and then everyone was screaming and rushing to their tents for their guns or to escape, but it was too late. The man and his people were everywhere, shooting anyone they could, laughing like it was all this big game, like the rest of us weren't even real.

"There were about twenty-five, maybe thirty, of us in all. Men and women. Some kids me and Jenny's age. The leader and his group killed all but us and a couple others. Then they put their guns away, took whatever supplies we had, and strolled back out of town."

A cold wind blew across the playground and made the trees around us moan. Jackson dug his hands into his jacket pockets.

"Whole thing didn't take but five minutes. When Mom and Dad came back, we took our things and ran as fast as we could, but no matter how far away we got, I thought they were right around the corner, ready to pop out again, just . . . smiling and shooting."

By now the dark of night was settling in. Everything around us — the trees, the houses, the curves of the land — was looming shapes, like animals prowling beneath dark water.

Jackson looked back at me, but I didn't know what to say to him. If we were friends, like Derrick had said, what did friends do? What did they say?

"Guess somebody like you has never felt like that," Jackson said quietly, turning away from me. "Afraid."

Shadows of leaves played over Jackson's drawn, pale face. I stared down at my lap. Something ached deep in my chest. The idea that I had never been afraid was ridiculous but I knew what Grandpa would have said. Never admit fear. Never admit weakness.

"I'm afraid all the time," I said. "After my mom died, I couldn't sleep. Not for months. I'd lie awake at night and think about Dad or Grandpa getting sick. One of them dying. Dad told me we'd be fine. He said nothing would ever change again, but then Grandpa died and he . . ."

I shut my mouth tight and closed my eyes. Saying all of that, thinking it, even, made the whole ugly mess real all over again. It was like this darkness that I could keep at bay most of the time, but if I got too close, if I touched it, it would seize up and have me.

"Hey."

I opened my eyes with a start. Jackson had left the swing and was standing right beside me.

"You're here now," he said. "We both are, right? No matter what happens. Me and my folks, all of us, we won't let anything happen to you."

I looked away from him, along the houses and up the street. How could I tell him that it would only be a matter of time before all of this was gone and we were scattered to the wind? Did a friend say that?

"Probably time for dinner, isn't it?" I said, slipping off the jungle gym.

Jackson lagged behind as I crossed the park and went up the stairs and into the house. The fireplace smelled smoky and warm. Timbers creaked above me. I stood by Dad's bed, looking down at him. His chest rose and fell weakly as he breathed.

"We've been here five years now," Jackson said from behind me in the hallway that led to the kitchen, half in and half out of the light. "I don't know if it'll be forever, but we've almost been wiped out by storms and droughts and bad crops and a hundred other things, and we've always made it. We just stuck together and never gave up."

Later that night, when I closed my eyes and headed to sleep, it was as though I could feel all of them: Marcus and Violet and Dad and Jackson and, somewhere outside in places of their own, Derrick and Martin and

132

Wendy and Carrie and Jenny too. I felt each of them like blooms of heat pulsing out in the night, separate but connected.

Instead of the tomblike stillness of the previous nights, the house felt warm around me, like all of us were settled underneath a thick blanket with the cold winds and the world safely outside.

Was Jackson right? Was it real? Could it last?

I didn't know. But right then, lying there in that quiet and warmth, I hoped. For the first time, I hoped.

SIXTEEN

The next morning before school I helped Violet carry tin buckets of hot water from the fire out back to a white tub in the bathroom upstairs. She said she figured *I* must be dying for a bath — meaning *she* was dying for me to take a bath but wanted to save my feelings. It was a good effort. And a few whiffs of myself confirmed that it was probably past due.

Once we were done and she was gone, I stripped and lowered myself into the tub. The homemade lye soap Violet gave me felt like it was taking a layer of skin off with the dirt. As I scrubbed, I thought how easy it must have been when she and my dad were my age, back before the Collapse. Turn a faucet and out came hot water. Flick a switch and there was light. It must have seemed like magic.

When I was done, Violet came back in with a razor and a pair of scissors. She cut my hair and shaved the light fall of whiskers on my cheeks, then sent me off to Jenny's room. There I found a pair of nearly new-looking jeans, a red button-up shirt, and a handmade black wool sweater. There was even a slightly scuffed pair of brown hiking boots. On the floor next to the bed were my old clothes: a dirty, heavily patched heap of greasy cloth I had been wearing almost daily for the last year or two. I knew every hole, every tear, every patch, wrinkle, and worn spot.

I lifted my old pants and turned them over. Sewn on the right knee was a rectangular scrap of red cloth with gold ducks on it. Dad had put the patch on when I'd worn through the knee a few months ago. The square of cloth had come from one of Mom's old dresses, her favorite one. After she died, Grandpa had insisted we trade her clothes away, but Dad had kept that one dress, hiding it like I hid my books.

Standing there, I didn't think I could do it — throw aside these old things for the new. I told myself I was being crazy. If I'd come across these new clothes on the trail, I'd have taken them. And if I'd come across my old clothes, I would've walked right on by.

"Stephen?" Violet called from downstairs. "You okay?"

I dressed quickly in the new clothes before heading out into the hall. When I turned to close the door, there were my old clothes, blue and black with a flash of red and gold. Dad's knife lying on top in its sheath.

They're just clothes, I told myself and shut the door.

When I came downstairs, Violet was sitting at Dad's side with a bowl of oatmeal in her lap.

"Hey, Violet, I . . ."

When Violet turned back, I saw the feeding tube down Dad's throat. He lay there, his mouth unnaturally wide, his teeth clamped down on the hard plastic. Something shuddered inside me, seeing him like that. Part of me wanted to run over and tear it out of him, to make her leave him alone, but I marshaled myself and crossed the floor slowly until I was just behind her.

"How's he doing?"

Violet spooned the last bit of food down the tube.

"About the same," she said. "I wish I could say more, but without tests . . ."

"I've been talking to him at night."

"That's good." Violet looked back over her shoulder and smiled. "You look really great, Stephen."

I pulled awkwardly at the new clothes. "Thanks."

"You ready?"

Jackson had just come down the stairs and was standing behind me.

I moved to the bed and squeezed Dad's hand tight. "Thanks," I said again to Violet before leaving with Jackson.

"Mr. Waverly!" Jackson announced cheerily as Martin and an extremely bleary-looking Derrick joined us. Jackson clapped him on the back. "How's it going, buddy?! Rough night last night?"

"Ugghhhh," Derrick groaned and halfheartedly pushed Jackson away. He trudged along behind us, grumbling as we made our way to school.

"You playing today?" Martin asked me.

"I don't know," I shrugged. "Stunk pretty badly at the end of the game yesterday."

"Yeah," Derrick said. "In fact, I think he was lying when he told me he was descended from a real New York Yankee. Don't let him play, Martin."

"We're not letting *you* play," Jackson said.

"Why not?"

"You're a mess."

"Quinn, buddy, I was just kidding about how much you suck. Defend me here. Am I a mess?"

I regarded Derrick carefully. His hair was a greasy tumbleweed. All his clothes were rumpled. "Definitely. A total mess."

"Ha!" Martin laughed and punched me in the arm.

"I liked you better when you didn't talk," Derrick grumbled.

Carrie and Wendy mixed in with us at the bottom of the hill as we all filed in behind the mass of little ones.

"Lookin' awful snazzy there, Steve," Carrie said with a grin.

"Oh," I said, looking down at my new clothes, strangely embarrassed. "Thanks. Marcus's old things."

Wendy reached across and drew her finger across the hair that fell just above my eyebrows. "Your hair's out of your face too," she said. "I can see your eyes."

I didn't know what to say. She was wearing a pink and white sweater and jeans, her hair loose and flowing coppery over her shoulders. I was surprised to find myself nervous as she fell into place next to me.

Once we got to school we all split up and the rest of that morning was pretty uneventful. Tuttle lectured and while everyone else was struggling to stay awake I leaned over my paper and took careful notes. He talked about math and poetry and the Holy Roman Empire. I had no idea there was so much world out there to learn about. At noon he let us out for lunch.

It had grown colder in the past few hours and some clouds had begun to pile up, signs of fall moving headlong toward winter. All of us spilled out onto the yard, pulling our lunches out of bags and buckets. The little ones immediately swarmed around the slide and swing sets, fighting over who got to do what first.

"Okay!" Martin announced as he pulled a wrinkled sheet of paper out of his back pocket. "Time to make the lineup! Waverly is benched!"

"What? No way!"

"Quinn is taking your place."

"You know," Derrick said. "You people don't appreciate me. I'm gonna start hanging out with Will Henry."

"Oh go take a bath, Derrick," Wendy said.

I laughed and the lineup talk went on. They all seemed so comfortable with each other, laughing and joking, trading mock punches. I looked around at everyone else in the school yard as they ate their lunches in their own small groups. The inside jokes and chatter of each one joined with the others into a low roar that somehow didn't seem as grating as it had just a few days earlier.

I turned back to the negotiations, and when I did, I saw Jenny. She was sitting under the big sycamore, facing away from the school, in her torn-up jeans and Red Army jacket with her knees pulled up in front of her, sketching furiously in her sketch pad.

My body tensed immediately. The note. I had almost forgotten. I tried to stay calm, nibbling at my sandwich and keeping my eye on her, waiting for an opportunity. All the noise and movement below her — the laughing and yelling and flirting, the squeak of the old swing sets — didn't seem to distract her in the least. She drew with great looping strokes and slashes, leaning down into the pad like she was wrestling with it and just barely winning.

When she was done, Jenny dropped the sketch pad on the grass and stretched out against the tree. She reached up and tucked a length of hair behind her ear, leaving the rest of it to blow over her face like smoke drifting over beach sand.

"I don't know why she even bothers coming."

Jackson had moved out of the lineup negotiations and was eyeing Jenny too.

"Does she always just sit up there drawing and stuff?"

"No, that one's new," he said. "She just started coming to school again the other day."

Up the hill Jenny leaned over her sketch pad, erasing, drawing again. I thought of that lone horse, locked in the classroom.

"Sometimes I wish . . ." Jackson's forehead wrinkled, his lips hardening into a tense slit as he watched her. Whatever he was going to say, he pulled it back before it could get loose.

"What?"

"Sometimes I wish she would go," Jackson said, his voice a harsh whisper. "Just leave. Before she does something that gets us all thrown out of here."

"Would they really do that?"

Jackson eyed me a moment like he was trying to make a decision.

"There was a family," he said, "a few years back. The Krycheks. Had a little girl, like nine, I think. Mr. Krychek used to be a soldier, but all he did was drink by the time he got here. He hid it pretty well for a while, but it got worse. One night he was drinking out in the woods and tried to build a fire. It went out of control and got within a few feet of spreading to the houses. Caleb called a meeting about it the next day. Mom and Dad tried to speak up for them, but Caleb had more than half the town ready to vote against them *and* anyone willing to stand up for them. In the end it was pretty much unanimous."

"Your parents . . . ?"

"Dad voted to send them away. He didn't want to but . . . I mean, the guy was dangerous, right? What choice did he have? Let the whole town get destroyed? Get us thrown out too?"

"What about your mom?"

Jackson's eyes went unfocused as he drew his fingertip aimlessly through the dirt. "She was . . . sick, I think. Didn't make the vote that day."

"What happened to them? The Krycheks?"

Jackson didn't look up. He shrugged. "Dad and some others insisted they at least give them some supplies but . . . it was the middle of January."

He didn't need to say any more. Middle of the winter and the dad a drunk and dragging along a nine-year-old. Only one thing could have happened. I looked down at the remains of my sandwich but wasn't hungry anymore. I could see that family clear as anything, huddled together and snow-blind, making their slow way out of town. A sick shudder went right through me.

I jumped as the bell rang and everyone started packing up their lunch things and heading inside.

"Let's go!" Derrick shouted, throwing up his arms. "It's time to learn, people!"

Jackson lingered by the door. "You coming?" he asked.

"Yeah," I said. "Sure. Just a second. I'll catch up."

The doors slammed behind them and the yard was quiet and empty.

Just me and Jenny.

Jackson's story hung with me. Now more than ever I had to be careful. If Jenny was going to be a threat to me, I needed to deal with it. I looked around, making sure I was alone before stalking up the hill. Jenny didn't notice me as I drew near, too busy sketching the landscape in front of her. The trees looked almost alive on her paper, caught in mid-sway against the gray clouds, the horizon ominous in the distance.

"You're different," she said without turning. "Your clothes and hair and stuff."

I froze. Jenny looked me up and down over her shoulder. Her dark eyes made me feel like I was a fish wriggling on the end of a spear.

"It was, uh . . . Violet. She gave me some clothes."

"Figures," Jenny smirked. "You look like one of *them* now. You come up here for a reason?"

I cleared my throat and tried to force myself back to business. "The note."

"Which note?" she asked innocently. "A? B? C major?"

"Your note."

"Oh, *my* note!"

"Jenny, whatever you think you saw —"

"Oh please," Jenny said with a flirtatious lilt. "Let's not play games that aren't any fun."

I felt my legs go weak. My mind was wiped clear like Tuttle's blackboard. Jenny chuckled.

"I need to know what you want," I said, trying to find the steel in my voice that was always in Grandpa's, but only managed what sounded like a strained squeak. For a second I thought Jenny would laugh, but she didn't. She dropped her pencil and shifted around, looking up at me like she was awaiting a lecture.

"Have you always been a scavenger?" she asked.

"I'm not —"

"Salvager. Whatever. You go north to south, right? To those trade gatherings?"

"Jenny, the note. I —"

"Do you take the same route every time or do you mix it up?"

One time Dad told me about how when they were building the railroads way back when, there would sometimes be a mountain in their
way and they'd have to decide whether to load it up with dynamite and
blow it up or just go around. I had the feeling that this was one of those
times and I was pretty sure I didn't have anywhere near enough dynamite for the first option. If I wanted the information, it looked like I was
going to have to play along.

"It changes."

"Why?"

"If you keep to one path, people can predict it. Set ambushes."

"Smart. How close do you get to the coast?"

"Not close."

"Why? Is it dangerous?"

"Some. Mostly it's just rubble."

"What about the West Coast? What have you heard about it?"

"Nobody goes there anymore," I said.

"Why?"

I gave her a look like it was obvious.

"What? Because that's where my scary Chinese brothers and sisters are?"

I crossed my arms over my chest. "Jenny —"

"You ever seen them?"

"No."

"So what are they *doing* out there?"

Jenny chewed on the end of her pencil, squinting a little in
the sun.

"You like your life, Quinn?" she asked, throwing me off base with the
sudden change in tack. "Wandering about this war-torn land of ours?"

No one had ever asked me anything like that before. Did I like my life? What kind of question was that?

"It's just . . . it's my life."

"Well, it's not a rock. You can have an opinion about it."

"You like yours?"

"I like parts of it."

"Which ones?"

"The parts where I get to break things."

"Why? Because that makes you feel like you're in control of something?"

For the very first time, I stopped her cold. It took everything in me not to throw my arms into the air in celebration. Jenny looked up at me blank-eyed, wriggling on a spear of her own. Slowly a smile grew at the corners of her lips.

"Oh Stephen," she said. "You *are* a pistol."

"What do you want, Jenny?"

Jenny's eyes glinted in the sunlight.

"I want a lot of things, Quinn. I'm just trying to decide which of them you can provide." She flicked her eyes to our left. "Uh-oh. Feel like a tussle?"

"Huh?" I turned and there was Will Henry, the redheaded giant, and one of the slug twins barreling our way.

"Come on," I said, backing away down the hill. "Let's get out of here."

"What? Are you kidding?"

"No, seriously, Jenny. They're trying to get me thrown —"

But Jenny wasn't listening. She jumped up and ran right at them. Will stormed on ahead.

"This isn't about you, Jenny," he said.

"Is it about the uses of symbolism in Melville's *Moby-Dick*?"

"What?"

As Will stopped to figure that one out, Jenny punched him in the face. A hard right, slamming into his jaw. It rocked him, but he came right back at her. Jenny laughed and danced away.

I edged back down the hill toward school. If Jenny wanted to fight, that was her business. I needed to play it safe, for me and Dad. For the Greens.

"This is my town," Will spat. "People like you and the spy aren't welcome, Chink."

Will planted both hands on Jenny's chest and shoved her to the ground. She landed with a dull thump.

I didn't even think. I just launched myself at him, slipping a fist past him and landing it in his stomach. He made a satisfying *oof* sound but recovered fast, throwing a punch that connected squarely with my jaw and spun me around. The next thing I knew, I was on the ground with a mouth full of grass. My head was ringing. I rolled over and all I could see was a wide expanse of cloudy sky cut in half by the dark shadow of Will Henry towering over me.

"You. Don't. Belong. Here," he growled.

Something behind me roared and Jenny flew past me, throwing herself at Will, her fingers stretched out like claws. He tried to shrink out of the way, but she got her arms around his neck and forced him to the ground. My vision was still a little hazy, but I could make out the two guys who were behind Will stepping forward and reaching for Jenny. I forced myself up, taking a fistful of dirt and grass with me. I threw the clump in Big Red's face and threw myself at the other one, using my body like a battering ram. I hit the slug twin full in the chest with my shoulder and he went down. Once we were on the ground, I brought my knee up between his legs. He howled, then curled up on his side, moaning.

I pulled myself on top of him, cocked my fist, and gave him a good one right on the nose. There was a sick crunch and blood spurted out between us. I reared back again, but someone's hands were on my shoulders, pulling me up and away from him.

It was the big redhead. He was strong but slow. I wriggled out of his grasp and got to my feet, backing away and getting my hands up in front of my face. I could hear another fight going on to my left. I wanted to look and see how Jenny was doing, to see if she needed help, but I had troubles of my own. Big Red was sizing me up, deciding on his next move. It was probably the dumbest thing he could have done. While he was thinking, I was moving.

I threw myself at him headfirst, right into his stomach. Even though I was pretty sure I knocked the wind out of him, he didn't go down. I kept pushing forward, hoping to get him off balance, but he grabbed my shoulders and used my momentum to toss me down instead. I hit with a thud, my head slamming into the dirt. I reeled again and a wave of nausea hit me. I reached for my knife, realizing too late that it was sitting on Jenny's floor guarding a pile of old clothes.

I tried to get up, but my arms felt like jelly, and before I could do anything else, Big Red was down on one knee beside me. He pulled his fist back, blocking out everything else in my vision. It was a pale comet hurtling toward me.

But then a look of surprise came over his face and his whole body shot back away from me, like he'd been grabbed up by an angel. There was shouting and a commotion, but my head was too swimmy to make it all out.

Someone grabbed my shoulder and tried to push me up, but it was no use. I was like a rag doll filled with lead.

There was a voice in my ear, close and rushed. "Come on, get up. We have to get out of here."

The world snapped into focus. Jenny was leaning over me. Her bottom lip was split and trailing blood down her chin and neck, soaking the top of her T-shirt. Her right eye was surrounded by a red and black bruise and nearly swollen shut.

"Did we win?"

"Ha! You are a pistol, Stephen," she said as she pulled me up. "Now let's get out of here."

"Jenny Tan!"

"Oh crap."

Tuttle stormed up the hill toward us, clutching his wooden ruler like a sword. He was being led by the second of the slug twins. I saw the plan immediately: Will starts a fight, then sends one of them to get Tuttle, no doubt blaming it on me and Jenny. *Idiot*, I cursed myself.

He was followed by a group of students, all excited to see what was going on. In the middle of the pack were Derrick, Martin, and, finally, Jackson. As soon as Jackson saw Jenny and me together, he stopped cold. The group broke around him, but he didn't move.

He was staring at my hands.

They were covered in dirt and bruises and blood. The new clothes Violet had given me just that morning were torn and stained. Jackson looked from me to Jenny and back again, his body rigid with anger, his hands knotted into fists. I knew what was going through his head. The last straw. A calm day was smashed to pieces and maybe this time it would lead to a vote that would turn his world upside down. I wanted to say something, tell Jackson it wasn't my fault, that it was Jenny, that it was Will, that everything would be okay, but before I could do anything, Tuttle barked, "Enough. Detention for both of you."

"But what about them?" Jenny asked.

Tuttle ignored her. He whirled around, sending the mass of kids behind him scurrying back toward the school. Jackson didn't move at first, but then Martin tapped him on the shoulder, whispered something, and pulled him away.

"You're done," Will said as he passed me, flashing that easy wolfish grin. He and his friends strolled down the hill in Tuttle's wake.

My hand curled into a fist so tight I nearly broke a bone.

"Easy, tiger," Jenny said. She laid her hand on my shoulder, but I jerked away.

"Get away from me."

"Oh come on. We'll get ours."

"Our what?"

Jenny's lips brushed my ear as she whispered, "Revenge, Stephen. We'll get our revenge."

"I don't want revenge," I said, pushing away from her down the hill. "I just want you to leave me alone."

SEVENTEEN

When the classroom was empty except for me and Jenny, Tuttle regarded us over the rim of his steel glasses. "*American History*," he said. "Chapters one through three."

"Read them?" I asked.

"Copy them."

I opened the book and flipped through the pages. Chapters one through three were about twenty densely worded pages. My bruised knuckles ached at the thought of it. Tuttle leaned over a stack of papers, making quick little check and X marks down the length of them. I couldn't concentrate. Every time I tried, I saw Jackson's face growing more and more angry as he looked from me to Jenny after the fight. I had tried to explain, tried to pass him a note even, but he'd ignored me, that hard fury like a wall between us. *Stupid*, I thought, over and over. *Why didn't I just walk away?*

What made it worse was Jenny, twirling a pencil in her bruised fingers, totally unconcerned.

Tuttle cleared his throat and I leaned over my paper. I swallowed the anger as best I could and started to write. I only had two pages done before something bumped against the side of my boot. When I looked down there was a folded piece of paper lying on the floor. I checked on Tuttle, then leaned down and picked it up, unfolding it onto my notebook.

How are the war wounds, tough guy?

Jenny had her head down in her book, copying away, the slightest shadow of a smile on her bruised face. I refolded the paper and went back to work, ignoring her. Minutes later another piece of paper knocked against my foot.

Awww, what's wrong, pal? Mad at me?

Leave me alone, I scrawled across the paper in heavy black letters before kicking it back to her.

Oh come on, Stephen, she wrote back. *You've been dying to hit somebody since the night you got here.*

Well, thanks, I wrote. *Now I'm in detention. Everybody hates me, and your whole family, my dad, and I are all one step closer to getting thrown out of here.*

She answered: *The sky's not going to fall because of one little fight! No one's going to throw you out. Jackson and his band of doofuses will get over it.*

I made sure Tuttle was still busy grading before writing back, *And if they don't?*

I could feel Jenny shaking her head as she read it. When the paper returned it was nearly torn through.

Food for thought. If someone can't handle seeing who you are — are they really your friends?

She was wrong, of course. Jackson and the others were my friends, and fighting those guys was not who I was. Jenny hadn't been there at the game or the quarry. She didn't know.

What would you know about who I really am? I wrote back.

Jenny wrote something immediately, then quickly erased it. Almost an hour passed before she kicked the paper back.

Sometimes I can't sleep, she wrote, her messy scrawl replaced by small deliberate letters. *Because it's like I can feel the whole world spinning so fast beneath me, and I'm thinking, what am I doing here? Is this where I belong? Do I belong anywhere? Some nights it gets so loud in my head that I want to break something, anything, everything, just to make it stop.*

I didn't move for several minutes. I just stared down at the words, the letters so tight, so precise and dark, they looked like they might rupture at any moment and tear the page to pieces. My pencil was near my fingers, and in one strange moment I thought, *Did I write that, or did she?*

I checked on Tuttle, then looked back at Jenny, but she was slipping out of her chair and heading toward the door.

"Miss Green," Tuttle called out, but she ignored him, didn't even correct him. "Miss Green, come back here!"

I wanted to stop her too, but the double doors behind me flew open and slammed shut. Tuttle settled into his chair, and I was surprised to see a strange look on his face, almost concerned. Maybe even a little bit sad.

"This does not mean that you are excused, Mr. Quinn," he said when he caught me looking at him. "Get back to work."

I read Jenny's note twice more before I did, lingering over each word. Tuttle cleared his throat pointedly, and I folded the piece of paper and put it in my pocket so I could finish my work. About an hour later, I finished the assignment and, my hand cramped into a claw, I set it on Tuttle's desk before turning to leave.

"A moment, Mr. Quinn."

I returned to my desk and slumped down while Tuttle took his time making a neat stack of graded papers and sliding it into a leather folder. The waiting was driving me crazy.

"Mr. Tuttle, we were just defending our —"

Tuttle held up his hand to silence me. He slipped a paper out of his folder, then crossed the room and dropped it on my desk. It was my *Great Expectations* quiz. Down one side of the paper was a long column of check marks and a single X. A large *A* was written at the top of the page.

"The question you must ask yourself, Mr. Quinn," Tuttle intoned, towering above me, "is this: Are you a boy or a man? Human being or savage?"

Tuttle's cool blue eyes were on me, unwavering.

"Obviously you've never had to make that choice before. Running around the ruins of this world as your sort of people do, you acted on instinct and self-preservation — an animal — no doubt quivering before rainstorms and amazed by fire and shiny objects. But you're here now, Mr. Quinn, and this is civilization, so now you *do* have a choice. So, what do you want to be?"

Tuttle waited for an answer.

"The fact that you pause does not fill me with confidence."

"Look, as soon as my dad is better, we're leaving, so you don't have to bother."

Tuttle surprised me by folding his long body down into the cramped desk in front of me. He twisted around to face me, his knees nearly pressing into his chest. "Do you like to learn?" he asked.

"I like to read."

Tuttle's thin lips curled into a tight smile. "Yes. So do I. Sometimes it doesn't seem like the world has much use for people like us, does it?

No, most of the world only has time for people who can build or break things. It won't always be that way, I think. A time will come when society, as it always has, will turn for its salvation to the learned. Now, to my surprise, you appear to be intellectually capable, but the question remains: Do you *want* to be one of them?"

It was a ridiculous question. Did I want to be one of the learned? I tried to think of an answer that would satisfy him, but he might as well have been asking me if I wanted to be an astronaut.

"The times we live in, Mr. Quinn, are teetering between the chaos behind us — an infancy made up of smoke and terror and withering plague — and what adulthood lies ahead for us. Wisdom? Peace? Oblivion? Whatever it is, to get there we must let go of the past. It is dead and gone. It will never return and it cannot be changed. All we have now is one another and whatever new thing we make together."

Tuttle unfolded himself from the desk and strode to a shelf along the wall. He pulled down a small stack of books, then laid it on my desk. *Mechanical Engineering. Chinese History. World Political Systems.*

"If you have a desire to be more than what you are, if you want the world to be more than it is, study these in addition to your regular work. If not, please feel free to escape to a warm cocoon of petty violence and team sports."

With that, Tuttle turned his back on me and planted himself at his desk to begin grading a new stack of papers. The books sat in front of me; I ran my fingers across their glossy covers.

This is how we got here in the first place, Grandpa would have said, sneering at the books. But then there was Dad's voice, whispering to me that night in the plane as we watched a doomed woman and boy.

Grandpa is gone.

In my head, it sounded like a fallen leaf blowing across a grave.

Out of the corner of my eye, I saw a thin smile grow on Tuttle's lips as I scooped the books up into my arms, and dashed into the twilight.

EIGHTEEN

I crossed the park, balancing the stack of books in my aching hands, strangely excited to start reading them, when the Greens' front door flew open and out walked Caleb Henry.

It was like I hit a wall.

Caleb was masked by the shadows of the porch at first, so all I could see was his tall frame in jeans, a flannel shirt, and boots. As he descended the stairs and stepped out into the yard, though, it was clear that he was smiling. He didn't acknowledge me or make a sound as he glided up the street.

My arms went weak underneath the pile of books. My stomach churned. *Of course. Where else would Will have gone after the fight?*

The Greens' door hung open. No candles had been lit yet, even though it was edging past twilight and into early evening. Inside it was gray and hushed. I set the books down by my bedroll and the neat bundle Violet had made of my old clothes and Dad's knife while I was away. Then, once I'd checked on Dad, I crossed the room and entered the short hallway that led into the kitchen.

Marcus and Violet were sitting next to each other in the gloom at the kitchen table. Marcus was hunched over a mug, his hands clamped around it, while Violet sat back in her chair, one hand covering her mouth and chin. The shadows of the room deepened the lines on their ashen faces. I kept to the darkness of the hall and listened.

"What choice do we have, Vi?"

"They can vote if they want to vote," Violet said. "We're not giving him up. We're not like that, Marcus. You're not like that."

"But what if we fight them again and Caleb decides to come after us this time?"

Violet had no answer. Her silence hung heavy as stone.

I backed away from the door. Whatever the people of the town thought of Jenny, she was family to the Greens and maybe that protected her. It wouldn't be the same with me or Dad. We were outsiders. Little better than vagrants, no matter how Violet tried to dress me up.

I eased back to the front room, then dropped to my knees alongside Dad's bed. I ripped my bedroll up off the floor and began shoving it along with the rest of my supplies into my backpack. I had put that pack together a million times, but my hands were clumsy now, rushed. I reached for the rifle's cleaning kit, but my knuckles slammed into one of the bed's legs and a jolt of fresh pain rocketed up my arm. Finally I just stuffed everything inside and yanked the flap closed.

There on my knees, I was eye level with the stack of books Tuttle had given me. Politics. History. Science. Little pieces of a larger world.

Useless, Grandpa's voice said deep inside me, disgusted, stronger than ever. I yanked my bag off the floor and stood up over Dad. A wave of sadness reared up. I told myself that Violet would take care of him, that if I didn't protect them, they couldn't protect him, but it was no use. The wave was too big and coming too fast.

How many days had it been now since Grandpa was gone? Eight? Nine? How was it possible that everything could have fallen apart so quickly? That our lives could turn over, again and again, in such a tiny packet of time? I longed for my old life, following Dad and Grandpa without question. Pack the wagon. Scan for salvage. Then make our way from landmark to landmark, a slumping mall and its rusted attendees, a parking lot cracked with yellow flowers.

I wondered if this was what it was like when the end of the world came. A sudden overturning that made every day like stepping alone into an empty room — everything you longed for, every handhold you used to pull yourself along, vanished.

My pack was heavy as I lifted it up onto my back and cinched the straps tight around my arms and middle. I threaded Dad's knife onto my belt and checked that the rifle was loaded before hanging it over my shoulder and walking toward the door.

"Stephen."

I stopped where I was. Violet was standing in the hallway, with Marcus in the dimness behind her.

"You're not leaving. We won't let you. We'll —"

Violet leaned forward, but Marcus's hand shot out from the dark and clamped around her wrist.

My eyes locked on Marcus's hand, rough and tan. It seemed to glow in the low light as he held her back.

"I'll be fine," I said. "Just take care of my dad."

I took the doorknob, but something stopped me before I could turn it. Dad was lying there in his bed, pale and still as always. There was a twist deep in my chest, a hand wrenching at my heart. There was something I still had to do.

"The second night I was here," I said, "I stole two bottles of medicine and some instruments. There's a lightning-struck tree overlooking the highway a couple miles to the west. You'll find them buried just behind it." I looked back at Violet and Marcus. Neither of them had moved. "Thanks," I said. "For everything."

Before either of them could say anything, I forced myself out the door and closed it softly behind me.

When I reached the foot of the steps, I turned and looked up at the house. Jackson's window glowed with a candle's flame. I hoped he was there, reading quietly in the calm of his room with no idea how close he'd come to another overturning, this one far worse than the last. I wished I could have said good-bye. I wished I could have explained.

I went out past the houses and driveways and neglected mailboxes until I came to the town's iron gates and let myself through with a rusty squeak. I stood on the other side, facing the long plain and the wall of the forest.

Where to now?

I put my hands in my pockets to warm them and skimmed the edge of a piece of folded paper I had forgotten was there.

Jenny's note.

I pulled it out and opened it. The dark letters shone in the moonlight.

. . . it's like I can feel the whole world spinning so fast beneath me, and I'm thinking, what am I doing here? Is this where I belong?

I folded the piece of paper, returned it to my pocket, and got moving.

NINETEEN

The trees grew thicker as I went, choked with deadfall and thornbushes. I pulled myself over the fence that marked the northern edge of town. All around me were the night sounds of the woods: owls hooting and lizards skittering through the underbrush. Farther out were the heavier steps of larger things — deer or wolves or bears — making their own way through the dark.

I leapt over a fast-running stream and then stepped out into a clearing, caught in the silvery wash of the moon. On the far side were the remains of a barn. Its arid wood slats were pockmarked with nail holes and overgrown with moss and creeping vines. There was a large ragged hole in the roof.

The whole place was surrounded by rusting farm implements, hoes and shovels and pitchforks, and what I thought was an old tractor that was covered in vines and weeds.

This old barn, Jackson had said. *North of town.*

I crept up to the barn and slipped in through half-opened doors. The inside was lit with a few flickering candles that sat near an old mattress in one corner. I looked around but there was no one there, just piles of hay bound into moldering blocks against the walls, and rakes and a long rusty scythe hanging on pegs. Something rustled in the loft above me.

"Jenny?"

An owl exploded out through the hole in the ceiling, startling me enough that I almost cried out. I steadied myself and crossed the barn to the mattress. It was covered with a quilt and a couple thin pillows. Scattered around it were scraps of paper, clothes and stubs of old candles, another dog-eared chemistry book. Near the head of the bed was Jenny's sketch pad.

I peered into the dark corners of the barn to make sure I was alone, then set the rifle to the side and knelt down. I opened the sketch pad, tipping its face into the candlelight. The drawings at the beginning were mostly of people. Tuttle glowered from one page, surrounded by a dark halo, his ruler in hand. Sam sat in soft candlelight holding a pipe, a half smile on his face and a book draped over one knee. As I got toward the end, the people began to disappear and were replaced by trees, the barn, the school building, empty fields. If there were any people at all, they were seen from far away, their backs turned — dark, faceless walls.

"What are you doing here?"

I twisted around so fast I lost my balance and fell in a heap onto the bed, scrambling backward away from the voice. When I looked up, Jenny was standing over me in a bloodstained T-shirt, with a cat's grin and a black eye.

"Nice squeal, tough guy."

"I didn't —"

"Whatever." Jenny snatched the sketch pad off the floor next to me. "What are you doing here?"

I stood up warily, awkward in my backpack and coat. I searched the ground for an explanation.

"I was . . . walking."

Jenny turned and peered into the dark outside the doors.

"There's no one else here," I said. "It's just me."

"I thought you were pissed at me."

I shrugged. Jenny set the sketch pad on a pile behind the bed.

"How's your hand?"

I raised my right hand into the light and flexed my fingers. The bleeding had stopped, leaving my knuckles crusted with dirt and blood. The joints ground together when I moved them.

"We should clean it up," Jenny said. She retrieved a plastic box from her bedside and stood in front of me. I just looked at her. "What? You want gangrene? Sit down."

I slipped out of my coat and pack and did as she said, sitting down on the edge of her bed. Jenny grabbed my hand, examined it, then started scrubbing away with a rag. I hissed and tried to pull back but Jenny held my wrist tight.

"Take it easy, you big baby. If it's not clean, I'll have to amputate."

I held my breath as she worked the dirt out of my wounds. Once my hand was clean, she spread some ointment from a small tube on it.

"How come Violet's not doing this for you?"

"Caleb was there when I got back after detention."

Jenny looked up with one arched eyebrow.

"They were going to have a vote tomorrow," I said. "I left before they could."

Jenny stopped what she was doing. Her dark eyes smoldered and she cursed under her breath. "I'm sorry. I shouldn't have —"

"You didn't make me do anything."

"Your dad, is he — ?"

"He's with Violet."

"Good," Jenny said. "They won't mess with her about a patient. Wouldn't dare."

Jenny tossed the tube of ointment back in the kit and took out a roll of gauze. She began carefully winding the bandage around my hand.

"Well, at least we denied them the pleasure of tossing us out," she said. "That's something, right?"

"Yeah, that'll show 'em."

Jenny smiled and her breathing slowed as she looped the bandage around my fingers and across my palm. It was strange to see her hard surface swept away. Before, she seemed like a giant. A hurricane. Here she was just a girl. The air around her felt still.

"So you're not going back?" she asked.

"No. You?"

Jenny glanced up at the rafters. "And leave all of this? It's easier for everybody if I don't. No place for me in their American fantasy camp." She shook her head with a dark laugh. "I mean, it's hilarious, right? Baseball games. Thanksgiving. American flags. They're the ones responsible for blowing all that stuff up in the first place, and now they love it so much and want it all back? They even took Fort Leonard and built themselves a little nemesis."

"Marcus and Violet aren't like that."

Jenny looked up from under her black hair. "No?"

"They took me in," I said. "Took you in too. They didn't have to do that."

"I know," she said quietly. "They mean well, I know they do, it's just . . . they only go so far. You know? They get right up to the edge and then back off."

I thought of Marcus's hand on Violet's wrist, holding her back. Violet yielding.

"Like with the Krycheks."

"Jackson told you about that? I'm surprised. It doesn't exactly paint Mommy and Daddy in the best light. I don't know. Maybe it's as far as they *can* go. Maybe it's safer to just keep things as they are."

Jenny secured the bandage with a pin, then put the rest of the gauze away and snapped the med kit closed.

"Well, I think you're all set. Should heal up in a few days."

"So no amputation, then."

"I'll keep my eye on it."

I took my hand back, a little sorry to see it leave the cradle of her palm. We sat there, silently, on the edge of her bed. I needed to go find a camp for the night, needed to search for supplies, but I didn't move. An owl hooted outside. The candlelight flickered.

"How is he?" Jenny asked. "Your dad?"

Her question brought a wave that reared up over me again. My throat constricted and there was a burning in my eyes that I had to fight back. But then Jenny drew closer and laid the flat of her palm against my back. Every curve of it, warm and rough, spread across my ribs and spine. There was maybe an inch between my leg and the calloused plain of her bare foot. A pulse of heat came off her, carrying along with it the scent of pine and spicy earth.

Everything in me calmed. The heat and noise faded away.

"Ever since we got here, I've been saying, 'when he wakes up,' and 'when he's better.' It's like I've been trying to pretend that Violet didn't say he might never wake up."

"Violet can be wrong," Jenny said. "She's not perfect. I mean, there used to be, like, tests and instruments and things that told us what was going to happen to us, but not anymore. Right? Now we don't know much of anything. The future just goes in whatever direction it wants."

She was right. I thought of the churn of the river tearing through rock and dirt. Who knew where it would go? What it would wipe away? Who it would spare?

"Did you really mean that stuff you said in the note?" I asked. "The stuff about the world spinning?"

"Yeah," Jenny said. "I did."

"What do you do about it?"

Jenny stretched across the bed behind me, curling around my back, and dug into a bag on the other side.

"What are you doing?"

When Jenny sat up, her hand was closed into a fist. "What I like to do in times like these. When the world's got you down."

"What?"

Jenny opened her hand into the candlelight. A pile of fat paper cylinders sat in her palm. There was a twisted white fuse attached to each one.

"If you thought punching people was good," she said, "wait till you try blowing things up."

Sitting there in the palm of her hand, the little explosives seemed distant, almost imaginary, but a tingling started through my whole body anyway, like that moment when my bat connected with the ball and I ran the bases.

"What did you have in mind?" I asked.

Jenny's grin shone all the way to the corners of her lips.

TWENTY

Minutes later I was running through the woods behind Jenny. There was no path I could see, so I had to struggle to keep an eye on her as she ran, slick as a deer, in and out of the pools of moonlight that littered the forest floor.

She knew the woods better than I did and made a game out of staying ahead of me so that I could follow but never quite catch up. It wasn't until we both had to slow down to scale the Settler's Landing fence that I got anywhere near her. She dropped down into a crouch just behind a thick stand of trees. When I came up, Jenny put her finger to her lips and motioned for me to get down. Both of us were breathing heavily, pushing out thick plumes of white steam.

"Where are we?" I whispered.

Jenny motioned forward with her chin. "Take a look."

In the clearing ahead was a house totally unlike all the others in Settler's Landing. It was enormous, more of a mansion than a house, with towering white walls and columns flanking the front door like marble generals. Two windows in the upper stories glowed with yellow light and filled the yard with a flickering glow.

"Casa de Henry," Jenny said.

"What are we doing here?"

Just then the lights in the upper windows went out. "Come on. We have to go around back."

Jenny took off deeper into the woods, heading to the rear of the house. As we moved around it, its size became even more overwhelming. The walls stretched back another hundred feet or so.

Behind the house there was a collection of fenced enclosures that looked recently built, homemade from scrap pieces of wood, split logs, and scavenged chicken wire. One held chickens, another pigs, and a third sheep.

"The horses and about twenty cows, mean suckers, are in different enclosures on the other side of the trees, but this'll do," Jenny told me.

"Do for what?"

Jenny wasn't listening. She had started to dig around in her bag.

"Take these." She dropped a handful of the fused cylinders into my hand.

"You want me to blow up the sheep?"

Jenny slapped me on the side of the head. "No! We're not gonna hurt them."

"But —"

"Look, the word *explosive*, when applied to these things, is a little grand. They're more like firecrackers."

"Jenny, I don't know. If we get caught —"

"What? We already tossed *ourselves* out of town. Right? Look, I swear to you, they'll never know it's us. Besides, what we are about to do is incredibly obnoxious but more or less harmless."

"What *are* we about to do?"

She smiled a razory smile. "We are going to make sure Will Henry has a really, really crappy night. Now go around to the sheep pen, open the gates, and toss them in. Oh! Matches."

Jenny shoved a cardboard box of matches in my hand and darted out from behind the tree to a spot between the pig and chicken enclosures. I made my way to the sheep's pen, one eye always on the house in case a light came on. I ducked down by the gate. Most of the sheep were in a knot at the center of their pen and didn't even raise their heads as I approached. I slipped the rope loop that held the gate closed up over a post. There was a sharp squeak from the hinge as I opened it that made my heart freeze. One sheep raised its head with mild curiosity but then lowered it again.

I shuffled the bundle of firecrackers in my palm. It was crazy. Utterly crazy. I peeked over the fence. Jenny was poised at the pig pen, firecrackers in hand. I swallowed hard and turned back to the sheep standing placidly in the mud. I saw Will Henry pushing Jenny to the ground. I saw his gold hair and his vicious smile.

I lit the fuse as Jenny struck hers, then tossed my bundle about five feet behind the biggest knot of sheep. One turned back toward the sparking pile of firecrackers.

"Baaaaa."

The explosions were so much bigger than I thought they'd be — a fast procession of booms, sizzles, and cracks, followed by great showers of sparks, red and green and yellow, shooting up into the sky and exploding again, creating umbrellas of fire that lit up the yard like a new sun.

"Cool!" Jenny exclaimed as she slid into the dirt next to me. "I had no idea they were going to do *that*."

The animals completely lost their minds. I had never heard anything like it — the clucking, the oinking, the . . . whatever it is that sheep do was deafening. In seconds they were on the move, pouring out of the gates of their pens. Most of them headed right for the Henrys' huge and beautiful home. Candles flared throughout the house and I could imagine what was going on inside: a confused jumble of Henrys shouting over the squeals of the animals, trying to get dressed, reaching for guns.

"Um, Jenny, I think we better get out of here."

Just then the back door opened and Will came running out in his underwear, a shotgun in one hand and a flashlight in the other. He was joined by a mix of relations, a group of much older brothers and a small girl with blond hair I guessed was his sister.

The animals made right for them, a tidal wave of flesh that curled around their legs, knocked them off balance, then scattered out in all directions. The smaller ones leapt onto the fine white porch and covered everything with a layer of mud and panicked excrement. A few even made it through the back door and into the house, eliciting a chorus of screams and smashing pots and pans. But the bulk of the animals tore right into the woods, crushing through the brush and disappearing. Caleb emerged from the house and shouted at the others to get after them. Will tried to comply but right then a particularly terrified sheep knocked him into the mud.

"Yes!" Jenny said. "Mission accomplished!"

"Hey! Who's there?!"

The beam of a big flashlight was coming Jenny's way. It would hit her any second.

I leapt up out of the brush. "Bow down to your new masters!" I yelled. "Fort Leonard forever!"

The flashlight jerked away and we took off into the woods, laughing just as a shotgun exploded behind us. We ran flat out, leaping over streams and dodging walls of thornbushes, pausing only long enough to fling ourselves up over the fence before racing on again. Even when the sounds of the stampeding livestock and the panicked Henrys were lost in the thicket behind us we kept running. Jenny was ahead of me when the barn appeared in front of us.

As we crossed the clearing, I gave a burst of speed and was right at her heels. I grabbed hold of her arm and tried to pull her back, but our momentum sent us both careening into the wall, landing hard enough to make the whole barn shudder. Jenny hit first and I piled into her, trapping her with my arms. She twisted around so her back was pressed up against the wall.

"I still won," she panted.

Her cheeks were bright red from the cold and slashed with strands of black hair.

The next thing I knew, we were kissing. I don't know if she started it or I did. My elbows collapsed, making a cage around her, pressing our bodies together so that when we fought for air our chests crashed together.

Her hands clasped around my back, pulling me in tight. My hand found her hip, then rose up until it touched the smooth fault line of her scar.

Her skin felt like it was on fire beneath my fingertips.

TWENTY-ONE

When I woke it was barely light out and freezing. Winter had finally arrived. Even in my sweater, flannel shirt, and jeans, I shivered as I pushed myself up on my elbows. Jenny was sitting on the floor of the barn, dressed in jeans and a black sweater, scribbling away on her sketch pad.

"Aren't you cold?"

She shrugged, focused on the paper in her lap, sketching, frowning, erasing, and starting over again. In the sunlight her black eye from the day before looked even worse, an oil slick spread of blue, black, and gray. I turned on my side and watched her, pulling the blanket up over my shoulder.

"What are you doing?"

"Drawing," she said without looking up.

"What?"

"You."

"Think you could make me taller?"

Jenny smiled. I turned on my back and rubbed the sleep out of my eyes.

"What do you do them for? The drawings. Do you sell them or trade them or something?"

"Oh yeah, I supply the entire town with moody line drawings."

"Seriously."

"I don't know. Violet found this set of drawing pencils somewhere and gave them to me. Everything seems a little quieter when I draw. Nothing else manages it. If I didn't, I think a lot more people around here would be sporting black eyes."

I looked up and traced the dusty lines of the timbers stretching across the ceiling, wishing I had something like that, something that would still the nameless feeling that was growing inside of me like a storm cloud, like something just barely forgotten.

Dad.

It was the first night of my entire life that I had spent apart from him. *And for what?* I thought bitterly, memories of the night before swarming in. *So I could run around having fun while he lay there alone in that house? What if our little prank made things even worse?*

I closed my eyes and saw a glint of gold shining in the dark. My grandfather's fist falling from the sky. Alive or dead, he was still there. His voice still in my ear. Our survival was all on me — and what was I doing about it?

I drew myself up out of the bed.

"What are you doing?" Jenny asked as I slipped one boot on and hunted for the other. "Uh, hello? Question here."

"I should be out looking for supplies," I said. "Making camp some-where."

"Funny, it seemed like you were making camp here."

My fingers froze on the strap of my backpack. I stood there stupidly, unable to move. It was like all the bones had tumbled out of my body. *How could I make her understand?*

170

"Talk to me, Stephen," Jenny said quietly. She was looking up at me over the edge of her pad. Her eyes, liquid and sharp at the same time. It was like she was always one step ahead of me. Grandpa had told me a hundred times to keep quiet. To keep things to myself. But I couldn't anymore.

"I just . . . I keep thinking I'm going to be . . ."

"What?"

A white star, crowned in gold, fell, and I shook from its impact.

". . . punished," I said.

"For what? Having fun? Being with me? Why would you think that?"

Jenny's pencil clattered to the floor as she charged across the room and knocked me back onto the bed. She threw her legs over my chest, holding me down.

"Jenny . . ."

She took both my wrists in her calloused hands, pinning me. Her hair fell down around us like a curtain, blocking out the rest of the world.

"No one is going to be punished for something as dumb as stampeding some pigs or wrestling with me. Not by God, not by anybody."

"Jenny, let me up."

"The world is not all on you," Jenny said, pushing me down, suddenly fierce. "I know it feels that way, but it's not. Not anymore." She dipped her head down and kissed me. "Not for either of us. Okay? Now say that the world isn't going to end if Little Stevie Quinn has some fun."

"Jenny —"

"Say it! I mean, you did have fun blowing things up and kissing me last night, right?"

Fun wasn't the word. Not even close. Suddenly Grandpa and that flash of gold seemed far away.

"Say it," Jenny repeated, a whisper, her face inches from mine. "The world isn't going to end."

I watched her lips move and matched them carefully, syllable for syllable. Something about it felt secret and shameful, but I said it anyway.

"The world isn't going to end."

Jenny's lips fell onto mine, and then we lay there gazing dreamily up at the high ceiling for I don't know how long. One of us would laugh and then the other, for no reason we could put a name to. Thoughts entered my mind and I said them and they all seemed to make sense to her.

The sun mounted steadily outside, filling the barn with an amber light.

"What time do you think it is?" I asked.

"Are you saying time doesn't cease to have meaning when we're together?"

"Seriously."

"I don't know," she said sleepily. "A little after dawn, I guess? Why?"

I turned so our faces were just inches apart on separate pillows. "I want to go back over to the Greens' for a second. Before everyone gets up."

"For what?"

"To see Dad. And get some books."

"Books?"

I paused. I had said it without thinking. I knew the mocking that I was in for, but what could I do?

"Some, uh, books Tuttle gave me."

Jenny chuckled. "He totally got to you with the save the world thing, didn't he?"

"He did not!"

"He did! You're going to help usher in a new golden age of mankind."

"I am not!" I said, and then, when her laughter had faded, "I don't know. I was mad when I left, so I didn't take them. But now I guess . . . I've just never had anything like that before. School and stuff, I mean. It's kind of cool knowing things other than how to avoid dying."

"No, I get that," she said, then added with a smirk, "you're coming back though, right? This isn't some clever little ploy?"

I laughed, struck for a second by the strange sound of it and how easy it felt when I was with her. Once I got myself together I stood there at the edge of the bed, hands stuffed in my pockets.

How does this work? Do I kiss her before I leave?

Over and over again I was falling into worlds I didn't know the rules for.

"So . . . I'll, uh, see ya later."

Jenny rolled her eyes at my awkwardness. I took a last look at her lying there in the half-light, then turned toward the door, knowing that if I didn't leave right away, I never would.

"I want to come with you when you go."

I stopped in my tracks inches from the door.

"When your dad is better," she said. "I want to come. I was going to be all subtle about it. At one point I was even going to blackmail you, since I spied on you burying all that stuff of Violet's that night, but now I thought I'd just come out with it."

Jenny rose up out of bed and moved toward me.

"Look, like you saw last night, I'm kind of a tactical genius, right? And I know where all the good stuff in this town is, so I could help you pick up some salvage before we go. What do you think?"

Jenny's face was inches from mine, but I was too stunned to say anything.

"You don't want me to," she said flatly.

"It's not that."

"What? You don't think I can handle it?" Jenny teased. "I could destroy you in a heartbeat."

"I know."

"Don't worry, Stephen — it's not like I'm asking you to marry me or anything."

"No, I didn't — I just mean . . ." I struggled, trying to come up with a reason her offer was so confusing. "Why would you *want* to?"

"Why? Because I can't live in this stupid twentieth-century museum anymore. I don't belong here, and neither do you! I want to be out there in the real world. With you."

"Jenny, it's not —"

"What? Easy? Safe? Uh, yeah, no kidding. We were out there for ten years before we came here and we saw all the same things you did. Worse, maybe."

I thought of that morning by the stream. She and Jackson playing cards and all the blood that followed. Who was I to tell her what the real world was?

"I know it will be dangerous," she said. "I just think sitting here in this barn playing dumb pranks isn't living. With or without you, I'm leaving. I'd rather it be with you. And I think that's what you want too."

She was right. I knew it as soon as she suggested it. I knew exactly what Grandpa would think, what he would say, but right then I didn't care. The idea of walking out of town without her seemed impossible.

"Yeah," I said. "Yeah. Okay."

"Ha!" she exclaimed. "Nice! It'll be great, you'll see. And your dad is totally gonna love me. Don't you think?"

"Yeah, I kind of have a feeling he might."

Jenny popped up on her toes and kissed me again, holding it longer this time, slipping her arms around my back so our bodies pressed tight together. "Still want to go get those books?"

I smiled. Our foreheads met, making a close little pyramid. "Yep."

"Jerk."

"I'll come back as soon as I get them."

By the time I got to the door, Jenny already had her sketch pad in her hands, drawing, lost in it. Her dark hair was a tangled mess, and in the growing light of the morning, her skin glowed. Her sweater slipped away from her shoulder, revealing a tiny island chain of freckles. I watched her for a second and then slipped out the door into the cold morning air.

I stood for a moment in the barnyard, then made for a path that cut like an arrow into the woods. Everything seemed golden and crisp around me and I felt I was close to touching something I had never seen, or even hoped for. The future.

TWENTY-TWO

I avoided the main road, following the decaying perimeter fence as it wound through the woods before jumping it and heading toward Settler's Landing. My steps felt lighter than usual as I walked through the bare trees. It was funny trying to imagine Jenny out with me and Dad on the trail. Somehow I couldn't see her trudging along, donkey in tow, picking up scrap.

Maybe we won't even go back on the trail.

I stopped dead in the middle of the woods, surprised by the thought. I rolled it around in my head like it was a jewel I had just discovered.

Was it possible? After all, Dad had been talking about it before the accident, and now with Jenny along, maybe we really could make a new start. Settle somewhere. Go west and see what there was to see. There was a whole world out there.

I laughed a little to myself. The idea would have terrified me just weeks ago. How had that changed? Was it Jenny? Was it Settler's Landing? Did it even matter? Hope was hope and I'd take it.

I clambered down a hill and leapt over a stream. The trees opened up above me. The sky was thick with looming gray clouds. The way the temperature was dropping, I wondered if I might actually see snow this year.

Usually we were down in Florida by this time of year, since real winter storms could sometimes last for weeks on end. The last time I'd seen snow was during a freak storm years before. We had just gotten to the Canadian camp in early April, when the day suddenly grew cold and snow began to fall. It had seemed like a miracle. The trading camp had buzzed around us, everyone rushing to celebrate before it was gone. There'd been a bonfire and food roasting on spits and a three-man band whose music had floated above the camp.

Mom and Dad and I had stayed behind while Grandpa went out looking for tobacco. We'd gathered around our campfire in a semicircle of folding chairs, cooking a skinny chicken on a spit, a plastic tarp angled over us to keep the snow off. We knew from experience that several hours from that moment we would have to take refuge to escape the drunkenness and the fights that inevitably broke out after a big party, but that was later. Right then the air was full of laughter and music and the clean-smelling snow that had painted the muddy camp around us a fresh, brilliant white. I had *The Lord of the Rings* on my lap but was listening to Dad talk about his days as a theater usher in San Diego while Mom talked of wild party after wild party and teased him for being a nerd.

"So how did you guys meet?" I'd asked that night.

Mom had glanced at Dad. I was maybe eight then and they'd only recently started talking to me about the Collapse and the war.

"P Eleven had just started up," Dad said. "There were rumors about a quarantine in San Diego, so your grandparents and I piled into the car, using Grandpa's military ID to get us through the roadblocks. We thought we'd head out east to this old army installation in the desert to wait things out. On our way out of town, we stopped for gas at the station your mom's parents owned."

"By then my whole family was gone," Mom said. "My sister, Sarah, went first, then Dad, then Mom."

Mom's face had darkened, remembering it.

"I heard the bell ding as your dad and his folks pulled up. I came out from behind the station to meet them. I was filthy. It's funny — I was such a prissy little thing when I was little, playing dolls and insisting everything I owned be as pink and frilly as possible. But by that point, I barely bothered to wipe the dirt off my face before going to fill up their gas."

Dad had held out his hand, stretching it across the space between them, and Mom had taken it.

"I pumped it for your grandpa, and when I was done, he dug down into his pocket to pay, but all he had was a hundred. When I told him I didn't have change for a hundred, he started yelling and screaming, claiming I was trying to cheat him! I laughed. I was like . . . the world is coming to an *end*, man! I mean, the sky is *falling*! I just buried my entire family out in the desert, and you're having an aneurysm over your eleven dollars and fifty cents in change? Finally I just said forget it. Go with God, Ebenezer!

"So he took his hundred and jumped in the car, but by that point your father here had gotten out of the car and said he wasn't getting in until his dad agreed to take me with them. Well, if you thought your grandfather had been impolite before, imagine the tidal wave of profanity that erupted when number one son decided to stage a little coup. Your grandpa screamed and hollered, he stamped his feet, even hit him! Can you believe that? Hitting something as adorable as your father? Didn't matter, though. Your dad was a brick wall. He wouldn't give an inch. Not one inch. I hadn't said two words to him yet! And here he was . . . my noble man."

"Why'd you do it, Dad?"

Dad had locked eyes with Mom over the orange flames. The snow swirled behind him.

"I don't know," he said. "Didn't really even think about doing it till then. It was just . . . the second I saw her, it was like a jigsaw puzzle. You know? You've got all these pieces and, on its own, each piece is a splotch of blue or a bit of green. But then a bunch of them click into place and you've got the sky or the grass and the whole thing just makes sense."

I'd recognized the look that came over his face then. He got it a lot when looking at Mom. It was like he was seeing her as she was right then, bright and rosy in the fire's glow, but at the same time seeing her as she was on the day they met, and when they'd first kissed, and when they'd snuck away from Grandpa to be married, and then as he imagined she might be ten years down the line, then twenty, then thirty, and finally as the old woman he had no idea she would never have the chance to become.

It was like he was looking at his whole life with her in that one moment.

I stepped out of the tree line and into the Greens' backyard. There were no candles lit in the windows and I couldn't hear any sign of movement from inside. Still, I skirted around the edge of their backyard garden toward the front door. I knew they wouldn't mind my coming, but I thought it would be better if they didn't see me. Hiding behind the corner of the house, I peeked out into the neighborhood.

It seemed strangely quiet, empty, almost as if everyone who lived there had picked up and moved on the night before. I told myself it was just my imagination.

I came out around the side of the house and went up the front steps, letting myself inside. Dad lay in his usual place, looking exactly as he had the night before. His face, more and more drawn as the days passed, was still framed with his great swirls of black hair, shot through with veins of white.

He had become a different person the day he met Mom, like a switch had been flipped inside him. He stood up to Grandpa in a way he never had before, and then they somehow managed to hold on to each other as the world tore itself to shreds around them. They even had me when the idea of bringing another person into that wreck of a world must have seemed crazy at best.

I thought maybe the man he was back in the plane, the one who rescued those two people, was the man Mom knew emerging again after being so long without her, the man who wouldn't admit that the world was really over.

She would have been so proud of him.

I realized, maybe for the first time, that I was too.

"Jenny wants to come with us when we go," I said quietly, my hand on his shoulder. "I think you'll like her. I was thinking maybe we won't even go back on the trail. You know? Like you said before we came here? Maybe we'll find someplace to have a house. Maybe we'll —"

I stopped myself short. It was fine when it was all in my head, but it felt foolish to imagine that life out loud.

Driving back the sadness I could feel swelling inside me, I knelt down by his bed and collected the books, piling them up in my arms.

"I'll be back soon," I said.

I reached for the doorknob, but as I did I noticed the coatrack that hung on the wall next to the door frame. Something about it struck me, but for a second I didn't understand what or why. And then I got it.

It was empty.

Each time I had seen the Greens come inside, they would take off their jackets and hang them on the coatrack's pegs. If Jackson or Marcus ever forgot, Violet would ride him until he took it from wherever he dropped it and hung it up.

The Greens should have been upstairs, maybe a half hour or so from getting up and starting their day. So why was the coatrack empty?

I set my books on the floor and stepped into the kitchen, listening intently for any sound coming from upstairs. Nothing. From the bottom of the stairs, I could see Jackson's door hanging open into the hall. The stairs creaked as I made my way up, but there was no answering sound from any of the rooms. There were clothes scattered on Jackson's floor and his bed was disheveled, like he had gotten up and dressed in a hurry. I made my way to the end of the hall, to Marcus and Violet's room, and found it the same way.

So what? Something came up and they all decided to get an early start. It's nothing.

It made sense, but I didn't believe it. Maybe it was that weird abandoned feeling I'd noticed as soon as I'd gotten to town this morning. I went downstairs and peeked out the front door. Just as I did, a door opened and slammed shut somewhere across the park. A man ran from his house and then down the road that led to the school.

I closed the Greens' door behind me and eased out onto the porch. I knew I should take my books and go back to Jenny. After all, what happened in this town was no longer my business but, curious, I went down the road toward the school.

I reached the edge of the parking lot just as the man threw open the school's front doors and disappeared inside. I circled around the side of the building, looking in each window as I had that first day, but saw nothing until I came around to the back of the school and looked in the window above the main classroom.

The room was packed with what I was sure was every single resident of Settler's Landing. A hundred people or more. The desks and chairs were pushed aside and everyone stood facing Tuttle's empty desk in tight groups. A murmur rose and fell in waves. I eased the window open.

Violet and Jackson were at the front of the mob. Violet stood behind Jackson with her hands on his shoulders. His face was cast down and his arms were crossed tightly over his chest. He leaned into his mom the way a scared child would. That was how everyone looked, afraid and waiting.

The doors at the back of the classroom flew open and Tuttle came in, followed by Caleb and Will and, behind them, Marcus. They all looked tired and pale. Their clothes were dirty and in some places torn. Each one of them was armed. The crowd hushed instantly as Caleb swept in front of Tuttle's desk. He bowed his head, his hands clasped tightly in front of him.

"Poison," Caleb said simply, letting it hang in the air without explanation. "The people of Israel were beset on all sides by the godless. Animals, starving and hungry for destruction. Unable to stand against the people of God in the field, they conspired to come into their land in parties of two or three as spies."

Caleb paused, searching the crowd. I pushed farther away from the window.

"The people of Israel took them to their heart. They dressed them in their clothes and gave them food and water and fellowship. After all, they thought, there were so few of them, what harm could there be? The people of God grew proud of their kindness and generosity, barely noticing the poison that had infected them, like a brackish stream pouring into a clear lake, until soon the water all around them was murky and foul. The people of God said to one another, 'But where is our home? Where is the land of God that was?' This is how the weak and the profane destroy the strong and the righteous."

The crowd held its breath as he scanned its faces.

"Last night, our home was attacked."

The crowd didn't move, except for some parents who pulled their children tighter.

"Two or more raiders from Fort Leonard, perhaps guided here by former members of our own community, came for our livestock, firing their weapons into the air to start a stampede. Whether their goal was to steal them or to simply run them off in order to weaken us before a larger assault, we don't know. My family gave chase but was unable to overcome them."

My first instinct was to laugh, it was so ridiculous, but the reaction from the crowd made it clear that this was deadly serious.

"Like you all, I know the danger of the world around us," Caleb continued, his voice softening, growing warm, "how it presses against us every day. For years now we have been safe in our anonymity, blessed by God in this place, but I fear, I fear deeply, that such a time may be coming to an end. These new times will demand not only vigilance but also action. It's my opinion that we cannot sit idly, waiting to be attacked again. If we are to be truly safe, we must act now before the danger grows. It gives me no pleasure to say this, but I propose the only course of action I feel is responsible. We must gather a force and, as quickly as possible, move to end the threat of Fort Leonard once and for all."

The people of Settler's Landing didn't hold back. Their agreement was absolute and automatic in a way that was frightening. Men yelled. Some stomped their feet and pounded on the walls. Down in the crowd, I saw Derrick and Martin and Wendy and the rest, all of them with their parents, and all of them shouting their approval.

Down at the front of the group, though, Jackson melted even farther into Violet's body, his skin waxy and pale as he imagined, I was sure, what was to come.

Caleb soaked in their approval as Sam entered the room, a rifle slung over his shoulder. He looked haggard, his clothes in disarray and a salt-and-pepper growth of stubble on his ashen face. Marcus leaned in, nodding, as Sam whispered to him. The two then slipped out the doors together and I moved away from the window to follow them. I thought that if I had the chance to stop the madness, this was it.

By the time I made it around to the parking lot, Sam and Marcus were talking to a small group of armed men. They spoke briefly, then Sam took the men east over the hill and out of sight. Marcus quickened his pace across the lot and toward town.

"Marcus!" I cried out. "Marcus, wait!"

Marcus turned back. "What are you doing here? You shouldn't be here, Stephen —"

"It was us," I said, catching my breath.

"What?"

"Me and Jenny. At the Henrys' last night. We didn't mean anything by it. It was just a stupid prank to get back at Will and them."

Marcus checked behind us, then yanked me off the road toward the shelter of the trees. "Someone said they were from Fort Leonard."

"That was me. It was dumb. I know. I'm sorry. Look, just tell Caleb. Tell him it was us. We'll go, we'll really leave this time. There's no reason to do what he's saying. Build an army? Marcus, that's insane."

"It's too late, Stephen."

"No it's not. Go back in there and tell them."

"No," he barked, almost knocking me back. "Caleb came and got a group of us right after it happened last night and we went out to Fort Leonard."

Something sunk inside me.

"What did you do?"

Marcus drew a shaky breath, then dropped his eyes to the ground between us.

"Marcus, what happened?"

"We found their settlement early this morning. Figured out one of the buildings was a food storehouse. Caleb had the idea we should raid it like we thought they'd done to us. It seemed simple; the whole town looked to be asleep, but . . . there were two guards. They fired at us. Caleb shot one. I got the other."

I jumped as the school doors boomed open behind us and the crowd started pouring into the lot out front.

"Maybe we can talk to them," I said. "Talk to Caleb, explain. Maybe —"

"The people at Fort Leonard were getting together before we even left," he said. "It won't be long before they come looking for us. Our only chance now is to get them before they can get us."

The rumble of the crowd grew louder as it reached the road.

"You should go. Take Jenny and get out of here. Go to the old casino on the other side of the highway. We'll come get you when things have calmed down."

"But, Marcus —"

"Did you listen to that speech? He thinks you two were a part of it, Stephen. That you helped them. We tried to tell him you weren't any harm, but I don't know what he's going to do. Just go, Stephen. Get back to Jenny. Now!"

Marcus left to join the mob as it swarmed up the hill. I slipped into the woods and ran as fast as I could, throwing myself over the fence and dashing off again. Jenny had been alone for more than an hour. The trees rushed by me as I ran leaping over rocks and brush.

I was little more than a mile out when I first smelled smoke.

The air thickened the closer I got. My eyes stung. My heart pounded and I ran until my legs burned, ran until I blew through the trees and came out into the clearing where I was faced with a wall of flame and gray smoke.

Jenny's barn was on fire.

TWENTY-THREE

"Jenny!"

I threw myself into the doors of the barn, scorching my hands and choking on a lungful of smoke.

"Jenny!"

Flames were spreading up the walls and tearing into the roof of the barn. I dropped low where the air was clearer and covered my mouth and nose with my sleeve. My eyes stung but I searched the barn, yelling her name as loud as I could. There was a flash of movement by the bed. I raced toward it, finding Jenny on the ground, coughing, her legs pinned under a pile of charred wood from the partially collapsed ceiling. She was trying to get out from under it but was weak and barely able to move. I grabbed her under her arms and pulled but she cried out.

There was a *whoosh* as the wall next to us caught fire, exploding into a curtain of red and orange. The smoke swelled and thickened.

I dropped to my knees at Jenny's waist and thrust my hands into the smoldering pile of wood, ignoring the feel of my fingers searing as I threw the timbers off. I shook Jenny by the shoulders, but by then she was unconscious.

I looked all around me. The doors I'd come in had caught fire, as had the walls on every side. Fire flowed over the ceiling. I was trapped. The old wood of the barn, dry and weak from years of neglect, popped and hissed, burning as easily as paper.

I rolled Jenny onto her back, then muscled her up over my shoulder. The ceiling groaned louder. There was no time to waste.

I stood up, eyes watering and lungs aching, then dropped my head and shoulder and ran as fast as I could, straight at one of the burning walls. There was a panicked instant when it resisted, but then the wood cracked and flames gouged into my shoulder and cheek.

Our momentum carried us out of the barn and to the tree line, where I stumbled and Jenny went spilling out into the brush. I collapsed, coughing and heaving beside her. Jenny moaned. Her one good eye was open, but barely. She was breathing.

"You're going to be okay," I said. "We're going to be fine."

"I thought it was Will and them," she rasped. "But it wasn't. It was a group of men. They didn't even say anything, they just —"

"It's okay," I said.

There was a crash behind us as part of another wall fell in. The relief of safety washed away, though, when I realized that everything we owned — my pack and supplies, Jenny's clothes, Grandpa's rifle — was all in the barn. We couldn't go back to Settler's Landing and without shelter or supplies, and with winter coming on fast, we were dead.

I could still make out the hole in the wall I had broken through, a splintering oval wreathed in flame. Fire had spread nearly everywhere, but the roof still hadn't come down. I had seconds. If that.

"What are you doing?" Jenny said as I pushed away from her. "Stephen!"

I ran for the barn and took a deep breath before jumping through the gap, stumbling toward what was left of the bed. My lips were sealed tight and my fingers pinched my nose closed. If I tried to take a breath, I was dead. I tripped over a pile of timbers and landed hard. The smoke had dropped almost to the level of the floor. I felt around wildly, squinting into the gray clouds until my fingers hit the side of my pack. I pulled it to me and threw it over my shoulder. My knife was in its sheath next to it. I stuffed it into my back pocket.

There was a *crack* behind me and the sound of falling wood. I caught sight of the rifle lying next to Jenny's sketch pad, its barrel pointed toward me. I reached for it but the red-hot metal singed my fingers and I had to yank them back.

There was a growl above me. The roof was coming down. I reached out again and my fingers closed around Jenny's sketch pad. I scrambled to my feet and ran toward the opening in the wall. The growl above me turned into a long moan. There was a *whoosh* and the wall behind me collapsed. Then the ceiling started to come down, forcing the smoke and heat down on my shoulders like two giant hands. Burning wood fell at my heels, popping and hissing.

The way before me was closing off. All I could see was gray and livid yellow. I thought of Jenny, lying out there alone, and threw myself into the air.

TWENTY-FOUR

We stumbled through the woods, our arms clasped around each other, until we crossed the highway and came to the parking lot that surrounded the Golden Acorn casino.

When we got there, I eased Jenny down inside. The lobby was musty and cold. A jumble of gaming tables, chairs, and slot machines, most of which had been stripped of anything useful years ago, littered the main room. I followed a corridor that branched off to one side and was lined on either wall with rows of identical-looking doors. I pushed on each one until I found a door that gave. The room was empty except for a mattress that lay on the concrete floor, stripped of sheets and its metal frame, and the husk of what used to be a giant television set. It wasn't much. I pulled the curtains back and saw that the big glass window on one wall was still intact. It would do.

I brought Jenny inside the room and we collapsed on the bed, both of us covered in small burns and soot. Jenny's legs had gotten the worst of it. I pulled out my first-aid kit and carefully cleaned and dressed her wounds. We'd have to keep an eye on them, but for now they didn't look serious.

Jenny patched me up and then we drank the rest of the water in my canteen. After that we were exhausted and lay down, our arms draped over each other.

Soon Jenny was asleep, but I lay awake for hours as the land outside and the hotel room around us dropped into deeper and deeper darkness.

For some reason I kept seeing the quarry. Me and Jackson surrounded by all his friends. My friends. I skipped back to earlier that day and felt the jolt as I connected with that ball and ran the bases. I felt the wind against my skin and heard the sound of those voices cheering me on.

But all of that was gone now, wasn't it?

I looked over at Jenny, who was sleeping fitfully, burned and slashed, and my nails dug into my palm. I grimaced at the pain but welcomed it. Because it had been me, hadn't it? I was the one who sent those people to Jenny's with torches in hand. If they had killed Jenny, it would have been my fault. If there was a war, it would be my war. The people of Settler's Landing were a bomb, but I was the one who lit the fuse.

I rolled out of bed and drew the curtains aside. I thought of Dad lying all alone at the Greens' and felt low and sick. If the war came to Settler's Landing, it would come for him too.

"They won't come here."

I turned away from the window. Jenny was sitting up on the mattress, watching me.

"Who?"

"Will and his family. They won't follow us here."

"Why not?"

"The square pegs are out of the round holes. They can do what they want now."

I leaned against the windowsill. "Do you think they'll really do it? Start a war?"

Jenny winced as she drew her burned legs up to her chest and wrapped her arms around them. Her face filled with moonlight as she peered out the window.

"I think they want the world to be like it was when they were our age. Maybe a war is just the last piece of the puzzle."

I left the window and pulled out my old bedroll, spreading the small blanket as best I could over us both. We sat up, huddled close together. Jenny laid her head on my shoulder.

"I shouldn't have gotten you involved," she said. "In any of it. The fight with Will. The thing at the Henrys'. It was stupid of me."

"You didn't know what would happen."

"I didn't care," Jenny said, a knife-edge of bitterness in her voice. She turned and stared out the window, her back to me. "Maybe I just wanted to get back at them and didn't care who got hurt in the process."

I reached out until my hand found hers and clasped it tight. She turned. Her cheek was silver in the moonlight.

"Come on," she said. "Let's get out of here."

We left the casino and Jenny led me down to a billboard on the side of the road. It was the tallest one I had ever seen and dwarfed the trees around it. We climbed to the very top, up rusty and vine-covered hand-holds — past the smiling, tanned family that claimed AT&T cell phones would keep them connected forever — and sat looking out over the miles of empty land around us.

The night had turned cold with banks of heavy clouds rolling in. Jenny craned her long neck and looked up at a field of stars that glittered in the black. If you looked close, it was almost as though you could see the stars moving, a sparkling dome, turning and turning.

"Used to be you couldn't even see them," Jenny said. "With the cities and their lights and pollution and all. At least that's what Violet said."

Jenny picked a leaf off a nearby tree and let it drop, watching as it helicoptered down through the emptiness. Jenny leaned into me against the cold and we sat and watched the moon. Far off in the distance the barest wisp of smoke rose like a ribbon from someone's campfire.

"Do you ever wonder what they're doing out there?"

"Who?"

"All the other people," Jenny said. "I mean, there's a whole world out there, right? Whole other countries. Who knows, maybe there's some place out there where the Collapse never even happened. Where people are just going about their lives."

Was it possible? Since we shared a border, P11 hit Mexico and Canada as badly as it did us. But what about everyone else? Were there places that the Collapse never touched? I looked out into the night and wondered.

"If you could make it so it never happened," Jenny said, "would you?"

I tried to imagine it. The Collapse. The horror of P11. What would this place be like if none of it ever happened? I imagined vast crowds of people packed shoulder to shoulder, scurrying about like ants, our silent world wiped away by electric lights and movie theaters and televisions and cars.

What would our lives be like? Jenny and I never would have met, for one thing. She would be thousands of miles away with a different name and a different family. And since my mom and dad only met because of the war, would I even have existed at all? I knew it was wrong not to wish all that death away; but how could I long for a life, a world, that I never even knew?

"I don't know," I said.

Jenny raised her lips to my ear.

"I wouldn't," she breathed.

Later, we walked back to the casino and slipped into bed. As Jenny slept, I laid my head on her chest and listened to the thrum of her heart. It sounded like a bird's wings beating at the air.

I opened my eyes hours later, fully awake, and stared up into the darkness. Jenny was on her side, breathing low and steadily. I dressed quietly and felt my way out of the room and down the hall to the brighter gaming area, navigating toward the front door. The edges around it seemed curiously bright for the hour.

I stepped up to it. Outside, the whole world had changed.

As we slept, the first snow of the year had fallen with a vengeance. It covered everything with a coat of white that was already inches thick. The snow fell lightly now with a musical clink as one crystal stuck to another and settled. With the full moon just visible through some cracks in the clouds the whole place glowed almost as light as day. I buttoned up my coat and made my way across the parking lot, my steps crunching and my breath a white plume trailing behind me.

I had no destination in mind, but I felt this pull to keep going so I followed the highway south for a while, then veered off into the trees.

There, I found a circle of land isolated from the snow by the heavy canopy of tree limbs.

I cleared a plot of ground, then knelt down and assembled a pile of brittle leaves and twigs for a fire. The movements Grandpa had showed me years before effortlessly flowed back to me. Soon a spark caught off the fire starter I had in my pocket and the leaves smoldered. I leaned in close and blew on it gently until smoke puffed up and a bit of flame peeked out. This was the most delicate time. Get excited, add too much wood too fast, and the whole thing would be suffocated. Go too slow and the flame would starve and die. I added thin twigs at first, until the flames grew and could sustain themselves, then layered on thicker branches. I watched it burn, the warmth and familiarity of it flowing over me.

"We're better off now," Grandpa had said one night as we sat together across a fire. He was shaping a tree branch into the trigger of a small game trap with his knife while Dad slept fitfully behind us. I was hugging my knees, my head down, my throat sore, exhausted from crying and wishing I could disappear.

I was ten. Two newly dug graves, one large and one small, throbbed in the darkness behind us.

For months I had watched Mom's stomach grow, drunk with wonder. Dad had sat me down and patiently, if awkwardly, explained exactly what was going on, but it meant nothing to me. Clearly, this little person, this little world growing inside her, couldn't be anything but a miracle. I tried to picture having a brother or a sister. Someone to talk to, to play with, to foist chores off on, to torture in more ways than I could imagine. It was too good to be true.

"What are we going to call it?" I asked Mom one day. "How about Frodo?"

"We're not calling the baby Frodo."

"Why not?"

"How about Agnes?" Mom suggested.

"Boring."

Dad piped up. "Hildegard?"

"Blech."

"Oh! Oh!" Dad hopped on his toes. "If it's a boy? Elvis. Aaron. Presley."

Grandpa, of course, was furious. It would be another mouth to feed. It would slow us down. He went on and on, but as tough as he was, Mom was tougher. She said if everybody thought like that, then the human race was going to disappear pretty fast.

We had planned on being at the Northern Gathering when the baby came — Dad said there were women there who knew about these things — but we were a month's hike away at best when Mom grasped her stomach and announced that it was time.

"But can't we stop it?" I'd asked. "Delay it or something?"

"Nope! When it comes, it comes!"

Dad was trying to seem unconcerned, dashing around to make Mom more comfortable, but I could tell he was worried. Mom too. Usually she joked through the worst of times — she always said that's what joking was for — but as she lay there on the grass that morning, her face was cut with lines of tension and sweat as she strained and cried out and fought. It was as though she was drowning and trying, more and more desperately, to claw her way to the surface of the churning water. Dad tried to help and so did I, but it was no use. There was so much blood.

Three hours into her labor, Mom's cries stopped.

Her face went slack.

"Bev?"

Dad knelt by her side.

"Bev?"

Her hand slipped from his, like a dove tumbling out of the sky.

Late that night, after the graves had been dug and Dad was finally asleep, I sat alone with Grandpa around that fire as he whittled at a piece of wood with his old hunting knife.

"Learn from this," he croaked.

"Learn what?" My voice sounded far away, like it was floating somewhere far above my head.

Grandpa glanced over his shoulder where the skeleton frames of the roller coasters rose into the sky. He turned and spit thickly into the fire.

He wasn't at all the stick figure he would become in just a few years. He was a twisted piece of metal, scarred and pitted and hard. His knife-edge crew cut was thick and gray. Even in the light of the fire his eyes were like pale blue marbles, small and cold.

"She's better off now."

Grandpa's ring glinted as he carved a bloodless gash in the wood and looked at me across the flames.

"We made a mess of things before you were born," he said. "P Eleven was just what we deserved. It was no plague. It was a blessing. Surviving it, that's the real plague. But soon it'll just be . . . silence."

Now, as my own fire hissed and sputtered, I wondered: *Was he right? Is this how we were meant to live — like animals? Living and dying and hoping for nothing until one day we all disappear?*

If we were, then what? Should I just go? On my own? Right then? Violet probably hadn't retrieved her medicines yet. I could take them, get my pack while Jenny slept, and disappear. Dad would be safe in Violet's hands. Jenny would be fine on her own. Maybe if we all went our separate ways, if we stayed low to the ground, no towns, no family, no friends, this new end of the world would pass us by. Maybe then we'd all be safe. Maybe Grandpa's only mistake was that in keeping us together he hadn't taken things far enough.

The wind surged, blowing the drifts off the ground and the low-hanging tree branches, whiting out everything around me, erasing it. I thought of Jenny lying there in that dark room, curled around the spot where I had been, a warm place in all that cold. I knew that leaving right then might spare us pain later, but I also knew that I was fooling myself if I thought I could do it. There was this chain that ran from me to her. I didn't know when or how it had come to be, but it was there. I could feel it. I didn't want to imagine what she'd be like in five or ten or twenty years. I wanted to see it. I wanted to be there.

Besides, in the end, who had Grandpa's rules ever saved? Not Mom. Not Dad. Not even himself. If it was true that all paths in our world led to only one place, then why not fill whatever path you chose with the best things you could find?

I wasn't my grandfather. I never would be.

I turned to go back to the casino, but before I took a single step, a dark figure crossed the highway in front of me and moved quickly toward the building, leaning in against the wind. I couldn't make out who it was, but it didn't matter. Jenny was alone in there.

My boots crunched through the snow as I raced back, wishing Grandpa's rifle hadn't been lost in the fire. I gripped the hilt of Dad's knife instead. It would have to do.

The figure, in a black coat with the hood turned up, was at the door when I got there, ready to go in.

"Stop!"

I gripped the knife's handle tight, ready to use it. The figure in black turned to face me and lifted the hood.

"Violet?"

She stepped into the white between us. "Stephen?" she said, moving toward me. "Thank God. Are you okay? Is Jenny? I didn't know they were going to do what they did. When I found out —"

"We're fine."

Violet said nothing for a moment. The snow surged, making her body waver, ghostlike and gray.

"What is it, Violet?"

A plane of snow drifted between us as she looked back in the direction of Settler's Landing.

"He's gone," she said. "I came to tell you he's gone."

"What? Who's gone? Violet, what are you —"

But then I knew.

TWENTY-FIVE

I stepped out onto the Greens' porch hours later. It was late and every-one was asleep. The snow had finally stopped.

I held a lantern I had found down in the Greens' basement. The land around me glowed a dazzling white. The roads were gone. The playground had disintegrated into a few ice-covered bars and odd-shaped mounds of snow. The lines that divided one yard from the next had been wiped clean.

I descended the steps and started south. The houses to either side of me were little more than snow-covered cliff faces. Walking through them was like walking along the bottom of a deep canyon.

It wasn't hard to carry him. As with Grandpa, death had taken Dad a bit at a time until there was almost nothing left. I passed the entrance to the town, the wall now just a long ridge, like a curving collarbone, bleached white in the sun. I crossed the lawn beyond the wall, then passed through the trees and out again until I came to the great empty plain on the other side.

The world had disappeared. There was nothing but white as far as I could see. The casino and the Starbucks were snowy hillocks. Even the towering billboards to the north had been nearly erased.

I walked out into the nothingness until my legs stopped moving. Then I set the lantern down and eased Dad onto a snowbank. As I did it, the sheet covering his face fell away. The crow black of his hair and beard was startling, lying in the middle of all that white. His mouth was slightly open and his skin was a bluish gray. He looked so small. Shrunken and old. People said that the dead looked like they were only sleeping, but it had never seemed that way to me. To me, there was nothing there at all. An empty house. An abandoned world.

I covered his face with the sheet and picked up the shovel.

Moving the snow aside was easy enough, but when the blade of the shovel hit the ground, it rang like a bell. My palms ached from the vibration. The ground was nearly frozen.

I had changed back into my old clothes before leaving the Greens' so when I pulled off my coat, the icy wind tore through my sweater and patchwork pants. I wedged the shovel into a crack in the ground, then leaned my weight into it, pushing the blade an inch or two farther in to break the icy shell. Once I had done that across the entire breadth of the grave, I was able to dig the shovel in farther and remove the dark soil inches at a time. As I got lower, the dirt became looser. The blade of the shovel scraped across rock as it tore into the soil.

Hours later, my muscles were burning and my chest was heaving. Each time I drew breath, the frigid air tore at my lungs. I couldn't feel my hands or feet. The skin of my ears stung. My body was slick with sweat despite the cold. I stopped digging. Hanging over the shovel's handle, exhausted, I caught my breath and then checked my progress.

I was standing only about two feet deep in the ground. The shovel fell out of my hands. I dropped back into the snow like a rag doll.

The cold reached up into my back, spread throughout my chest, and curled its fingers around my heart.

"Stephen?"

Jenny stood behind me, our blanket wrapped around her shoulders. When I didn't say anything she reached for the shovel, but I yanked it away from her and held it to my chest.

"I have to do this myself."

Jenny stared at me, her hair whipping past her reddened cheeks.

"No you don't."

I ignored her. Using the shovel like a crutch, I got back to my feet. I raised the handle painfully over my head and dug down another foot before faltering again and collapsing into a heap. I forced myself up and began again.

When I was finally done, I sat at the foot of the open grave and pulled Dad to me, wrapping my arms around his thin chest.

I closed my eyes and could see his face as it was, lit from the inside as he held up that first slice of pear in the darkness of a dead plane, then the iron look that came over him when he decided he was going to be a hero for the first time since Mom left us.

I heard his booming laugh and his shuddering sobs as he sat by his father's grave and Mom's and the daughter's he would never know. I felt his chest rise and fall alongside mine, his breath like the dry turning of pages in a book.

All of that had come to this.

Stillness.

A yawning silence.

Like none of those things had ever been.

Jenny helped me lower him down until the white glow of his shroud disappeared in the darkness at the bottom of the grave. He looked like a child, curled up and helpless. Alone. I reached into my back pocket and found the sharp edge of our family photograph. I raised it up into the dim moonlight, tracing the lines of me and Mom and Dad smiling together for one of the last times, before holding it over the grave and dropping it in. It fluttered like a leaf and settled onto his chest.

I stood there for some time, feeling the pull of the grave, like a cold arm wrapping itself around my shoulders and drawing me down with him.

I took up the shovel and filled the hole.

When it was done, I stumbled and fell back onto the ground. A new swirl of snow appeared out of the gray, lightening sky. It seemed like the body of a great white bear tumbling down onto me, its claws out-stretched.

I shut my eyes, and let it have me.

PART THREE

TWENTY-SIX

There was a crash as I fell into one of the gaming tables that littered the casino floor. *How did I get here?* I wondered distantly, then Jenny's hands dug into my shoulder and pulled me up. She threw my arm over her shoulder and pushed me blindly through the dark. My bones ached from the cold. My skin burned. I couldn't stop shivering. I remembered kneeling by the grave in the snow. I told her to leave me with Dad, but she wouldn't listen. I wanted to tell her again, but now I couldn't speak.

Jenny dropped me down on the bed in the back room and covered me up with all the blankets we had, tucking them tight around my body like a cocoon. I lay there in the absolute dark and quiet of the room. The blankets had my arms pinned to my sides. I couldn't move. I couldn't see. It was like being a thousand miles under the ocean with the immense weight of it pressing down on my chest.

But I wasn't afraid. I was relieved. Finally, after all my running, I had arrived at the place I was meant to be, at home, at peace, in the nothingness and the dark and the cold.

The door opened and Jenny was at my side again, leaning over me.

Was it hours later? Days? I didn't know. I couldn't see her, just feel her arms digging under my shoulders and lifting me up.

I groaned, struggling against her touch, trying to keep still. "I'm fine. Leave me alone."

"Stephen, you're freezing to death. Now move!"

Jenny managed to get me up from the bed and out of the room, shoring me up with her shoulder and driving me down a long hallway. I couldn't fight. I faltered along beside her, my legs stiff and awkward as a foal's. We moved deeper into the casino toward a distant light. A fire. Jenny had built it in the center of a tiled atrium. Its smoke twisted upward to the shattered remains of a skylight.

She dropped me within inches of it. Its brilliance made my eyes ache, but I couldn't feel its warmth. It reached out but couldn't touch me. Jenny wrestled me up into a sitting position and arranged the blankets over my shoulders. I tried to push her away, but I was too weak. All I wanted to do was lie down. All I wanted was to sleep, to be in the quiet and alone in that black nothingness, but Jenny wouldn't let me go.

There was a crash somewhere out in the casino, then the sound of shattering glass. Jenny stiffened. Dad's knife appeared in her fist as she crouched beside me like an animal, peering into the dark, listening for more.

"There's no one out there," I said thoughtlessly, my head lolling onto my chest.

"Maybe I was wrong. Maybe Will and them aren't done with us. They could still come."

"They're dead."

Jenny's eyes left the empty dark and fell back on me.

"What? Who's dead?"

I looked up from the tiled floor. Jenny's face, streaked with ash and pockmark burns, was framed in fire.

"Everyone," I said, my voice rising up from the deep in a cold rasp. "Marcus. Violet. Dad. My mom. Even you and me. We thought the Collapse was over but it's not. It just keeps going. It doesn't matter where we go or what we do. We're all dead. All of us. We just don't know it yet."

Jenny said nothing. She eased down beside me, bringing her body alongside mine. She brushed my hair aside with the tips of her fingers. When I flinched away from the warmth of her lips on my cheek, she wrapped her arms tight around me and leaned me in toward the fire, rocking us back and forth.

The heat from the fire pounded against my skin, but it was useless. My body was a gate of iron and I would not let it pass.

All that night, she left my side only to get more wood for the fire or to dart out into the darkness to check on the crashes and groans that seemed to be our constant companions. She was sure that each one was Will or Caleb or some faceless mob with torches in hand, ready to burn us down. But each time it was simply the old building settling into the brunt of winter. Broken glass. Creaking walls.

"We can't stay here," she said.

It had stopped snowing. A thin, watery light began to show through the clouds. The first traces of dawn.

"It isn't safe."

I turned toward the dim outline of the casino's front door. Outside, across the parking lot and through the trees, was the clearing where Dad lay, buried deep underground. There was no cross. No marker. Jenny had pulled me away before I could make one. If we left, I knew I would never be able to find him again.

"You can go," I said.

"I'm not leaving without you."

Somewhere behind us, the roof of the casino groaned under the weight of the snow. I traced my finger along the hills and valleys of the wrinkled blanket piled up in my lap, marking out a meandering path on its folds. *Never the same path twice*, I thought. *That way you're safe. That way no one finds you.* I saw myself on the trail. I saw worn ground and the mall and the neighborhoods, crumbling and covered in vines. I could hear Dad, his shuffling footsteps, his bright babble like water coursing over smooth river rocks. I saw his hands so clearly — long-fingered and strong, a hairline scar running down the index finger of his right hand.

"Steve?"

Jenny laid one hand over mine, blotting out the trail. She used the other to lift my chin up to her, so I couldn't look away, couldn't not see her.

"Maybe there isn't anything better out there, but . . . your dad and your grandpa handed you this life, right? Just like Marcus and Violet handed me mine. This is your name. This is where you live. This is who you are. We never chose any of it. So whose lives are we living? Ours or theirs? Haven't you ever thought about that? Don't you, just once, want to choose something for yourself?"

I pulled my chin out of her hand and looked deep into the darkness of the casino.

"I have," I said.

Jenny stared at me, her eyes wide and hurt, waiting for more, but I said nothing. She let go of my hand.

"I'm sorry about your parents," she said. "But at least they died while they were trying to live. They didn't just sit around waiting to die."

Jenny pushed herself back from me and stood up.

"It's not safe for us here, Stephen. I think you know that. There's an old hospital a few miles west that's still pretty intact. I'm going to leave for there today. I want you to come, but even if you don't, I have to go."

Jenny waited for a response, and when there was none, she walked away from the fire and was gone.

Without Jenny, the immensity of the casino's silence was overwhelming. This was what I wanted, wasn't it? On my own in the dark. I sat there while the fire died out, then stumbled back to our room. Before I drew the curtains shut, I surveyed my little world. I had shelter. I could find food and water easily enough. I had everything I needed.

My eye fell into the corner of the room by the window, to a large white square. I didn't recognize it at first, but I moved closer and saw that it was Jenny's sketch pad. It fell open to the end as I lifted it, to the last picture she had drawn.

It was like a small, soft hand had reached inside of me and pulled the air out of my lungs.

It was the picture Jenny drew our first morning together as I huddled, freezing, under the blankets. All the details of the barn were there: the patched-together plank walls, the early morning sunshine, the rumpled bed. You could almost feel the chill in the air. I was staring up into the rafters and my feet were sticking out of the cover, hanging slightly over the edge of the mattress. I smiled despite myself.

She had made me taller.

I kept coming back to the look on my face. I almost didn't recognize myself. She caught me just as I was waking up, before my worries about Dad and the town had flooded in. I had, not a smile exactly — it was harder to place than that — but more a look of stillness, of thoughtfulness. Of peace. On my face was the look of someone who was exactly where he wanted to be with no thought of the future or the past. Nothing but that moment.

Jenny said that drawing quieted something inside her. I said I had nothing like that, but was I wrong? Wasn't that what being with her did for me?

I thought back to that night out by the snowy highway, wondering if the answer was to walk away and disappear. If being alone might spare us the pain of feeling anything like Dad felt the day Mom's hand slipped from his in the shadow of that amusement park. Maybe if we never built anything, then nothing could ever collapse.

We have to be more than the world would make us.

Mom's words were like a warm breath blowing past my cheek.

The sketch pad fell out of my hands, and I drifted from the room and down the hallway, following the dim morning light toward the exit. I could just barely see Jenny standing outside.

The unbroken snow was dazzling, clean and white. She didn't turn as I stepped through the door and came up beside her. The back of my hand grazed hers. Her fingers fell and intertwined with mine, locking together. I felt a deep sigh in my chest as something settled into place.

"I'm so sorry about your dad," she said.

A chill spread over me again, but I pulled Jenny close. My heart thumped hard in my chest.

"They destroyed their world," Jenny said, looking out over the vast plain of snow. "But this one is ours."

"We should leave," I said. "Today."

We said nothing more for a while. I wished Dad could be there with us. Wished he could leave and come find whatever it was we would find. I wondered if there would always be this empty, aching place inside me where he used to be.

Jenny nudged me with her shoulder. "Come on, then. We've got some packing to do."

She reached for the door, but before we could go in, there was a crunch of snow to our right. Tree branches shook. We jumped back into the doorway and out of sight.

"Probably just a deer," I whispered, but then we saw two figures slide behind the curtain of trees. Once they passed, Jenny motioned me forward. I took her wrist, but she turned back and held up one finger.

Just a second, she mouthed.

I followed as Jenny moved to the corner and we both dropped down low to peer around to the back of the building. Two men emerged from the woods. I could tell immediately that they weren't Will or Caleb or anyone we knew from Settler's Landing. They moved in precise glides, short automatic rifles held ahead of them, communicating with crisp hand signals. They were both wearing some kind of black uniform, their shoulders and waists crisscrossed with pouches of equipment. They looked ex-military to me.

What are they doing here?

The two men circled the building, then disappeared around the other side. Jenny looked at me. I nodded. We moved along the back wall until we saw them climbing the hill toward the highway and Settler's Landing.

"Scouts," I whispered.

"For who? Fort Leonard doesn't have any military."

A buzz of nerves started to rise in my chest. "Come on," I said. "We'll pack up. Go. Like you said, this isn't our —"

Before I could finish, Jenny leapt up from her crouch and ran for the highway.

"Jenny!" I hissed, then scrambled to my feet and went after her.

The scouts were a ways ahead of us by the time we made it to the woods, but we could follow their tracks easily enough. We didn't catch sight of them again until we came out of the trees above Settler's Landing's gates. The men swept down the hill toward them, but instead of passing through, they veered sharply north and into the forest across from us.

"We should see how many of them there are. Maybe they're camped nearby."

"Jenny —"

"If it was just Fort Leonard against Settler's Landing, I'd leave it, but if they've brought in help, we need to tell Marcus and Violet it's not going to be a fair fight. Right?"

. I hated the idea but had to admit she was right. I agreed, and we trailed the two scouts from as far back as we could. They followed pretty much the same path Jenny and I had the other night. I thought they were making straight for the Henrys' house, but before they reached it they cut around it and went farther east, disappearing into thick trees.

When their footprints finally petered out, we dropped down onto the snowy ground and crawled up to a fallen tree that lay at the edge of some brush. Voices came from the other side, a mix of languages and accents. We glanced at each other, then peeked over the edge of the tree.

Less than a hundred feet from where we lay was a camp made up of black tents arranged in precise rows. Twenty of them, at least. Men like the two scouts we'd seen milled around, bristling with as many weapons and as much ammunition as they could carry. A fire burned at the center of the camp, and behind it sat a central tent that was flanked by three large dark shapes that sat just outside of the firelight.

Jenny looked at me, but I shrugged, unable to tell what they were. The forest curved around the north edge of the camp, so Jenny and I pulled back from our hiding place and crawled until the three dark shapes became all too clear.

The one closest to us was a flatbed truck. On its back there was an immense metal canister with a hose running from one side of it. A fuel truck, I guessed, meant to service what sat next to it — two hulking black jeeps, their sides and fronts plated with armor and an open back where heavy machine guns were mounted on rotating tripods.

It was like looking at two prehistoric monsters. Both of us stared in awe, speechless at what was looming over Settler's Landing as it quietly slept just a few miles away.

"How could Fort Leonard afford mercenaries?" I whispered. "Aren't they smaller than Settler's Landing?"

Before Jenny could answer, there was a commotion in the camp as the black flap of one of the central tents opened. Two figures walked out and everything inside of me froze.

No. It can't be.

The black man's dreadlocks were longer than the last time I'd seen him, and so was his beard. The white man with the scar seemed, if anything, bigger. There was no doubt who they were though. Their faces were seared into my memory.

Not mercenaries.

Slavers.

The air rushed out of me as I realized exactly what Fort Leonard would have offered them in exchange for ending the war once and for all. They offered them Marcus and Violet and Jackson. They offered them Tuttle and Martin and Derrick and Wendy. They offered them everyone and everything in Settler's Landing.

"Stephen?" Jenny whispered.

She grabbed my arm and pulled me deeper into the forest, away from the camp. Once we couldn't hear them anymore, we eased down the back side of a slope, pressing our backs into the snow.

"We'll tell Marcus," Jenny said. "Warn them. Maybe if they know what's coming —"

I almost laughed. The thought that they had a chance against these people, that they could even risk that, was ridiculous.

"They'll have to go," I said. "All of them. Take what they can and leave."

"Leave Settler's Landing? They won't. Marcus and Violet? They'd die first."

My fists curled in on themselves. She was right. God, what had I started? Were they here because of me too? Had they come looking for me and Dad and found Fort Leonard instead?

We sat there, a moat of empty space between us. Jenny chewed on her thumbnail, staring at the ground. We both knew what was coming.

I had seen it in the belly of that plane and she had seen it in a mass of men with their guns and their wild, hungry looks.

"It's not our fault," Jenny said. "What we did was stupid, but it was Caleb who went to Fort Leonard. Not us. *He* started this."

I murmured something in agreement, but I didn't believe it and I knew Jenny didn't either.

A light snow began to fall again, whipping through the trees and tapping against our shoulders. A laugh, loud and throaty, rose from the slave traders' camp. It was like the grunting of an animal ready to hunt.

I took Jenny's hand and we fled through the woods.

Violet and Marcus were at the kitchen table when we arrived. Violet was at one end, knitting distractedly, while Marcus leaned grimly over a mug of tea.

"What is it?" Violet asked.

Before I could speak, Jackson came thundering down the stairs. I felt a flash of happiness to see him again but as soon as he saw me and Jenny, he stopped where he was, grasping the rail and eyeing us sharply.

"What are they doing here?"

The way he spat it out, I knew instantly that Marcus told him everything about our raid on the Henrys'. How we had started all of this. My mouth went dry. I felt sick. Ashamed.

"Come sit down, Jackson," Violet said. "Stephen and Jenny say they have something to tell us."

Jackson crept down the stairs, then took a seat at the far end of the kitchen table. He didn't look at me and I found I couldn't look at any of them. How could I? I'd abandoned Jackson, stolen from Violet, and betrayed Marcus and everyone else in the town.

"Well, Stephen?" Violet said.

They all sat there watching us. Waiting. I clasped Jenny's hand under the table and told them about the slavers that Fort Leonard had hired. The jeeps. The weapons. That they were the same ones my Dad and I had fought. Everything.

When I was done, Marcus rubbed his hand over the thick collection of stubble on his chin.

"Slavers," Marcus said carefully. "You're sure?"

I nodded. "I'm sure."

Marcus looked across the table at Violet, but she stared down into her lap, all the color drained from her face.

"I know you don't want to leave," I said. "But you don't know what these people will do. They —"

"They won't do anything," Jenny interrupted.

I turned to where Jenny sat beside me.

"What do you mean? Of course they —"

But Jenny wasn't looking at me. She was focused on her parents. Her parents, who wouldn't meet her gaze.

"Will they?" Jenny asked, holding the words out like bait.

Marcus and Violet said nothing. Jackson didn't move.

"I don't . . ."

And then I got it. I saw what Jenny saw.

Ever since the night of our raid on the Henrys', they should have been expecting the forces of Fort Leonard to arrive at any moment. But if they did, then why was Violet sitting at the table knitting? Shouldn't she have been preparing for the coming fight? Shouldn't Marcus's rifle be close at hand instead of sitting in its rack on the wall?

And when I told them that a small army of slave traders was bearing down on them, they didn't seem scared. They didn't pack up. They didn't flee town.

Most of all, they didn't seem surprised.

I felt something like a barbed hook sinking into my gut and in that instant I knew.

Fort Leonard didn't hire the slavers.

They did.

TWENTY-SEVEN

"Caleb told us they were mercenaries," Marcus said, looking down into his tea. "Ex-soldiers. I don't know where he found them. He said they'd run the people at Fort Leonard off so they wouldn't come back. That's all. He said no one would get hurt."

"What are you supposed to do for them?" Jenny asked.

"They want to expand west. Caleb said we'd be like a way station. Nothing more. They'd store fuel here, food. He didn't tell us they were slavers, I swear."

"When does it happen?"

"Tonight. Sundown. We're supposed to meet them at the gates and then we all go together."

"We have to talk to Caleb," Violet said. "Now."

Marcus looked up at her. "And say what? You don't think Caleb and his friends know what these people are already?"

"Then we talk to everyone else. Sam, Tuttle — we'll have a vote."

"You think if we have a vote and we actually win, they'll just leave?"

We all sat there, still as statues as it sunk in. Slavers were no different from starving animals. Deny them Fort Leonard and they'd eat Settler's Landing just as happily.

"Then what?" Violet asked.

Marcus turned to face the swirl of white outside. It was mounting steadily on the porch and bending the trees until their branches hung down miserably, nearly ready to snap.

"We did well this year, but you know the winters as well as I do, Vi. We'll lose at least ten people from the cold and lack of food alone. If we have to deal with Fort Leonard picking away at us too, we could be done for. Our home. All of us. Gone."

"What are you saying? We let this happen? Marcus —"

"I'm saying we don't have a choice, Vi."

"We do," Violet said. "We have a choice about what we become, Marcus. Maybe it's the only thing we *do* have a choice about."

"Do you want to be out there again? Us and not them? Is that what you want?"

"How many times have we come close to doing the right thing," Violet asked, "and then stopped because we were afraid? This. Sean and Mary Krychek —"

"Violet."

"— that girl of theirs, just nine years old?"

"We did the best we could for them."

"We stood up for them for an hour before giving them an old blanket and a day's worth of bread and sending them on their way! Because we were afraid!"

Violet was red with anger and shame, leaning up out of her chair, her nails digging into the table. Marcus had no answer for her.

The wind howled and the snow mixed with hail that sounded sharp and metallic, like fingers tapping on a tin roof.

"You remember that day we played Go Fish, Jenny?"

Everyone turned to Jackson. His back was to us, caught in the half-gloom at the edge of the kitchen, looking out past the marble-topped counter to the storm outside.

"Yeah," Jenny said. "I do."

"Everyone in Fort Leonard is just waking up," Jackson said, almost to himself, the words tumbling out. "They're talking. Starting fires for breakfast. Wishing it wasn't snowing. But then these people, us, will appear and some of them won't live through the day. Some of them have maybe a few hours left until they're gone, or their families are gone and they're alone. And they have no idea it's coming. They think it's just another day."

Jackson's voice hitched in his throat. A redness crept into his cheeks like leaves of flame.

"Jack," Marcus urged. "Listen to me. I don't like it either, but it's us or it's them. It's —"

Jackson turned from the window and faced Marcus head-on, searching his face. Marcus deflated. He dropped his head, looking down at his hands. They seemed so small now, framed against the hardness of the table.

Violet moved over to Jackson, wrapping her arms tight around him from behind.

"I'm afraid too," Violet said to Marcus. "But if fear's all we've got, then we're building this world on the same rotten foundation as the last one. What good are we doing Jackson or Jenny or Stephen? What good are we doing anyone?"

Marcus turned and regarded each of us one by one, like we were a jury deciding his fate, before struggling up out of his chair and gathering his rifle and his coat.

I stood up at the table. "No," I said, urgently. "You can't fight them. If you try to be a hero —"

"Caleb lied to us," Marcus said. "And he did it so he could turn this place into something none of us want it to be. This is our home. If this isn't worth fighting for, then what is?"

Jackson left his mother and crossed the room to stand with Marcus. Together they went out into the front room. A moment later, the door shut with a deep *boom* that shuddered through the house.

No one moved for a time. The wind moaned. The finger-tap hail pattered on and on.

Violet went without another word to her cabinet. She lit candles and then opened each drawer one by one, taking inventory with crisp practiced motions, preparing for whatever was to come.

Beside me, Jenny sat with her chin resting on her fists, absorbed in the whirl of white. I pushed away from the table and went out the front door.

A rush of wind and snow blew toward me as I stepped outside and dropped down onto the front steps. Across the street, Marcus and Jackson moved from one house to the other. They'd disappear inside for a time, and when they came out they'd be joined by one or two others and they'd all move on, snaking their way through the town.

With their dark coats cutting through the snow, they reminded me of an army of black ants gathering to make a valiant stand against a farmer's boot.

Behind me, the front door opened and closed. Jenny descended the steps and went to stand beyond the porch's roof, looking from house to house, taking it all in.

"You're staying," I said. "Aren't you?"

Jenny lifted her chin, examining the cottony sky. "I thought I could leave," she said. "I thought it'd be easy. But I can't. Not if they don't."

Everything in me ached. Of course Jenny would stay. She'd join with whoever Marcus could raise to fight Caleb and the slavers, and they'd all suffer.

And what could I do? Only one thing.

"I should get our things," I said, looking down at the brick steps beneath my feet. "From the casino. Before anything starts."

"Want me to come?"

I turned back to face her. Jenny stood on the porch with her hands jammed in the pockets of her coat, her hair a cloud of black. She was looking over my head, scanning the neighborhood, her eyes focused to a knife's edge. There was no stopping her.

"It's okay," I said. "I'll do it myself."

Jenny darted in and kissed my cheek. "Hurry up. It'd be a shame if the cold killed you before the slavers had a chance."

I nodded and Jenny threw open the front door and went inside. I stood there a moment looking at the blank face of the door, listening to the falling snow, before I crossed the Greens' front yard and went out into the street.

The walls to either side of the Settler's Landing gates had never seemed more like two gravestones as I passed them and went into the forest. Looking out over the crumbling highway and the casino, everything seemed so far away. Jenny. Jackson. All of my friends. I wished the chain that bound me to them could be cut, but it was there, strong as ever.

I bypassed the casino and trekked some miles until I found the clearing where I'd buried Dad. In the center there was a swell in the blanket of white. My hands stung as I knelt in front of it and scooped the piles of snow away until I reached the loose dirt at the top of the grave. I pressed my palms deep into it. My breath dropped to a whisper. A yawning emptiness opened inside me.

I'm here, I thought. *I'm right here.*

I used Dad's knife to cut a thick branch down from one of the surrounding trees, stripped it of its bark, and flattened one side. I held it in my lap and carved the letters of his name before plunging it deep into the ground at the head of his grave. When I was done, I traced my fingers over its surface.

STEPHEN R. QUINN.

I thought of Grandpa lying out alone in the woods so far away. If we had left a marker for him, it would have said the exact same thing.

And soon so would mine.

I started to speak, to say good-bye, but it was like my mouth was stuffed with dead leaves and sand.

The wind rose, carrying the scent of pine and earth, and for a second I felt Jenny's lips, soft and warm, against my cheek. She lingered there, her forehead at my temple, her breath on my neck. I had to shake her ghost away.

I drew my knife and tested its dark edge with my thumb. Though its surface was pitted and scarred and worn with age, it was still sharp. It killed me to lie to Jenny, but I knew that what I had to do, I had to do alone.

TWENTY-EIGHT

I slipped into the trees as quietly as I could, staying low and in the shadows. I had to stay hidden for as long as possible.

The snow had stopped and the day had grown warmer, leaving slippery patches of ice and snow and mud. As I drew closer to the slavers' camp, I caught metallic clanking noises and snatches of voices, faint at first. Despite the cold, sweat was dripping off my forehead. When I slid Dad's knife from its sheath, my palms were slick on the handle. A heavy thump shuddered through my chest.

I closed my eyes and was once again cowering in the back of that plane, choked with the musty smell of dank water and the tangles of weeds and dirt all around us.

I wiped my hands off on my jeans and stood up, surveying the last stretch of woods between me and the slave traders' camp. I gripped the blade tight and began to step over a fallen tree, but a pair of hands grabbed me from behind and yanked me backward. I struggled to get away but my knees hit a stump and I toppled over it. The knife shot out from my hand. I thought of Jenny and the Greens. I couldn't lose like this, not when I was so close. I tried to get myself up again, but before I could, my attacker vaulted over and pinned me down. A face framed with long wisps of black hair darted down toward mine.

"Jenny?"

She put her fingers to her lips, then dragged me away, farther from the slavers' camp. We stopped on the other side of a fallen tree and she dropped down in front of me.

"What are you doing here?" I hissed.

"What am I doing here? Following you, that's what I'm doing. Man, I've known you for, like, a week and I can already see right through you. 'Going to get our things from the casino.' Yeah, right. Why didn't you tell me you had a plan?"

"There is no plan," I said, picking Dad's knife up out of the snow. "Go back to town."

"Oh sure. I'll let you waltz into camp and stab their two psycho leaders on your own. I'm sure that'll work out just great. Are you insane? This was your plan? Why didn't you tell me?"

"'Cause I didn't want you to follow me! Look, just go home. I don't want you involved in this. This isn't your problem. Let me —"

"That isn't how this works, Stephen."

"How what works?"

Jenny stared at me.

"Us," she said. "If you're going to do something stupid, then so am I."

My hands went weak on the handle of the knife. "Jenny —"

"Marcus gathered about forty others," Jenny said in a hush. "They're meeting Caleb and the slavers at the gates at sunset. If they can't call it off, they'll fight. I figure the best we can do is slow them down, hobble them a little to give Marcus a chance. Without those jeeps, things would be a little more even. Right?"

I wanted to argue but she was that hurricane again, ready to tear through whatever was in her way. How do you fight a force of nature?

"Right," I said. "But how —"

An explosion of light came from the direction of the camp, piercing the gloom with razor-thin fingers. Jenny and I fell flat in the snow. We glanced at each other, then Jenny crept forward before I could stop her. I scrambled along behind, and together we peeked over the edge of the fallen tree.

The jeeps' headlights washed over the camp, throwing the shadows of the slavers onto the trees. Their engines roared. The men were making final preparations, fueling the jeeps, strapping on their gear, and checking their weapons.

There were at least twenty of them. With just the two of us and practically no weapons, I didn't see any option for us that didn't look like suicide. I was about to tell Jenny it was impossible, but before I could, she nodded out to our left where a lone backpack sat by the side of a tent.

At first I didn't see why, but then I looked closer. Hanging from the side of the pack was a string of black baseball-size orbs with pins sticking out of them. Grenades. One of the men must have set them aside, meaning to grab them on the way out. I looked across the camp. The pack was a good ten feet from where the slavers were gathering for their instructions, but at least forty feet from where Jenny and I were.

"We'll never get to them before they get us."

Jenny was silent, chewing on it. She kept her eyes fixed on the camp. The man with the scar climbed into the driver's side of one of the jeeps just as it was finished being fueled.

"This isn't going to work," I said. "We should just —"

Jenny pulled off her heavy coat, revealing her old Red Army jacket beneath. She started buttoning it up.

"What are you — ?"

"I'm taking care of the first part." Jenny pulled her hair back tight and secured it with a leather thong she took from her pocket. "Second part's on you."

"Jenn —"

Before I could finish, Jenny kissed me quick, stepped out from behind the tree, and walked right into the middle of the slavers' camp.

TWENTY-NINE

My heart seized. The slavers saw her immediately and raised their weapons, but for a strange moment no one fired. It was as if Jenny's sudden appearance was so unexpected that they were all trying to make sure they weren't dreaming. Jenny stood ramrod straight, her arms clasped crisply behind her, a scowl on her face.

With her hair back and her army jacket, she looked like the picture of a grim and fearless Chinese soldier.

"Ching-ma!" she shouted. *"Cho wen dow! Cho wen dow. Ching-ma!"*

As the men looked, puzzled, from one to the other, I got up and started moving to our left. Jenny kept shouting in her nonsense Chinese, but the distraction wouldn't last long. I had ten seconds, tops, before the men put it together that she was not being backed up by an entire Chinese regiment and then started shooting.

The man with the scar was starting up his jeep while the man with the dreadlocks moved off toward the one parked on the opposite side of the fuel truck.

"Ching mow don! Kai! Kai!" Jenny called forth her imaginary soldiers, then took off into the trees. There was a split second of confusion

before shots rang out as about half the men chased after her. Leaving her on her own felt like a knife twisting in my gut, but I had to stay focused.

I leapt into the camp, running as hard as I could to the grenades. Out of the corner of my eye I saw the dreadlocked man yanking the steering wheel hard, trying to get his jeep moving. Smart. Not even a little bit interested in Jenny's distraction. I pushed through the burn in my legs and drove toward the bag, skidding to a stop and grabbing it before taking off again the way I had come.

"Hey! You! Stop!"

There was a sharp *crack*, then a bullet tore past my shoulder and cut into the branches next to me. I pumped my arms, running hard until I was even with the fuel truck and stopped. I took a grenade and yanked out the pin.

I pivoted to the camp. The dreadlocked man had the jeep turned around now and was only seconds from getting away with it.

I thought of John Carter pitching as I wound up and threw the grenade at the side of the fuel truck.

The boom of the explosion was deafening. A yellow flash blinded me as the shock wave tore through the trees and knocked me to the ground. I lay there, arms over my head, as three more explosions rang out one after another. Deep, hollow booms. After that, there was a moment of silence when everything hung, suspended, like the world was holding its breath and waiting. Then all at once everything came crashing back. There were shouts and cries and the sound of burning that seemed to be everywhere at once.

The camp was in chaos. The air was thick with black smoke that smelled sickeningly of chemicals and burned my throat and eyes. The men who hadn't chased after Jenny were battling the flames that had erupted with the explosions. One main fire at the eastern edge of the camp was out of control. I could just make out a dark skeleton of twisted metal deep in the yellow flames. One of the two jeeps burned next to it.

The other was gone.

"Stephen!" Jenny was standing behind the first rank of trees. "We have to get out of here," she cried. "Now!"

I ran toward her. The oily smoke had already seeped into the woods, mixing with shafts of moonlight and the hellish glow of the fire, turning the forest into a confused maze. I had no idea if we were even headed in the right direction, but Jenny pushed on.

"Hey! Hey, you over there! Stop!"

A string of shots crackled behind us. We dodged to our right, following a sharp ridgeline. More gunfire came from behind us. Men shouted and we ran flat out, as fast as we could, sometimes missing trees by just inches.

"This way," Jenny said. We ran for a mile or more, turning back for Settler's Landing only when we were sure we had lost our pursuers. We came out of the trees at the crest of the hill that led into town. A thick haze of black smoke filled the air and dirtied the snow. The slavers had beaten us there. Everything reeked of burning wood and gunfire.

"God," Jenny breathed.

I took her hand and we moved on, past the front gates and down the road into town. The first two houses we came to were on fire. Orange flames poured out of the smashed windows, throwing awful jerking shadows onto the dark road and the woods. We passed a green house with an American flag just as its roof collapsed with a moan.

"Stephen, what if . . . ?"

I nodded down the road, toward the distant sound of gunfire. "I think they all pulled back that way. Everyone probably left their houses before the soldiers even got here. Those houses are empty."

I was amazed by how sure my voice sounded, given that I had no idea if what I said was true. I prayed it was. We leapt over tire-shaped scars in the grass and past the swing sets and slide that were lying smashed in the mud.

We followed the sounds of gunfire down the road, turning off to the left and down a short hill. I suddenly realized where they were leading us. The school. We slowed as we got close, staying low, finally taking cover behind the brick corner of the building. We flattened our backs to the wall. It was hard to make anything out in the fog of gun smoke, but I saw one group across the playground by the swing sets. It seemed to be a row of people on their backs and someone who moved quickly among them. In the lulls between the gunshots I could hear steady moans coming from them. Beyond them, lying in a rough line behind the crest of the hill that led up to the baseball field, were thirty or more townspeople with rifles, taking the only cover available. The slavers' men must have been just over the hill.

"Stay here," I said to Jenny as I started around the edge of the wall. "I'm going to go see if I can help."

"Did you just meet me?"

"Jenny, if it wasn't for me, this wouldn't —"

She darted out into the darkness.

Right. Should have known. I shot out from behind the school as a volley of gunfire erupted from the crest of the hill, lighting the playground in flashes of yellow and orange. I ducked my head and ran, passing within feet of the swing sets.

A voice called out from my left. "Stephen, over here!"

It was Violet, kneeling down among a group of ten or more people.

"Violet, I have to get to —"

"Later." She pushed a flashlight into my hand and pulled me down next to her. "Shine that here."

I looked up the hill, searching for Jenny.

"Now, Stephen!"

I flicked the light on, shining it down onto someone on the ground. As soon as I did, my hand shook.

All I saw was blood, shockingly red against the white of the snow.

"Steady," Violet said.

I didn't know the man on the ground in front of me. He had been shot as many as three times. There was so much blood it was hard to tell where. He was unconscious. Violet leaned over him, probing a wound on his shoulder with a small pair of pliers until she pulled out a big piece of shrapnel. As soon as she did, blood welled up in the gash and coursed down his arm. I was sure I was going to be sick. Violet grabbed a towel off the ground next to her and pressed it deep into the man's shoulder. My stomach turned again as the towel grew damp with red. I turned my head away. Others were laid out to Violet's left, a line of wounded men, women, even kids my age. Some unconscious, some twisting and moaning.

"The soldiers didn't expect us to fight. Neither did Caleb and his people. His family and a few others joined with the slavers. We let them chase us back here to get away from the houses and then we turned on them."

I fumbled for a roll of bandage on the ground and handed it to her, still holding the flashlight on the figure in front of me. I got a better look at him. He was young, maybe even my age, wearing a dark T-shirt and jeans. He had fine features and his hair, where not matted and red with blood, was golden and flopped down over one eye.

Something inside of me went cold.

It was Will Henry.

"But . . . he's with them," I said. "With Caleb and the slavers. He — "

Violet gritted her teeth and yanked a bandage tight. "He's dying, Stephen. It doesn't matter what side he's on."

"Is he really going to . . ." I couldn't finish. My throat had closed up.

"I don't know," Violet said. She wiped her hands on her jeans, then moved down the line. "I've got it from here." She took the flashlight from my hand. Another volley of gunfire roared behind us and we ducked instinctively.

As Violet moved along the line of wounded, I wiped a splash of blood off Will's cheek with the edge of my sleeve. For an awful moment I thought I would never be able to leave that spot. There was a time I probably would have claimed that I wanted Will Henry dead, but now, seeing him lying there pale and covered in blood, all I felt was emptiness, waste, and stupidity.

I pushed myself off the ground and ran up the hill, anger crashing through me. When I got to the crest I dropped down into the grass and peered over the edge. Out across the field, near second base, was the black shadow of the remaining jeep. A line of low swells in the grass stretched to the right and left of it. The soldiers and Caleb's people, I suspected, dug into shallow pits.

Jackson was lying to my left, a rifle in his hands. Marcus and Sam were on the other side, their eyes steady on their rifle sights. There was another barrage and we all ducked our heads. Bullets whistled past inches from us.

"Where's Jenny?" I asked.

"She said she was going back to town to help look after the little ones," Marcus said.

Right, I thought, looking all around trying to find some trace of her, but seeing nothing.

A roar of machine-gun fire rose from up ahead and was answered with shots from the line to either side of me. The bullets slammed into the ground between the two sides, kicking up a fog of snow but doing no damage.

My mind raced. When I was little, Grandpa would sit me down almost weekly for one of his endless lectures on military tactics. I'd humored him, barely paying attention, but I struggled now to bring some of it back. Marcus had numbers, but the slavers were so well armed it more than evened things out. I scanned the snowfield and surrounding trees ahead, looking for a way out. Suddenly something fell into place.

"You're pinned down," I said. I could almost hear Grandpa's voice in my head. "You need a smaller group to go out into the trees, around to their flank, and distract them so the main force can move in."

"I can't spare anyone to —"

"Don't worry about it," I said. "When the flanking group attacks, the soldiers will be distracted. That's when the rest of the line has to get up and rush them. It's the only way."

"Wait, where are you going?" Marcus yelled. "Stephen!"

But I was already on my way, hurtling down their line toward the woods, staying as low as I could. There was no time to worry about where Jenny had gone. It was best we were apart, given what I had planned.

As soon as the soldiers noticed my movement, they let go with a hail of bullets that Marcus and the others quickly answered. The mud and snow made it tough going, but I made it into the trees and out of sight. I thought I was home free until I heard someone running after me. I turned and there was Jackson, his rifle slung across his chest.

"Jackson, go back!"

He ignored me and kept coming. I ran as fast as I could, putting some distance between us, but I could still hear him behind me, his footfalls mixing in with the gunfire and shouting. There was no time to try to turn him back. I prayed that I'd either lose him or, when he saw what I was planning to do, he'd turn back on his own.

I ran until I was sure I'd made it as far as the soldiers' line out in the field, then jogged to my right. My heart sank when I saw who was waiting there.

"What are you —"

Jenny put her finger to her lips, then motioned me over next to her.

There were only a few thin ranks of trees between us and where the soldiers lay. It had gone quiet out in the field. The jeep was maybe fifty yards away, surrounded by about twenty men arranged in a half circle. One man stood at the back of the truck behind an armor plate, operating the swiveling machine gun and shouting orders. I could tell from the hulking outline that it was the man with the scar.

The underbrush behind us crunched. Someone coming. I slipped my knife out of its sheath and turned, but when the trees parted it was Jackson, rifle in hand.

"Oh great," Jenny whispered. "The cavalry's here."

"What are you two — ?"

We both shushed him and motioned for him to get down.

"What are you doing here?" Jackson said, pulling close to us.

"Up and at 'em," Jenny said. "You in?"

"No," I said sharply, then dropped my voice down to a whisper. "We're not doing it. We're going back and joining Marcus's line."

"That's stupid, and you know it," Jenny snapped.

"It's not."

"Then what did you even come here for? God, Stephen," she said. "These people have more guns and more ammunition. They can just wait us out. I mean, think about it — the only reason they're firing right now is so Marcus and them will waste ammo shooting back. Right? Am I right?"

What could I say? Of course she was. From the other side came the rustling of soldiers adjusting in their places and the metallic clinking of reloading from both sides. It was about to start again.

"Okay, then," Jenny said. "How about it, Jackie boy? You up for some mischief?"

Jackson nodded. He looked terrified, but he was serious. He was going to do it. They both were. It was pointless. I knew we wouldn't get ten feet before that machine gun swiveled our way and chopped us down. I peered into the brush I had come through, my mind scrambling for another idea, some alternative. If I'd been alone, I would've been running right out into the field, no matter what my chances were. Seeing Will had settled that. But now Jenny and Jackson would be right there with me, and they'd be cut down as fast as I'd be.

Jenny hopped up off the ground. Jackson slung his rifle over his shoulder.

"You coming, Steve?" Jenny asked.

I had no choice. If they were going, so was I. Whatever was going to happen to Jenny and Jackson, I wanted to happen to me too. As I pulled myself up off the ground, something about the brush surrounding us made me stop short.

Mischief.

"What's on the other side of those trees?"

"The Henry house," Jackson said. "Why?"

My mind raced. I turned back to the soldiers arrayed along the ground.

"Steve?"

I felt what I always imagined Dad and Grandpa felt in times like these, a moment when all the twisting confusion and uncertainty collapsed into a simple straight path.

A moment of being sure.

"Come on," I said, pushing between the two of them and up the trail. "Follow me."

THIRTY

I led the two of them at a run through the woods.

"Where are we going?" Jackson asked from behind me, more insistent now that it was the third time he'd asked without me answering. I ducked beneath a low-hanging branch and took the last leg at a sprint. The rocky ground gave way to the snow and grass that surrounded the house, and I had to stop, unsure where to go next. Luckily, as soon as we made it to the yard, Jenny knew exactly what we were doing.

"Stephen, you're a genius," she said. "Come on, it's this way."

She took off. I started to follow her, but Jackson grabbed my coat and jerked me back.

"What are we doing here?"

"There's no time to explain," I said, but he wasn't backing off. The mix of fear and anger in his eyes was electric.

"Why should I trust you?" he asked through gritted teeth. "After what you and Jenny did — you just left. You didn't even say anything. I thought we were friends."

"We are."

"Then why —"

"I was trying to protect you!"

"Well, I don't need your protection!"

"Look, this whole thing was my fault. I know that, but I need your help to fix it. I'm sorry I left. I am. I didn't know what else to do."

Jackson didn't relent. He held me there, sure that I was lying; sure that it was a trap. The distrust in his eyes bored through me. Some part of me that was still Grandpa's wanted to push him away and finish things with Jenny, but I held my ground.

"It's not going to be like before," I said. "We're not going to let them have this place, Jackson. And we're not going to run. I swear."

Jackson fixed me hard with his eyes, looking deep for the lie. A clatter of gunfire rose behind us, followed by three deep booms that lit up the sky in orange flashes. Jackson pushed me aside and ran after Jenny. Praying I was right, I followed.

We found Jenny at the northern edge of the Henrys' big house, kneeling down and peering out around a corner of the wall. In the darkness all we could see was the sharp outline of two paddocks and the wall of trees that separated them from the Henrys' pigs and sheep. Inside the pens, the horses and cows, anxious after the night of gunfire, were a confusion of restless shadows, snorting and attacking the ground with their hooves. The sound of it, angry and wild, made a piece of my heart lodge firmly in my throat.

Jenny nudged Jackson with her shoulder. "Whatcha think, Jackie boy?"

Jackson's forehead furrowed as he put it together. "Will it work?"

"Did last time," I said, earning a glare from Jackson and Jenny. "What? It did."

Jackson stared into the darkness, his hands fidgeting and seizing into fists, relaxing, then doing it again.

"We can do this," I said quietly, just to him, hoping it was true.

Jackson turned to me and something seemed to click inside him. He stood up and swept the rifle off his shoulder. Without another word, he tore out into the open.

Jenny and I followed him, running out across the Henrys' yard, slowing as we came to the pens. Closer up, I could see how panicked the animals really were. The horses paced and bucked fitfully in their small area, thousands of pounds of muscles and fear, the whites of their eyes flashing in the low moonlight. Near Jenny, the group of twenty or more cows lowed and snorted and dug their hooves into the ground, swinging their horns wildly around them. My stomach twisted with nerves as I set my hand on the flimsy latch that held the wooden gate closed. Whenever one of the horses so much as touched a rail the whole thing shook. Jenny looked up at me. I took a deep breath and nodded.

"Okay!" Jenny called out. "Now!"

Four shots from Jackson's rifle exploded into the air across from us. The animals reared up and crashed into one another, filling the air with their high-pitched squeals. When they started moving, the ground beneath us shook. Jenny and I yanked the gates open, scrambling to get out of the way as the animals came boiling out as a single mass, like water exploding from a burst dam. They trampled through the mud and snow past the house, headed for the trees, throwing up a haze of debris all around them, their dark bodies shooting through it. I pressed my back against the wooden gate until I saw a flash of Jackson through the dust. He was moving south, firing his rifle into the air, herding them along.

I left the pen after the last horse had cleared it and followed along behind. I didn't see Jenny anywhere — the cloud of mud and smoke was too thick and the roar of the animals was deafening. I was swept away with it, running, stumbling, barely able to see the ground beneath my feet, my mouth and nose clogging with dust. I thought I heard someone calling my name, thought I saw someone up ahead, but then it would all disappear in the gray churn and all I could do was run and hope I didn't fall.

It was worse when we moved out of the field and into the woods. There, the rumble and blare of the stampede were enclosed in the trees and focused, like an avalanche finding its course. The animal surge tore apart everything in its path: brush and leaves, exposed roots and saplings. All of it was shredded and sucked into the deluge, leaving a barren strip of land in its wake.

The herd spread out as it poured into the field. When the firing and screams began, I knew they had found their mark. Out in the open now, I could see the animals breaking around the body of the jeep. Most of the soldiers had heard them coming and fled, but as I ran I passed the few who hadn't, lying beaten and bruised on the ground, the conscious ones gasping for air as though they'd nearly been drowned.

I didn't know if Marcus and his people were taking the opportunity to attack or not — there was too much confusion to be sure — but up ahead I did see the one thing that mattered.

Somehow the man with the scar had managed to hold his place on the machine gun at the back of the jeep. He was no fool either. He knew what was happening and wasn't paying the slightest attention to the stampede around him. He was aiming squarely ahead, fully prepared for Marcus and his people to attack.

I ran toward him as he leaned into the gun and a tongue of orange flame roared out of it. Taking three quick strides, I leapt up to the lip of the jeep's bed. My foot hit the edge of it and I pitched forward, piling into him. He jerked around and, not missing a beat, dropped his fist like a hammer. The breath shot out of me. I gasped but somehow managed to hold on to him. He struggled, squirming and punching, until his feet hit a pile of shell casings that littered the floor of the jeep and he went down. I fell on top of him, my legs landing on either side of his chest. He looked up at me and a sudden burst of recognition shot through him.

"You," he growled.

Before he could say anything more, I braced my forearm on his throat and pressed down with all my weight.

I stared down at his white face, craggy and pitted and hard as Grandpa's. His teeth were bared, his eyes burning but empty. I saw him coming at us in the plane, drunken and full of hate. For so long I had blamed Dad for what had happened. But I knew right then, leaning over that monster, that it was this man's fault, everything was. All Dad had been trying to do was be a better man than him.

I grabbed my wrist and leaned in, pressing down onto his throat. His fists slammed into my sides but I barely felt them. I wasn't going to miss my chance. He gasped and his eyes widened, but he was far from giving up. He struggled even harder, his balled-up fists beating at my ribs, then grabbing at my shoulders. His hands went white, trying to tear me off. His left hand made it to my throat, his fingers clamping down as his right braced against my chest.

I had to let go of him to pull his hand from around my neck. As I thrashed, his other hand closed around my throat as well. He pushed me over onto my side, then rolled on top of me, both hands on my throat.

"Stupid kid," he said as he squeezed. "You may have helped that woman and her brat, but looking for you and your dad led us right here where we made some nice new friends. I should thank you."

I threw my fists into him, but they bounced uselessly off his thick shoulders. I gasped for air as he put me down on my back and leaned over me, squeezing his big hands tighter and tighter.

Gunfire crackled around me as the world tripped into darkness, collapsing until there was just his face, twisted into a snarl or a smile — I couldn't tell which — hanging over me like an awful moon.

The shouting and gunshots faded, receding farther and farther away. As darkness seeped in, I saw Mom and Dad. He had his arm around her, drawing her in close to his side. They were standing in a sun-drenched field against a blue sky, smiling, skin bronze and shining. Mom was in her red and gold dress, her hair blowing in the breeze.

Mom's hand grazed my cheek, then took my shoulders and brought me in between her and Dad so I could feel the warmth of their bodies and the steady rhythm of their breath, in and out, in and out, all around me.

I looked up and saw the flash of her smile like a winking star.

Then there was a *crack*, like thunder, and everything went black.

THIRTY-ONE

I was being dragged across the ground by my wrists, my arms thrown over my head, aching badly. *Shackles. I'm in shackles.* Rocks and shell casings scraped my back, and when I tried to breathe, the air was thick with smoke and my throat was wrecked. My head pounded.

I was alive. How? I opened my eyes, but they stung from the smoke. All I could see were hazy blooms of light in the sky. Orange and yellow and then a smear of bloody red. I wrenched my head back, hoping to see who had me, but I couldn't see any farther than my own wrists and the pair of hands that were clamped around them. Not shackles. Hands. Pulling me. But to where? I writhed, trying to free myself, but I was too weak.

"Who are you?" I croaked. My throat was ragged, dry, and swollen like it was full of thorns. "Where are you taking me? Where's Jenny?"

A canopy of trees closed over us and whoever was pulling me dropped my hands and stalked a few feet away. I tried to sit up, but my back screamed in pain, so I lay there catching my breath, trying to ready myself for whatever was next. The fighting was a distant series of thumps and cries somewhere out on the field.

A shadow fell over me and I cringed, attempting to get my hands over my face to protect myself. But all that came was a cool rush of water sweeping down over my forehead and across my eyes, wiping away the grime and the burning. I opened my mouth to let the water rush down my throat. Once I drank all I could, I opened my eyes again.

Sitting behind me, a canteen in his hand, was Jackson. He wasn't looking at me. His arm was wrapped in a bandage that was soaked through with blood. There was a clatter of gunfire way out in the field and then the yellow flash of an explosion that lit up his dirty face.

"You okay?" I asked.

Jackson nodded.

"Where's Jenny?"

"With Dad and the others. They're chasing the last of them out now."

I urged myself up to my elbows painfully. A low fog hung over everything, and a column of smoke billowed into the sky from the corner of the school's roof that was visible.

What had once been a baseball field was pitted and torn. A few animals stood here and there, lost. Some lay dead on the ground. The fighting had moved east into the woods. The jeep sat in the middle of the field.

"What happened to . . ."

And then I saw him. Just behind the jeep lay the man with the scar. He was facedown in the mud, his arms thrown over his head. The snow around him was stained a deep red.

I turned to Jackson. His rifle lay on the ground next to him. He stared across the field at the man, looking hundreds of miles away.

Jackson shuddered, then dropped his head into his hands, his chest heaving as he sobbed.

I dragged myself closer and put my hand on his shoulder. I wanted to say thank you. I wanted to say I was sorry. I wanted to say a lot of things, but right then it seemed best to say nothing at all, so I sat there with him until his breathing slowed, thinking how the end of the world had made so many of us unrecognizable, even to ourselves.

Soon, Jenny came running across the field and dropped down beside us. Her clothes were torn and dirty and there was a smear of blood on her forehead, but I couldn't tell if it was hers or someone else's.

"Are you —"

She lunged across me and grabbed Jackson into a hug. He seemed surprised at first, but then his hands tightened around her back, grasping her to him.

"Mom and Dad are all right," Jenny told him breathlessly after they parted. "After the man with the dreadlocks ran, the rest started to fold. There are a few stragglers, but we're pushing them back."

"How many of our people —"

"Don't worry about that now. We can —"

"How many?" I insisted.

Jenny looked at her brother, then at me. A tattoo of rifle shots crackled through the air, followed by the boom of explosions like a waning thunderstorm.

"Twenty," she said. "Maybe more."

"Will?"

Jenny turned to track a low rumble that rose in the east.

"He's dead."

It was like the deep toll of a bell, leaving us silent, kneeling together under that stand of trees.

We all turned as some kind of commotion broke out down the hill on the way to town. The few adults who remained were racing up the road past the school, shouting back and forth to one another.

"What's going on?"

Jenny helped me and Jackson up, and together we trotted across the field and down the road. We reached town just behind the gathering group of people. They were all hurrying into the park, but the three of us froze where we were.

Sam's house was a wall of fire. Three houses down the road from it were smoking, their windows lit a livid orange from inside. Trees were burning like torches and spreading the fire from house to house. The slavers may have gone but we had a new problem now.

Settler's Landing was in flames.

THIRTY-TWO

Jenny pulled at my hand and we all raced into the crowd that was gathering in the park between Sam's house and the Greens'. Others flooded in behind us, returning from the fight only to find their homes close to destruction.

Tuttle stood at the center of the crowd shouting instructions I couldn't make out over the roar of the fires and panicked voices. Buckets were passed out and people began filling them with snow and rushing off to the houses that hadn't caught yet. Another group took axes and ran to the stands of trees between houses, hoping to fell them and create firebreaks.

It seemed hopeless. The air was thick with smoke and the smell of burning. There was screaming as the crowd surged and pushed. Tuttle tried to keep people organized, but his voice was getting more and more drowned out.

Someone forced a bucket into my hand and I was pushed on by the crowd, Jenny beside me.

"We're going to the school," she shouted into my ear. To her right were Jackson and Derrick and some others.

"They sent the little ones there," Derrick said. "Thought they'd be safe there during the fight. We think some of them are still there now!"

I remembered the plume of smoke I'd seen rising from the school roof and broke into a run. There were about twenty of us, some with axes and some with buckets. We tore down the hill and across the parking lot to the school.

It was better off than many of the houses, but smoke was seeping out of the cracks of doorways and some of the windows were lit up with flames. Derrick led a group to a snowbank nearby where they began to fill their buckets.

"Where are they?" I asked Derrick. "The kids?"

"Toward the back, I think."

I dropped the bucket and once Jenny, Jackson, and I made it to the school's front doors, I slammed my shoulder into them. The doors gave with a screech and a wave of heat. It was worse inside than it looked. Jenny motioned some of Derrick's team into the doorway and they began tossing loads of snow onto the walls to try to keep the fire from growing. There was a hiss and gasps of steam as some of the flames were squelched.

"Stay low," Jenny called.

The three of us covered our mouths and noses and ducked down, crawling along the floor where the air was clearer. We checked all of the small classrooms we passed, but each was empty except for overturned desks and chairs. The smoke was already massing in my throat and burning my eyes. We had to find them fast.

The three of us finally reached the main classroom at the end of the hall and tumbled through the doors, coughing. The air inside was clearer, but still just as hot. I doubled over and sucked in a painful breath. At first the room seemed empty, but then I saw a leg poking out from behind Tuttle's big desk.

"There!"

We found ten of the little ones cowering behind the desk, all of them stained with soot and looking terrified. Jenny dropped to her knees by their side.

"It's going to be okay, guys," she said calmly. "Just come with us and we'll get you out of here."

The kids shied away at first, like scared animals, but she was finally able to pull them to their feet and lead them back to the doors. I paused by the desk as she went. Jenny turned back.

"Take them out of here," I shouted.

"What are you going to do?" Jenny asked.

I turned toward the far wall of wooden shelves. Each level was stacked with row after row of books. Science. Government. The arts. Everything.

"Are you crazy? We don't have time, this place is coming down!"

Over her shoulder I could just see Jackson leading the kids into the smoky hallway.

"Then go! Help Jackson with the kids!"

I knew Jenny would keep protesting, so I turned from her and ran for the bookshelf, weaving through the lines of desks and pulling books off as fast as I could, filling my arms with them. I reached for a copy of *To Kill a Mockingbird*, but Jenny got it first.

"One more stupid thing I have to do because of you," she said with a sooty smile as she yanked down a score of books.

Our arms were full when there was another moan from behind us. The far wall of the classroom was blackening and about to go. Soon the whole place would be on fire.

"Think we're out of time, pal. Let's get out of here!"

Just as we turned to the doors, a curtain of flame appeared, blocking our way. The wall alongside it had begun to smolder too. Smoke was now seeping into the room.

We both stood there, our arms weighed down with books, looking for some way out. The walls around us groaned. Tinder deep inside them crackled and popped. We were trapped.

"Well, Stephen? Any more bright ideas?"

I looked all around the room. I had nothing. The only doors out were blocked and the fire was only growing stronger and hotter. The books felt like lead in my arms. How could I have been so stupid? We were going to die for these? As the smoke grew thicker all I could think of was the whole town wiped away, little more than a smudge of ash in the woods. All they had done, all they had built, would be lost, forgotten.

"We have to just run for it," Jenny said. "Drop the books and jump through the fire. It's the only way."

It was insane. The fire had grown too big, feeding off the old wood. "Jenny, no. We can't —"

"Just do it!"

Jenny dropped the load in her arms, but then someone screamed my name from behind us. I turned to see Jackson leaning through the open window high up on the back wall.

"Come on," he shouted. "This way!"

I looked up at the window. It was narrow and set a good fifteen feet high. We'd never make it. I spun around the room, hunting for a solution, but all I saw were desks and chairs and . . . something snapped. I had it.

"The desks!" I shouted to Jenny. "Come on."

Jenny started grabbing desks out of their neat rows and dragging them over to the window. There, we stacked desk upon desk until we made a ladder leading up to the window. Jackson knelt at the window's edge and held out his hand. I pushed Jenny up first. When she reached the top she turned and held her hand out for me, but instead of starting the climb I reached back and gathered the stacks of books.

"Come on!" Jenny urged.

"Hey, remember how I promised Tuttle I'd bring about the new golden age?"

"Stephen!"

"I'm not moving until you take them!"

Jenny grimaced but held out her hands as I dug into the piles and handed up as many as I could. She passed them off to Jackson, then dove through the window and reached down for my hand.

"Okay, now you!"

The desks were shakier than I'd thought. The thin metal legs quivered as I climbed. I could feel the heat of the fire singeing my back, growing by the second. I made it up one desk, then two, but as I reached for the third, there was another collapse behind me and I felt the bottom desk shift and falter.

"Jump!"

My legs shook. There was a crash as the desks tumbled beneath me and then I was falling, my arms pinwheeling as the hands of gravity pulled me backward, down into the smoke. There was a strange moment as Jenny's face seemed to rush away from me and everything else slowed down. I felt weightless and weak and I knew there was nothing I could do. I would fall and the smoke would swallow me whole, but at least Jenny and Jackson and the kids would be safe. I closed my eyes, accepting it, but then I jerked to a stop.

I opened my eyes and there was Jenny leaning halfway out of the window, her hand locked onto my wrist.

"Gotcha," she said, and then other hands appeared, latching on to me and dragging me up toward the window. As I got closer, Jackson took hold of my sleeve. I grabbed on to them, pushed against the wall with my feet, and climbed, the fire licking at my heels.

When I made it to the window more hands reached out: Derrick's, Martin's, Carrie's, and others'. I felt the cold, fresh air rush into my lungs and I bent over, coughing, then fell onto my side. Behind my friends were the ring of little ones and a stack of books mostly untouched by the fire.

I had only a moment to rest before Jenny lifted me up and we all stumbled away from the building and out to the battlefield. Once we were far enough away, we stopped and turned back to the school.

Flames had consumed most of the west wall and were spreading around to the front. Soon the roof groaned and fell in. When it did, the fire surged, lighting up the gray sky and filling it with columns of smoke. It seemed as though only minutes passed before there was nothing but piles of burning wood and scattered bricks.

I remembered sitting inside that first day, desperate to flee, feeling alien and alone amid all those kids who seemed nothing like me. I looked around at the group of us now. Everyone was streaked with ash and peppered with burns and trails of blood, our clothes torn into ruins. Carrie was leaning into John Carter's shoulder while Derrick and Martin sat on a snowbank on either side of Wendy, helping her wash the ash out of her eyes. Jenny's hand fell into mine.

Standing there as the school burned, that group of us drew together into a tight little band that felt solid as iron. The houses could burn and the school could fall, but maybe together we'd survive.

"Look," someone said.

We turned toward the field just as a group of people emerged from the trees opposite us, maybe forty in all.

"Are they ours?" Derrick asked.

"All of our people went back to fight the fires," Jenny said.

The group moved slowly, weaving their way past the bodies and the wreckage of the jeep. They definitely weren't slavers, but as they got closer I made out the thin silhouettes of rifles in their hands.

Whoever they were, we still weren't done for the day.

THIRTY-THREE

Jenny, Jackson, and I moved the younger kids back into the woods with Derrick and the others.

"Should we go get Mom and Dad?" Jackson asked.

Jenny shook her head. "There's too much to do down there. Looks like it's just us."

The three of us made our way through the carnage, our boots sliding on the muddy and blood-soaked snow. As soon as the others saw us coming, they unslung their rifles and lifted them. The three of us slowed.

"Just stay calm," I whispered. "Don't make any sudden moves and keep your hands where they can see them."

It was a ragged group, a mix of old and young. They weren't clothed or fed as well as those in Settler's Landing, but we couldn't mistake that for weakness. Some looked just as scared as I imagined Jenny and Jackson and I did, but some also looked hard and ready for whatever might happen. They would use their weapons, no doubt about it.

This looked especially true of the one I took for their leader. He was a tall, rail-thin man with a scraggly black-and-white beard and a patch over one eye. He had a chrome revolver attached to his hip but was so calm he hadn't even drawn it yet, just moved across the field with his hand resting on the pistol's grip.

We kept our approach slow and easy until there was only about ten feet separating us. Everything around us stank of blood and fire. Jenny and Jackson and I stopped where we were; the man with the patch lifted one hand, and his people stopped too. Gun barrels dipped slightly but did not drop.

No one said anything for a moment as we took a measure of one another. I looked back over my shoulder. No one in sight. Everyone was still in town fighting the fires. A shot of nerves quaked through me. I'd have given anything for Marcus and the others to appear, but we were on our own.

I took a step forward. My mouth felt full of cotton. My hands shook.

"You're from Fort Leonard," I said.

The man nodded slowly. "Looks like you all had a bit of trouble here."

"Yes sir."

The man appraised the field around us and spit on the ground. "Slavers. We passed a bunch of them retreating on the way over. No coincidence they were here, I guess."

"No sir."

"You all hired them to take care of us."

I looked over at Jenny and Jackson. I could tell both of them were scared, but they were putting on stony faces. I felt their strength bleed into me, straightening my spine, making me even more sure of what I had to do.

"Yes sir," I said. "We did."

"Guess it didn't go as planned."

"Some of us thought the folks who hired them shouldn't be running things anymore," Jenny said from beside me. "When we told them and the slavers to take off, they went after us."

"You think I'm going to thank you for deciding *not* to turn all of me and mine into slaves?"

"No sir," Jenny said.

It went quiet again and I had to fight to keep still. This wasn't going right. *What were we thinking, coming up here?*

"Stephen, Jenny, Jackson — step away from there!"

The three of us whipped around to see Marcus and Sam and about ten others appear on the field behind us. Each of them had a gun trained on the people from Fort Leonard, who in turn raised theirs with a metallic clatter. The man with the patch had his gun out now and was pointing it right in Marcus's face. The chrome hammer was drawn all the way back.

"Stephen," Marcus said slowly, "take Jenny and Jackson and move out of the way."

I swallowed hard. "They're not here to fight," I said.

"Stephen."

I turned to the man with the patch. "Are you?"

The man tightened his grip on the revolver.

"They killed two friends of ours. We will fight if we need to, son."

"Tell them it was an accident," Jenny pleaded.

"Just get out of the way!"

I turned away from Marcus and back to Fort Leonard's leader.

"It was my fault," I said. "Okay? It was a dumb prank. I made everyone here think your people were attacking us and that's why they sent the group that shot your friends. So if you want to shoot someone, then shoot me, but we're telling you the truth. The ones who sent the people who killed your friends, the ones who hired the slavers, are not in charge anymore. I swear they're not."

The man with the patch considered this as we all held our breath.

"Look," I said, as steady as I could, "the people who came before us nearly destroyed the whole world, but that was yesterday. This is today, and today we've got a choice, right?"

The group from Fort Leonard gripped the stocks of their guns like they were trying to keep their heads above water. If the wind blew wrong, they'd fire. And if they did, Marcus and his people would too.

"Marcus," I said, "have everybody put their guns down."

"Them first," Marcus said. "We're not —"

"Just do it," Jackson commanded, turning around to face his father. "You've come this far. Just go one step further."

Marcus gripped the rifle to his shoulder, sweat cutting channels through the soot on his face.

Jenny took a step toward him. "Please, Dad," she said, and reached out to lay her palm over his rifle's sight.

Painfully slow, Marcus lowered the barrel of his rifle, keeping his eyes on the people from Fort Leonard the entire time, looking for any hint they were about to take advantage. When they didn't, he lowered his gun all the way and then motioned for Sam and the others to do the same.

Jenny turned to the man with the patch. "Now you."

The man looked back at his people and gave a slight nod. All around us gun barrels wilted and fell until we stood there, two divided fronts without a war to fight.

Marcus took a tentative step forward and held out his hand.

"Marcus Green," he said.

The man holstered his revolver, then lifted his own hand to take Marcus's.

"Stan Allison."

The two stood silently for a moment. Marcus looked back over his shoulder at the smoke rising above the trees.

"If you all could spare it," he said, "we could really use some help."

Stan nodded, then waved his people forward. Marcus and Sam and the others from Settler's Landing led the way, but soon the people from Fort Leonard had caught up. They all mixed together, one side indistinguishable from the other as they marched toward the fires.

We watched them go, then Jenny took my hand and Jackson's, and once we gathered up the little ones, we followed them back to town, all of us hoping there would be something left.

EPILOGUE

It was a Saturday, but there I was anyway, sitting at the edge of Tuttle's new desk, a copy of *Charlie and the Chocolate Factory* in my hand, facing a crowd of kids who were looking up at me expectantly.

"Who wants to read the next chapter?"

Everyone's hand shot up, everyone's except Claudia's, of course. She was a small girl with long blond hair and freckles. She almost never spoke in class and seemed paralyzed by shyness. Tuttle said that sometimes you have to force them to do what they need to do.

"Claud? How about you read some to us?"

The little girl shook her head vehemently. I left the edge of the desk and sat down on the dirt floor beside her, slipping the book into her lap and leaning in close to her ear.

"How about you just read it to me?"

Claudia's blue eyes shone as she sucked back the fear.

"It's okay," I said, nudging her shoulder with mine. "Go ahead."

Claudia lifted the book up off her lap. Her first words came out in a halting trickle. There were snickers and I threw out some hard glares to silence them. She stumbled over the next three words, then let the book fall into her lap.

"Claud . . ."

The book fell to the floor and she ran out — crying, I was sure. Great.

"Eddie, can you pick it up?"

Eddie, the oldest in the bunch, nodded, and I went off to find Claudia. I left the log cabin schoolhouse we had built on the site of the old school and walked out into the grassy field. It amazed me that, even months later, I could still smell the smoke.

I had been doing the little ones' Saturday classes for the last month or so while Tuttle healed from his broken arm and smoke inhalation. He did the weekday classes himself, gasping and wheezing, but he said the weekends were too much. I was hesitant at first, but once I got into it, I found that there was something strangely comforting about being in the new school and, despite what Jackson and the others thought, the little ones were actually kind of fun.

I found Claudia out under the big sycamore tree at the top of the hill, her chin in her hands. Across from her, a crew of twenty or so people raised the roof on one of what was going to be a few new cabins behind the school. Claudia was lying on her stomach, staring not at the construction but at what lay beside it.

Twenty-three wooden crosses.

They were set out in neat rows in the grass, most of them surrounded by bouquets of wildflowers, cards, or keepsakes of the person who lay beneath them. Twenty had died that night, along with three injured who followed soon after. Claudia's dad was there. Her brother too. Her mother had died years before.

"Hey," I said, landing nearby.

"Hey," Claudia said, pulling at the grass and tossing it aside.

"You okay?"

The little girl nodded, her pigtails swinging. "I don't know why we have to come here on Saturday too."

"Makes you one day smarter."

"My mom told me when she was little they had Saturdays and Sundays off."

"It's a brave new world."

"What does that mean?"

I picked a strand of grass and twirled it around my finger. "I don't know," I admitted. "Something Tuttle says."

"Are you gonna teach us when Mr. Tuttle dies?"

"Jeez, Claud."

"Well?"

"I'm pretty sure Mr. Tuttle will live forever. Like a vampire."

Claudia laughed, and I figured this was my chance. I reached around to my back pocket and threw my own copy of *Charlie and the Chocolate Factory* down in front of her. She leaned back from it like it was diseased.

"I think you'll like it," I said.

"But . . . why?" Claudia asked, looking out at the graves. "I mean, it's not even real."

I searched for something Tuttle might have said then, but found nothing. I looked from the graveyard up to the roof as it was carefully nailed into place by a work crew that was half Settler's Landing and half Fort Leonard, distinctions that were fading more and more by the day.

"I don't know," I said. "I guess . . . maybe it makes you realize that other worlds are possible."

Claudia considered that and, even if she didn't seem totally convinced, she opened the book to the first page and began to read. It came slowly at first, like the words were nettled things too large for her mouth, but gradually they tripped out more and more easily. She read as the workers muscled up the roof and the wind blew the smells of sawdust across the grass.

Other worlds.

I hoped it was true. That the leap of faith we all took was a beginning and not just a blip, soon to be wiped away like so much had been wiped away before. Like Mom and Grandpa and Dad. As much as things had changed, I still heard their voices and felt their hands guiding me, though their grip seemed looser each day.

Another family had already stepped forward to take Claudia in, just like the Greens had done for me. In time I hoped she would feel at home and the world would move on for her, leaving everything else safely behind.

By the time Claudia reached the second chapter, I could tell she had forgotten I was there. The words moved from the page and out of her mouth, like a mill wheel dipping into the water, lifting it up and casting it down again in a glittering shower. After a while, the workers took a break, moving off into the shade of the trees and swatting the sawdust off themselves. Even when the rest of the kids broke free from the school and poured into the yard in a riot of shrieked laughter, Claudia didn't move.

Her words rose up into the air, up beyond the trees and into the sky.

I walked into town, past the scars from the fight with the slavers. The fires had spread quickly and destroyed more than half of the houses in town. The ones that couldn't be saved were torn down and replaced by what were little more than rough log cabins, neat and warm but small.

They were integrated with the houses that still stood, giving the neighborhood an odd mixed look of past and future. Though sometimes it was hard to tell which was which.

I headed out through the front gates and crossed the forest to the highway. Once I got to Dad's grave, I knelt down beside it and carefully cleaned away the week's accumulation of leaves and twigs and discarded acorns. The wood marker that sat at the head of the swell in the grass looked old and dry, the letters in his name already fading. I'd need to replace it soon. I used to come every day, but soon the demands of school and of a town that needed to be rebuilt kept me back.

Once I was done cleaning the grave I stayed there for a time and then leaned over the grass, pressing my hands deep into its waxy depths.

"Hey."

I jerked my hands back and turned around to find Jenny standing over me, in a T-shirt and jean jacket. The bill of Violet's old baseball cap was pulled down low over her eyes. Back near the tree line, her horse, Wind, was tied up and munching on grass. His sandy flanks glistened in the sun.

"You must have ridden him far."

"Farthest yet," Jenny said, pulling off her rawhide gloves and stuffing them in her belt before flopping on the ground next to me. "I swear I could see the Rockies."

"You could not."

"Well . . . it was something."

"Any trouble?"

"Oh yeah," she said. "Always."

"You didn't have to shoot anyone, did you?"

Jenny pulled off her cap and leaned on her elbows in the grass. The sunlight hit her face like a splash of cool water. "Not today, Steve-O. Not today."

Jenny closed her eyes and lay down next to me, her chest rising and falling gently, a glisten of sweat like a mist of diamonds on her forehead.

As soon as things calmed down, Jenny had set about tearing apart the Starbucks down the highway and hauling it in pieces back to town. It had taken her weeks, but when it was done, she'd been able to trade it all for Wind and a rifle of her own. From that day on, she'd throw herself onto her horse and disappear, always heading west, always pushing a little farther each time, stretching the boundaries of her world like a rubber band.

Every time she came back, we would stay up late and she would tell me stories of the things she had seen, so excited you would have thought she'd uncovered a field of gold when it was no more than a new tract of houses, or an abandoned car rusting in the woods.

"You should have seen it," Jenny murmured into the air above us. "Animals everywhere. *Everywhere*. I saw elk and mountain lions and beavers. I even found this whole herd of buffalo. Hundreds of them. Thousands maybe. I ran Wind right through them. It felt like flying."

Her eyes were distant, locked on the cloudless blue, glazed with joy at remembering.

"Is today the day?" I asked . . . and immediately regretted it. Jenny's eyebrows drew together, making a gloomy little wrinkle. She checked on Wind over her shoulder.

"I think so," she said. "Maybe. I don't know."

I turned on my side to face her. I had said it a hundred times before and I'd say it a hundred times again. "It's still dangerous out there."

"I know that."

"Dealing with the slavers wasn't magic. There are others — the army and a thousand other —"

"I know, Stephen."

Jenny turned onto her stomach. I plucked a blade of grass and settled it between my teeth. We had had this fight before. I knew when it was over.

"So, how's shaping the minds of the next generation going?"

"I'm just helping out."

"Then what?" Jenny asked. I could feel her staring at me. "Have you thought about it anymore?"

Jenny laid her head on my chest. Her breath went in and out, reminding me of a swing arcing up toward the sky and then falling again, over and over.

"Okay," she said, and after a long while she drifted off.

I lay there, the heat of Jenny's body beside me, the far-off smell of sawdust floating through the air.

Behind us, Wind shook his mane and stamped his foot into the grass, eager to be on his way.

"You ready, tough guy?"

When I opened my eyes, Jenny was adjusting Wind's saddle and harness. Her rifle sat in a handmade leather case along his side. She pulled it out, checked it over, and replaced it. Then she drew on her gloves and cap and mounted Wind in one smooth, liquid motion.

Jenny guided Wind over to me. I pulled myself up onto the back of the horse between her and her rolled-up gear. Jenny turned Wind around and we trotted off toward Settler's Landing, racing him when we reached the main road, his hooves making a machine-gun rattle against the asphalt.

We came to a halt out in front of the Greens' just as Jackson stepped down off a ladder that led up to the house's gutters. "Hey, cowgirl!"

Jenny slid down off Wind's back. "Hey, Jackie boy! What's happening?"

"I'm a gutter slave today," he said, wiping the muck of wet leaves from his hands before giving her a quick hug.

"Mom and Dad inside?"

"Yep." Jackson pulled the ladder off the house and carted it around back. After Jenny got Wind tied up in the park across the street, we went inside to the smell of baking bread.

"Hey, you two!" Violet called out from the kitchen as we came in.

Marcus was coming down the stairs and grabbed Jenny as soon as he saw her.

"Whew! Somebody smells like a horse."

"Yeah, I gave up on trying to make it go away."

"Well, sit down," Violet said. "We'll have lunch ready in a minute."

"So what's out there these days?" Marcus asked once we'd all sat down and passed plates of food from hand to hand.

"It's mostly quiet," Jenny said, handing me a bowl of potatoes. "I hear about more towns going up though. Little ones, but it won't be long until it gets crowded around here."

"Are you talking to people?" Violet asked, trying to sound casual but under the table she was probably twisting a napkin into tight knots.

"Only if they look friendly, Mom."

"And if they don't?"

"I shoot them on sight." Jenny grinned, but then pulled it back when Violet didn't so much as crack a smile. "If I see more than a couple people together, I run and hide. I've gotten pretty good at it. It's fine. I promise."

We ate lunch while Marcus quizzed Jenny about how many people she had seen, what kinds of animals and plants, any sign of a government. Then we lingered there, drinking glasses of sweet tea that Violet made from an herb she'd discovered growing wild in the woods. It was my favorite time, everyone sitting there with the afternoon sun streaming in from the porch window, yellow as a dandelion, voices mixed with the bright clinking of forks and knives on plates.

The months after the fight hadn't been easy, even for us. It had taken time to mesh back together again. But, like everything, it couldn't last. I knew that as soon as Jenny slid her plate out in front of her.

"I'm going to go past the mountains."

The silence was like a granite wall. Violet looked over at Marcus. He swallowed and set his fork down neatly next to his plate. "To do what?"

"To see what's there."

"It's not a vacation," Marcus said.

Jenny leaned across the table on her elbows. "Look, you need a scout —"

"Why does it have to be you?" Jackson asked. He was sitting across from Jenny, his fork still in his hand, his fingers white around its metal body. He was trying to cover it, but I could hear what was in his voice. Something welled up in Jenny's eyes, but she pulled it back.

"Because I want to," she said. "And because there's no one who will be better at it than me. We can't sit here with our heads down and hope everything's going to be okay. The slaver, the one with the dreadlocks, is still alive, and there are more like him. You need to know if there's danger out there, or people like us we can join forces with."

Marcus and Violet exchanged a look and entwined hands.

"You know it's true."

Violet pulled in a shaky breath. "You weren't meant for one place," she said. "I know that, but . . . we just got you back."

Jenny set her hand on top of Violet's, and along with Marcus they held on to it.

"I'll come back," Jenny said. "I'll always come back. This is my home."

There was more talk, but the sound of it dropped away for me. I dug my thumbnail into the soft wood at the edge of the table and wondered if it was true, if she really would come back or if there would be a time when that rubber band stretched as far as it could go and would snap, releasing her into the world, never to return. The thought of that was more than I could stand.

"I'm going too."

I didn't even know I'd said it out loud until the talk at the table went silent. When I looked up, everyone was staring at me.

"Stephen . . ." Violet began.

"I've thought about it a lot, and it's what I want to do."

Violet glanced at Jenny, who dropped her hand onto mine, squeezing my palm under the table.

"Well . . ." Violet said after a long pause. "I guess we better get both of you packed up, then."

Violet pushed away from the table to gather things for Jenny, and I went up to my room, Jenny's old one, and packed my things. Soon

Jackson drifted into the doorway. I folded a shirt and a sweater that Violet had knitted for me and placed them down in the bottom of my bag.

"You're really going?" Jackson asked.

I picked up the rest of my clothes and tucked them in the bag. "I'll be back," I said. "We'll be back."

"What books do you want to take with you?"

"Those are yours."

"Yeah. I know. It's just . . ."

I pulled my tent out of the closet and started folding it up. "What?"

Jackson leaned against the edge of the door and crossed his arms, his eyes on the messy carpet at my feet. "Nothing," he said, and disappeared back into his room.

I got the tent into its pack and lashed it to the outside of my backpack, then went back through the closet, looking for anything I'd missed. The bat and glove that Jackson and Derrick had given me as a present at the start of the season sat in the corner. I ran my fingertip down the face of the bat, dipping in and out of its dents. The well-seasoned leather of the glove smelled spicy and sharp. I left them there at the back of the closet.

I was about to close my pack when Jackson reappeared with a stack of paperbacks in his hand.

"Take them," Jackson said. "If you don't, you'll have to spend all your time talking to Jenny. I've read them all. That Piers Anthony is really good. And the Peter Straub."

"Thanks," I said, stuffing my bag with the books. "You guys have a good game today."

Jackson studied me with that penetrating look of his, the same one I had seen for the first time as he'd struggled along behind the wagon that brought me here. He'd changed so much since then, and I was sure he would change more. I wondered how long it would be until Jenny and I would be back this way and who he would be then. I wondered if I'd even recognize him. If I'd recognize any of them. Or if they'd recognize me.

Jackson ran his fingers down the door frame. "Yeah. We'll try," he said quietly. Then his shoes whispered down the carpeted hallway and he descended the stairs, leaving me there alone.

I took my bag's straps in my hands, but it felt like it was full of bricks. I couldn't move. I stood listening to the hollow silence of the house until Violet's voice drifted up the stairs.

"Stephen?"

"Coming," I called weakly, but it was a struggle to lift the pack up off the ground and place it on my shoulders, a struggle just to reach the door. I stopped in the doorway and ran my hand down the smooth wood alongside it. Marcus had covered over the spot where Jenny had caved in the wall months ago. All that was left now was a small depression in the plaster.

The house was empty by the time I got downstairs. I moved through the silent place like it was a museum, remembering the strangeness of it all when I'd first come there: the smell of the food, the sounds of people talking.

I made it through the kitchen and the front room to find everyone waiting outside, gathered around Wind and finishing their good-byes. I threw my pack down at the horse's feet and hugged Violet and Marcus. Sam appeared from his house and shook my hand. I didn't know what to say. Violet squeezed my arm, then hugged me tight again. Her eyes began to glitter with tears that she sniffed back. Marcus gave me a firm handshake before laying his arm over Violet's shoulder and walking her across the park along with Sam.

Jackson hugged Jenny again. "Be careful."

"I will."

"Come back, okay?"

"I will," Jenny said. "I promise."

Jackson didn't move away or take his hands from her shoulders.

"Yo! Jackson! Quinn! Time's wasting! Let's go!"

Derrick and Martin and Carrie were crossing the park, heading toward the road that led to school and the baseball field. Martin was throwing the ball up high into the air and racing to get under it. There was a snap as it fell into his glove.

Jackson's hand slipped off Jenny's arm and he glanced at me one last time.

"See ya," he said, then ran off and joined his friends, disappearing down the road with them and a wave of others who followed.

"You ready?"

Jenny was standing with Wind's reins in her gloved hand. I nodded and lifted my pack up off the ground to load it onto Wind with Jenny's equipment, her tent and rifle and provisions. I stopped when Jenny's hand fell on my arm, holding it down.

"What?"

Jenny looked at me evenly. "Go," she said.

"What are you talking — ?"

Jenny nodded over my shoulder. A stream of kids stormed out of their houses and surged down the road toward the school to join Jackson and the others. Claudia trailed the group, tossing *Charlie and the Chocolate Factory* into the air and catching it over and over. I couldn't lie — I felt a pull toward them. But then, behind them, came Sam and Tuttle and Mr. Allison, who still looked fearsome with his scraggly hair and eye patch.

"They're talking about building a church," I said, watching them go. "Forming a government. Mr. Allison even thinks he can get some of the electricity back up. It's just like you said. They're going to start the whole thing all over again. Take us right back where we started."

"Then maybe they need someone to keep an eye on them."

"Jenny —"

She pulled me close. "Look," she said. "Forget the future. Forget them. Forget me. You spent your whole life following somebody else. This is your world now. What do *you* want?"

My heart thumped. Jenny placed her palm in the center of my chest, covering it. Everything that had happened to us spun through my head.

After the storm and the deaths and the fires and the guns: What did I want? I closed my eyes, desperate to hear Grandpa's voice, or Dad's, or Mom's, but there was nothing.

There was just me.

"I want a home," I said.

I don't think I knew it was true until right then, but it was. Jenny leaned in and set her lips lightly on mine. The sweet, spicy smell of her mixed with the clean wood of the town surrounded me.

"This is your home," Jenny murmured into the small space between us. "You fought for it. Don't be afraid to take it."

My breath caught in my throat. I thought I could stay right there with her forever, but I knew that she had a path and so did I. After so long, mine had led me here and hers led . . . out there.

I kissed her and stepped away. Wind jerked and snorted as Jenny glided up onto his back, and the muscles in her arms stood out as she tried to hold him still. He was as ready as she was.

"Hold the fort down while I'm gone. Okay, Stephen? Don't let them do anything too stupid."

I nodded. A stone, thick as a fist, was resting in my throat.

Jenny twisted around in her saddle and took a last look around the town, the houses, the park, the road.

"My God," she breathed, then gave the reins a quick shake. Wind exploded out across the park and up the road. Jenny paused at the top of the hill and raised her hand high in the air and then there was a great joyous *whoop* and that was it.

She was gone, but she'd be back. I believed. I hoped.

I turned to face the park. The neighborhood had gone soundless and empty, like a ball suspended, weightless, in midair. I could have believed that there was no one else around me for miles until a voice snapped through it all.

"Yo! Stephen! Let's go! We've got work to do!"

Derrick had come back to the head of the road to school and was standing there with his arms out, a ball cap arranged messily on his head.

I started walking, slow at first, then faster, following what felt like a string fastened to my chest, yanking me forward.

Derrick broke into a run, so I was alone when I reached the field. An excited chatter overflowed the small wooden risers that had been built earlier that month. I let my hand slide across the wood of the stand as I passed. It had been planed smooth and smelled powdery and clean. Everyone was there: the Greens, Sam, Claudia with the book balanced on her knees, Tuttle with a stack of papers to grade.

I dropped my bag near the stands. Violet nudged Marcus and shot me a wink. Jackson was off in the outfield having a catch with Martin. They stopped when they saw me. Jackson was still for a moment, unsure, then he raised his arm and waved, a broad smile on his face. I waved back and trotted out onto the field.

"Let's do this, people!" Derrick shouted as we all converged on home plate, pushed forward by the cheers from the seats behind us. We formed into a tight knot together, Jackson on one side of me and Martin on the other. Carrie and Wendy and John Carter stood opposite. "Now, I need everybody to keep in mind that Stephen has decided to join us today, so we'll all have to up our game to compensate for how much he sucks."

Martin popped Derrick on the back of the head. "Jeez, Derrick, shut up already and let's get going!"

As the group broke up and everyone moved to their places, I looked past them, out toward where the forest shrouded the Henry house in green and shadow.

After the fight with the slavers, a trial was organized with a judgment of banishment seeming all but sure for the Henry family. Sure, that is, until Marcus stood up and, to everyone's amazement, spoke on their behalf. He said it would be too easy to send them out into the world like some gang of unruly children, only to become someone else's problem. It was Settler's Landing's responsibility, Marcus said, to make sure nothing like this ever happened again.

And so they were stripped of any power they had and were made to work and contribute like anyone else. So far it had worked, but like many of the wounded from that night, I wondered what would happen when Caleb finally recovered. Would Settler's Landing's mercy and Will's death really make him a different person, or would he still hear dark voices as I had once heard Grandpa's?

"Hey, man, you ready?"

Jackson was at the end of our team's line, holding a bat out to me.

"You're up," he said.

Maybe Jenny was right, I thought. Maybe they really did need some-one to keep an eye on them.

But there would be time for that.

The bat seemed to vibrate in my hands as I took it and stepped up to the plate. John Carter checked the bases, then wound up and set the ball tumbling through the air. When it was time, I unfolded my arms in a smooth arc. There was a *crack* as the ball sailed out into the air over everyone's heads, streaking past the houses and across the wide emerald field. A roar went up from the stands and from my friends massed behind me.

The outfielders scrambled for the ball as I dropped the bat and ran, tagging first and second easily. As I strained past third, Jackson yelled for me to stop, but I just threw my arms into the air, laughed, and dove toward home.

ACKNOWLEDGMENTS

So many folks to thank. Up first, thanks to my wonderful family, Lara, Wyatt, and especially Mom and Dad, for insisting I read as a kid (even if it was just Batman comics) and for supporting me through all the twists and turns of my life. Also, to Mom and Dad for acting as, respectively, Official Medical Adviser and Official Agriculture and Animal Husbandry Adviser on this book. Thanks also to Patty, David, Bryan, and Amanda Sauer for all their support.

Thanks to my agent, the delightful Sara Crowe, who made me see I was thinking too small. To David Levithan, Cassandra Pelham, and everyone at Scholastic for their belief in the book, their enthusiasm, and most of all for making this thing so much better. For early encouragement and much needed criticism a big thank-you to Deborah Halverson, Ken Weitzman, and Ryan Palmer. For constant support, inspired silliness, and being a living link to my own days as a teen, thanks to Dave Denson, Ken Fortino, and Chris Ham. And to all the fine folks at the Society of Children's Book Writers & Illustrators who supported the writing of this book early on with a Work-in-Progress grant.

Lastly, thanks to Gretchen because, for me, it's turtles all the way down.

DON'T MISS JEFF HIRSCH'S NEXT NOVEL,

MAGISTERIUM

A MYSTERIOUS DIVIDE BETWEEN TWO WORLDS. ON ONE SIDE, A TECHNOLOGICAL PARADISE. ON THE OTHER, THE UNKNOWN.

Sixteen-year-old Glenn Morgan has lived next to the Rift her entire life and has no idea of what might be on the other side of it. Glenn's only friend, Kevin Kapoor, insists the fence holds back a world of monsters and witchcraft, but magic isn't for Glenn. She has enough problems with reality, and she dreams about the day she can escape. But when her scientist father's work leads to his arrest, he gives Glenn a simple metal bracelet that will send Glenn and Kevin on the run — with only one place to go.

Read ahead for a special sneak peek.

"Glenn! Glenny! Wake up!"

Glenn bolted upright, twisted up in her sheets, Hopkins beside her. A dark figure stood over her bed.

"Dad?"

"It works, Glenny," he said. "It actually works."

Glenn rubbed her eyes. "What are you talking about? What works? What time is it?"

"Get dressed and come see."

Her father leaned into a shaft of moonlight. Glenn jerked away without thinking and gasped. His hair was disheveled and his clothes were stained with oil and soot. There was a long gash on his arm that oozed blood. Hopkins reared back and hissed as Dad reached down and grabbed Glenn by her shoulders.

"We're really going to do it, Glenn."

"Do *what*? What happened to you?"

He knelt down beside Glenn's bed. His skin was sweaty and pale, ghastly as melting plastic.

"We're going to get her back," he said. "We're going to march right over there and bring her back."

"Go where? Get *who* back?"

"Your mom," he said, his voice trembling. "We're going to rescue her, Glenn."

It was like a fist slammed into Glenn's chest. Her breath stopped. Suddenly it seemed like he was too close to her, kneeling there on the floor. Glenn could feel the fevered heat radiating off of him.

"Rescue her from what?"

"It's not something I can just — you have to come see!"

Before she could respond, he had leapt up and was running out of the room. Glenn stumbled out of her bed and followed, Hopkins trailing behind.

"Everything you've been told is a lie," Dad said as they descended the stairs and went out into the yard. "The Rift wasn't an *accident*. And it's not some kind of wasteland over there. Ha! I can't believe they've gotten away with this for so long!"

"What are you talking about? What does this have to do with Mom?"

Dad tore into the workshop. He drew a stool from the corner and sat down between Glenn and The Project.

"Okay," he said, one hand tugging nervously at the other. "Now, how to . . . yes. There's a set of rules — physical rules — that govern cause and effect, gravity, nuclear and chemical reactions, time, momentum. All of those rules come together and we call the result reality. Is that right?"

The workshop was more of a wreck than usual. Tools lay everywhere. Half of The Project lay in pieces on the floor, and the other half had been radically altered. The generator was now directly hooked into it, and the whole thing glowed a livid blue as if it was alive.

"Glenn?"

"Of course. But what does that —"

"Think of a set of playing cards. The cards are always the same — King, Queen, Ace, Jack — but the game you play changes depending on what set of rules you decide to invoke. Use one set of rules and you're playing poker. Choose another and you have solitaire. What we think of as reality is no different. It's a card game. Change the rules and you change reality."

"Dad, that's not possible. You can't —"

"Yes you can. That's just . . . that's the thing: it is, Glenn. Possible. That's what I'm trying to tell you. The rules can change. They *were* changed. That's what the Rift *was*. They've been so good about keeping it all under wraps. The border. The stories. The fake satellite pictures! They've made us so afraid of what's on the other side that no one even thinks about going over and actually looking to see what's there."

"Who are you talking about?"

Dad leaned closer in to Glenn. She could smell sweat and the blood that oozed from his arm.

"Authority. They've been lying to us for a hundred years. But that's not important, what's important is this" — he took a rattling breath — "on the other side of the border there are people like us, except for one thing — they live in a reality based on an entirely different set of rules."

ABOUT THE AUTHOR

Jeff Hirsch graduated from the University of California, San Diego, with an MFA in Dramatic Writing, and is the *USA Today* bestselling author of *The Eleventh Plague* and *Magisterium*. He lives in Beacon, New York, with his wife. Visit him online at www.jeff-hirsch.com.